Dream Walker
The Tale of the Sleepless Knight

Kevin Horwitz

Dream Walker
The Tale of the Sleepless Knight

Editors: Gloria Wall and Chastity West
Logo design: Devin Muldoon
Cover design: Patricia Lupien

First edition: September 2015

This book was typeset on Ubuntu GNU/Linux and LaTeX. Many thanks to the free software contributors who make these and other projects possible.

Published by Onyx Neon Press, http://www.onyxneon.com/. The Onyx Neon logo is a trademark of Onyx Neon, Inc.

ISBN-13: 978-0-9854519-5-0

http://onyxneon.com/books/dreamwalker/

The Sleepless Knight

"...And Michael Everway takes the snap from the center...takes a few steps back...he narrowly escapes one lineman...he throws the ball to his receiver...and the receiver drops it! He drops it! It's now fourth and ten with one second left on the clock. What will the Carter Cougars do now? They're down 14–10 with one play left in the National Middle School Football Championship. What will Coach Weaver do? His players look tired. His players look beaten. What could he be thinking?"

Eighth-grader David Calloway watched as Coach Weaver took off his glasses and wiped down his face with a towel. Whatever the Coach was thinking about, it couldn't possibly be him. He'd ridden the bench almost the whole season, grateful for the chance to be on the field for even the occasional kickoff.

"Calloway!" The coach screamed. "Get your butt off the bench and get out there!"

Dave jumped to his feet and quickly ran toward the field, but just before he could, the coach grabbed him by the arm.

"Where do you think you're going, Calloway? Aren't you forgetting something?" Coach Weaver said, holding Dave's helmet.

His shoulders slumped as he took the helmet from his coach's hands.

"Get out there, Calloway, and kick some ass. We just had the horns on those helmets cleaned, polished, and sharpened, so use 'em if you can!"

Dave nodded and noted the sharp bony horns sticking out of the sides of the helmet. It didn't really need to be sharpened or cleaned. After all, when did he have the chance all season to run headfirst into somebody when he was riding the bench?

David entered the huddle and looked at their star quarterback, Michael Everway. Michael smiled and nodded as David joined the group.

"All right people, listen up," Michael said in a forceful voice. "Are we ready for this? Nothing complicated here. The pass is going to David. They'll never expect it. The Jaguars will think we're going to Bullington or Grasso. This is it! Let's do it! Cougars on three... one, two, three!"

"COUGARS!"

Michael and the rest of the squad broke the huddle and lined up as the crowd in the stadium fell silent, the sounds of swords being drawn by the players on the field the only noise. David took position and held his breath. He didn't want to move lest a penalty be called. He didn't want to ruin his team's chances of winning this game. The coach and the entire team were counting on him and he wasn't about to let them down! He looked across the line of scrimmage and saw Terry Williamson, the Jaguars cornerback assigned to defend him. Terry was a shutdown corner—no one caught a pass against his defense.

Dave suddenly realized that the quarterback had taken the snap a second ago. He wasn't paying attention! David took off down the field, finally exhaling. He easily dodged his defender who was frozen in surprise since Dave hadn't moved when the ball was hiked. Maybe Dave didn't have the strength of most of the guys on the field, but he knew he was one of the fastest, even against Williamson. The cornerback turned to catch up to him, but by that time David was ten yards down the field and quickly losing him. Suddenly, a roar like an airplane engine and a flame burst from Williamson's shoes and his speed suddenly tripled. A few steps later and he was right behind David.

"Oh no!" shouted the announcer. "Williamson has upped the ante and hit the button for his Burst Shoes! There's no way Calloway will get open now!"

David just smiled. "Burst shoes, eh?" David yelled. "Not a problem. Check this out!"

Dave pushed a button on his jersey and it split down the middle as a jetpack emerged from his shoulder pads.

"See you later!" Dave said as fire shot from his back and launched him toward the end zone.

"And Calloway responds with a trick of his own! The ol' jetpack trick! Shoulda seen that one coming!" the announcer yelled, losing his breath.

Michael saw him separate from the defender and launched the ball downfield. It flew high into the air, and Dave calmly steered his jet pack toward it, but before he could get there, another engine roar filled the air. Williamson had unveiled a jetpack of his own, one that was even faster than Dave's and he quickly caught up. Both boys lunged and grabbed the ball. Dave pulled. Williamson wouldn't let go. As they wrestled for control, their jet packs shot them straight up, then sideways, then plunged them straight toward the ground again."

One chance, David thought as he pulled a cord on his jersey. The jetpack ejected from his back and a parachute shot out in its place. Williamson couldn't react in time and screamed past him as he made one last slap at the ball, knocking it out of Dave's hands, before smashing into the ground. Dave grabbed for the falling ball and managed to get just his fingertips underneath and flicked it upwards. It was just enough to roll it into his hand as he landed safely in the end zone. He looked down and smiled. He had scored a touchdown! The Cougars had won!

"David Calloway has done it! He has won the game! The Cougars

3

are national champions! David Calloway has become a hero!" shouted the announcer growing hoarse.

The entire offense rushed him tackling him to the ground and screaming that he'd done it! He'd won the game! The team picked him up off the ground and put him on their shoulders, marching him up and down the field, their arms raised in victory. The sky lit up as fighter jets streaked across the night's sky shooting out fireworks to celebrate. David smiled and let out a victory yell, not caring that the crowd was cheering so loudly his ears were ringing. It was all so unreal. He never would have imagined this.

*
* *

Later in the evening, Dave was still feeling the euphoria of winning, but it was getting close to his curfew. Most of the players and fans had already gone, leaving only the clean-up crew and a few players and their friends. He stopped at mid-field to say goodbye to the rest of his team and Michael Everway extended his hand to Dave.

"Dave, I know I've acted like a real jerk to you in school. I know it's not going to make it any better if I say I was just doing it as a joke, but I completely regret everything I've done. You are one hell of a player and honestly, you're actually a pretty cool guy. I think it's because you're dating Emma Ashford. I'm actually kind of jealous. I've had a thing for her for years and you dating her made me... well, kind of envious. But, hey, we've all grown up. I just wanted to shake your hand and try to put everything behind us. Dave, I'd really like to be able to call you my friend."

David looked at Mike in shock. Mike had always seemed to be one of those annoying jock bullies who picked on everybody. But here he was, offering his hand in friendship. Dave took his hand and shook it.

"Yo, Mike. My brother's car won't start," a deep voice called from the edge of the field. "We gotta get it started if we're gonna get to Kurt's party. The key is in the ignition, but he said it won't start."

Dave recognized that voice. That was Mike's friend, Cole Dutton. He played linebacker for the Cougars and was very good at his position. He walked over to where Mike and Dave were standing. Cole was an intimidating figure with his shaved head and towering muscular frame made—in contrast to Mike who, while in shape, was a thin boy with good hair and looks that never seemed to get ruined despite any hits he might have taken in practice or in games.

"Cole, did he try...you know...turning the key?" Mike asked, turning toward his friend.

"The key won't fit if he turns it around, idiot!" Cole responded. Dave stifled a small laugh as Mike patted Cole on the back.

"Don't worry. I'll fix it for you guys. But it'll cost you," Mike said walking with Cole.

"How much this time?"

"Fifty bucks sound okay?"

"Fifty? Come on, Mike! Can't you cut my brother a break?"

"Cole, remember, those mechanics are gonna charge him about two hundred just to look at the car."

"Yeah, you're right, Mike. Fifty is fine."

"Great! Now let's go fix the car! We wouldn't want to interrupt the two lovebirds anyway."

Confusion crossed David's face as the two guys walked away.

"I think he means us, silly," said a girl's voice. She hesitated for just a second before the last word.

He turned around to see a very beautiful girl. It was Emma Ashford, his girlfriend. Beside her was her dog, Max, a cute golden retriever that was mouthing a leftover football.

"Congratulations, hero!" She said, running into his arms and giving him a hug before planting a huge kiss on his lips. Dave kissed her back, wrapped her up in his arms and lifted her up off of the ground a few inches. Emma broke off the kiss and let out a loud laugh as she let go of Max's leash so that she could run her fingers through Dave's short brown hair before kissing him again.

And then the lights to the arena went out.

With the sudden moonlit darkness, Emma jumped out of his arms, almost landing on Max. Dave laughed and pulled her back towards him.

"Heh, afraid of the dark?" Dave asked, a big smile on his face.

"No, you jerk, don't make fun of me!" She said, punching him on the shoulder, "Hey, listen, there's something you have to do," Emma whispered into his ear.

"Anything, just name it," Dave said, now curious.

Emma leaned in closer to his ear and whispered, "You have to defeat the Sleepless Knight."

"Excuse me? The whatless knight? I have to defeat who?" Dave asked, utter confusion replacing his curiosity.

Emma backed away and pointed behind Dave. He slowly turned and saw a human shape standing in the end zone. In the moonlight, it was hard to see what or who was there, but it looked enormous. Dave turned back to ask Emma, but she was no longer there. A loud bark from the sidelines drew his attention. There was Max sitting in the grass. Still, there was no sign of Emma.

"Max, where's Emma?" Dave asked, as if expecting an answer from the dog. Max simply barked again, but then looked in the direction of the shape and whimpered. Max lay down, as though trying to hide himself in the grass.

"What do you want?" Dave asked as he turned to face the shape. In response, the shape began to march deliberately toward him each footstep echoing the across the field with the cold clang of metal on metal. *Is he wearing armor?* Dave wondered, as the thing grew closer. When it was within twenty feet, it stopped. There was a loud click and the arena lights flashed on again. Accustomed to the darkness by now, Dave shielded his eyes from the glare and finally took a good look at the shape in front of him. Standing about seven feet tall and encased in black glittering armor, the thing crossed its arms and looked down at him. At only five feet and five inches tall, Dave had to crane his neck in order to see the face of this thing. There wasn't a single opening in the armor to see out or even to breathe. The face, like the rest of it, was polished black metal. It reminded Dave of the sky on a clear night full of shimmering and twinkling stars.

"Are you the Sleepless Knight?" Dave asked the armored figure. It nodded in agreement.

"What do you want with me?" he asked again. It said nothing, but reached toward its side and pulled out a gigantic sword—apparently made from the same black metal—and pointed the blade directly at Dave. At that moment, a cheer erupted from the arena. Startled, Dave took a step back and looked around him. The seats were filled with people who had just seen him win the championship! He saw his friends and classmates. He saw Emma, sitting there and cheering. On the other side of Emma were Michael Everway and Cole Dutton holding a large sign between them that read *Calloway Rulez*!

"Emma, what the heck is going on?" he asked as he took a step towards her. Just as he started to move, the knight's blade swung into the earth in front of him nearly cutting him in half. Dave fell backwards and landed hard on his back. After shaking off his shock, he looked up to see the knight bringing the sword back up as the crowd began to boo. Dave began to get up, but ducked down as soon as he saw the sword swing again, this time horizontally. If he hadn't just ducked down just then, his head would have been in the end zone. He quickly got back to his feet as the knight began winding up for a third swing. Dave slowly backed away a few feet and once he knew that he was beyond the reach of the Sleepless Knight, he turned and ran, much to the shock of the crowd who let out what sounded like a loud sigh. The arena was built with a horseshoe design. One side of the end zone was open and led right to the street. However, that way led right into the Sleepless Knight. Unfortunately, he couldn't climb up into the seats as the arena walls were purposely built high to protect the fans. Dave breathed deeply and ran to the side of the arena, running up the ramp way leading towards the locker room while reaching into his pocket for his cell phone. Pulling it out, he quickly dialed 911 and listened as it rang.

"Nine-one-one, what is the nature of your emergency?" A man with a deep voice answered.

"This is David Calloway. I'm at the Hughes Arena. Some psycho guy dressed like a medieval knight is attacking me! I need cops down here fast!"

"Sir, calm down, who is attacking you?"

"Didn't you just hear me? Some psycho guy dressed up in black medieval armor is attacking me. If you don't get some guys out here soon, this psycho is going to cut me in two."

"Wait a minute. Is this the same David Calloway who just won the National Football Middle School Championship?"

David paused for a second and looked at his cell phone then slowly put it back to his head as he entered the locker room and shut the door tight.

"Yes. How do you know that already?"

"And you said that a guy dressed in medieval armor is attacking you?"

"Yeah, that's what I said!"

"Tell me, is this armor black as night?"

"Yeah, what does that matter? Send out the cops fully loaded! This guy is going to take a lot to—"

"Is the armor glittery, giving off an almost...oh...how to say it? It gives off a starry night effect?" The person on the phone said, cutting Dave off.

"I guess so," Dave said, looking for a way to barricade the door. "Listen, I can give a full description after you save me, okay?"

"Tell me, is it the Sleepless Knight that you're facing?"

"Yeah! Yeah! That's the guy! So, you guys have heard of him before, right? You know how dangerous he is?" Dave said, not believing the conversation he was having, his eyes searching for an exit that wasn't there and then looking toward the closed door of the locker room.

"Sir, please calm down. Just because you won the championship

8

for your team does not mean that you get to call the shots here, all right?"

"What the heck is going on? Can you help me or not? What should I do here?"

"Sir, calm down. This is what you need to do if this is in fact the Sleepless Knight."

The door to the locker room began to open. Dave quickly threw his full weight into the door, slamming it shut, and hoping it would hold. He tried to imagine that somehow the door could withstand the weight of the Knight or the sharpness of the sword.

"Sir, are you still there?"

"Yeah, have you sent the cops?" Dave screamed into the phone as the thing behind the door kept trying to force itself into the room.

"Sir, in order to rectify this situation, you're going to have to let the Sleepless Knight kill you."

Dave looked at his cell phone in shock. Suddenly, on the display screen of the phone, it began displaying, 'KILL KILL KILL KILL KILL KILL KILL.' Dave dropped the phone onto the ground where the glass screen broke into many little pieces. From behind the door, came the distinct sound of a sword being drawn. Dave looked nervously at the door. He wanted to move, but his legs wouldn't let him. Suddenly, the Sleepless Knight's sword sliced through the door. Dave barely moved in time, but not before it nicked him on the shoulder. He backed up as the sword was withdrawn, leaving a gaping hole in the door. He clutched his shoulder in pain and felt something wet. He brought his hand back and saw that it was coated in blood. His eyes widened as he backed up a few steps, and the sword cut through the door again. He could see the Sleepless Knight through the massive gouges. Dave stumbled backward a few more steps and tripped over something. He lost his balance and slammed his head into a locker. Clutching his head in pain, Dave slumped to the floor. He looked up to see what he had tripped over and heard a loud bark. He gasped in confusion when he realized it was Emma's dog.

"Max, how the heck did you get in here?" Dave asked as he stroked the dog's head with one hand while holding his own head in the other. "Well, Max, I don't know how to tell you this, boy, but I think we're both going to die."

As the slicing sounds of the sword cutting through the door continued, Max licked Dave's face and barked.

"You, maybe, but not me," Max said in a scratchy voice. Dave's eyes widened as he heard the dog speak. He looked up at the locker where he hit his head and then back at the dog.

"Max? You can speak?"

"Much better than you can, thank you very much."

"When did you learn how to speak?"

"Listen, we can sit here and talk about how Mrs. Hirsche taught me in first grade, but I think we have bigger things to deal with right now."

"Mrs. Hirsche? But that was my first gr—"

"Hey, Sleepless Knight, remember? Focus!" Max yelled at him. Dave shook his head in disbelief and looked up at the shredded door. He crawled backward and behind one of the rows of lockers that were hidden from the door's sight as Max walked along beside him.

"What can we do about the knight? There's no way I can take him, and unless you've got Scooby Snacks somewhere, I don't think you're taking it out unless you're going to kill it with your doggy breath!" Dave whispered.

"Oh, ha ha. Talking about my oral hygiene at a time like this. Listen, there's no way you can defeat the Sleepless Knight right now and trust me, it means business. It's definitely not supposed to be here and that makes it even more dangerous."

"Like I don't know that! I was kissing Emma and next thing I know, I'm staring down some freak from the medieval ages."

"I wish I had gotten to you sooner. I can only hope that it's almost time," Max said as the Sleepless Knight pushed down the remnants of the door and squeezed its massive frame through the opening.

"Gotten to me sooner? Almost time for what? Max, what are you talking about? He's going to kill us!"

"Why do you automatically assume that it's a man? Remember the whole women's rights movement? Geez."

"Max, what are you talking about? What do you mean by 'it's almost time'?" Dave yelled as the Knight came around the corner and found the two at the back of the lockers. It pulled its arm back and then quickly snapped it forward swinging its sword toward Dave's neck.

Looking For You

Bzzzzz

Dave opened his eyes and was instantly blinded by the sun shining through his window.

Bzzzzz

He looked around him and saw that he was in his room lying in bed. It was all a dream.

Bzzzzz

Dave reached over and slammed his hand down on the alarm clock silencing its annoying buzzer—the buzzer that had woken him up every school day for the past ten years. As he did so, he grabbed his left shoulder as a stabbing pain shot through it. It was the same shoulder that the Sleepless Knight had slashed in his dream. He brought his hand back to see if he was bleeding, but there was nothing. He heard a knock on the door, but before he could say anything, the door opened and his mom peeked into the room.

"David, time to get up for school. Is everything all right? I thought I heard a scream," his mom said, a slightly concerned look on her face.

"Yeah, I just hit my alarm clock a little too hard. That's all," David said hoping that his mom wouldn't ask any more questions.

"Oh, okay. Well, jump in the shower. I'll make you some breakfast," she said closing the door.

Dave turned on the shower and let it warm up as he brushed his teeth. *That was a really strange dream,* he thought as he rinsed his mouth. *Why does my shoulder hurt? Was it one of those things where I hurt myself in real life and the pain showed up in the dream? Or the other way around? Weird... I'm going to have to ask my friends about it.*

He jumped in the shower and closed his eyes as he put his head under the spray of water. As he did, he thought of winning the championship game and how good it made him feel. He thought of how the crowd was cheering his name. He thought of Emma kissing him. In reality, most of it would never happen. He's only on the team because he's extremely fast. Even so, he was still a third-stringer. He just didn't have the skills that the other players on the team had. He was fast, but he just didn't have the coordination or the strength. He occasionally ran kickoffs, but the other team usually pulverized him. And as for the crowd cheering his name—that was just ridiculous. That wasn't the only problem though.

He was average.

He knew he was the middle of the pack in terms of popularity. He had friends and at least a decent social life. The only problem was that he faded into a crowd. People would recognize his face, but they couldn't remember his name or anything like that. He just wasn't memorable.

Dave got out of the shower, dried off, finished up in the bathroom, and then got dressed in his bedroom. He went downstairs and gulped down his food before kissing his mother and saying goodbye to his father before walking to school. His father sometimes offered to drive him, but unless the weather was bad, he liked to walk. It gave him time to think and if necessary, cram for a test. Besides, if he timed it just right, he'd run into Emma.

He had been dating Emma for the past few months. They were each other's first relationship. They were nervous about everything. Even a little kiss on the cheek was considered a big deal.

As soon as he walked outside, he could see his breath in the cool October air. It was just at the point where you could still wear short sleeves, but you might regret wearing shorts. The trees were turning different shades and all around him was the smell of wet leaves. Fall was his favorite season. He loved the color of the leaves and the smell of fireplaces and the light scent of burning leaves. Along with the warm weather left over from summer and just a nip of cold in the air, it was shaping up to be a great Pennsylvania fall.

As he set out, he saw his friend and next-door neighbor, Andrew Bays, leaving his house as well. Andy considered himself Goth. He was decked out in black from head to toe wearing a shirt with huge things that resembled wooden safety pins where the buttons should have been. His hair, while technically supposed to be a light brown, was dyed black and spiked straight up.

"Hey, Andy," he said catching Andy's eye. Andy walked out to the sidewalk as Dave caught up to him.

"Dave, you missed the BEST Null Spiders show on Friday. They kicked ass!" Andy said, turning around to show off a giant dark gray spider on the back of his shirt.

"Andy, when are you going to understand that every band you listen to sucks and all of the music I listen to rocks?" Dave said with a laugh that came mostly through his nose.

"Probably when you realize that all of your music is force fed through corporations and has no creativity whatsoever," Andy said.

"I'm just joking. Anybody go with you? Cynthia?" Dave asked.

"You mean, Siiiiiin-thia? Yeah, she went with me and so did Jake, but his girlfriend bailed on him, so we were stuck with him all night. The only time we got rid of him was when he went to the bathroom," Andy said.

"Third wheel, huh?

"Literally."

Dave and Andy laughed at that as Dave spied Emma walking in the distance.

"Hey, there's Emma. Let's catch up to her."

"Uh, speaking of third wheels, I'm not interested in being one. I'll meet you at school," Andy said, slowing his pace.

Dave shrugged and jogged to catch up with Emma. After about fifteen seconds, he noticed that Emma was picking up her pace as well. She turned her head slightly and gave him a little smirk. Dave smiled and went into a full run. Emma kept her quickened pace knowing there was no way she could outrun him. As he caught up with her, he pulled out a pen from his backpack.

"Excuse me, miss, you seemed to have dropped this," Dave said, a big smile on his face. Emma turned around, looked him up and down, and then looked at the pen.

"Uh, that can't be mine. That has some other girl's name on it," Emma said in an irritated tone. Baffled, Dave looked down at the pen. All it said was the pen maker's corporation name.

"It...doesn't say any girl's name!" Dave exclaimed, pointing to the pen. Emma just rolled her eyes.

"Oh Dave, you're so silly. I can't believe you actually looked. Do you mean that you MAY have a pen with some other chick's name on it?" She asked as she punched him on the shoulder. He winced and dropped the pen.

"Are you okay? I thought football was supposed to toughen you up?" Emma said, "Here, I'll give it a kiss."

Emma kissed his shoulder, and while it didn't lessen the pain, it made Dave feel good inside. She giggled and turned slightly red as she pulled away.

"Thanks. I think I just slept on it wrong last night. It hurts like heck though," Dave said making arm circles with his left shoulder and wincing as pain shot through the shoulder.

"Well, let's cause more pain by working out the shoulder more, why don't you?" Emma said, taking his left hand into her hand. "Let me keep that hand busy for a while."

"No problem," Dave said, smiling as he felt the warmth of her hand. "So, how was hanging out with your dad?"

Emma took a few steps in silence before answering. "It was okay.

My dad doesn't really get out much right now, so it's kind of depressing."

Dave opened his mouth to speak, but Emma cut him off. "I'd rather not talk about it, okay?"

Since Emma's parents had gotten divorced about a year ago she spent every other weekend with her dad who lived a few towns away. Right about then, she had distanced herself from all of her friends, even going as far as to eat alone every day at lunch.

That was why Dave was a little surprised when Emma had plopped down in the seat next to him at the movie theater near the end of the last school year. She hadn't intended on meeting anybody, especially Dave. She just wanted to get away from home for a while, but after the movie, they recognized each other from school and started talking. After that, they talked on the phone, by email and text, and it would have been smoke signals if they'd known how. However, when Dave tried to take it beyond friendship level, Emma seemed to back off. Later that summer, though, just before they both went to a summer party at a lake a few miles out of town, Emma kissed him. It was more than a little peck that a friend could give another friend. From then on, Emma and Dave were a couple.

They walked in silence for a while until the school came into sight. Dave looked behind them and saw Andy walking in silence, the cords from his headphones apparent even at this distance.

"Hey Emma?"

"Yeah?"

"Remind me later to tell you about the craziest dream I had last night," he said, opening the door for her before following her in.

"Give me the short story now. I wanna know if I was in it or some other hot chick!" Emma said, turning back to face him.

"Heh, nah, nothing like that. Well, you were in it, but I was having this crazy dream where I had just won the national championship for the team."

"That IS crazy!"

"Hey, quiet!" Dave said, giving a brief smile. "Right after we won, you and I were uh...talking while on the field when suddenly we were attacked by this dude called the Sleepless Knight who was decked out in this crazy black armor. He attacked me with his sword and I barely escaped," Dave asked, shrugging. "I mean, I can fight, but it's not like I'm going to be breaking through metal armor. Anyway, just when I thought I was going to get stabbed, you know who started talking to me? Your dog, Max! He started talking to me and giving me advice on what to do. Then I woke up. I'm telling you, if food is what causes weird dreams, I'm saying 'no' to taco night from now on!"

Dave glanced at Emma to see what she thought of the dream. However, Emma was standing still, staring at Dave.

"Em, what is it?" Dave asked, putting his arm around her waist.

"You said that you fought the Sleepless Knight in your dream last night?" she asked, looking past him and waving to one of her friends.

"Yeah, why?"

"Last night, I dreamt that I was working in the garden with my mother when somebody in black armor calling himself the Sleepless Knight came out of nowhere and demanded to know where David Calloway was."

"What?" Dave said, backing up a step, accidentally hitting somebody with his bad shoulder.

Emma's eyes brightened as a smile crossed her face. "This is soooo weird! You know what this means?"

"What? What does it mean?" Dave asked.

Emma grabbed his hand. "You and I were meant to be! I mean, we have a psychic connection!" Emma said, giving his hand a squeeze. "Anyway, I've got to get to class! I'll see ya!"

Emma gave his hand another squeeze and let go walking down the hallway toward her class.

"Yeah...weird," Dave said, staring at Emma as she walked away before walking off in a different direction for his own class.

One-In-A-Million

Dave could barely pay attention in any of his morning classes. It took the math teacher three attempts to get his attention to come to the blackboard and work out a geometry proof. In French class, he ignored the teacher's lessons so that he could flip through the English-French dictionary to find out how to translate Sleepless Knight into French. In Biology, the teacher talked about cold-blooded reptiles like alligators and snakes, but Dave just doodled in his notebook what the Knight looked like. He knew it was a dream, but it was so intense that it felt real.

Finally, lunch came. He quickly walked to the cafeteria and peeked in. The cafeteria was filled with long brown tables connected to orange stools. While there wasn't officially assigned seating, everybody generally sat in the same seats everyday and ate with the same people. All the jocks and incredibly hot girls hung out at a table in the back corner. Dave had already made the mistake of sitting at that table once. No one said anything directly to him, but the pointed looks of irritation communicated plenty. At the table next to the jocks, the stoners spent their lunch period discussing which jam band concert to go to next week and what they were going to do before the concert. On the other side of the cafeteria, the gamers debated the latest in online role-playing game tactics.

Dave and his friends had a table that was almost dead-set in the middle of the room. He liked that. He liked the fact that he wasn't in the ultra-popular groups but had a reasonably good social life. People wouldn't go out of their way to invite him to parties, but he wouldn't have a problem if he decided to go.

He looked down at the table and saw Emma there, just beginning to open up her packed lunch. He smiled and leaned in to talk to her when he felt a slap on his back.

"Buddy, I know you want her and all, but get some food first, all right?"

Dave turned around and saw his friend Eric Graham standing there. Eric and Dave were friends pretty much from birth thirteen years ago. Their mothers gave birth at the same time at the same hospital, and later their parents met while staring at the babies in the nursery. A simple joke between them about the two children being destined to be best friends turned out to be true. Their parents spent time with each other regularly which meant that he and Eric had to hang out too. Luckily, they shared similar interests and hobbies, and if they didn't, they'd often change their minds. When Dave got into video games, Eric brought over the game controllers. Eric took up camping, and Dave asked his parents to get a tent so they could camp in the backyard or in various parks. Dave became interested in paintball, so Eric made sure to ambush him on the way to school with his new paintball gun. Eric started football, and Dave signed up with him.

Eric was a stocky kind of guy. He wasn't fat, but he definitely wasn't thin. He wasn't weak, but he wasn't the most muscular guy. His short brown hair and serious eyes made him look like a fairly aggressive guy, and although his mouth sometimes got him into trouble, he usually was one of the calmest guys around. It hurt him on the football field sometimes though, as he wanted to play on the defensive line and it was hard to get him pumped up to play to the best of his ability.

"Eric, you're lucky I recognized you as quickly as I did," Dave said, his voice slowing and deepening as he turned to face Eric. "Otherwise, I'd have to use my kung fu skills on you!"

Dave threw a slow punch at his friend. Eric, even slower, blocked with his forearm.

"Your tiger skills are no match for my crane style!" Eric yelled as some smiling students watched while making their way into the cafeteria. Eric kicked his leg in slow motion, but Dave easily caught it. Just then, the massive Cole Dutton walked right in between them, the duo separating just before Cole collided with them. Cole kept on walking past them.

"What the hell, Cole?" Eric yelled as Dave backed up to the wall.

"Eric, don't...not now. Let him walk away," Dave said, shutting his eyes for a second, realizing it was too late. Cole, hearing his name, turned around and smiled, revealing a mouthful of crooked teeth that looked like they had never seen a dentist.

"You want to start something, Graham?" Cole said, walking up to Eric, easily towering over him by at least half a foot. Dave wanted to say something. He wanted to do something. However, caught in the moment, he hesitated. Eric's eyes lit up like he was about to do something, but he just couldn't make the first move.

"Leave the dork alone, Cole," Michael Everway interrupted, appearing from behind Cole. Cole turned around and looked at the Mike.

"Why? He's a loser. Who cares?"

"Cole, come on, if one of the teachers sees you doing that crap, they might get you in trouble with the coach. Go eat lunch. I think the coach wants to talk to us about the game on Saturday during our free period." Mike said, his head nodding towards the cafeteria. Cole turned and made a sudden move towards Dave. Dave flinched and backed up to the wall. Cole laughed, turned, and walked to the cafeteria. As he turned away, he slammed into another person, knocking their books to the ground. The student who dropped their books looked up at Cole, but thought better of saying anything instead just picking up his books and continuing on his way. Mike shook his head and turned toward Dave and Eric.

"Guys, can I talk to you?" Mike said, stepping closer. Eric and Dave swapped a quick glance.

"Uh, sure, what's up?" Dave said, both of them moving their heads forward off the wall. Mike immediately smacked their foreheads with the palms of his hands sending their heads crashing back into the wall.

"Have fun riding the bench on Friday!" Mike said, laughing as he went into the cafeteria. Eric and Dave clutched their heads in pain.

"That son of a bitch!" Eric said. "We should go kick his ass!"

"Screw it! Let's go do it!" Dave said, feeling for blood and finding none, "Crap, but my parents are going to kill me if I get suspended for fighting," Dave said as they walked toward the cafeteria, "Maybe we'll just key some swear words into his locker. Yeah, that'll probably work better."

"Next free period?"

"Sure thing. I'll meet you at his locker," Dave said.

"Oh crap, I can't do it. I promised Cynthia I'd help her with her science project," Eric said, grabbing a tray.

"Don't you mean Siiiiiin-thia?" Dave said with a chuckle.

"Dude, Andy's an ass. That name drives her crazy."

"Crazy bad or crazy good?"

"Uh...what do you mean?" Eric said as the two placed sandwiches and drinks on their trays.

"Does it get her mad crazy or all hot and bothered crazy?"

"Dude, mad crazy. I don't want to even think of my sister getting hot and bothered. That alone will give me nightmares," Eric said, shuddering.

Instantly, an image of the Sleepless Knight standing over him, sword raised, flashed through Dave's head. He shook it off as he paid for his food and went to sit down.

"Still being the overprotective brother, eh?" Dave said.

"Andy's a friend, but you know what's going to happen if they break up, right? Especially if he's the one that causes the breakup. I've got to choose between my friend and my sister."

"Well, your sister is hot, so if she needs a shoulder to cry on, she knows I'm available, right?" Dave said loudly, making sure that Emma heard it as he sat down next to her. Emma smiled, blinked a few times, and then punched him on his bad shoulder. Dave's eyes widened and began to tear up. Everyone else laughed.

Dave recovered and looked around at the table. Most of his friends were here. Emma and Eric sat next to him while Andy led Cynthia to her seat and sat down. As Dave bit into his sandwich, Todd Maggio arrived, plopping his tray down, pasta sauce splattering onto the table. Cynthia and Andy instantly jumped up to check whether any sauce had landed on their clothes.

"Todd, watch out!" Cynthia yelled out as they sat back down. Cynthia, like her boyfriend Andy, was Goth and dressed from head to toe in black. She wore a tight Null Spiders t-shirt that showed a bit of her flat stomach. She always enjoyed showing off her body. It was "sexy Goth-wear" as Andy liked to put it, much to Eric's nausea. She was really nothing like Eric, her older brother by a year. She was thin, almost too thin. She was usually a very sweet, but also outspoken girl. Getting her riled up was fairly easy, but it was getting her to stop talking after you got her going that was the tough part.

"Sorry, sorry. I didn't realize how much sauce I had on there," Todd responded, digging deeply into a huge pile of spaghetti.

Dave and Andy made eye contact and rolled their eyes. Todd was a friend, but basically a pity friend. Todd was picked on for being clumsy and for saying things that made everybody just shake their heads. He didn't make it easy on himself like the time when he wanted to drop out of school to become a professional card player because he once won a poker tournament in summer camp or the time he wantied to ride in the trunk of Dave's parent's car because it would be roomier than squeezing in between a few people in the back seat during a ride home.

No one remembered exactly how he joined their group, but they were pretty sure he just randomly sat down at their table one day and somehow ended up hanging out with them after school. They realized pretty quickly that he was a strange and fairly annoying guy, but occasionally he had some good moments of being legitimately funny or helpful. Todd's good moments always fooled them into believing he'd changed and always came on the day the group had resolved to tell him they didn't want to hang out with him anymore. However, after a few days, the real Todd was back along with all his awkwardness. They tried to ignore him and hope he'd get the point that no one really wanted him around, but he seemed to enjoy the company, even if they weren't talking to him. He would laugh at their jokes, be the extra guy when they needed another person to play basketball or a video game, and would be the target of their insults when they needed to let off some steam. They did feel bad about using him that way, but he almost seemed to enjoy it. It was as if he relished any kind of human contact, even if it wasn't the nice kind.

After Andy and Cynthia calmed down, Todd reached over with a napkin and started wiping something off Andy's shoulder. Andy slapped his hand away, but Todd pointed to his shoulder. Andy pulled down on his shirt and saw that a bit of the sauce had splashed his shirt. Andy opened his mouth to say something, but then just turned his head and closed his eyes as if doing so would hold back the words of rage he was planning on unleashing.

"Em, I want to talk about the dream you had last night," Dave said watching Emma shake her head as Eric stepped in between Todd and Andy. Todd was holding a napkin, obviously trying to clean up the sauce, but Andy wanted none of it.

"Dave, are you seeing this?" Emma said, briefly glancing at Dave who turned to look at his friends again.

"Yeah, classic Todd," Dave said. "Either Todd's going to get the point or Andy's going to kill him."

"It's only a matter of time," Emma said, turning toward Dave. "Anyway, what did you want to talk about?"

"The dream. Remember? Sleepless Knight?" Dave said, glad that he finally got her full attention.

"Okay, whatever. Uh...let's see. Gardening with my mom. Then I heard a really heavy pounding noise. I turned around and I saw this huge black thing in the middle of the yard. It was the middle of the day and the sun was shining on it, but it's almost as if the armor absorbed the light. It came up to me and sort of stared at me for a little bit. It was kind of creepy, but it just stood there. I tried to get my mom's attention, but she was intent on getting things to grow, so she just ignored me. So, I asked it what it wanted. It said it was looking for David Calloway. I told it that I didn't know where you were. So, the knight took out his gigantic black blade and asked me where you lived. I didn't want to tell it. That thing scared the hell out of me. But, I told. I told it exactly where you lived. It then turned away from me and headed off in your direction. Then I went back to planting in the garden."

"Didn't think to maybe, you know, call me? Warn me?" Dave asked, his eyes widening.

"Nah, it made much more sense to plant stuff with my mom!" Emma said, giving Dave a big smile. However, the smile quickly dissolved when she saw that Dave looked worried.

"You'd rather plant than warn me that I was in danger?" Dave asked, leaning closer to Emma.

"Dave, you're freaking me out! It was a dream! It made way more sense in the dream to just hang out with my mom," she said, pulling back. "What's the big deal?"

"Well, let's see. I had a dream about a guy calling himself the Sleepless Knight and as it turns out, my girlfriend had a dream with the same darn thing in it," Dave said raising his voice. Emma looked around to make sure no one was watching them.

"Oh, come on. We probably saw it in some movie or on TV. It's just one of those one-in-a-million shots. Kind of like if we both dreamt tonight about Todd spilling spaghetti sauce. That's all," Emma said, pointing over to Andy and Todd arguing.

"I don't know. I don't remember seeing any medieval guy recently."

"I'm sure we've seen it somewhere. Davey, you've got to chill out! I mean, how many times have you had a dream that freaked you out, like a nightmare or something?" Emma asked.

"I dunno. A few times, but this felt way more real!"

"Dave, seriously, it's a dream, that's all. You probably ate something weird last night and it gave you an intense dream," Emma said touching his shoulder. "Hey, listen, why don't we hang out later tonight after practice?" Emma said with a small smile and slowly leaning closer.

"I-I—" Dave said, sure of his answer, but not able to say it. However, before he could say anything, their friends returned.

"Sure thing, let's hang out! What are we doing?" Eric interrupted, looking back and forth between Emma and Dave. Dave chuckled and Emma turned toward Eric, still holding onto the same smile from before.

"Looks like we're hanging out at your place tonight," Emma said, her smile growing.

"Why my place?" Eric asked, a confused look on his face.

"Because then we get to interrupt YOU!" Emma said as Dave let out a small laugh.

*
* *

After school, Dave met Eric outside his last class, and they made their way down the long blue hallway and gray stairs to the locker room. They geared up for practice and made their way onto the field, where they found Michael Everway throwing the ball around with his main receivers, Wes Bullington and Evan Grasso. On the other side of the field, Dave spotted Cole Dutton's massive frame already running drills, getting into a three-point stance and then running shoulder first into the goal post. Eric slapped Dave on the back and pointed over to Emma who was just coming onto the soccer field, which was right next to the football field.

Emma was a great soccer player and looked awesome wearing a short sleeve shirt and shorts and running onto the soccer field. Dave smiled and waited for her to make eye contact as she talked and jogged with some of her friends. As if reading Dave's mind, she turned around and began jogging backwards. She saw Dave, smiled, and waved before turning to rejoin her friends. Dave watched her jog out of sight, then suddenly the blunt impact of a football hit him square in the lower back. He stumbled a few steps and almost fell, but Eric caught him and stood him up.

"I heard they still have slots open on the girls' soccer team, ladies! There's still time to sign up!" Michael Everway yelled.

Dave turned towards the quarterback and without thinking, he marched towards the quarterback. *This time,* Dave thought, *I'm going to do it. I'm going to make him pay.*

He could see Mike's laughing face through his helmet. Dave was determined to show that Mike wasn't so tough and that he was just all talk. But just as Dave got within a few yards, Coach Weaver walked between them blowing the whistle and telling them to fall in. As the players formed a circle around the coach, he overheard Mike and Cole talking.

"I bet I nail Emma before he's even figured out what to do with a girl," Mike said, casting a sidelong glance at Dave. Dave tried to ignore him by listening to the coach.

"Yeah, Mike," Cole said, a hungry look in his eyes. "Just make sure you save some for me,"

"Don't worry, Cole. The way I hear it, she'll put out enough for all of us," Mike said, turning toward Dave. "But you wouldn't know anything about that, would you Dave?"

Dave couldn't take it anymore and charged. Eric tried to stop him, but it just caused Dave to stumble. Cole quickly stepped in Dave's way tackling him to the ground. Cole stood up and roared like a wild animal. Mike slapped Cole on the back, pointed down at Dave, and laughed.

"Oh, look who just went down just like—" Mike started, but the coach blew his whistle.

"That's enough, Everway. Dutton, get the hell away from him. Calloway, are you okay?" Coach Weaver asked, offering his hand. Together, Eric and Coach Weaver helped him to his feet.

"Coach, are you going to let Everway and Dutton get away with that?" Eric screamed, pointing at the two players. "Those two jack-asses are going to kill somebody one of these days!"

"Graham...Calloway...listen to me. I told everybody this very same thing at the beginning of the season. Leave your personal grudges off the field. When we play, we need to be a team. We need to be one huge, oiled machine. If we're not, we're going to get our asses kicked! Whatever problem you two and those guys have, settle it off the field, otherwise I'm going to have to get rid of some of you to stop this from happening, and I can tell you this right now...it ain't gonna be my starting quarterback and my star linebacker. Do we have an understanding?" Coach Weaver said, a seriously angry look in his eyes.

"Coach, those guys are—" Eric started, but the Coach's face turned red as he faced-off with him, his large sweatshirt-covered belly backing Eric up a few steps.

"Do we have an understanding?" the coach yelled.

"Yes coach," Eric said looking defeated.

"Calloway?"

"I understand," Dave mumbled.

"Good, now fall in and start your stretches."

Coach Weaver turned toward the rest of the team yelling at them to start stretching in preparation for a long practice. Dave and Eric looked at each other. Eric shrugged and walked toward the practice.

Dave took a deep breath and shook his head to clear it before following him.

*

* *

After practice, Dave went into the locker room showers. He made sure the hot water hit every new bruise and hoped it could magically wash away the pain. It was days like this that made him want to quit the team. He knew he would barely have any playing time in an actual game on Saturday. He was a third-string benchwarmer. He was the backup's backup. Combine that with the fact that sometimes at the end of practice he felt like he wouldn't even be able to physically make it home because of how beaten up he felt, it sometimes was hard to stay motivated.

After the shower, he tossed on his clothes, grabbed his bags, and left. On his way out, he passed a row of lockers and heard voices. It was Mike and Cole talking. Mike turned and looked at Dave, his mouth opening and closing constantly as he chewed some kind of gum.

"Trying to sneak a peek of us getting dressed, Calloway?" Mike asked digging around in his locker. "If so, you definitely should hold onto this."

With a sudden movement, Mike threw something white at Dave hitting him square in the face, and it fell into his hands. He looked down and saw that he was holding Mike's jock strap. Dave instantly dropped it to the floor, while Mike and Cole laughed.

"Gross!" Dave said, wiping his face with his shirt.

"Emma will probably want to see it too," Mike said in between the laughs.

"So would Emma!" Cole said, laughing even more. Mike stopped laughing and stared at Cole.

"Dude, I just said that!" Mike said.

"Huh?" Cole said, looking over at Mike.

"Never mind," Mike said, shaking his head.

As the two continued to bicker, Dave slipped out the door, meeting Eric and Emma just outside. He saw a car waiting in the school driveway. Even from the entrance to the school, Dave could see the large hair of Eric's mother over the top of the driver's seat. Even though they only lived a short distance away from the school, with practice running them ragged, she always offered to drive them home, which Dave saw as a welcome benefit of being Eric's friend. His mother insisted on being involved in almost every facet of Eric's life. Sometimes that meant she'd be watching his games from the stands, which was nice, but other times she insisted on being the chaperone at dances or insisted that social events be held at her house.

They all tossed their stuff in the trunk and got into the car, Eric in the front with Dave and Emma both sitting in the back.

"Hello, Mrs. Graham, thanks for giving us a ride again!" Emma said.

"It's no probem at all, Emma," Mrs. Graham said. "How was practice today, Eric?"

"Not too bad. I think I'm one practice away from officially being one giant bruise," Eric said looking back over at Dave.

"You got that right," Dave said. Emma quickly threw out a poke to his ribs and managed to catch a sore spot.

"Quit it!"

"Not in this car, you two!" Mrs. Graham said, turning briefly to look at them before looking back at the road.

"Mom, do you mind if people come over after dinner?" Eric asked.

"After dinner and homework, you mean?"

"Yeah, of course!"

"Well, it is a school night, so I don't think..."

"We won't be up late. I promise."

Mrs. Graham paused at a stop sign and after making sure that there were no other cars coming, she turned down the street to Emma's house. "Oh, alright. But, they've got to be out of here no later than nine-thirty, okay?"

"That's great! Thanks, mom!" Eric said giving the thumbs up to Dave and Emma.

The car pulled to a stop and Emma got out, but not before giving Dave a quick hug. She closed the door and the car pulled away. A minute later, they arrived at Dave's house and he got out after thanking Mrs. Graham. He opened the screen door to his house and turned the doorknob. It was locked. He shook his head and looked for his key in his pocket. His mother was always doing this. They lived in a fairly quiet and safe neighborhood. The police reports usually consisted of various wildlife sightings and the occasional teenager picked up for doing something he shouldn't have. However, his mother always kept the door locked. It didn't matter if he was gone for five hours or even five minutes. As soon as he left the house to go somewhere, he could hear the loud click of the lock sliding into place. Dave unlocked the door, pushed it open, and walked in. Instantly, he was hit by the smell of cooking chicken. He peeked into the kitchen and saw his mother's head, with its short curly brown hair, stirring one of two pots she had on the stove.

She saw him and immediately said, "Put your stuff in your room and then come downstairs. Dinner's almost ready."

Dave grunted and heaved his gear over his shoulder as he went up the stairs and turning to the first door on the left. He threw open his door and tossed his gear onto the rug in the middle of his room. When he turned around, he saw somebody peeking a head into his room. It was his younger brother, Nick. At eleven years old, he was already showing signs of growing into one of the tallest kids in school. Pretty soon, Nick, with his dirty-blond hair, would be bigger than Dave. Dave hoped that by then, Nick would have forgotten all the mischievous older brother pranks Dave had pulled on him throughout his younger years.

"Dave, dinner! Mom's making fried chicken!" Nick said, his eyes wide with the excitement that any kid would have when one of his favorite dinners was being served. Dave looked at his bed and wondered how much time he would have on it before he'd have to get up and eat dinner. Deciding against it, he followed Nick downstairs and sat at the round white dinner table in the kitchen. As they sat down, he looked over at the empty seat where his father should be sitting. His father was late again. The rule was that dinner happened at precisely six o' clock, not a minute before or after. If you showed up late, you have to deal with "mother-wrath" as Dave liked to call it.

His mom looked up at the clock, then down at Dad's empty seat, before finally speaking up, "Dig in, it's getting cold! We can't wait for your father all night!"

As if on cue, the front door swung open and Dave's father walked in, wearing his usual brown suit, white shirt, and dark brown tie. He rushed upstairs pausing only to say that he would be right down. Meanwhile, Dave and Nick and both helped themselves to a plate of fried chicken, mashed potatoes, and baked beans. His father quickly came down the stairs, kissed his mother on the cheek, and sat down to eat. She wouldn't even look at him and started to eat, shaking her head. Dave and his father looked at each other and shrugged while Nick stifled a laugh.

"Mom, is it okay if I go over Eric's house tonight?" Dave asked, grabbing another drumstick.

"Tonight?" She asked, exhaling loudly. "It's a school night. You'll see him tomorrow."

"Please? Eric and I really need to go over some football stuff or we'll never get a chance to play. I promise I'll do my homework first." Dave said, his eyes occasionally shifting over to his father.

"Do your homework and then let me see it. If you do a good job, then yes, you can go over. But you have to be home by ten, all right?" His father said.

"Steven, I don't think he should be going out on a school night. He'll barely touch his homework."

"Lisa, Dave's grades are pretty good and he's never gotten into any serious trouble. Well, none that we know about. If his grades start to slip, then bring down the hammer on him. Until then, as long as he's in by ten and does his chores like we ask, then what's the big deal?" His father asked.

"Fine," she said, looking at Dave. "I'll give it a chance. But one little screw up, mister, and you'll be lucky that I even allow you out of the house to go to school on a weekday, you got that?"

"Yes! Absolutely!" Dave said.

"Eat your dinner," his mom said, "Steven, tomorrow you need to be home at six on the dot. Otherwise, I'm not setting out a plate for you."

All three Calloway men chuckled, but soon silence descended again as she glared at all of them.

Snakes and Alligators

As soon as dinner finished, Dave ran upstairs and finished up his homework. Luckily, he had finished most of his work in study hall earlier in the day. After showing all of his homework to his dad, Dave threw on a light jacket and was out the door before his mother could say a word.

When he ran outside, he was glad to have grabbed the jacket. It was dark and the temperature had dropped what felt like twenty degrees since he'd gone inside for dinner. He stopped and breathed out hard watching the breath form a white vapor in the air. Smiling, he inhaled the scent of fall like he did in the morning before setting off down the road. It was a clear night so he spent most of the time looking up at the sky. His street was not that well lit so there was little light to prevent the stars from showing through.

As he rounded the corner to Eric's street, he heard a loud engine and saw bright headlights speeding toward him. The car was coming down the road at a very fast pace with detal metal screaming out of the open windows. That could only mean one thing: It was Rake and his cronies.

Raymond Argus, known to his classmates as Rake, was one of those guys who, every two to three weeks, went missing from class—usually to serve some kind of suspension for fighting, vandalizing, or things of that nature. Dave wasn't above doing some goofy prank like putting a thumbtack on a vacant chair, but Rake liked to pick fights for no reason other than the fact that he didn't want to go to class. Nobody, except maybe some of the jocks, could say that Rake had never harassed at some point in time. It was as if he had a check-list of people he wanted to annoy each day, and he had to do it, otherwise he wouldn't get any dinner. No one could ever figure out why he hadn't been kicked out of school yet. Dave's only idea, crazy as it was, was that every school needs one of those unpredictable menaces. It was like a quota that the school had to fulfill. Unfortunately, over the course of his life, Rake picked up a few cronies to help him out. Combine that with the fact that one of them somehow passed the test to get a driver's license and everybody in the town was now aware of Rake.

The car sped past him and suddenly screeched to a halt. It backed up, turning slightly to force Dave off of the street. The light blue car had taken a lot of beatings. A huge crack scarred the rear windshield. The passenger-side door was brown with rust, and the bumper barely managed to hang on. One of the back seat windows rolled down, and a shaved head emerged followed by the upper half of Rake's skinny body. He wore a leather jacket and impenetrably dark goggles and pinched a lit cigarette between his lips."

"Calloway, izzat you?" Rake said clumsily as he worked to keep the cigarette in his mouth. Inside the car, the music lowered to a reasonable level.

"What do you want, Raymond?" Dave said glaring at him. He could see Rake's crew in the car. He saw the short, spiky pink hair of Rake's girlfriend Alexis, who Rake just called Ale. But Dave couldn't remember the real names of the rest of his gang, just their nicknames. There was the driver Jax, whose idea of a good time was setting things on fire and was the only kid in middle school old enough to have a driver's license. Also, there was also big, bulky Grey who probably could give Cole Dutton a run for his money in terms of size.

"Ooohooo, he called me Raymond," he said, looking back into the car. "Whatcha doing, Davey? Out looking for a date?"

"Whatever, Raymond. Go to your Hitler rally or whatever you guys do," Dave said, in no mood to deal with them right now.

Rake took his cigarette out of his mouth, opened his mouth to say something, then smiled and flicked the cigarette at Dave. It only nicked Dave's shirt, but it was enough to burn a small hole in his shirt. Rake laughed and the car sped away, the music cranked up to a ridiculous volume again. Dave kept brushing at his shirt in case any hot ashes were still there.

After making sure he wasn't on fire, he walked to Eric's house, staring down at the hole in his shirt until he reached Eric's driveway. He walked down the driveway and went around to the back of the house and heard Eric and Emma's voices, both laughing loudly. Instantly, the events of the last few minutes faded from his head as he opened the sliding glass door and stepped into the room. There was a large table in front of him with a few bottles of soda and a few open bags of chips. Beyond that were a few chairs and a small couch right next to a TV and Eric's Zeus, the current state of the art home video game system.

"Hey Dave," Todd said, almost hiding in the back corner of the room by the snack table. Dave nodded in his direction and then went to the front of the room where he found Eric, Emma, and Andy sitting around staring at the screen. He looked down at Emma who saw him and instantly gave him a huge smile. Eric saw that and moved off of the couch where he was just sitting with Emma. Dave plopped down next to Emma who hooked his arm and held his hand. Andy made a choking sound and barely avoided a kick from Emma.

"What happened to your shirt?" Emma asked, poking a finger through the hole.

"Rake happened. He and his buddies tried to start something just down the street."

"Did you beat them up?" Eric asked, a smirk on his face.

"There were four of them. So, yes!" Dave said, smirking back.

"You know, if you ever want to get back at them, we've got your back," Andy said, making a stabbing motion.

"Yeah!" Todd yelled out from the back of the room.

"Todd, keep your voice down. I don't want my parents to get pissed," Eric said, pointing to the ceiling. Todd quickly covered his mouth.

"So, what are we doing tonight," Dave asked, looking around at the room and then at the screen. "Hey, isn't that Lord Battler? Didn't we beat everything in that game?"

"Sure did. But this isn't Lord Battler, David," Andy said.

"Wait, you don't mean that this is..."

"Ultimate Lord Battler!" Eric loudly said. "Whoooo!"

From the kitchen directly above them came the sounds of stomping feet. "Sorry mom! We'll keep it down!" Eric yelled to the ceiling.

Dave smiled and grabbed the game controller.

"Let's play."

"Okay, let me run you through the character creation," Eric said.

Lord Battler was the name of their favorite video game. It was a one-on-one fighting game where players chose a warrior to take into a fight against another player or a computer-controlled opponent. Unlike other fighting games where players chose a premade character, in Lord Battler, a character is designed from scratch and launched into tournaments to gain experience and money to improve the warrior's fighting ability.

While Eric ran Dave through the character creation process, Dave tried to remember all of the details of his last warrior, Hypnos. Usually, he set up Hypnos to be covered from neck to toe in black leather. However, after encountering Rake's gang, he didn't want to deal with black leather. So, he changed Hypnos to a dark blue leather, gave him a paintball mask and goggles like he had before and picked several attacks for him to use, including his "finisher" called the "Hand of God" where with a wave of Hypnos's hand, a beam would shoot out of the sky towards his enemy and evaporate them.

As he was selecting the attacks, Eric went over some of the differences between Lord Battler and Ultimate Lord Battler.

"So, there's the Hero/Villain system. You could develop your warrior as a hero or villain depending on several choices you make between battles. Your old characters from Lord Battler can occasionally show up as warriors that you battle against. So, Lord Battler's Hypnos can actually show up and challenge you."

"Sweet," Dave said as Emma yawned and leaned her head onto Dave's shoulder.

"Plus, they put in this system where if you play against another player in a non-tournament game, you can click on the G button and it'll automatically boost your guy to match the other player. That's sweet because Andy decided instead of being patient and waiting until we all got together, to play on his own and get his guy up to Rank 3," Eric said, throwing an empty soda can at Andy.

"Why didn't you wait, Andy?" Todd said.

"Because I bought it a week ago, and I wanted to see how my guy, Andruseth, played," Andy said, not looking back at Todd back in the corner. "Besides, I knew about the warrior matching feature anyway."

"Isn't half the fun the fact that we all get to play it together?" Todd asked.

"No one wants to play with you, Todd" Andy said.

"Guys, guys, who gives a crap? Let's just play," Eric said, shaking his head, "Dave, are you done already? Just press the Arch-Enemy button."

"Oh yeah, I completely forgot about that. My enemy from last time was that fishy dude with that magical trident. He was goofy, but when we both got experienced he was a... well, a tough fish to fry," Dave said.

"Yeah, but if he didn't get tough, we would never have seen the biggest Hand of God attack ever," Eric said, chuckling.

"How long did you spend in tournaments attacking with just the Hand of God to get it to that level?" Andy asked leaning forward.

"Jeez... It was a long time. I think I spent two or three weeks on it. But man, when I finally maxed out that move, old fish brains had no chance."

Dave clicked the Arch-Enemy button and watched as the screen began assembling parts and powers to the character which would be his equal throughout the game and would try to get in his way at every opportunity.

"I got some crazy telekinetic and pyrokinetic chick. Her name's Ragecage or something like that. Probably some really bad Japanese translation just like the bad translation 'Lord Battler,'" Andy said sinking back into his chair.

"Oh, give it a break, Andy. How many times are you going to remind us that it's a bad translation? Who cares?" Eric said, rolling his eyes, "Oh, and I got this guy with this enormous afro as an arch-enemy. I'm talking unnaturally huge. And he can launch out these weird electrical tangles from it. It's really weird, but I think he's a one-trick pony. As long as I build up Third Degree's defense to stop that one attack, I should be fine. He's called Afro Storm or something like that. Anyway, let's see what you got."

The computer screen kept randomly popping characters onto the screen at a fast pace and then kept slowing down. Slower... slower... slower... and then it stopped. Dave's eyes widened when he saw who was his arch-enemy. Staring at Dave was a person clad in black, glittering medieval armor with a gigantic sword made out of a metal similar to his armor. Below the picture of the character flashed its name:

SLEEPLESS KNIGHT

Dave looked down at Emma who looked back up at him in shock.

"Aw, that sucks," Andy said. "That was Jake Warlick's arch-enemy from the old Lord Battler. They either have a crappy random character generator or we need to go to Las Vegas and put you on the roulette table."

"He... was Jake's arch-enemy?" Dave asked, slowly turning his head away from the screen.

"Yeah, don't you remember? He's pretty nasty. He kicked Jake's ass a lot in the beginning. Remember when I told you that Jake broke one of my controllers? Good ol' SK caused that one. As I recall, he was just some strong man with a sword, but the damage he can deal out with a sword is pretty nasty. Man, Jake's going to bash his head into wall once I tell him who your arch-enemy is! Anyway, watch out, you get right into a fight with him," Andy said as the fight loaded up.

"Oh, that's so weird," Emma said.

"What's so weird?" Todd asked.

"Dave is just freaked out because he dreamt about the Sleepless Knight last night," Emma said, covering a laugh. "And he's freaked out because I had a dream about the Sleepless Knight last night as well."

"You did? Weird, you two must have some kind of psychic connection or something." Todd said as Emma laughed.

"Shut up guys! Thanks Emma. Thanks a lot!" Dave said as she continued to laugh and then pinched him on the leg. He tried to pinch her back and they started to wrestle around a little bit. All of a sudden, he heard Eric and Andy gasp as they looked at the screen. It showed Hypnos on the ground, badly burnt, and bleeding with the Sleepless Knight standing over him raising his sword in victory as the screen declared, *You Lose!*

"Wait for the replay of this, Dave! You got beaten down worse than Todd does in dodgeball."

The replay came on and showed Hypnos standing there occasionally moving slightly to the left or right as the controller moved while Dave and Emma wrestled. Then the Sleepless Knight lashed out with his sword, impaling him through the stomach, draining most of Hypnos's life to disappear. The Sleepless Knight then lifted him up above his head as a huge beam of light came down from the sky. It hit Hypnos and instantly burnt him to the bone eliminating the rest of his life to deplete. The replay ended, flashing the *You Lose* screen along with awarding a small amount of experience points that Dave could spend on upgrading his character.

"Ouch," Dave said.

"Wasn't that the Hand of God?" Andy asked.

"Dude, he used your own specialty against you! That has to hurt!" Eric said, breaking into a laugh. Dave tossed the controller to Andy who barely caught it.

"I think that butt-kicking told me that I'm doomed tonight. You guys use your characters. I'll catch up some other day," he said, leaning back into the couch. Emma did the same thing and cuddled next to him.

"Whatever," Andy said as Eric picked up another controller.

They played several battles with Todd occasionally loading up his character and getting soundly thrashed before going back to his corner. Meanwhile, Dave and Emma leaned on each other and watched. It wasn't long before he noticed that he was having a hard time staying awake. The weird dream from last night combined with football practice must have really wiped him out. He turned and noticed that Emma had her eyes closed, fast asleep. He smiled, tried one last time to stay awake, and then fell asleep. His last thought was, *It's all just a coincidence.*

*
* *

Dave smiled and breathed in the warm air. He heard the sounds of a slow moving river lapping against the shore while the leaves of dozens of palm trees rustled in the wind.

"All right class, open your books to page thirty-three. It's time to start today's lesson."

The nasally, high-pitched voice of his biology teacher, Mrs. Strawn, snapped him out of the hypnotic effect that this environment was having on him. He looked around from his desk and marveled at the sight of his entire classroom setup on the shores on an enormous river surrounded by miles of jungle. He looked up and quickly closed his eyes as the sun shone down on him, heating his face.

"Mr. Calloway, eyes front! Your parents didn't pay all this money for you to just stare at the sun," Mrs. Strawn said as the entire class turned to look at him.

"Sorry," Dave said opening up his three-ring binder to his biology section as the rest of the class turned around to the front.

"Now class, we're going to talk today about a species that you will find only in this part of the Godoy River, the snarling rabid whiptail alligators," Mrs. Strawn said, her eyes still on Dave.

"Excuse me, Mrs. Strawn," said a girl in glasses. "The what?"

"Adrienne Desmond, surely you read the textbook I assigned yesterday. The snarling rabid whiptail alligators, one of the most dangerous species of alligator in all of the Godoy River. Now then, if I may go on."

"Yes, sorry teacher," Adrienne said, flipping through her notebook.

The class continued for what felt like forever to Dave. The sun, that at the beginning was a welcome surprise, had soon become a source of irritation as sweat now poured down his face forcing him to constantly wipe his brow. Still, beads of sweat rolled into his eyes, forcing him to squint to see what the teacher was doing. He kept looking at the Godoy River, thinking how nice it would be to simply dive into the water and cool down. However, every time he thought about it, a few bubbles would rise up from the water. Was it a snarling rabid whiptail alligator? Just some frog? Was it worth the risk to get out of this heat?

Before he could come to a decision, the school bell rang. The people in front of him started getting up and putting their books away as did Mrs. Strawn. Dave, however, stayed in his seat trying to figure out where the bell was actually located. Not finding it, he stood and put his books and papers away. He turned and saw Mrs. Strawn and the rest of his classmates walk into a mass of palm trees behind him and then vanish out of sight. He dashed over to the trees to follow them. However, he couldn't find a trace of anybody beyond the tree line.

"Dave?" He heard Adrienne say. He turned and saw her long,

light brown hair and familiar baggy clothes, standing close to the river. He walked over to her, still glancing over his shoulder to see if any of his other classmates were nearby. As he got close to Adrienne, she walked away from him, moving toward the river, twice stumbling over her baggy clothes, and took out a bag of bread from her book bag. She opened it up, grabbed a slice, ripped it into a few pieces and then tossed them one by one into the river. The bread stayed on the surface for a second and then disappeared underneath as a fish came up to eat it.

"Dave, how long have we known each other?" She asked, turning to face him, pausing only to push up her glasses.

"Geez, pretty much all of our lives."

"Why don't we hang out any more?"

"Uh, I dunno. You used to live right across the street, but your parents moved across town. Besides, they moved when we were what? Seven? Eight? We were just kids then. I think everybody hung out with everybody back then."

"So, you wouldn't hang out with me now?" Adrienne said, moving closer to Dave. He took a small step back on instinct. Adrienne wasn't a bad looking girl, but she was always considered the weird girl in class and because of that, most people avoided her. Rather than playing at home with dolls on a rainy day, she would be outside without a raincoat looking for worms. She had an obsession with all things fantasy, particularly fairies. Fairies covered her book bag, her binder, and her shirt. Dave distinctly remembered sitting next to her in history class last year and watching her draw pictures of her favorite fairies all over her notebook. When she noticed he was looking at the notebook, she just smiled at him and turned the page.

"It's not that I wouldn't want to hang out with you, but..."

"But what?"

"Buuuut, I'm with Emma now. I don't think she'd like it if I started hanging out with another girl. I—"

"Ooooo! Look at that! It's so cute!" Adrienne said, looking down at the river and ignoring what he had just said. Crawling out of the water was a baby alligator. That was another thing that bugged everybody about Adrienne. She would get excited about random things and then go nuts and call everything cute, even if no one in the world but her thought it was cute.

Adrienne immediately stepped closer to the river's edge to get a closer look at the gator. Dave followed her, but kept a few steps behind.

"Adrienne. Be careful. It may be one of those rabid raketail things."

"Snarling rabid whiptail alligator, you mean? I think it is!" She bent down and picked up the creature. As she held it in her hands, its mouth started to bubble over with white froth. As soon as its mouth was covered with the white froth, it started snapping its teeth at her.

"Oooo! Aren't you a feisty one?" She said, smiling and offering it a finger before pulling it away just before it was chomped.

"Adrienne, come on. Put it down," Dave said, worried that Adrienne would get bit.

"Think I can smuggle it back and keep it as a pet? I'm sure I'll be the only one in town with one!" She said, opening up her backpack.

"I don't think that's a good idea. Do you even know how to take care of an alligator?"

"I had a turtle once. I'm sure it won't be too different."

"Come on, Adrienne, put it down. You don't know what to do with that thing."

Just then, he looked to the river and saw several dozen pairs of black eyes poking out of the water, staring at him, and gliding closer to the side of the shore where Adrienne and Dave stood.

"Uh, Adrienne. I think it's time to put the baby down."

"Why?" she asked, confused. However, her confused look turned to shock as she saw the eyes. She slowly put the baby down as it growled at her and took a quick bite at her shoe, but it couldn't even make a small indentation. It then scrambled back into the water. "What now?"

"I think we back away slowly," Dave said, backing away, putting his arm across Adrienne, and forcing her to move backwards as well.

"Slowly...slowly...slowly," she said as they backed up. The eyes approached even closer to the shore. One of pairs of eyes turned to inspect the baby that had just crawled into the river and then turned back to face the two teenagers. Dave and Adrienne backed up a few more steps when Dave's legs caught in the legs of a chair, and he tumbled over it. His face slammed into a desk and he hit the ground hard. As if on cue, the river erupted as dozens of frenzied alligators dashed out of the river, their mouths foaming over. Adrienne darted over to him, but Dave pushed her away.

"Adrienne. Run! Don't stop running! RUN!" Dave yelled. Adrienne looked at him and then took off running, constantly glancing over her shoulder to see how he was doing. As she entered a thick patch of trees, she disappeared just like the rest of her class.

Dave got to his feet and found himself surrounded by the alligators. A few of them hissed at him and opened their mouths, ready to strike. He looked for a small opening, but the ground writhed with the angry gators. Taking a deep breath, Dave leapt onto one of the chairs, and the space he was just in was filled with gnashing teeth. He saw another alligator lunging for him on the chair, but he avoided that by jumping on top of one of the desks as the chair was toppled over. He knew that the desks were pretty flimsy. One good push by a gator and it would topple over. Out of the corner of his eye, Dave spied a tall tree near one of the desks. Dave viewed a tree right on the edge of the forest that was close to one of the desks on the corner. He took a deep breath and took off running, leaping from desk to desk as the gators came crashing through each one he had just left behind. He reached the last desk and then leapt with all of his remaining strength. He stretched out and grabbed a limb of the tree with one hand. He swung his other arm around and grabbed it with a second hand. Breathing a sigh of relief, he looked down and saw the gators massing below him. As long as he kept to the trees, he'd be fine. They'd eventually grow bored and go away. Just above his head, however, Dave heard a hissing noise. Dave slowly turned his head up and saw a massive orange snake slithering down the tree toward him. Dave's whole body began to tremble and he began to lose his grip. The snake slithered its way onto the limb he was on and came right up to his face. It opened its mouth, baring its fangs and hissed, its tongue flicking on Dave's nose. Dave tried to slowly back away down the limb, but the snake followed him down. It then did an amazing thing. It spoke.

"David, we have to talk about what happened last night. I think somebody is coming after you," the snake hissed.

"What?" Dave said looking at the snake, looking at his hands, and looking at the gators below.

"Your mind is going nuts right now and you're just going to hurt yourself again, like you did last night. I can't deal with you in this condition and you're not going to be able to deal with the Sleepless Knight when it comes back to finish you off," the snake said, eye-to-eye with Dave. "All righty, why don't you go get eaten by the gators and then come back tomorrow when you're a bit more relaxed and have rested that noggin of yours a bit. In this state, you're worthless to me. So, for now, get going!"

With that, the snake began snapping its mouth at the Dave's hands, coming dangerously close to biting him. Dave shimmied even further as the limb bent from his weight. The snake looked back at the limb and then back at Dave.

"Time to go!"

With that, the snake snapped its head at Dave's hands and landed a bite right on his left hand. Dave screamed in pain and let go of the tree limb, falling into the pile of gators. He opened his eyes and screamed as a gator charged at his head, its mouth opened wide, and its teeth closing in around him.

*
* *

Dave woke with a jolt, letting out a yelp and waking Emma in the process. Andy and Eric turned toward him and after seeing that he was all right, they began to howl in laughter. Todd and Emma soon joined in. Dave hit Emma over the head with one of the couch pillows and then threw it at Eric.

"Quit it, Dave. Check this out! Other people's arch-enemies can come after other players! Look at this!" Eric said, pointing to the screen.

Dave looked at the screen and saw the face of the Sleepless Knight staring at him. At the bottom of the screen he read the text, *"I've defeated Third Degree and now I'm coming after you!"*

"Cool, isn't it? Man, they really amped up the quality of their games after their other crappy ones since the original Lord Battler!" Andy said, clicking a couple buttons to get into battle with the Sleepless Knight. Dave watched as Andy pulled off a few really neat moves. However, one bad move by Andy allowed the Sleepless Knight to grab him with an armored hand, raise him to the sky and choke him. Andy rapidly pressed a variety of buttons as he saw his life bar rapidly depleted. Finally, his character, Andruseth, kicked the Sleepless Knight hard enough so that he got out of the chokehold. However, as Andruseth clutched at his throat to regain his breath, the Sleepless Knight raised his hand to the sky.

"Oh crap! Recover, Andruseth! Recover!" Andy screamed mashing the buttons."

The Sleepless Knight lowered his hand quickly. The sky opened and a beam of light show down from a rip in the sky and enveloped Andruseth. A few seconds later, the beam disappeared as did Andruseth's remaining life. All that was left was a roasted corpse.

"This sucks! Why is the Sleepless Knight so hard? It's only on the beginner fights, even with me up a few levels on you guys!" Andy said, tossing the controller onto the carpet.

"So there's a stiff learning curve. No big deal," Eric said, saving the game.

"I think it's ridiculous when a game is so hard so early on. It makes me not want to play it anymore," Andy said, putting on his coat and gathering his things.

"Oh, not again," Eric said, shaking his head.

"What?" Andy asked.

"Every single time we play these game, once it gets a little tough and you start losing, you start spouting off about how ridiculous the game is and how it shouldn't be that difficult. It's supposed to be challenging!" Eric said, chuckling a little.

"Yeah, you say it every time!" Todd said from the back.

"Shut up, Todd. Why are you here anyway?" Andy angrily said, glaring at the TV.

"I'm just hanging out. That's all," Todd said.

"Yeah, but who invited you?"

"Guys, guys," Eric said, standing up, "Calm down. Listen, my parents are going to freak out if you guys are here for much longer, so I gotta kick you out."

As everybody around him stood up and began putting things away, Dave stared at the screen as the Sleepless Knight stared back. Below the knight was the text, *"I'm not through with you yet. In your worst nightmares, I will be there."*

You're In Control

When Dave got back home and climbed into bed. His eyes stayed wide open as he began to ponder the events of the evening. Was his mind so focused on the Sleepless Knight throughout the day that his dreams kept bringing it up? Why did it feel like it was more than that?

Eventually Dave's eyes became heavy and his eyes closed. Just as he was about to fall into a deep sleep, he saw the snake from the Godoy River lunge at him.

"Tomorrow," it hissed as Dave's eyes snapped open, his reflexes forcing his arms to block his face. But, there was no snake. He was just in his room, the only light coming from the moonlight shining e window shade. Dave shook it off and closed his eyes again. As soon as his eyelids shut, the snake lunged at him again.

"Tomorrow," it hissed again, his eyes springing open. Dave sat up, looked around his room, and listened. The only noise he could hear was the creaking of the bed from the occasional tossing and turning of his younger brother in the room next door.

"Get a hold of yourself, Dave," he whispered, trying to reassure himself. "It's just a dream. A weird one, but just a dream. That snake isn't real and it can't hurt you."

Dave closed his eyes, and again the snake lunged.

"Tomorrow," it hissed at him a third time. Sleep never came for Dave for the rest of the night.

*
* *

"Time to get ready for school," Dave's mother called from outside the door. Dave's first thought was that he had actually fallen asleep and his mother's voice was just part of a dream. There was no way he stayed awake for the entire night. He sat up, but then immediately collapsed back into his pillow. His mind was in a fog, and his eyes felt like they had been lifting weights all night. His eyes drooped, but as soon as they did, he thought he heard the snake hiss. Sitting up, he quickly surveyed the room. Seeing nothing out of ordinary, he got up and jumped into the shower. The hissing hot water helped rid him of the haze in his head, but his eyes still felt heavy. He slapped himself a few times trying to shake it off, but nothing helped.

After the shower, he dressed and went downstairs for breakfast. His little brother was already down there eating his cereal. Dave plopped on his seat as his mother put a bowl of oatmeal in front of him along with a glass of orange juice.

"Dave, you look like you didn't sleep a wink last night!" his mother said, concerned. "Are you feeling well?"

"Yeah, Mom. I'm fine. Just had trouble sleeping last night. I'm sure I'll be fine." He considered saying something about his strange dreams, but he was too tired to discuss it.

"All right, but if you start feeling like you're coming down with something, give me a call. I don't want you spreading it all over school," she said, wiping off a bit of cereal that somehow had ended up on his brother's arm.

"Sure thing. No plague for the school," he said. His mom responded with a smirk and walked away.

After Dave finished his breakfast and messed up his brother's hair with a playful slap to the back of his head. He walked out his front door for school, hoping that he left early enough so that he could avoid Andy and Emma and could have some time alone to think. Unfortunately, Andy saw him from his kitchen, grabbed his things, and went outside to walk with him.

"Mornin', Mr. Screamy," Andy said with a completely straight face.

"Don't start," Dave said in between yawns.

"Man, you look like crap today. Well, crappier than usual. What happened to you?"

"I couldn't sleep last night. No matter what I tried, I just couldn't fall asleep."

"Meh, insomnia happens to everybody every once in a while. My cousin had it for a few weeks," Andy said, putting an earbud into one ear.

"Don't you, you know, die from it if you can't get to sleep? Shouldn't your cousin be dead?"

"Well, maybe it wasn't a few weeks, but it was at least a few days in a row that she couldn't sleep," Andy said with a shrug.

"Did they find out why?"

"Some bad sleep disorder. She has to wear some screwed up mask every night, but she's okay now."

"So, anyway, what are you going to do with Andruseth?" Dave said, changing the subject, not wanting to talk about anything to do with sleep anymore.

"Andruseth? I'll just keeping winning tournaments and getting experience points to spend. I'll take on Ragecage once Andruseth is more powerful," Andy said. "Ragecage is a cheap-ass arch-enemy. As soon as I hit Rank four, he gained this sick move that does mega-damage to me and heals him in the same move. It's totally a cheap move."

"I'm sure there's a way to counter it. Hey, Rank four? Man, I've got to get the game so I can get up to Rank two!"

"Is Emma going to let you play?" Andy said, chuckling.

"Emma had nothing to do with it! Shut up!" Dave said, stopping and turning to face Andy.

"Calm down, I'm just joking around. Geez, get some sleep or something!" Andy said.

"Sorry," Dave said, starting to walk again. "You're right about the sleep thing though. I don't know how I'm going to get through class."

"We'll stop at Krazy Koffee before we go to school and get some caffeine in you. If you have money, you can buy me an energy drink too since I'm helping you out," Andy said, stopping mid-chuckle, making it difficult to figure out whether or not it was a joke.

"Oh, it'd be my pleasure," Dave said, pushing him into one of the bushes.

"Jerk!" Andy said, jumping out of the bushes and chasing him all the way to Krazy Koffee.

Dave and Andy opened the door to the Krazy Koffee café and were immediately overcome with the smell of hot coffee and fresh pastries. Andy took a deep breath and smiled.

"Smell that?" Andy asked.

"Smells like coffee," Dave said.

"No, it smells like pure happy," Andy said, stretching out as if the smell of coffee was loosening him up.

"Happy? I didn't realize that was in your vocabulary," Dave said.

"Please, I can be happy. You guys just don't bring it out of me often," Andy said as Dave rolled his eyes.

When they got to the front of the line, they each bought a large energy drink. The two didn't really like the taste of coffee, but the smell of it always perked them up. Andy got his and quickly took a sip of it.

"Man, that's good," Andy said before downing the rest of the drink

"How can you drink it that fast?" Dave asked.

"My body needs the energy it has been deprived of for so long," Andy said, stretching out each word.

"Oh, stop the drama," Dave said, turning to leave. As he did, he accidentally bumped someone in line, almost dropping his drink.

"Sorry about that!" Dave said, looking up at the person he'd bumped.

"No problem. I understand how important caffeine is to students," the man said in a deep voice. "Though it's not often I see a middle school student in here before class."

"Uh, I just prefer coffee. It tastes better," Dave said, getting a good look at the man. He was dark-skinned, with a mixture of short black and grey hair. Dave recognized him, but couldn't quite place where had seen him before. The man chuckled.

"You probably know my face and you should know my name, but most students don't. I'm Mr. Laws, the school counselor. And you are?"

"Dave...er...David Calloway. "

"Well, nice to meet you Dave," Mr. Laws said.

"Same here. So, you're a shrink or something?" Dave said as he watched Andy pour mounds of sugar into his coffee.

"Basically, yes," Mr. Laws said, nodding his head.

"Really? Hmmmm..." Dave said, catching himself before he went further. Should he talk about it? It's just a couple of weird dreams—strange to him, but nothing to alarm other people about.

"Yes, is there something I can do for you, David?"

Dave was silent for several seconds. "Ummm...maybe. Nah, don't worry about it," Dave finally said.

"Well, if there's anything you want to talk about, my door is always open," Mr. Laws said, moving to the front of the line.

"Umm...sure...thanks," Dave said smiling. "Well, I have to get to class now."

"I will talk with you later, Dave," Mr. Laws said, turning and placing his coffee order.

Dave managed to get through his first class without a problem. Luckily, the teacher didn't care if they brought in food or drinks. The caffeine was helping—even just the motion of drinking the coffee was helping. However, after first period, the coffee was gone and at about the mid-point of second period, he felt the caffeine buzz wearing off. Along with it went his ability to concentrate. It took all he had to keep his eyes open during class. Unfortunately, ten minutes into his third period history class, his eyes wavered and finally closed. For a second, there was nothing but darkness and quiet peace. Then the snake emerged from the darkness and struck. Dave awoke with a gasp drawing stares from the entire class and the teacher.

"Yes, Mr. Calloway, the Industrial Revolution was incredible, but try to keep the noises to a minimum," the teacher said as the class chuckled. Adrienne kept laughing for several seconds after the rest of the class had stopped. Emma poked him on the shoulder with the end of her pen and tossed him a note. It hit the side of his head and fell onto his desk just after the teacher had turned away. The note had a big smiley face with the words: WAKE UP, SLEEPYHEAD!

He smirked at Emma and mouthed the words, "I'll try."

The rest of the day was a blur. When the bell rang ending each class, he'd look at his paper to see one or two lines of well-written notes and then just random scribbled words from the lecture. His friends tried to keep him awake at lunch, but when that proved futile, they moved onto other things. Andy and Eric discussed their plans for Ultimate Lord Battler, ignoring Todd's input, as usual. And the girls raved about their new favorite TV show—its hot host and sweet outfits. To Dave, it was all just a jumble of words.

Later, during practice, he could barely remember the routes he had to run. Tony Krantz, the backup QB, kept trying to throw passes to him, but he kept running the wrong way or dropping the ball. After about a half hour of this, the coach pulled him aside.

"Calloway, is there some kind of problem with you today or are you just screwing up on purpose to piss me off?" Coach Weaver asked, already out of breath from walking and talking.

"I'm sorry coach. I'm just exhausted."

"If you're exhausted now, how do you expect to ever play in a game, son?" the coach said, his voice rising and spittle flying at Dave.

"Sorry, I just didn't get much sleep last night."

"You've got to set your priorities, son. Either put down the comic books and stop playing video games with your friends all night or get the hell off my team. Do you get me?"

"Yes," Dave said, looking at the ground.

"Do you get me?" The coach repeated, louder this time.

"Yes, sir," Dave said, a bit louder than before, staring the coach in the eye.

"Good, shower and go home early. Get eight hours of sleep and be ready to play tomorrow," the coach said, turning his back to him.

"Coach, I think I can play some more today," Dave said, moving towards the field. The coach reached out and grabbed his jersey.

"I said go home, Calloway," Coach Weaver said, shoving him away. Dave looked around the field and saw Mike and Cole pointing at him and laughing. He shook his head and headed toward the shower.

"Dave, wait up!"

Eric ran up behind him, still in full gear.

"What?" Dave said through clenched teeth.

"Coach is a butthead, but he's right, man. I think even Todd could have defended you today."

"Trying to make me feel better by telling me I'm worse than Todd? Thanks, man!" Dave said, throwing his arms up in frustration.

"Don't be an ass," Eric said, punching his shoulder pad.

"Sorry. I'm just going to go, okay?"

"Don't you want a ride home?" Eric asked.

"Nah, I'll walk. See you later," Dave said. Eric shrugged and stared at him as if waiting for Dave to change his mind. But Dave turned and walked off the field, his pads giving him the look of a defeated warrior.

After a quick shower, Dave noticed something out of the corner of his eye as he walked past the coach's office. He came to a full stop and entered the coach's office, glancing down the hallway to make sure no one was looking.

Hanging on the wall of the coach's office was a giant poster of an orange snake slithering along a jungle tree branch. Below the photo was some motivational message about not having legs doesn't mean you can't move. Dave didn't fully understand the message itself, but the snake looked just like the one from his dream.

Weird, Dave thought to himself. *My mind is pulling out all sorts of old stuff. I've got to be coming down with something.*

He put down the photograph on top of some warnings from the principal's office about the low grades of some of the players and left the room. He headed out of the exit, but just as he was reaching for the handle, he realized that he had forgotten his science book in his locker. After spending a few seconds contemplating whether it was worth it to just forget about the book and deal with the consequences of not doing his homework, Dave kicked the door lightly to open it and headed back to his locker. Along the way, he heard someone yell from behind a closed door.

"You think I give a crap what you say?"

Dave noticed the name printed onto the wooden door: MR. PETER LAWS, COUNSELOR.

Just then, the door was thrown open. Much to Dave's disappointment, Rake stepped out. Rake stormed past him, making sure to slam his shoulder into Dave's. However, before Dave could say anything, the counselor came out from behind the door.

"Raymond, I expect to see you back here tomorrow afternoon as agreed."

"Whatever... " Rake kept walking without looking back.

The counselor shook his head, looked at Dave, and smiled.

"Mr. Calloway, is it?" he asked, his eyes occasionally looking around to see whether Rake had left the building.

"Yeah, that's me," Dave said, turning to leave.

"Come on in," the counselor said, pointing toward his office.

"Me?' Dave said, quickly turning his head towards the counselor. "Oh, sorry, I don't have an appointment."

"But, you have something to talk about, don't you?" the counselor said, his face taking on a very serious look.

"I...uh..." Dave said, trying to think of some excuse.

"Come on in. I can't force you to talk, but it looks like you want to talk to somebody who wants to listen."

Dave stared at the counselor's office—the oak desk, the black leather chair, and a nice comfy-looking couch. Dave remembered how tired he was and just wanted to flop down there and take a nap to get some energy to walk home. He then scanned the bookshelf in the office. Most of the books mentioned different behavioral issues in children and teenagers. However, there was one book on the third shelf that caught his eye. It read *My Dreams, My Worlds*, by Alan Cudney.

Dreams. Maybe this will make sense to me, Dave thought.

"Maybe I do have something to talk about," Dave mumbled.

"Good. Have a seat on the couch. You can either sit or lie down. Whatever is more comfortable for you."

Dave sat and instantly realized that the couch was just as comfortable as he'd imagined. He sank deeply into the cushions, which were as soft as a blanket fresh from the dryer. He had to fight the urge to relax his head on the soft pillows, close his eyes, and just go to sleep.

The counselor sat behind his desk, took a deep breath, and opened a spiral bound notebook. He jotted down some notes, then looked up at Dave, staring at him for a few seconds before going back to his notebook again.

"Seventh grade?

"Eighth"

"Soccer?"

"Football."

"Well, I got that one half-right. If we were in England I would have been right!" the counselor chuckled as he said that. Dave laughed through his nose.

"So, anyway, what can I do for you, Dave?"

"Well, Mr. Laws..." Dave hesitated. He turned his eyes toward the bookshelf and looked at the dream book again.

"Dave, I'm not here to pass judgment nor am I going to send you to detention. Things that you say here will stay in this room."

Dave nodded. "It's my dreams," Dave finally said, still staring at the book.

"Your dreams?"

"Yeah, I know it must sound stupid. Everybody has dreams, but mine have been really weird these past couple of nights."

"Weird how?"

"Like the one I had two nights ago. I was playing football when all of a sudden, this crazy armored freak with a sword starts coming after me."

"And what did the crazy armored freak do?" Mr. Laws asked, writing down some notes.

"He managed to slash me right on the shoulder," Dave pointed to his hurt shoulder. "I woke up soon after that."

"Well, Dave, it's not unusual to have dreams where you're hurt or worse. However, they're harmless. Now, some people do think that dreams mean something beyond what literally happened in your dream, including me. That being said, in this case, it's probably just your stress from football. I imagine Coach Weaver is really running you ragged," Mr. Laws said, putting his pen down, as Dave nodded in agreement. "Did he look familiar?"

"The armored guy?" Dave asked as Mr. Laws smiled at his answer. "Well, I'm not sure if it's a guy, but it was wearing this freaky black armor."

"And have you seen this freaky armored person before?" he said, picking up the pen again and starting to write again.

"I found out later on, yeah, I saw him in a video game earlier. Like, years earlier."

"There you go!" Mr. Laws said, throwing up his hands. "Your mind sometimes goes into long lost memories to create a dream."

"Yeah, but when I woke up, the place where he slashed me hurt," Dave said, rolling his shoulder and wincing in pain.

"Dave, have you ever started to go to sleep and just when you're on the edge of sleep, you start dreaming and just when that happens, something happens that made you lash out with a punch or a kick?" Mr. Laws asked, making a punching motion.

"I guess. Maybe?" Dave said, thinking about it.

"That could be what happened here. This guy tried to stab you. Your body tried to get out of the way. You probably ended up twisting it in your sleep."

"But, it felt just like it did in the dream," Dave said.

"Dave, did you wake up with a bleeding slash wound?"

"I don't think so."

"Hmmm...you know, normally when I wake up bleeding heavily from a shoulder wound from my dreams, I remember it," Mr. Laws said, smiling.

"What? Oh...no, I wasn't bleeding," Dave said, following it up with a small laugh.

"Good! Excellent! It was just a dream!" the counselor said, slapping his hand down on his desk.

"Well, there's one more thing."

"Really?" Mr. Laws said. "Another dream?"

"Yeah. The dream was weird, but not anything I couldn't deal with. It's what happened at the end. I met a talking snake who told me if I don't rest up and relax, the armored guy is going to come back and kill me," Dave said, returning his gaze to the bookshelf.

Mr. Laws allowed for a few seconds of silence before answering. "Dave, what I tell everybody who has strange dreams is to remember that they are *your* dreams. *You* control them. If you don't want that snake there, tell it to go away. If you can't make it go away, then at least open up your desk and pull out the bazooka you've been storing there. Use it to get rid of the snake *and* the freaky dude. It's your dream," he repeated, raising his voice near the end as Dave turned his back to the counselor, listening intently. "Your mind made the snake just like it did the armored guy. Use your mind to unmake it. That snake is bossing you around? Go up to it tonight and tell it that *you* are in charge, not it. You'll find your dreams a lot more pleasant after that resolves. Got it?"

"I do. Actually, that makes a lot of sense," Dave said. In actuality, while it did make some sense to Dave, he wasn't exactly sure whether he could pull it off.

"Great! Tell you what. I have an opening tomorrow just before your football practice starts. I want to see you tomorrow and hear about the results. How about it?" he asked with a big smile, walking over to Dave, and offering his hand.

"I'll give it a try tonight and let you know tomorrow if it works," Dave said, shaking his hand.

"Excellent! I'll see you then! And remember that it's your mind and it's your dream. You are in control."

When Dave arrived home, his mother poked her head out from the kitchen.

"Dave? What are you doing home so early?" she asked.

Dave thought about it for a second before answering. "I have a lot of homework to do, so I told the coach that I had to leave early," Dave said, taking off his shoes.

His mother smiled. "I'm so proud of you. You're finally taking your school work seriously," she said on the verge of tears of joy.

"I just don't want to fall behind," he said smiling.

"Well then, since you're home now and have a lot of work, march yourself right upstairs and do your homework," she said, the smile on her face gone, replaced with a very serious *Mom* look.

Dave peered down the staircase at the TV where his little brother was playing the Zeus. He wanted to go down there and relax a bit, but he had backed himself into a corner with that little white lie. He slowly made his way upstairs to do his homework.

Sitting at his desk, he found it hard to concentrate on his books and his paper without his mind drifting. *Was it all just some normal, run-of-the-mill whacky dream? It must be a regular dream. How could it be something different?* Sure, one dream referred to the other, but that was probably his mind playing tricks on him.

Dave looked at his clock and saw that he had been in his room for nearly an hour and had barely made a dent in his homework. He leaned back in his chair, relaxed his head, and let out a sigh. Just as he did, he heard his mother yell that dinner was ready. Within seconds, he heard his brother running up the stairs from the living room to the kitchen. Dave slammed his science book shut and left his room to get some dinner.

Finally around eight o'clock that evening, Dave finished his homework. He thought about playing the Zeus, but his body forced out a yawn, as if telling him to not even think about doing anything except sleeping, despite the early hour. Climbing under his soft blankets, he had no problem falling asleep.

Guardian

Dave walked through the open gateway quickly catching up with his parents. The carnival came to his town once a year for a weekend and his family always went. It wasn't a matter of whether any of them were too old or too young to enjoy it. His brother was quickly getting ahead of the family and his mother yelled for Nick to slow down and wait for them. Nick, now at the age where he was finally tall enough to ride most things, raced ahead of his family, excited to try everything. Dave smiled as his mother chased Nick. His father approached him and said two words that Dave would have said if he hadn't said them first.

"Ring toss?" His father pointed towards a booth only a few steps away.

"Ring toss," Dave agreed, walking towards the booth. "Only this time, the bet is washing dishes for a week."

"Getting a little cocky, I see! Play a little football and suddenly you think you can beat your dad, eh?"

"I think you stopped being able to beat me a few years ago," Dave said.

"Oh, is that right? Alrighty, big man, how about this? If you win,

I'll do the dishes for a week. But if I win, which I will, you can't play the Zeus for a week. How about that?

"The Zeus? That's—."

"Cruel and unusual, yes, but if you're so confident, then put your money where your mouth is," his father said, crossing his arms while nodding and smirking. It was always a game of one-upmanship with his father. He remembered hearing his mother saying that eventually they'll be betting houses and cars on the carnival games.

"Fine, Zeus versus dishes. You're on," Dave offered his hand to his father. His father faked a spit into his hand and shook it. "Gross!"

"That's how you did it in the old days."

"Great! You know, I didn't come to the carnival to get a history lesson. I came here to keep my football hands from doing the dishes."

"And I'm here to keep those football hands from getting ruined from too much time on the Zeus."

Father and son laughed together and then walked over to the ring toss. There was a fat man in full clown garb at the ring toss who looked like he slept in the costume every night. His face was a mix of make-up and dirt, and it looked like both had run directly into his now colorful, and dirty, beard. Without blinking an eye, the clown waddled up to the front of the booth.

"Howmanyringsdoyouwantthreefiveten?" the clown said, speaking quickly yet still slurring his words.

"Ummm...what?" Dave asked.

"Isaid...howmanyringsyouwant?"

"We'll take three each, thanks," his father said, putting down ten dollars. As the clown reached out with a dirty glove and took the money, Dave got a feeling that he was forgetting something. Did he forget to do his homework? Nope, it was a Saturday so he didn't forget it yet. Did he forget to call Emma? Nah, she was out with some of her friends.

"All right, Dave. Concentrate. Be the ring. Throw it over one of the milk bottles and you'll have those extra few minutes a day to not do dishes. But, I have every confidence in the world in you...I have every confidence in the fact that you'll miss and you won't get to use the Zeus for a week!" his father said, picking up his rings.

"Nice parenting! Aren't you supposed to be encouraging me or something?"

"Not when we're on the battleground, son. Today, I know you only as the enemy."

"You're a pretty weird guy, Dad," Dave said, chuckling as he picked up his rings.

"Thank you! I try my best! Anyway, remember that it's not just for our bet. Win this and you get one of those little mustache combs as a prize," his father said tossing his first ring in between the milk bottles. "Darn. Almost got it."

"You would have missed hitting reality with that shot!" Dave said throwing his first ring. It landed on the milk bottle, spun around, and then jumped off, landing on the floor. "Almost! I almost had it!"

"Almost isn't going to do it, buddy!" his father said throwing the ring. It clipped the top of one of the bottles, bounced into the air, and landed in the clown's hand.

"Niceshotmaybenexttimetryaimingatthemilkbottleinsteadofthe-clown," the clown said, following up with a long belch and lip smack. Dave looked at the clown and tried to think of something to say to the clown, but a nasty smell came over him. He realized that it was coming from the clown. It smelled like hundred-year-old feet. He felt his stomach want to retch, but he fought it and threw the ring without even looking. It clanged off two milk bottles and fell between them. As soon as the ring stopped moving, he got that nagging feeling that he was forgetting something again.

"Uh oh! One more ring each," his dad said aiming with his last ring. He took some deep breaths, trying to make the situation as dramatic as possible and flipped the ring high into the air. It hit the side of a milk bottle in the first row and fell to the ground.

"Ohsosorrywannatryagain?"

Dave ignored the clown and breathed deeply. He saw his dad

give him a smile and he gently threw the ring up into the air. The ring landed on top of one of the milk bottles on the very edge of the table right near the clown. It spun around a few times and stayed put.

"YES! I WON!" Dave yelled as his dad congratulated him. The clown looked at Dave then down at the ring. With a flick of his wrist, the clown knocked the ring off of the bottle.

"Ohsosorrywannatryagain?"

"What?!" Dave and his father screamed.

"I saaaaaiiiiiiiid. . . sosorrywannatryagain?" the clown said, making sure to talk very slowly and to say the first part of his sentence very slowly before speeding up again.

"Hold on here," his father said. "My son won this game fair and square."

"Nohedidn't."

"Yes he did!"

"Doyouseearingonthebottle?"

"No, but that's just because you knocked it off!" his father said, pointing at the ring on the ground

"Didnot."

"Did too!" his father said, raising his voice and slamming his hands on the counter.

"Didnot!"

"Listen, buddy, I know we're just talking about that stupid little comb, but give us the comb," his father said, calming down.

"Nowaythatcomesoutofmypocket!"

"And the money that we just spent came out of my pocket. Get over yourself and give us the comb!"

"Imgoingtocallsecuritytheydonottakekindlytocheaters."

"Like yourself? Dave, I'm sorry, let's just go. Apparently there are some people in this world that no matter what you do, they just like to be a pain in the butt to everybody else," his father said walking away. Dave turned to join him when the clown reached out and grabbed his arm.

"David? DavidCalloway?" the clown asked. His breath was horrible and smelled like he brushed his teeth with old cheese.

"Yeah, that's me. How do you know my name?

"Ihavesomethingforyouholdon," the clown said, ducking beneath the booth for a second. He emerged with a beaten up cardboard box stained with grease. On the side of the box, written with red crayon in horrible handwriting was *David Calloway*.

"What the heck is this?"

"Openit!"

"Uh, you open it!"

"AlrightyI'llopenit," the clown said, opening up the box. "Neat!"

Dave peered over the side of the box to look in. As he did, an orange snake lunged at him from inside—the same snake that attacked him on the tree the other day. Dave tripped over his own feet and fell backward into the dirt. He quickly tried to get to his feet. He looked around for his father but couldn't find him. He turned to see the clown hop over the wall of the booth with ease, as if his weight didn't matter. Most of the snake's body was out of the box. It was hissing as it stared at Dave. The clown seemed to move as the snake did, twisting and turning his body in sync with the reptile, which looked very odd considering the clown's shape.

"What are you doing?" Dave screamed.

"Thisisyourpackagewhatareyoudoing?" the clown asked, getting closer.

"Who are you?" Dave yelled, scooting backward while still trying to stand up.

"I'm... your... worst... nightmare," the clown said very slowly, enunciating every word.

Nightmare? Why did that sound so familiar? What was I forgetting? Nightmare? Scary thoughts? Dreaming? Dream! Mr. Laws! What did Mr. Laws say? It was my dream! This was my mind! I could do anything I wanted to... in my dream!

He looked up at the snake as it hissed. Suddenly, it lunged at him.

"This is my dream!" Dave said loudly as he reached out and grabbed the snake in mid-air. The clown started backing away as the entire length of the snake's body slipped out of the box. Dave and the snake met eye-to-eye. It hissed and tried to bite him, but Dave wouldn't let him.

"This is my dream, snake. You're part of my dream. You do what I say in my dream," he said as the snake stopped hissing and then just nodded. Dave smiled and looked at the clown. "I think the clown might be tastier."

He let go of the snake. The snake looked up at Dave, flicked his tongue at him, and then turned and hissed at the clown.

"Whatareyoudoing?"

"I told you. It's my dream!" Dave yelled as the snake lunged at the clown. As he did, the clown tripped and fell to the ground, the snake just missing his head. Then, the clown did something that surprised even Dave. He clapped.

"Very good, boy! I finally got through that thick head of yours! It took a while, but hey, it's not like I get to pick who I'm a dream guardian for," the clown said, getting to his feet.

"A what?"

"A ddddrrrreeeeaaaammmm… guardian," the clown said. "You're in a bad situation. Therefore, I'm allowed to reveal myself. OW!"

The clown turned around to show that the snake had latched onto his behind. The clown tugged and pulled on the snake, but it didn't want to let go.

"Would… ow… you… ow… mind?" the clown said, pointing to the snake.

"Who are you?"

"I'm your damn dream guardian! Are you really that dense? I mean, I thought I was just joking about the thick head, but I guess I was really serious. Call off your snake and I'll tell you what you need to know."

"I think I'll leave him until you tell me what I need to know," Dave said, crossing his arms.

"Oh crap, you suck, you know that? This really hurts! You want to see a sad little clown in pain?"

"You tried to attack me!"

"No, the snake did. It's a vicious snake! Look what it's doing to my poor costume," the clown said, pulling apart some of the ripped clothing.

"You're my dream guardian, eh? What are you guarding me from?"

The clown kept pulling on the snake, trying to get it off of him, "Who do you think? The Sleepless Knight!"

Dave uncrossed his arms, "Snake, off of him, now."

The snake dropped off and slithered away, going underneath the booth.

"Oooohhhh, so now you believe me because I'm talking about the knight!"

"Were you the dog? Were you Max?" Dave said, staring straight into the clown's eyes.

"I was Max in a lot of your dreams," the clown said, poking a hole through his ripped pants.

"I'm talking about recently. A few nights ago when the Sleepless Knight attacked me," Dave said, getting close to the clown.

"Yeah, that was me and I was the snake from last night as well. Man, you should have seen your face. *Help me, help me*, you were screaming. Hell, I was even the 911 phone operator!" The clown said as Dave felt a wave of anger come over him. "Oh don't worry about it. I was the 911 operator because I figured you were dead anyway. May as well have some fun!"

"Shut up. Aren't you supposed to be my dream guardian?" Dave said, raising his voice.

"Yup, that I am."

"Then what the heck is your problem?"

"Listen, buddy, I'm your dream guardian, not your dream buddy. Think of me as your schoolteacher. I don't have to like you. It's not part of the job description. However, I'll make sure that you know everything you need to know," his dream guardian said, a disgusting-looking smile coming across his face.

"Can I get a new guardian?"

"Can you get a new guardian? What? What's wrong with me? And no, you can't get a new one. Every dreamer comes with their own personal dream guardian. I'm yours, kiddo," the clown said, dragging a chair from his booth and sitting down.

"Just great. Even in my dreams I've got somebody who wants to harass me."

"Hey, listen up kiddo, I've got your best interests in mind. If you go kaput in your dream, I have to pay attention to the person who ummm... kaputed you," the clown said, pulling out a soda from underneath the booth.

"Kaput as in dead? Is the Sleepless Knight trying to kill me? I thought he was just something I made up in my head," Dave said, confused.

"Trying to kill you? Sort of. And hey, how do you know that it's a guy?"

"I don't, but..."

"It's this sort of crap that prevents women from being equals in society."

"Can we please not have a political discussion in my dream?"

"Whatever you want, boy," the dream guardian said, his voice turning serious. "Welcome, kiddy, to the Dreamscape!"

The dream guardian spread his arms wide, splashing his soda all over the prizes.

"The what?"

"The Dreamscape. The land of the dreams."

"There's a land of dreams?" Dave said, noticing that nobody was around. The amusement park was empty except for the clown and himself.

"No, you're the only person who dreams. Of *course* there's a land of dreams. Where else do you think the dreams go?"

"Sorry, but I didn't plan on having a philosophical discussion about dreams today, okay?" Dave said, looking around. "So, there's a land of dreams? This is the fair from my childhood."

"Well, the Dreamscape is less of a land and really more of a dimension. Well, actually a series of interconnected dimensions, but whatever," the clown said, rubbing his chin, some paint coming off.

"Whatever. All right, dream guardian."

"Bags."

"Where?" Dave said, looking around.

"No, that's my name, you idiot. My name is Bags," he said, giving a big smile, revealing several broken rotten teeth.

"Bags the Clown?"

"Bags the Dream Guardian!" Bags said, raising his voice. "Crap, that school doesn't teach you much, does it?"

"About dreams?"

"About anything!" Bags said, shaking his head.

"Whatever. So, dream guardian..."

"Bags!"

"So, Bags," Dave said, scratching his head in disbelief that this conversation was actually happening. "How are you going to help me against the Sleepless Knight?"

"Right now, you're a sitting duck. You've got nothing. But, with me at your side, I'll make sure that if you do go kaput against the Darkity Dark Dark Knight, it won't be because of a lack of training."

"Stop joking around. Do you know who the Sleepless Knight is?"

"She's a bad sort of Dreamer," Bags said. "She's probably a Trauma Guild member or at the very least, a Harvester, but sometimes you can never tell."

"Trauma Guild? Harvester? What are you talking about?" Dave

69

asked, grabbing the clown. Bags just shook his head, sighed, and got to his feet, slipping out of Dave's grasp.

"Take a seat, boy. I don't want you fainting and hurting yourself once you hear this stuff."

The Dreamscape

Dave sat down in the chair once occupied by the clown. Bags stared at him briefly before shaking his head.

"I can't believe that some Harvester is going after you. I mean, why? Because you're easy pickings? It can't be because you're good looking," Bags said, throwing his arms into the air.

"Excuse me? I thought you were going to tell me about the Dreamscape, not insult me," Dave said, trying his best to stay calm.

"Ah yes, the Dreamscape," Bags said. "Mr. Fancypants here wants to know what the Dreamscape is all about. Well, understand this, once you understand that your dream is more than just a dream, you probably will never want go back to just dreaming any old dream anymore. You'll want to experience everything that the Dreamscape has to offer, and let me tell you... there is a lot out there!"

"Like what?" Dave asked.

"All in due time, boy. Now, what am I?"

"Um... my dream guardian who looks like a clown? Get to the point, I know that already!" Dave said.

"Patience is a virtue, boy. I'm the one who is supposed to be watching out for you. However, while I'm your guardian, that doesn't mean I have to take a bullet for you. No way. Bullets hurt."

"Then, what do you do?" Dave asked. "Obviously you didn't try to help me against the Sleepless Knight or those alligators, so what's your deal?"

"Okay, if you were some normal kid, you probably even wouldn't notice that I'm here in your dreams. In fact, dream guardians make sure that they're never noticed by the dreamer. However, there are circumstances that come up where a guardian has to talk to its dreamer."

"Like what?"

"Like another dreamer entering your dream," Bags said.

Dave moved closer to the edge of his seat. "Say what? So, you're saying that the Sleepless Knight was..."

"Somebody who actually exists in your reality. Someone put on the Sleepless Knight suit and tried to skewer you."

"Why would someone try to skewer me in my dream?"

"Who knows? I mean, you're quite an annoying boy, so that's one reason. But in truth, it could be many reasons. It could be a dreamer not knowing what they're doing and not realizing that they're in somebody else's dream. It could be a Wraith, it could be a Living Dream, it could be a Harvester, it could be an Ino—."

"Stop it, stop it, stop it!" Dave said. "Let's go through this slowly. A Wraith? A Living Dream? Harvester? Where the heck am I?"

"You're in the Dreamscape, duh!"

"I'm about one second away from knocking you out."

"Oh please. Threat, threat, threat," Bags said. "That's all that comes out of you."

"I'm serious."

"Well, I know you well enough to know that you are *not* serious about knocking me out. Now, would you like to find out what the hell I'm talking about?"

"Yeah, that's what I've been trying to get you to do," Dave said, as he could feel his blood pressure rising.

"Alrighty, let's do the easy thing right now, okay? Now where did that snake go?" Bags said, getting on his knees and crawling underneath the booth. "Ah! Yes! Here it is!"

Bags got back onto his feet holding the orange snake from before. Dave took a step back as the thing hissed at him.

"What are you doing?" Dave screamed as Bags smiled and looked at the snake.

"What a good snake you are," Bags said, petting it as if it were a puppy. He sniffed it and his nose wrinkled up. "Pew! It stinks! You know what? We need you to smell better, isn't that right Dave?"

"Uh, what? I guess," Dave said with a confused look on his face.

"Good! Dave, what smells nice to you?"

"Um..."

"Don't think too hard," Bags said.

"Uh, flowers?" Dave shrugged.

"Good! Flowers! How about a rose! How do you like a rose's smell?"

"It's all right, I guess."

"He guesses, Mr. Snake. Mr. Snake should smell like a rose, don't you think?" Bags said, looking at the snake.

"What are you talking about, Bags?" Dave asked in a frustrated voice.

"Listen, if you can't trust a figment of your imagination, who can you trust?" Bags said, smiling at Dave. "But anyway, listen to me, boy. I want you to imagine that this snake is not a snake at all, but a rose. A nice smelling orange rose. Can you do that for me?"

"Why?" Dave asked, not sure whether he really should have followed Mr. Laws' advice.

"Boy, just answer the question!" the clown yelled.

"All right, all right. I'll try," Dave said, looking at the snake.

"And I don't want you to just imagine an orange rose. I want you to imagine that the orange snake transforms into the orange rose and that it makes complete sense that it does so. Orange snakes turn into orange roses all the time!"

"Um, I'll try," Dave said in an unsure voice.

"He'll try, Mr. Snake. You're going to be a pretty-looking rose soon," Bags said in the same voice you would address a dog that you adored.

Dave thought about the snake. He thought about the scales. He thought about its tongue. He thought about what the snake would look like with petals for a head. He imagined what it would look like if the snake's body were the steam of a rose. He imagined a bouquet of roses.

"Good, boy, good! You've almost got it! You—ACK!"

Dave looked at the snake as its head split open with a sickening cracking noise. Emerging from the opening was a new snake, but this time it had multiple heads, one for each rose that he had imagined. The multi-headed snake lunged at Bags who dropped it before it could sink its fangs into his hand. The snake turned around and saw Dave. The mere sight of the multiple heads lunging at him made him fall to the ground. All the heads hissed at Dave before the body flung itself into the air, going for his throat.

"Dave! The snake is a rose!" Bags screamed. Dave looked at the snake as it flew into the air. He imagined all the heads as the head of a beautiful flower and the body as a stem.

"The snake is a rose, the snake is a rose, the snake is a rose..." Dave repeated as he closed his eyes, waiting for the pain of the bite. However, the snake's bite came softly as it gently caressed his neck and then landed in his lap. Dave opened his eyes and quickly felt around his neck for the bite. Feeling neither a wound nor any blood, he looked down at his lap and saw no snake. There was only a bright orange rose with an orange stem. He picked it up and looked at it in amazement as Bags began to clap.

"Good! I would have lost a hundred bucks betting against you, but good!" Bags exclaimed.

"What did I just do?" Dave said, amazed at the flower in his hand.

"Transfiguration, transformation, whatever you want to call it. You changed the snake's shape."

"I can do that?"

"It's your dream! You can do whatever you want! While you're in your dream, you can do anything, create anything, and be anything. See an ant on the ground? Wouldn't it be great if it weren't an ant, but a giant bazooka? You can do it. You can even turn the air you breathe into something. It's like pulling something out of thin air. Instead of using the ant, you just wish for a bazooka and WHAM! A bazooka is formed out of the air and bye-bye bad guy! Wouldn't that be fun? Of course, to do it you have to have some creativity, some imagination, and some brains. Looking at you, I'm zero for three! Crap, I'm screwed!" Bags said, laughing as he clutched his huge belly.

"Stop laughing, Bags. I thought you were supposed to be helping me," Dave said, moving closer to the clown.

"Didn't I just teach you a new trick? Next one is learning how to roll over," Bags said, laughing harder than ever.

Dave thought about the snake trick. He thought about being able to transform the things within his own dream. "All right, fine. So, I can just walk into my dream and start changing things? Can I control what I'm dreaming about?"

"Almost no dreamers can control what they dream about when they go to sleep," Bags said, still clutching his enormous stomach. "It's usually a mishmash of what you saw today, what you did yesterday, along with some screwed up things from your past. But, as soon as you arrive in your dream, hey, you can start changing things and rebuilding."

"What about you?" Dave asked, smirking.

"Me? What about me?" Bags said, raising an eyebrow, now fully paying attention to Dave.

"Can I control what you are?" Dave asked.

"What are you getting at, boy?" Bags said, his hand on one of

75

the rings from the game, almost as if he was thinking about using it as a weapon.

"You heard what I said, Bags," Dave said, smiling. "Can I control what you are? Are you part of my dream?"

Bags looked down at the ground. "I'm your dream guardian, but I'm still part of your dream, as much as it pains me to say so."

"That can't be," Dave said.

"Why not?" Bags asked.

"Because I don't remember any fat smelly clowns from today, yesterday, or any other day!" Dave said.

"Hey, listen, if you don't want to learn anything else and you want to get skewered by the Sleepless Knight, by all means go ahead and don't believe me. But at any rate, I'm simply a part of your dream. If a form hasn't been pre-chosen for me by the dreamer, I pick a form that blends in with the scenery," Bags said, pointing to his clown suit.

"A fat smelly clown blends in?" Dave said.

"What's your point, boy?" Bags asked, emphasizing the end of the sentence.

"Never mind. What's this about a pre-chosen form?"

"Uh, never mind about that one, let's talk about Pathways next."

"No, no, no. You brought it up," Dave said, a big smile on his face.

"Uh... well, as this is your mind and your dream, you can choose the form that best suits me. Something that you're comfortable with. Like a clown, or a giant robot, or a super-soldier. Those things are great! Anyway, once a person becomes self-aware in a dream as you have, you can select a form for me. Once I'm in that form, I stay that way until you change me to something else."

"Wow, can I really transform anything in my dream?" Dave said, faking his amazement.

"Whatever your little imagination wants, kid," Bags said, eyeing him suspiciously.

"You know what I'm picturing now?" Dave said, smiling.

"What? Your blanky?"

"No, I'm imagining Bags as a small furry animal. Hmmm... kind of like a ferret."

Bags' eyes widened as Dave saw the clown's body quickly distort and resize itself to the long brown furred weasel-like creature.

"Wow, it worked!" Dave said, laughing between his words as he picked up the ferret. "You don't look so tough now, do you?"

"What the hell?" Bags said, still with the same deep voice as he had when he was the clown. "Change me back this instant."

"Nope, not gonna do it," Dave said, laughing. "I like you in this form. There's less risk of you eating me this way."

Dave pulled him close and mussed up the ferret's hair. Just after he did that, Bags nipped at Dave's nose. Dave winced in pain and dropped the ferret. Bags landed on his feet and ran under the booth.

"Ferrets may be cute and cuddly, but they still have sharp teeth!" Bags yelled. Dave checked his nose and noticed a small amount of blood. In an instant, Dave was on the ground, looking underneath the booth for the ferret. As he peeked underneath, Bags darted out and latched onto Dave's head with his arms and legs.

"Get off me!" Dave yelled as he pulled Bags off, leaving little scratch marks on his face.

"Change me back!" Bags yelled.

"No!"

"Then you're not getting any training!" Bags yelled back. Dave put the ferret back on the ground, and they looked at each other in silence for several seconds.

"Then I guess you don't care if I go kaput then. Wait, what happens if I die in here?" Dave said. "Do I just wake up?"

"There's going to be one pissed off ferret, I'd imagine," Bags said. "Listen, I don't want to be a ferret!"

"Bags, seriously. What happens?" Dave said as Bags sighed.

"It's all gone. All your dreams. All your hopes. All your ideas. All your creativity. The person who defeats you gets all of them and you're left with a blank slate. It's called harvesting and while sometimes it's necessary as a form of self-defense, taking somebody's dream by force is an evil, nasty act. There are some out there who harvest without a need or necessity. They do it for the thrill of it. Those dreamers, called Harvesters, are a seriously bad lot. If your Sleepless Knight friend is aware of what she is doing, then I'll bet my ferret-form she's a Harvester," Bags said, trying to look Dave in the eyes as best he could from just a few inches off the ground.

"So, the Sleepless Knight is trying to harvest my hopes, dreams, and creativity? He's trying to take them all away?"

"Every last bit. And because they've got your dream, they get me as well."

"Is it permanent?"

"Unless you take them back by defeating the guy who defeated you, yup. But, people have long lives. They can grow new hopes and dreams, but they start over from scratch."

Dave opened his mouth to say something meaningful, but all that came out was, "That sucks. But, if that's all that happens, is it really that bad?"

"Think about it this way. Imagine if Shakespeare's dreams were destroyed? Imagine if Leonard Da Vinci's dreams were destroyed? Imagine if Martin Luther King's dreams were destroyed? Imagine if all their hopes, dreams, and ideas were gone."

"Are you saying that killing your dream makes you stupid?"

"No, you idiot. Your brainpower is still there. But your inspiration is gone. Your urge to achieve your goals will be gone. You'll go to school as normal and you'll see your friends. However, when your friends ask what you want to do after school, you won't be able to come up with any ideas. When your teacher asks you to come up with a thesis for a research paper, you won't be able to do it on your own. Sure, you can read a book for the paper and you'll be able to write about the facts, but there will be no life in it. To the people you know casually, you'll be known as the guy who is as dull as a door-knob. To your friends, you'll have completely changed," Bags said, doing his best to try to climb to the top of the booth. After several attempts, he finally made it to the top and took a deep breath as he stared at a wide-eyed Dave.

"Let me put it in a way that you can understand," Bags said. "Imagine playing Ultimate Lord Battler, but you have no desire to design your own character. You'll have no desire to learn new moves to beat up your friends with. Hell, to put in better terms, imagine if you no longer could say any of those idiotic sweet nothings that you say to Emma. Imagine if you went out on a date, but you constantly took her out to a dinner and a movie, repeatedly. When she tells you to come up with a new idea, you do a movie and a dinner instead of a dinner and a movie. Imagine if you couldn't see a future with Emma. Imagine if you could only see the relationship as exactly the way it is as it is now."

"So, let me get this straight," Dave said, trying to take it all in. "I don't die if I die in here?"

"Holy crap," Bags said. "Is that all you learned from my little speech there?"

"Well, losing your hopes and dreams isn't so bad if they come back, right?"

"No! It's NOT GOOD! Everything you hoped and dreamed for in your life will BE GONE... You won't hope or dream for a long, long time," Bags said, pounding his little paw on the booth for emphasis.

"What happens here in my dream when I come back the next night?"

"You'll have a new dream. A new dream guardian... and don't even think about cheering for that one. But, the dream will be basically blank. Every memory that your dreams would normally bring up would be gone. Everything. Remember the carnival smells? It's gone. You'll have to experience it anew to be able to smell it in your dream."

"Wait, does it affect my memory?"

"In a way, yes. You won't forget names or faces, but you may forget why you feel love for Emma or how it felt when you beat Lord Battler for the first time. Your love of football? Gone. Your skill is there. Your passion for it? Gone."

Dave took a second to take that all in. "Okay, okay, I can see how that could be a bad thing."

"No crap. Now, will you turn me back?"

"In due time," Dave said, taking a deep breath. "You treat me right and do what I say, I'll turn you back. It's my dream after all."

"You little..."

"Little what?" Dave said, glaring at Bags.

"Nothing," Bags said, defeated.

"Great! Now that we have that going for us, tell me more. I'll have to be careful about getting killed in here. But, wait a second," Dave said, looking up to the clouded sky. "I remember getting killed in a dream before. Heck, dozens of times in some creepy dreams. Have I lost my dreams dozens of times?"

"Possibly, but I doubt it. It looks like you still have some of your lame ass memories and dreams from early childhood in here. We can talk about the psychological implication of your dream killing you, but overall it's no big whoop. It's just when another Dreamer kills you that you really get screwed up. If your dream gets you, it's no big deal. Well, as long as it's not a Nightmare," Bags said, cocking his head as if he just came up with an idea. "Anyway, if a Dreamer gets you, you lose your dreams. But, it gets worse."

"How does it get worse?"

"The Dreamer who killed you gets your dreams and passions. Remember that book idea you had? The other Dreamer has that idea now. Remember the reason you love Emma? The other Dreamer knows it now and you won't. Remember that fantastic dream you had when you found out your dad is secretly a ninja? The other dreamer has it now." Bags said in a very serious voice. Dave looked back down at his feet and thought about what Bags had just said.

"So, this Sleepless Knight guy."

"Or woman," Bags reminded him.

"He wants to take my dreams away?" Dave said, looking back at the ferret. "Why?"

"Well, just look at you? Who wouldn't want to beat you up? But at any rate, it could be a zillion different reasons. She may not even know that she's doing it."

"Seriously?" Dave said.

"Seriously," Bags said, nodding. "This knight could be just some random girl who happened to walk into your dream and tried to kill you."

"Why would this guy want to kill somebody?" Dave continued on without taking a breath as he saw Bags open his mouth. "Seriously."

"All right, so if you're in a dream, you're a Dreamer," Bags said. "If you're a Dreamer who knows that they are in a dream, you are Aware. If you go into somebody else's dream, you are called a Dream Walker or Walker for short. You can be a Walker that is not Aware. So, she may not know that she's in a real dream. She may think that she's in a video game. To her, you're just points in some game."

"Seriously?"

"Seriously."

"All right," Dave said, trying to take it all in. "I can kind of see that. But, let's say that he knows what he's doing and he's that Harvester thing. But how would he get in?"

"She would get in via a Pathway," the ferret said, getting up on its hind legs and stretching its arms wide.

"Which is...?" Dave said, trying to lead Bags into finishing the sentence.

"Come with me," Bags said, starting to run, "I'll show you."

Bags quickly bounded away, his little ferret legs moving so fast that it was hard for Dave to keep up. They ran past roller coasters, arcades, food stands, and a variety of mascots, all of which looked exactly how Dave remembered it from his younger days.

"Hold on, Bags," Dave said, starting to slow down a little bit as his legs screamed at him in exhaustion. "Slow it down a bit."

Bags turned his head and stuck out his tongue while he ran, "You're the one who turned me into a ferret!"

"Yeah, but I've never seen a ferret run this fast!"

"Listen, you can make me into whatever you want, but I'm just a dream! I don't get tired!" Bags said. As Bags turned back to face the way he was running, he saw that he was quickly heading for the sidewall of one of the booths. He tried to stop as quickly as he could, but he lost his balance and then tumbled, rolling a few feet before landing on his back. "A ferret? A ferret!" Bags yelled. "Why not some kind of giant robot or something? Something's wrong with you, kid! I know they're fun pets and all, but you make your guardian a weasel?"

Dave caught up with Bags and picked him up, making sure to avoid getting bitten this time. As soon as he picked him up, Dave doubled over to catch his breath.

"Wait a minute," Dave said in between breaths. "If this is a dream, why am I getting tired?"

"Your physical body doesn't tire, but your mind does," Bags said, finally calming down and not trying to bite him. "Exhaust yourself here and you'll wake up exhausted in the real world. Well, at least mentally exhausted. But hey, it's not like you used that ol' noggin of yours before anyway."

"Bags."

"Yes, boy."

"You're lucky I'm not cruel to animals."

"Good to know. Just so you know, I don't feel the same way towards Dreamers."

"You know what? I think I'm going to change my mind about cruelty to animals," Dave said, as Bags slithered out of his hands and landed on his feet.

"Oh please. I can maybe see you beating up some dweeb who has been really pissing you off, but a ferret? Even you have morals and I know you stand by them," Bags said. "Besides, we're at a Pathway now."

Dave looked up and just saw several blue portable bathroom stalls.

"What is this? I thought we were going to a Pathway. These are Port-A-Potties."

"The stalls ARE Pathways, idiot."

"Well sure, it's obvious, isn't it?" Dave said, rolling his eyes.

"Are you sure you don't want a giant robot for a dream guardian?" Bags pleaded with him.

"Very sure, why?"

"Because I was hoping to have giant lasers to fry off those fuzzy eyebrows of yours," Bags said, shaking his head.

"Nope, ferret form. And just for that, I'm keeping it on for longer than I had planned," Dave said, smiling.

"Jerk," Bags said, shaking his head. "All right, now then, do you see a name on the door on the toilet nearest to you?"

Dave leaned closer and saw printed in white that there was a name:

ANDREW BAYS

"Andy?"

"All right, that's another hundred I would have lost," Bags said, going up to the doorway. "You can read the name on the door."

"What do you mean? Why wouldn't I be able to read it? What's Andy's name doing on this door?" Dave looked at the door, re-reading the name.

"Because this is the Pathway to Andy's dream. He must be sleeping right now."

"What? Andy? But it's only like nine o'clock. He's a night owl."

"Time is a bit different here. Each person's dream can feel like ten minutes to get eight hours of real sleep, or it might feel like eight hours to get ten minutes of sleep. It's kind of random."

"Okay, I sort of get it," Dave said, but then turned his head in confusion. "Then how could you tell I was going to wake up?"

"Untrained Dreamers usually wake up at tense moments. Did you ever wonder why you always wake up when things are getting really good?"

"Actually, yeah."

"Well, now you know. Once you know what you're doing, the good parts don't end when you don't want them to. You know what that means, right?"

Dave thought about it for a second, thought of his girlfriend, and then got a goofy grin on his face, "Yeah, I think I can imagine."

"That's right. Imagine not waking up when you're in battle with undead, acid-spitting panda bees! Whoo!" Bags said, pumping his little ferret fist to the sky. "That's what you were thinking, right?"

Dave looked down at the ferret and thought about saying something else. Instead he kept grinning and thinking of Emma.

"Anyway, so this leads to Andy's dream?" Dave said, pulling himself out of a trance.

"Yup. Everybody that you've ever seen in your life has a Pathway to and from your dream. However, only the people that you interact with on a daily basis actually have Pathways that you can reliably find. Everybody else that you've ever met is in here; most of them are just about impossible to find them. The guy who you bought a pack of gum from when you were 10? A pathway of his is around here somewhere. Your teachers, your parents, your friends, your coaches, your clerks, your doctors—everybody is in here!"

"So, I can find the Pathways to all of my friends here?"

"That's affirmative. In fact, since you have a close gathering of loser friends, all of their Pathways should be around here somewhere," Bags said, looking around.

"Sweet! Let's go find them! Where's Emma's?" Dave said, starting to look around as well.

"Focus! Let's concentrate on Andy first. We're going to go into the Pathway for his dream, but there is something that you need to know first."

"What's that?"

"Number one: I can't come with you."

"Oh that's the best news I've heard all day!" Dave said, looking up and throwing his arms into the air.

"Number one, subsection one: You can still hear me," Bags smiled as he said, revealing his sharp ferret teeth.

"Darn it."

"All right, dummy, it's time to go in, but first you're going to need to take something," Bags said, getting up on his hind legs and looking around. "There! The teddy bear!"

"Teddy bear?" Dave said, looking around. His eyes found the stuffed animal lying on the ground by one of the carnival games. It was covered in dirt, looked wet, and one of its little black eyes was hanging by a thread. "Hey! I remember this little guy!"

"Awww... your first friend, right?" Bags said, sniffing the bear and then jumping back, wrinkling his nose in disgust. "That guy stinks like a sewer!"

"I lost that guy on some vacation when I was five years old or something like that. I'm pretty sure my mom ended up throwing it out because I left it out in the rain, but she kept saying that they couldn't find it when they unpacked."

"Ouch. Your mom got rid of your best friend?"

"Hey, I was five! Give me a break!" Dave said, picking up the bear.

"What was your friend's name?"

"The bear?" Dave asked, as the ferret nodded. "Uh, Beddy Tear I think."

"Teddy Bear, Beddy Tear? Nice. Real creative."

"Bags... five years old, remember? Anyway, what am I doing with Beddy Tear?"

"You're taking... help me out here, is your best friend here a guy or girl?"

"Guy," Dave said, looking the bear over, flicking the hanging eye.

"All right, take him with you into Andy's dream," Bags said, returning to the door.

"Why? I don't think I need a teddy bear in Andy's dream. The last thing I need is Andy making fun of me tomorrow."

"Trust your guardian, boy. You may annoy me, but my objective is purely to make you stronger in your dreams," the ferret said, looking up at Dave. "And besides, unless he's actually aware that he's in a dream, he's not going to realize that you're anything more than a figment of his imagination. If he's unaware and making fun of you for something you did in his dream, then he's got some serious personal issues that you should have that Mr. Laws fellow check out. The worst thing he could do is say, 'Dude, you did the strangest thing in my dream last night'," Bags said, imitating Andy's voice.

"You're sure?" Dave asked.

"Kid, I have to make sure you're prepared to defend yourself against Ms. Creepy Knight. Now, open that door. Some doofus made me too short to open it," Bags said, reaching up as far as his little ferret body would allow him and finding himself well short of the door handle.

Dave reached out very slowly, his hand trembling as if he knew that this was going to hurt. He put his hand on the door handle, twisted, and pulled on the door. He took a step back when he saw what the door led to.

Nightmare

On the other side of the door was a classroom from his Middle School. It looked like it was his English class. He could see some posters of Shakespeare as well as the window that overlooked the teacher's parking lot.

"Go in, boy. You're letting the cold air in," Bags said, pushing on Dave's calf with his paw.

"Huh?" Dave let out the only thing his mouth would let him say.

"It's a joke, dummy, go in," Bags said, scratching Dave's leg a bit with his paw.

Dave ignored the ferret's scratching and cautiously put one foot into the room. Once his foot was firmly planted, he felt a wave of relief come over him. He took a few more steps into the room and then turned around.

"Bags, what am I supposed to do?" He asked, turning around to face the ferret in the doorway.

"Go explore. Wander around. I'll explain along the way. Just remember that this is somebody else's dream. Oh, one more thing. Don't touch yourself," Bags said with a chuckle, but continued on before Dave could respond. "If you see yourself in Andy's dream, you don't want to touch dream Dave in any way, not even an accidental brush of the shoulder. It could have very bad consequences. It's one of the risks that all Dream Walkers run. By the way, congratulations. You're officially a Dream Walker. You have entered somebody else's dream. Not too many people can say that they can do it nowadays."

"Yeah, great, I'm a Dream Walker. But what are the bad consequences if I meet myself?" Dave asked.

"You could create a Wraith, a type of living dream," Bags said as Dave took a few more steps into the room. Suddenly, he heard a familiar voice.

"Mr. Calloway, I certainly did not expect to see you during your free period. Have you come to drop off your homework or are you just trying to bribe me with a gift?"

Dave turned and looked at the far end of the classroom. Sitting at the teacher's desk was a middle-aged man with small round glasses and graying long hair tied back into a ponytail. It was Mr. Burke, his English teacher. Dave looked at him and realized that even while sitting, Mr. Burke was taller than he was in real life. Even while in his chair, he was a good foot taller than Dave.

"I'm sorry, wrong room," Dave said, noticing that he had come out of the closet of the classroom. Thankfully, Mr. Burke didn't ask about that. Mr. Burke was a fairly decent teacher. He split up his class so that half of the semester was just spent on creative writing while the other semester was spent on literature such as Dickens, Shakespeare, and the like. He wanted everybody to experience the trials and tribulations of being a writer first so that they would better appreciate how the classics were written.

Dave put the teddy bear on one of the student's desks and walked up to Mr. Burke's desk, looking up to his teacher. He then had a wave of fear come over him. Had he forgotten to do his homework?

"Where are you trying to get to, Mr. Calloway?" The teacher asked, looking down at some papers on his desk.

"Uh, have you seen Andy?" Dave said, not even thinking about adding in Andy's last name. The teacher looked up at Dave and stared at him. Out of the corner of his eye, Dave could have sworn that he saw the teddy bear twitch.

"You just missed him, actually. He forgot his twenty page story that was due today and he was going home to retrieve it," he said as he looked down and began flipping through his papers. Finding what he was looking for, he looked up at Dave. "*The Hand of God*, by David Calloway. Well, Mr. Calloway, I'm sure that I'll enjoy reading your story tonight."

"My story?" Dave asked.

"*The Hand of God* is your story, is it not?" The teacher asked, looking down to check the name.

"Uh, yeah," Dave said. Seeing the teacher look doubtful, Dave kept talking. "Of course it is! Why wouldn't it be?"

There was that twitch again, Dave thought as he caught a movement from the corner of his eye. He turned his head toward the desk where he put the bear but didn't see it move.

"I'm just making sure," Mr. Burke said, quickly scanning the story. "After all, you need to get a good grade on this story in order to pass."

That comment brought Dave's attention back to the teacher.

"That's not true! I know I'm not the best writer around, but I'm at least getting a C, right? That's some kind of mistake, right?" Dave said, stepping closer to the teacher. Mr. Burke flipped open his grade book.

"No, I see that you've handed in everything, but if you think you deserve a C with those stories, you're dreaming," the teacher said, putting the paper back into the pile of other stories.

"Dreaming?" Dave asked, breathing a sigh of relief. "Uh, I understand. Don't worry about the story. It's top notch."

It's just a dream, Dave reminded himself. *Not only that, but it's just Andy's dream. But does that mean Andy thought I was failing English?*

"I hope so," Mr. Burke said, pulling another story out to read.

"If you're still having trouble, you should talk with your friend, Mr. Maggio."

"Todd?" Dave said, pulling himself out of deep thought about what Andy's dream meant.

"Correct. He is an excellent writer. Have him send you the story about the Null Spiders. It is quite a good read."

Nobody in Dave's circle of friends was doing well in the class except for Todd. If there was one thing Todd had going for him, it was that he was unbelievably creative when he was writing. Dave looked at the teacher, but as he had practically buried his face in the stories, Dave took it as a cue to leave. He stepped into the hallway, nearly getting trampled by a student running by screaming that he was late for class. He saw other students walking with friends, boyfriends, and girlfriends. He could hear the sounds of lockers opening and slamming shut as students grabbed their books for the next period. Dave walked down the corridor and saw the familiar black trench coat of Andy's. As Andy began putting books into his locker, Dave walked up to his friend and patted him on the back.

"Hey Andy!" Dave said with a loud voice.

Andy quickly turned to face him and a look of utter shock came over his face. He looked over his shoulder and then back at Dave.

"Okay, how the hell did you do that?" Andy asked.

"Do what?"

"You just walked that way," Andy said, pointing behind him. "And now you show up coming the other way. I know you're a fast runner, but damn that's fast. But, crap, man, did you get my paper?"

"Your what?"

"I forgot my twenty page story. I asked you to get it out of my house," he said, looking somewhat confused. "Did you already forget?"

"Now why would I get your paper? Get your own darn paper!"

"Fine," Andy said, slamming the locker door shut and holding his hand out. "Gimme my keys back."

It's just a dream. In his dream, for some reason it made sense for me to go to his house to get his papers, Dave thought.

"Keys? I don't have any keys," Dave said, pulling out his empty pockets.

"I gave them to you! Where are they?"

Great, Dave thought to himself, *there's a dream version of me around here somewhere. That means that I've got to be careful or else I'm going to create a Wraith or whatever Bags called it.*

"Come on, I've got to get to class. You have my paper, right?" Andy said.

"Um, I don't think so," Dave said, patting his jeans pockets.

"Seriously? You said you'd get it if I paid you five dollars, which you're not getting now, by the way," Andy said, still holding out his hand.

"I would never do that! Especially not for five dollars!" Dave said, trying to get a laugh out of Andy. However, his friend was very serious. Suddenly, he heard a voice in his head, almost as if he were listening to music on his headphones.

"Kid, don't worry about him. Turn around and start walking away," Bags said in his head. Dave turned and started walking away, quickly putting distance between Andy and himself. He looked over his shoulder and saw Andy staring at him.

"Bags, what is it?" he asked as confused students noticed him talking to himself. He could overhear them talking about him, saying that he was a weirdo for talking to himself.

"Best not to argue with the unaware. Anybody who isn't aware that they're in a dream is not worth the time and effort to deal with. Anyway, even if you decide to argue with the unaware, don't take anything personally that the dream does. Those people that are making fun of you, while they're justified, in the end, they're just scenery in a dream made by Andy's little mind. Just remind yourself that they're not real. Unless they're physically trying to stop you, just walk on by," Bags said.

"I'll try. By the way, there is a dream version of myself around. Don't worry, I haven't seen him yet."

"Remember, don't touch him. Laugh, cry, spit, whatever you want. Just don't touch him. If he does, he's going to realize that he's a dream and you're real."

"Okay, weird, but what's the big deal?"

"Imagine you've been stuck in a windowless room for all your life. Suddenly, poof! There's a window. You can see trees, cars, and kids playing baseball in a field. Wouldn't you try to find a way to get out and play baseball? To drive? To climb a tree?" Bags said. "Bottom line, it wants to get into reality."

"What?" Dave said, "How does it do that?"

"By taking over the dream of its true self. It will try to take over your body. You will become lost in the Dreamscape while it takes over your body in reality. We call them Wraiths when they do that."

"Can I ever get my body back?" Dave asked.

"Yeah, but you'll have to find the Wraith while your body sleeps and defeat it."

"So, if I get taken over, it rides around in my body until I defeat it in my—its dream?

"You got it. Hell, one of the Dreamers thought the concept of a Wraith was good enough for a movie in reality. You know the movie? The guy with a claw glove? Burned face? Unfortunately, the guy got almost all of it wrong. He started the Wraith in reality and screwed it up by then sending him to the Dreamscape as some murderer. At least, that's what I hear from others in the Dreamscape who heard it from other dreamers. We thought it was going to be a documentary," Bags sounded disappointed.

"A documentary on Wraiths?"

"Sure, why not?"

"I think I know what movie you're talking about. I kinda liked the movie, it was pretty freaky," Dave said.

"Just not realistic."

"It's a movie!" Dave yelled.

"I know, doofus!" Bags yelled back.

"A dream is NOT realistic!"

"To me it is," Bags said, "It's my life. My entire life."

Dave was silenced by that comment. That silence was only broken by a loud crash in the distance followed by a woman screaming. A few seconds later, Dave heard dozens of other screams as well as stampeding footsteps. He emerged from behind the stairs and was immediately caught in a tidal wave of his classmates, everybody sprinting in the same direction—away from something apparently horrible. Several teachers ran with the students, though it seemed as if they were a good two feet taller then he remembered. He watched as Cole Dutton pushed his way through the crowd, knocking people into the wall, not caring about anybody but himself. At the last second, Dave grabbed hold of one of the railings on the stairs and pulled himself through the railings on to the stairs.

"Bags, I think we have a problem here," Dave said, "Something has scared the heck out of everybody."

"Weeeeelllll, maybe you should check out the problem, boy. It might be interesting," Bags said.

"Yeah, uh... okay," Dave said, not exactly sure of what to do. He looked out in the hallway and his eyes caught the black trench coat he was looking for.

"Andy! In here!" Dave yelled. Andy turned toward Dave and swam through the crowd, pushing and shoving his way through them.

"Dave, if you have my keys, now would be a good time to give them to me!" Andy said.

"Why, what the heck is going on?

"What's going on? There's some freaky-ass monster that just busted out of a classroom," Andy said, looking down the hallway as another loud crash could be heard and the students got louder and faster.

"Monster?" Dave said as he felt his heart beat faster.

"Yeah, a friggin' monster! This is crazy!" Andy yelled.

As the last of the students went down the hallway, something let out a roar, just like a hungry wild animal. Then, there was a strange noise:

Click-clack, click-clack, click-clack

"Let me guess, Biology class?" Dave asked.

"No, Mr. Burke's English class. Why does that matter?" Andy said, grabbing Dave's shirt and pulling him toward the hallway. Dave's heart skipped a beat as he registered what Andy had said.

Click-clack, click-clack, click-clack

As they stepped into the hall, Dave turned to look in the direction the students were coming from. Nothing. Just a few open blue lockers along with some books and papers strewn around during the mayhem. Dave was just about to leave when the wall ahead of him was knocked down by something powerful on the other side, sending bricks and dust flying everywhere. The shock of the noise jerked Andy's legs out from under him, dragging them both to the ground.

Andy and Dave crawled backward to get away. Mouths agape, they couldn't take their eyes from the horror emerging through the huge hole in the wall. It was an oversized desk, its rusted legs curved and sharp like blades. Fused to the top of the desk was the upper half of a giant bear. Its head just grazed the ceiling. It was covered in dirt and dust and one of its eyes hung from its socket, dangling by a tendon. Dave looked closely at the bear and thought about what Andy said. It came from Mr. Burke's class? The class he just came from? His eyes widened as he recognized the creature.

"Beddy Tear?" Dave asked the creature as if expecting a response. The bear creature turned toward him and growled.

"That's not a teddy bear, Dave! Let's get out of here!" Andy said.

"That's Beddy Tear!" Dave yelled. "What the heck is going on?"

Dave and Andy tried to get to their feet but slipped in the rubble, and they ended up back on the floor. With its four legs, the creature closed on them in no time. Andy and Dave glanced at each other nervously. Then Andy lashed out his foot at the creature's leg, kicking it out from underneath the monster. It fell onto that corner of the desk and roared in anger. Andy let out a victory yell and jumped up. As he turned to run, however, the bear grabbed him with its paws. It righted itself and raised Andy into the air. He struggled to get free from its strong paws, but it was no use. Dave tried to kick out its legs again, but this time it readied itself and did not buckle under. It put Andy in one paw, looked down at Dave, and swatted him away, sending him crashing into the wall. He collapsed onto the floor, but he managed to look up just as the desk opened, revealing a mouth filled with lines of pointy teeth. The bear tossed Andy into the mouth and chomped down on him. Andy screamed in pain as the bear chewed several times and then swallowed. Then there was just silence.

"The bear is a rose, the bear is a rose, the bear is a rose," Dave chanted as he closed his eyes to the horror before him. He felt hot air blasting him as he said the phrase over and over again. He opened his eyes slowly to see the creature standing before him, staring him eye to eye as it leaned over the desk.

"Bags, it ate Andy! It ate him! It's going to eat me!" Dave said, managing no more than a whisper.

"You're looking at a Nightmare, kid," Bags said, "That's exactly how I wanted it. We'll talk more about it tomorrow."

"Tomorrow? What about tonight?!" Dave screamed. He looked up as the creature roared and opened its desk mouth and swallowed him whole.

School Drama

Bzzzzz

Dave's eyes opened wide. His lungs burned like they hadn't held a breath in several minutes.

Bzzzzz

He took a deep breath and held it for as long as he could.

Bzzzzz

He threw off the covers, sat up, and looked his body over to make sure there were no bite marks or bruises. Finding that he was okay, he let out his breath and collapsed back into bed.

Bzzzzz

Dave slapped the alarm clock to turn it off. As he got ready for school, all Dave could think about was whether or not it was a random dream. Was it his mind just playing tricks on him?

As he left for school, he saw Andy going through his own book bag at the end of his driveway. Andy looked up at Dave and mumbled a greeting as Dave did the same.

"I am so exhausted today," Andy said, zipping up his bag.

"Same here," Dave said, adjusting his bag on his shoulder. "Couldn't sleep?"

"I never sleep well," Andy said as they began to walk. "But, I had this weird-ass dream. It was seriously messed up. You know those dreams where you forget your homework or something like that?"

"Yeah sure," Dave said as he felt his heart beating faster.

"Yeah, well, I can't remember the entire dream, but I remember that I forgot some story I was supposed to hand in to Mr. Burke. Anyway, I was hanging out in the hallway talking to you when suddenly the wall next to me blew apart and standing there was—and you won't believe this—but there was this crazy-ass monster that was like a bear fused with a spider," Andy said, wiggling his fingers as if trying to simulate a spider.

"A bear spider? Cool!" Dave said, trying to act like he didn't know about it. "So, what happened?"

"I remember that I saved you from being eaten and then I did some weird kung fu stuff and kicked its ass!" Andy said, shadow boxing for a few seconds. "That thing was so weird. You know how in elementary school the desks open up so you can put your books and stuff in there? Inside the desk was its mouth! There were some seriously sharp teeth in there," Andy said, now opening and closing his hands to simulate a mouth.

"But, you beat it? You killed it?" Dave asked, as one eyebrow rose. Andy looked at him and shrugged.

"Yeah, of course I kicked its ass. I mean, I think I did. It definitely ended up eating you, but there's no way it took me out," Andy said as Dave walked beside him in silence. After a few steps, they saw Emma just down the street from them. They walked a little faster and to catch up with her. When they were about ten steps behind her, she turned around and smiled.

"Morning, boys!" She said as she stopped to let them catch up. Dave walked up to her and hugged her. He went in for a kiss, but her eyes glanced toward Andy and her face turned slightly red.

"Don't mind me," Andy said, rolling his eyes. "I'm not here."

Emma leaned closer to Dave's ear and took his hand. "We'll continue this some other time."

Dave smiled. "I'll hold you to that, you know."

Emma smirked and opened her mouth to speak, but Andy went first. "Emma, you've got to hear about this weird-ass dream I had last night," Andy said, as he repeated the story to Emma.

"Uh, yeah, that sounds pretty weird," Emma said, turning to Dave with a face of disinterest.

After a quick stop at Krazy Koffee, they continued to school and went their separate ways. However, right before lunch, Andy and Dave both sat down in Mr. Burke's English class. Just to make sure he wasn't going crazy, Dave noted that Mr. Burke was not in fact seven feet tall like in Andy's dream. He was hovering around six feet, just as Dave remembered. He glanced over at Andy who was doodling in his notebook.

It's just a regular old dream to him. But, I was IN his dream last night! I walked from MY dream to HIS dream! Dave looked down at his notebook then over at Mr. Burke who began handing out graded stories from the previous day. He took his story and saw a *C* on it with some notes on how the plot was creative, but all the characters had the same voice, and the description was vague. He glanced over to Andy who had a *B* on his. Andy never seemed to have trouble with creative writing projects, though his stories always were about vampires and zombies.

Meanwhile, Mr. Burke had the students with the three highest grades get up and read their short stories to the class so that the other students could hear what he was looking for. As usual, Todd was called up. Dave could hear other people groaning when Todd went up to the front of the class. He always wrote long stories. When the minimum was five pages, he would write fifteen. In the end, it was great that Todd was so creative, but even the people who enjoyed fantasy and science fiction, Todd's specialty, were bored to hear him read his stories week after week.

When the bell rang to end the class, Mr. Burke assigned them homework to write a new five page story to hand in on Monday. Most of the class groaned, but Todd just smiled and packed up his things. Andy and Dave left class quickly to go to lunch, but Todd caught up with them as they entered the cafeteria.

"So, what do you think you're going to write about, Andy?" Todd asked.

"I don't know," Andy said in an irritated voice, "I'm not going to think about it until the weekend."

"Oh," Todd said, disappointed, "I think I'm going to write about some guy who rides a diamond dragon into battle against evil dragon-riders using dragons that are made up of other gemstones. What do you think?"

"I think it sounds lame," Andy replied.

"Really? I thought it sounded neat," Todd said his forehead wrinkling in concern.

"You're the only person who thinks your stories are neat, you realize that, right?" Andy said, looking up to the ceiling and shaking his head. Todd went silent, but then looked at Dave.

"Uh, I'm writing umm..." Dave thought about it for a second then used the first thing that came to his mind. "I'm writing a story called *The Hand of God.*"

"Wow! Like your Lord Battler character's move?" Todd said excitedly.

"Yeah, like that," Dave said as he heard Andy laugh. "What's so funny?"

"You know that weird dream that I had last night?"

"Yeah, the one where you got beaten up by a bear?" Dave said, smirking.

"No, I beat up the bear, remember?" Andy said in a serious voice.

"Sure, whatever," Dave said as they got into line at the cafeteria to get some lunch.

"Anyway, that was the exact title of the story that you were writing in the dream," Andy said, looking at Dave. Dave looked at Andy in silence for a second as they moved down the lunch line, loading up on milk, sandwiches, and fruit.

"You know me way too well, buddy," Dave said, pushing Andy along.

"A little too well," Todd agreed.

"Shut up, Todd," Andy said, glaring at him. Suddenly, a large shape slammed into Andy's side, knocking all of Andy's food onto Dave's tray. Andy turned around and began to say something, but then he saw that it was a familiar chunky dark-skinned friend.

"Jake Warlick," Andy said. "I heard reports that some giant lizard was attacking Tokyo. Now I know it was just you hunting down something to eat! I can hear all of those people now 'Help! Warlick is attacking! Somebody save us!'"

"I only went there because your mom isn't cooking for me anymore," Jake replied, pushing his massively overweight frame in between him and Dave, squeezing out Todd.

"Where were you yesterday?" Andy asked. "Didn't see you at school."

"Sick," Jake said, piling on three sandwiches. "Came down with a nasty cold."

"And apparently you're trying to drown your cold in calories, right?" Andy said, putting his own food back on his plate.

"Again with the fat jokes. Get some new material!" Jake said as Todd tapped him on his shoulder. "What is it, Toddy?"

"So, I bought Can't Reezist's album yesterday. It was pretty good!" Todd said with a smile. Jake, Andy, and Dave all turned to look at Todd.

"Todd, how many times do I have to tell you," Jake said, getting close to Todd. "Just because I'm black doesn't mean that you have to tell me every time you buy a rap album."

"Yeah, but I thought you'd like to know," Todd said, reaching into his bag. "Here, I'll show you the album!"

"Not necessary, Todd, not necessary!" Jake said, turning to look at Dave and Andy with a bewildered look on his face. "So, Andy-Dandy-McFandy, a little birdie told me that you have the new Lord Battler game. Is that right?"

"Yeah, I picked it up this weekend," Andy smiled, reached into his bag, and pulled out the strategy guidebook for the game. "I've been learning some of the new tricks they put in there. Apparently your arch enemy can now have minions."

"Minions?" Dave asked, raising an eyebrow. "Like, soldiers it can send out?"

"Yeah, so that Sleepless Knight guy that you're fighting could have dozens of weaker guys that it sends on its behalf to fight you."

The group sat down at the lunch table and began to eat as Jake made plans to hang out with Andy after school. When Jake wandered off to sit with another group of friends, Dave's friends sat down. Eric slapped Dave on the back as he sat down next to him.

"You ready for practice today?" Eric said, lowering his voice to sound manlier.

"Ready as I'll ever be!" Dave said, elbowing Eric hard.

"Boys, boys, boys," Emma said, putting her arm around Dave. "That's enough. Stop hurting my boyfriend."

Eric rolled his eyes and Emma blushed after she said that, her arm retracting from around Dave and hanging by her side.

"Hey Andy, why don't you ever ask Jake to sit with us?" Dave asked, reaching under the table and taking Emma's hand. Andy looked over at Jake and back to Dave.

"Because he wants to sit with his other friends," Andy said, stealing a French fry from Cynthia's tray. "He usually sits with the Strack brothers, that Craig Lui guy, and whatshername... Christine Spriggs."

"Yeah, all the video game nuts," Cynthia said, stealing a tater tot from Andy's tray. "It's Final that, Mortal this, Legend that, Fighter this. You wonder why my boy is so pale? It's not because he's my dear goth-boy. It's because the Zeus has sucked my poor boy's life completely away. It's tragic, really."

Andy turned towards Cynthia, "Yeah that really stops you from playing with me all the time."

Cynthia rolled her eyes. "That's allllll we do. Unless you've got tickets to some band you like or something like that. Otherwise, boooorrrrrinnnng. You're so boring!" Cynthia said, just looking at her tray.

"Fine, I'll get out of your way then," Andy said, picking up his tray. "Guys, I'll see you later."

"Andy, learn how to take a joke!" Eric yelled, but Andy just rolled his eyes, walked over to Jake's table and sat down. Dave watched as Andy pointed over at Cynthia and then shrugged. She looked over at Andy and her eyes filled with tears. Eric quickly stood up to console his sister, but Emma waved him off.

"What did I say to piss him off THAT much?" Cynthia said.

Before any of the guys could speak, Emma jumped in. "Sorry, girl-talk time," Emma said, going over to Cynthia. She whispered something her ear and they both got up and left the cafeteria.

"I'm going to kill Andy," Eric said, looking over at Andy.

"I've got your back," Todd said, cracking his knuckles.

"Shut up, Todd," Dave said, quietly.

"No, you know what?" Eric said. "I'm going to hurt him. I'll break his legs or something. Then, I'll have Cynthia finish him off! That'll make her feel better."

"That guy loves his Zeus, what can I say?" Dave said. "He and Jake already have plans to try to design some games for it. Still, it's not like he had to walk off like that."

"What's the name of the game, Gothboy vs. Fatboy?" Eric said, "That'll be a blast. I swear, if Andy doesn't apologize to her, there's going to be problems."

"It seems to me that she should apologize as well."

They both turned around to see Adrienne, holding a half-eaten apple in one hand. Mounted onto her shoulder was a stuffed fuzzy alligator. From the way she was standing, the alligator looked like it was staring right at Dave.

"Adrienne, eavesdrop much?" Dave asked, staring at the alligator instead of Adrienne.

"Why should my sister have to apologize?" Eric asked.

"Awwwww, sibling love. That's so cute!" Adrienne said with a smile, starting to pet her alligator. "Anyway, she was the one who started it. She didn't have to do that in public. She just wanted to make it seem dramatic. Unfortunately, so does he. That's why he stormed off. Way too much melodrama in your group."

"So they're both dramatic. But, he made my sister cry!" Eric said, raising his voice. Adrienne pulled the alligator off of her shoulder. There was a noticeable ripping sound as Dave saw that there was Velcro on the bottom of the alligator as well as on her shirt. She pointed the alligator at Eric.

"Jimmy Chestnut says that your sister was wrong to say that in public. At the very least they both should apologize to each other."

"Who the hell is Jimmy Chestnut?" Eric said, looking around.

"Eric, it's the—." Dave tried to speak, but Adrienne cut him off.

"Who's Jimmy Chestnut? He's only the cutest and most adorable alligator in the whole wide world!" Adrienne said, clutching the alligator to her chest.

"Seriously? Get lost, weirdo," Eric said, shaking his head. Adrienne looked at Dave, made Jimmy Chestnut take a bow, and then walked off.

"Bizarre girl," Eric said, taking a bite from his sandwich.

"She's right, you know," Dave said. "Your sis just basically said to all of his friends that he sucks and is the most boring guy on the planet. I mean, yeah, Andy just really overreacted, but I can kind of see why he walked away."

Eric looked at Andy and then back to Dave, "You may be right. I'm still going to go over there and make Andy apologize."

"Dude, dude, dude," Dave said, grabbing Eric by the shirt as he began to walk over. "Let them take care of it themselves."

Eric sat down in his seat and took a large gulp from his bottled water, "I hate having you as my voice of reason. You know that, right?"

"If it weren't for me, Eric, I think you'd be six feet under by now... or at least, friendless," Dave said, receiving a quick punch on the shoulder by Eric.

The rest of the day, Dave was distracted. Not only because of the Beddy Tear incident from last night, but also because of the argument between Andy and Cynthia. Those two breaking up could lead to a whole bunch of awkwardness in the group. Their plans would inevitably have to leave out one or the other of them. They couldn't be in the same room at the same time. They couldn't just all go to the movies. Dave was closer to Andy, but Emma was close to Cynthia, so he was kind of stuck.

Luckily for Dave, his distraction didn't matter when playing football. The coach, remembering how worn out Dave was yesterday, brutalized him by having him run countless laps and drills. Every time he dropped a pass, the coach would scream at him to get his lazy butt in gear. Not even the situation with Andy and Cynthia could distract him from the soreness in his body.

Finally, the starters scrimmaged against the backups. Backup QB Tony Krantz called the first play, a quick pass to Dave. The team lined up at the line of scrimmage and faced off with the starters.

"Hey! Girls can't play football!" Michael yelled. "Oh crap, sorry! That's just David Calloway! I'm sorry, I thought I saw a bra strap!"

Dave turned to Michael to say something, but Tony hiked the ball. Dave turned back just as the cornerback slammed into him. Dave stumbled and fell down. Tony looked toward him then downfield. Seeing that nobody was open he turned to run down the field, but by that time several of the defensive linemen had broken through. Two of them grabbed Tony and threw him to the ground with little effort. The coach blew his whistle, calling the play dead.

"Calloway, you idiot! Pay attention to the play, not to Everway!" the coach yelled.

"Sorry, coach, but..." Dave started to say as he got up.

"But WHAT? Do you think the away crowd is just going to cheer and boo? They're going to say some nasty things. Nasty things about you, your mama, your papa, your brother, your sister, your dog, your cat, your turtle, your Chia pet, whatever the hell they want. It's your job to faze out the crowd and catch the damn ball! DO I MAKE MY-SELF CLEAR?" the coached yelled, getting right in Dave's face, grabbing one of the rungs on the helmet.

"Yes sir," Dave said, unemotionally.

"Good. Now, Krantz. Second down and ten. Go!"

The team huddled up and called the next play. It would be another quick pass to Dave. The rest of the team look a bit surprised at that.

"Look, Dutton's crew would never expect it to go to Dave after that," Tony said, looking around at the players in the huddle. "Plus, if Dave catches it and hangs onto it, it'll get the coach off his ass."

Dave smiled briefly as they clapped their hands in unison. They all lined up on the line of scrimmage with Dave to the left of the quarterback. Dave stared down the cornerback for a second before turning his head toward the quarterback and holding his body still. Tony took the snap as Dave nimbly sidestepped the cornerback who tried to crash into him again. He ran about five yards and made a sharp right turn toward center field. Immediately as he made that turn, he saw Tony throw the ball toward him. Dave leapt up and snagged the ball out of the air. He landed on his feet and a sense of relief washed over him. He had caught it! He turned to run up the field, but as soon as he did, a huge shape slammed right into him. Dave felt his feet leave the ground and he sailed through the air at least a few feet before landing on his back. Looking up at his attacker, he saw the massive frame of Cole Dutton, who laughed and pointed down at him.

"The little girl held onto the ball!" Cole said in between laughs as he walked away. Tony ran over to Dave and knelt down.

"Dave, are you okay?" Tony asked, checking to see if he was even conscious. "I'm sorry, man, I should have thrown that so you would have been able to see him and get out of the way."

"Everybody, let's give the two lovebirds a minute to make out, okay?" Michael said loudly and the team laughed.

"I can't believe you held onto the ball there!" Tony yelled, slapping him on his shoulder pads. They both got up, Dave a bit more slowly than Tony as they saw Coach Weaver running up to them, red faced and belly wagging.

"Calloway, are you hurt? Are you seeing double? Do you remember your name?" He asked in between breaths.

Dave took a deep breath and exhaled it slowly. Thankfully he didn't slam his head into the ground. If he had gotten a concussion, or even if there was a reasonable chance at one, there was no way he was playing until he got evaluated.

"I'm fine, coach," Dave said. "My head didn't even touch the ground."

The coach smiled and slapped him on top of the helmet. "Excellent! Great hands! Let's run that play again! Krantz, fantastic play-calling! You've got a future here, boy! You keep improvising those play calls and ideas like that and you'll be the starting QB once Everway gets his scholarship and goes off to some Division 1 college. Dutton, way to use the body, but WRAP him up next time! I want you to plant this guy into the ground! "

"Yeah! Plant him like a piece of candy!" Cole said, mimicking a body slam. The coach looked over his shoulder at Cole and then just shook his head.

"Just tackle them, Cole, just tackle," Coach Weaver said, turning back toward Dave.

"Yessir, coach!" Cole said, going back into a huddle. Coach Weaver put a hand on one of Dave's shoulder pads and sighed as he looked over at Cole.

"Calloway, you may start someday or you may ride the bench until you graduate. Hell, you may end up being great at football, but if there's one thing you should be happy about is that you have options. You'll get to make a choice about what you want. That boy, Cole, he's an incredible player, but sometimes it amazes me that he knows that socks go on his feet. He may hit you and trust me, he'll hit you hard, but he's one broken leg away from having no future. This is all he's got. Do you understand what I'm trying to say?"

Dave smiled and nodded.

"I think so, Coach," Dave said.

"Good, now get into your huddle," the coach said, turning around to look down the field. "And next time, try not to run into the guy who weighs twice as much as you, all right?"

After practice, Dave and Eric sat on the curb by the school drive-way waiting for Eric's mother to pull up.

"I can't believe you actually got praised by Weaver for catching that pass. I thought he was trying to get you to quit," Eric said, slapping Dave on the back.

"I know! I can't quite believe it myself," Dave said, leaning forward, trying to see if a certain sitting position could take away some of the pain and soreness from practice. A breeze picked up and the boys were silent until the wind died down.

"So, you really still think that I shouldn't kick the crap out of Andy, right?" Eric asked. Dave wondered for a moment if he should even answer the question.

"Yeah, let them be. Andy didn't do anything too bad. I mean, he annoys me sometimes, but he means well. Unfortunately, and it really kills me to say this, but I agree with Adrienne. They're both being overdramatic. In the end, Cynthia basically told all of his friends that he's boring. That's gotta hurt, especially from your girlfriend!" Dave said, watching cars drive by and pick up some of the other players.

"Yeah, I guess you're right. But, promise me one thing," Eric said as he waved to his mother as she drove up.

"What's that?"

"If he really truly hurts her, we break his legs?" Eric asked, smiling. Dave laughed as they both stood up. As soon as he did, he felt someone hug him from behind. Dave looked over his shoulder to see his girlfriend.

"Uh oh, guys, just remember, I'm under eighteen, okay? You can't do those things in front of me. I'll go blind or something," Eric said, his face brightening up as he opened the car door. Dave took Emma's hand and led her into the car. She sat down and moved all the way over. Dave turned to say something to Eric, but as he did he remembered that he had forgotten to talk to Mr. Laws today.

"Aw no, I forgot some stuff that I need for some homework tonight," Dave said, closing the door as soon as Emma got in. All three people in the car turned to him.

"Do you want us to wait here for you?" Eric's mother asked.

"Thanks, but it's okay. It's not too bad outside, and I'm sure the coach would like to hear that I'm taking the hard way," Dave said as he smiled at Eric's mother. He then turned to Emma. "I'll call you tonight, okay?" Emma smiled and nodded and the car pulled away, her eyes not leaving his until the car turned out of the driveway.

He quickly walked back into the school and as he turned the corner he slammed shoulder to shoulder with the leather-clad Rake. Rake quickly shoved Dave who stumbled back a step before regaining his balance.

"What the heck are you doing, Rake?" Dave asked standing up to his full height, which was just a bit taller than Rake. Rake smiled at him.

"Oh crap, for a second there I thought I just ran into a football player, but it looks like I was wrong. I just ran into some doofus who loves to ride the bench and play towel games in the locker room," Rake said, imitating a towel snap. "By the way, how's the shirt?"

Dave shoved Rake on the shoulders knocking him back a few steps. His heart started beating faster as he readied himself for a fight.

"You're a dead man, Calloway, you know that, right?" Rake said, putting a cigarette in his mouth.

"Why? Are you going to cry to your chick so that she can fight me?" Dave said, his heart beating so fast it felt like it was heating up his entire body.

Rake was about to respond when Mr. Laws' door swung open and he stepped out.

"What the hell is going on here? Raymond, go home now," he said, pointing to the door. He then pointed at Dave. "David, you're late. Get in here."

Rake stepped in closer to Dave, "Have fun with the ax murderer," he said motioning to Mr. Laws before turning around and leaving. Mr. Laws just shook his head and let Dave in.

"And here I was thinking that you had better things to do today! Take a seat," he said, motioning to the couch. "How are things?"

"Fine," Dave said, sinking into the comfortable couch, letting his heart rate calm down. "Um, I'm not really late, am I? I didn't think that we had an appointment."

Mr. Laws chuckled. "No, you didn't. It was just an easy way to get you two separated, that's all. Anyway, how are the dreams?" Mr. Laws said, pulling out a yellow notebook. Dave looked over at the bookcase and noticed that the dream book was gone. "David?"

"Oh, um..." Dave noticed that the dream book was now on Mr. Laws' desk. "I think I did it."

"Did what, David?"

"I took control of my dreams," Dave said, remembering Bags and facing Beddy Tear.

"And what happened when you did that?"

"Things got a lot easier, I guess," he said, watching the counselor write some things down in his notebook.

"Tell me about your dream," Mr. Laws said, looking up at Dave.

"Well," Dave said, suddenly not wanting to talk about the dream. "I...uh..."

"David, remember that there's nothing to be embarrassed about. I'm here to help you, all right?" Mr. Laws said, putting his pen and notebook down, smiling.

"Yeah, but you're not on the other side of the desk! It's kinda tough sometimes."

Mr. Laws sat back in his chair. "You know, when I was about your age, I had regular appointments with the school counselor. It was tough for me as well."

"You went to the counselor?" Dave asked, leaning forward. "Does that have anything to do with you being an ax murderer?"

Mr. Laws started to laugh loudly, "Raymond really is a piece of work, huh?"

Dave smiled but stayed silent.

"Well, all right, since the cat is out of the bag, I was having a heart to heart talk with Raymond. As you know, that boy is... oh, how to put it... he's a bit on the violent side of things, and I wanted to try to bond with him a bit. I also wanted to let him know that just because he's this way now doesn't mean he needs to be this way later," Mr. Laws said, putting his hands behind his head. "Back in the day, I was a pretty obsessive kid. I remember back before I was a teenager, I was a goody-two-shoes. I would never break the rules, and if I saw you doing it, I'd be the first to report it. As you could expect, I was bullied quite a lot."

"You were a snitch?" Dave said.

Mr. Laws laughed. "Yes, I broke the law of the playground many times. Anyway, once I hit my teenage years, I started rebelling. I did a one-eighty and started breaking some rules. Showing up late for class, picking fights, graffiti, and so on. During that time, slasher movies like *Friday the 13th* and *Halloween* were pretty big. I actually started dressing like those guys from the movies."

"You're kidding me, right?" Dave said, his laughing coming to a stop.

"Nope."

"Mask and all?"

"All right, you got me there. I didn't wear a mask. Not that I didn't consider it. My mother drew the line there! However, I certainly dressed like one of them. People avoided me before because they thought I was a loser. Now they avoided me because they thought I was going to take a machete out," Mr. Laws said, mimicking a slashing motion.

"Doc, you're freaking me out a bit," Dave said, still not sure if the counselor was serious or not.

"Listen to me, David. While that whole speech was for Raymond, it still holds true for anybody around his age. I'm telling you this because you, like all your schoolmates, have still yet to discover who you really are. Did I end up a goody-two-shoes or an ax murderer? No. Later on, I made a few friends. I started lightening up. I went to college. Turns out, I really enjoy talking to people and finding out how to make their lives better. Even now, seeing people leave my office happy completely makes my day."

"Will Raymond change to be a better person overnight? No, but sometime in his life I'm hoping that before he tries to beat somebody up or vandalize somebody's property, that he'll think of what he and I talked about. Slowly but surely, he'll come to realize that doing the horrible things he does doesn't do anybody any good, including himself."

Dave let what the counselor said sink in for a few seconds, "But, wait a minute, I'm not like Rake—I mean, Raymond. He needs to change or he's probably going to be spending his whole life locked up behind bars. But me? I'm just a bench-riding football player who does okay in his classes and has an okay social life. I mean, what's there to change? I don't do anything that needs to be changed!"

Mr. Laws leaned in closer, "I'm trying to show you that you can be better than what you are. Sure, you're getting by, but you're in your comfort zone. You're coasting. But, don't you want to be the starter for your team? Don't you want to come home to your parents with all A's on your report card? Don't you want to have a fantastic social life and get invited to all of the parties?"

"Well, sure, but nobody's perfect. I mean, sure I'd like to do all of those things, but it's not happening," Dave said, pausing between the last two words.

"And why not?" Mr. Laws said, sitting back.

"I don't know," Dave said. "Maybe, because there isn't enough time in the day to do all those things."

"So, you're saying that there's no way you can be a star football player, get good grades, and have a great social life? So, if you're a star football player and go to a couple of parties, you can't get good grades?"

"Well, I guess you could, but it would be pretty tough,"

"But, not impossible?"

"No, what's your point?"

"Listen, what I'm saying is that while there's no shame in coasting by and being average, you've got to think about it. Think about what your point in life is. Is it your goal to be average? To get by?" Mr. Laws said, pausing for a brief second. Dave opened his mouth to say something, but the counselor kept going. "Of course not. You may end up doing so, but you WANT to be more than average. Tell me, why do you play football?"

"Because my friend Eric and I really like it," Dave said without hesitation.

"So, you like it, so you joined up. Does that keep you there?"

"Yeah, sure," Dave said, looking toward the books on the shelf, avoiding the counselor's eyes.

"Even though many of your other teammates harass you?"

"Well, that kind of sucks, yeah, but I...uh..."

"Why do you stay?"

Dave looked at the counselor, down at his own feet, and back to the counselor, "Because I want to prove to them that I'm just as good or even better at it than them. Or at least, I'm better then they think I am."

Mr. Laws clapped his hands, "That's what I wanted to hear from you. Your drive is to prove to your teammates as well as yourself that you are just as good or even better than them at football. Rise above being average. Don't be content with it. Can you do that for me, David?"

David looked at Mr. Laws directly in the eyes for several seconds before responding. "I can try."

Mr. Laws nodded and smiled, "Excellent! Now, by the end of the school year, I'm expecting you to say 'I'll do it' instead of 'I can try'."

As Mr. Laws began flipping through some of his papers, Dave again reviewed the books on the shelf.

"So, David, tell me about your dreams. Did you do what we discussed?"

Dave turned back to face the counselor, "Actually, yeah... I did."

"And?"

"It... It worked out pretty well actually. I confronted the things in my dream and made sure that they knew that it was my dream. That I was in control."

"And then what happened?" The counselor said as he scribbled more notes.

"It was kinda strange. It was almost like once I was in control that I could start doing anything I wanted. It was like I was in a video game or some movie," David said.

"A video game?"

"Yeah, I was turning snakes into roses, going into other people's dreams. It was pretty cool, actually." Dave said spreading out on the couch.

"Entering other people's dreams, eh?" Mr. Laws said, opening up the dream book in front of him and skimming through a few pages. "What happened when you entered another person's dream? And whose dream was it?"

"My friend Andy's. It was really weird. All the teachers there were gigantic!" Dave said, putting his hand a few feet above him. "Then Andy and I had to fight some monster, but I think we lost. I woke up just when we were fighting it."

"Now, you know, David, that you weren't really in Andy's dream, right?"

"Are you sure?" Dave asked. "It sure did feel like it. I know it was a dream and all, but it felt so real."

"Now Dave, you know just as well as I do that a dream is all in your own mind. It may have felt like Andy's dream to you, but in reality your mind just made you think it was Andy's dream."

Dave thought about it for a few seconds. "I know, but it just felt so darn real."

"I know, I know. Now, those teachers. That's an easy one. You simply find teachers to be intimidating. An easy way for that to be reflected in your dream is simply that they're bigger than you are."

"So, Andy is afraid of teachers?"

"No, you're afraid of teachers."

"Right. It's my dream," Dave said, correcting himself. "But, it felt like it was Andy's."

"Tell me about this teacher."

"Uh, it was Mr. Burke," Dave said, looking back at the books.

"The English teacher?"

"Yup, that's the guy. Strange, isn't it?"

"Nope, not if you dreamed it. To your mind, it makes sense. Now, do you do well in Mr. Burke's class?"

"I do okay,"

"Interesting," Mr. Laws said, looking at his watch and closing his notebook, "Well, Dave, it looks like we're out of time. I'm glad to hear that we fixed your dream issue. Just keep remembering that it's your dream and your dream only. Also, remember that you can be better than average. Be the absolute best possible. Finally, show up on time next time."

Dave nodded and stood up from the comfy couch. Mr. Laws stood up with him.

"Now, Dave, stop by any time you like if you have any issues. Dreams, problems at school, problems at home, whatever you need, okay?" Mr. Laws said, extending his hand. Dave shook his hand, grabbed his things, and left the office.

During the walk home, Dave kept thinking to himself about what Mr. Laws said. *Was it Andy's dream I was in, or was it just my mind making it seem like it was Andy's dream?* It must be Dave's dream, and his mind was just playing tricks on him. He entered Andy's dream because he wanted it to be Andy's dream. It's the same thing with Bags. Bags was Max, the snake, the clown, and the ferret because Dave wanted them to all be the same thing. He wanted it to all make sense. So, his mind made it that way. The whole nightmare thing was just some random thing. It must have been. Even so, Dave was actually looking forward to going to sleep tonight.

Rampage of a Teddy Bear

Later that evening after he ate dinner and completed his home-work, Dave called Emma to apologize for bailing on the car ride. Emma forgave him, but had to run as her favorite TV show was just getting back from its commercial break. After hanging up, Dave dis-tracted himself and played on the Zeus for a bit, but soon decided to give up on it to go to bed. As soon as he climbed under the covers and closed his eyes, he fell asleep.

The next thing Dave knew, he was lying in a pile of dirt and debris. He stood up and brushed himself off, but as soon as he did, a man dressed in camouflage tackled him to the ground. Dave tried to throw off the attacker, but the man covered him completely with his body. Before he could do anything, a loud explosion blasted nearby. Dave felt the tremors and heat as well as a few bits of gravel. Dave looked into the face of the person who had just shielded him from the blast to discover that it was Jake.

"You've got to be careful, Dave. Remember your training!" Jake said, getting up and pulling Dave up with him. As he got to his feet, Dave quickly looked around and found that he was in a long trench with several other people. The trench was covered in netting. Guns and bits of blown apart military equipment were scattered ev-erywhere. Lined up against the wall of the trench were Andy, Eric,

Todd, and even the lunch lady from the school cafeteria. Each person in the group was holding a rifle and was dressed in the same camouflage as Jake.

"What the heck is going on?" Dave yelled to his friends.

"What do you mean? It's war! Those punks from Somerset Middle School launched a nuclear strike against our school. We and the rest of the survivors are fighting back!" Eric screamed back.

"They had nukes?! How did they get nukes?!" Dave asked, ducking as bullets flew over his head. Andy stood up and filled the air with bullets from his gun. Todd stood up soon afterward and did the same. Eric crouched down and made his way to Dave. Once he reached him, Eric grabbed Dave by the shirt and slapped him across the face.

"Remember?" Eric yelled right into his face. "Remember how they always beat us in football, baseball, soccer, and hell, any other sport? We always joked that they were on steroids? We were wrong! They weren't on drugs. They were cyborgs!"

"Cyborgs?!" Dave said, his eyes going wide.

"Yes, cyborgs!" Eric said, shaking Dave. "And once they knew that we found out, they launched the nuke to shut us up!"

"But, that doesn't make sen—" Dave and Eric hit the ground as an explosion hitting nearby sent both of them for cover.

"Get back to HQ!" Eric screamed over the explosion. "You've gone into shock! See a medic!"

Eric pointed behind Dave. Dave turned around and saw a huge hole in the wall of the trench where a bright light was pouring out. Eric pushed Dave away and ran to the edge of the trench, aimed his rifle, and shot. Dave ran over to the hole, keeping his head down to avoid the jets and mortars all around him. He dove into the hole as he felt the heat and impact from yet another explosion.

He landed on a tiled floor instead of dirt like he had expected. Instead of hearing gunshots and explosions, he heard pop music.

"You really did your school proud, boy," Dave heard a familiar voice say. He looked up and saw a large water fountain in front of him that sprayed water in neat designs. It looked so familiar. He looked to his left and saw a few storefronts. He was at the mall! He looked to his right and sitting on a bench in front of the Hot Day For Ice Cream stand was Bags, still in his ferret form, but dressed in full army gear, wearing camouflage, helmet, small gun, even a small backpack. If it weren't for the fact that it was Bags, Dave would almost have considered it cute.

"So, it wasn't just a bizarre dream. It wasn't just a coincidence, was it?" Dave said, sitting down on a bench near Bags, brushing off the remaining dirt and various bits of metal from his shirt and pants.

"Actually, it's still a pretty bizarre dream. I mean, you pissed off a disgusting looking clown at a carnival, turned a snake into a rose, went into your friend's dream, and fought a teddy bear combined with a desk. What's not so bizarre about that?" Bags said, while taking out and inspecting his little gun.

Dave got to his feet and brushed the dirt from his clothes. He turned around and saw that the hole where he had entered was gone. "I guess this is another bizarre one then. I went right from a war zone to a mall."

"That's what happens when you're infested with a nightmare. Things tend to jump around, especially when the nightmare has had time to look around for a bit."

"Beddy Tear, you mean? Why is Beddy Tear my nightmare?" Dave asked, looking around and realizing they were alone at the mall. The silence and emptiness of the mall gave Dave the chills.

Bags holstered his gun and looked up at Dave, "Oh, that's right. You gave it a name. Great. Wonderful. Well, the Beddy Tear is wandering around your dream right now. It's learning more about you."

"To do what? Scare me?" Dave asked, looking quickly at the storefronts, expecting to see Beddy Tear walking around.

"Damn right it's just to scare you. Anyway, nightmares are like a cold or a flu," Bags explained. "It's almost like it's contagious. If you encounter one, it may be able to find its way into your dream.

If it actually kills you in a dream, well, it's pretty much guaranteed access to your dream."

"So, I caught a nightmare from Andy?"

"Bingo! Nightmares are somewhat like dreamers, but all they have to do is to infest more dreams to get more powerful. And the only way to get rid..."

CLICK-CLACK, CLICK-CLACK

Bags and Dave looked at each other and then slowly looked around.

"It's Beddy Tear, isn't it," Dave whispered, looking to his left and right as his body tensed.

"Yeah," Bags whispered back. "I've been waiting to see when it would make an appearance. Hell, I was wondering if the darn thing was going to form after you put the doll on the desk."

"Huh?" Dave said, raising his voice. "You helped create a nightmare on purpose?!"

Bags stepped back a few steps and then stood up on his hind legs.

"You have to learn and learn fast if you want to be able to defend yourself against other dreams and dreamers. This is the best practice," Bags said, raising his voice to match Dave's as he took off his little helmet.

"Learn what? How to create monsters?"

"No, you need to..."

CLICK-CLACK, CLICK-CLACK

From somewhere above him, Dave heard the sound of rope unwinding as something slammed into him from above, crushing him to the ground underneath its weight. He turned his head to one side trying to see what had landed on him. He could only to see the underside of a large desk with blade-like legs.

Before Dave could react, Beddy Tear's legs snagged him in a claw-like grip and began re-ascending, the blades digging into Dave's flesh.

"Bags! Help!" Dave screamed as he rose closer to the roof.

"Kid!" Bags yelled from below. "Remember that it's your dream! You have what it takes to beat your first love!"

Beddy Tear reached the rafters at the top of the roof and tossed Dave into a corner. Dave landed in a pile of something wet, slimy, and mushy. As he looked around, he saw that it was mounds upon mounds of wet lined notebook paper. Dave then realized something else. He was stuck.

His torso was stuck on the paper, his feet dangling on the top of a long fluorescent light bulb holder. Dave struggled to free himself, but the notebook paper was covered in some kind of sticky substance that kept him in place. Beddy Tear pulled up the rope that it used to crash into him, opened its desk mouth, and shoved it in. Dave noticed as it closed its mouth that the rope was made of the same notebook paper that was holding him up. It swished it around, sounding like a dishwasher for several seconds, and then opened its mouth, pulling out a wad of wet paper. Using its legs, it placed the paper all around Dave, covering him completely from the feet to the middle of his chest before running out of paper. Seeing that Dave's arms were still free, Beddy Tear began making a noise that sounded like a lot of hiccups. It then opened up its desk mouth and pulled out a new wad of wet lined paper and mashed it onto Dave, covering him up to his chin.

"Dave!" Bags screamed. "Don't get eaten! You don't want to keep this thing in your dreams! Remember the snake! Remember what you did to it! Remember that it's your dream!"

Dave looked at the bear's mouth as it slowly opened revealing a nasty set of paper-covered teeth. He closed his eyes and breathed deeply.

"The bear is a rose, the bear is a rose, the bear is a rose," Dave repeated desperately as he opened his eyes. The bear, however, was still there. It came closer, sniffing at his face.

"No, you idiot!" Bags screamed. "You're not THAT good yet! You can't change the nightmare directly!"

Dave quickly looked around the ceiling. Rafters, lights, a banner... lights!

"The light bulbs are bombs, the light bulbs are bombs, the light bulbs are bombs," Dave repeated as quickly as possible, envisioning in his head that the bulbs were actually small explosives. Beddy Tear roared and its wide mouth lunged toward Dave's head. Just before it could chomp his head, an explosion from beneath them launched Beddy Tear into the air. The creature cried out in a high-pitched whine.

Dave's wet paper restraints seemed to have protected him from the blast, but he noticed the paper was ripped in several places. Dave held his breath and pushed off the wall with all his might. Encouraged by the tearing, he pushed again, finally releasing himself completely from the paper goop. Too late, he realized it was the only thing holding him up there! He fell screaming from the ceiling. He saw a rafter below him and screamed in a panic, "The rafter is soft, the rafter is soft!"

Dave slammed into the rafter chest first. Expecting to bounce off, he instinctively reached around the rafter and grabbed on, but as he did, he began sinking into it.

"It's a sponge!" Dave cried out.

"Of course it is, dummy! You wanted something soft you got something soft. Do you get it now?" Bags said as Dave pulled himself up. "It's not over yet, kid. Here it comes!"

Dave looked up to see Beddy Tear descending on a paper rope toward him. Dave tried to stand on the sponge rafter, but his feet only sank into it. Every time he tried to pick up his feet, they just sank back into it. He looked up to see the hungry mouth of Beddy Tear coming down for him. Finding nothing around he could use to defend himself, he did the one thing he knew he could definitely do. He jumped.

Dave screamed all the way, unsure where he would land. He looked down just as he landed in the fountain, water filling his mouth as he sank into the water. Once he surfaced and regained his breath, he saw Beddy Tear reaching the sponge rafter. It glared down at him and the bear portion growled.

"Bags, what am I supposed to do against that thing?" Dave asked, climbing out of the fountain.

"You've got to face your fears, kid, but you may want to arm yourself first," Bags said, loading his small pistol.

Dave examined his options and found the local sports equipment store, Sporty's. Dripping, he ran to the store as fast he could, threw open the door, and raced inside.

"Good morning, welcome to Sporty's. Can I help you?" asked a nasally kid behind the counter. Dave recognized him from school but couldn't place the name.

A quick glance around, and Dave found what he wanted. He tossed on some football shoulder pads then grabbed an aluminum baseball bat and a few baseballs.

"The baseballs are buy one and get one fifty percent off today, sir," the kid behind the counter said.

"Good to know. See ya!" Dave said, dashing out the front door as the kid screamed after him to pay for the items. He looked around the rafters, but he couldn't find Beddy Tear.

"Sir, come back here!" Dave heard the kid screaming behind him. Dave turned toward the shouting store clerk and just above him Beddy Tear balanced on the store sign with its legs hooked around the logo. It leapt at him, but at the very last second, Dave managed a weak swing with the bat to the right side of the desk. Both mouths whined in pain as Beddy Tear came up short and crashed to the floor.

Dave hesitated, unsure what to do next. Beddy Tear recovered from the hit and roared at Dave from the bear's mouth. Dave swung the bat and it connected with the bear portion, but it just sank harmlessly into the stuffed animal's soft body. He swung again, but it reared on its hind legs and blocked the bat with its metal legs, the two metals meeting with a clang. Its mouth opened and out launched a wet ball of paper that hit Dave in the chest, knocking him off of his feet. Beddy Tear hiccupped and a sticky ball of paper shot out covering Dave's legs. His heart pounded as he found that despite his best wiggling, he could not move his legs. He was stuck again!

Beddy Tear moved over him so that its legs were outside Dave's legs. He flailed with the bat, but the hits were ineffective against Beddy Tear's legs.

I need something. Something stronger! I need something to destroy it. I need something to destroy my nightmare! Dave thought to himself as Beddy Tear roared.

"The bat is an ultra sharp sword, the bat is an ultra sharp sword, the bat is an ultra sharp sword," Dave chanted as he imagined the bat in his hand thinning out and turning into a sharp blade. He felt the bat wiggle in his hand. He glanced down to see his fingers wrapped around the hilt of a sword about the same size the bat was.

Beddy Tear roared again and swooped down to chomp Dave's head. Just before impact, Dave swung the sword and gouged out a huge chunk of its metal leg. Beddy Tear reared again and roared as a strange black dust burst from the wound. As it lowered onto its four legs, Dave thrust the sword upward, driving it straight into the middle of the desk. Beddy Tear roared and whined all in one breath as black dust poured out and coated Dave. He quickly used the sword to free himself from the paper and stood as Beddy Tear struggled to stay on its feet.

"Sorry, Beddy Tear, but I gave up on you a long time ago," Dave said, swinging the sword with all of his strength. The blade connected right at the point where the bear's torso merged with the desk. The bear roared as it separated from the desk in one stroke, spraying even more black dust. As the bear hit the ground, both halves began to whine as Dave saw a black hole form between the two parts. The two halves began to slide towards the hole as if it was sucking them into a vacuum cleaner. But Dave felt no pull. The desk and the bear gouged their claws into the floor to stop from entering the hole, but the pull was too strong. The bear looked at Dave, bared its teeth, and then disappeared into the hole, the desk following soon after. The black hole disappeared with a thunderclap as Beddy Tear was no more. Things had returned to normal.

Dave fell to one knee and dropped the sword, his lungs screaming for breath and his heart rattling in his chest. As soon as the sword hit the ground, he heard the sounds of people walking, talking, and shopping. He saw people moving in and out of stores as if it was just a nice weekend day of shopping.

"You know what," the Sporty's clerk said, "keep the bat. I think you need it more than I do!" The clerk ran into the store without looking back.

Bags stood on his hind legs and wriggled his nose sniffing the air. "You defeated the nightmare, kid. You had me worried there. I thought you were a goner for a while," the ferret said, marching up to him as if following a military march. Dave quickly reached out and snatched the ferret.

"Hey, get the hell off of me!" Bags yelled, twisting in his hands.

Dave held the ferret high into the air. "You tricked me into creating that thing," Dave said, lowering the ferret to meet it eye-to-eye, making sure that he kept his nose away from biting distance.

"Yeah, I did. So what?" Bags said, not a bit of emotion in his voice.

"Are you kidding me? I got eaten by that thing last night! I got EATEN! Heck, it almost happened again tonight!" Dave said.

"But you beat it, didn't you?"

Dave looked away shaking his head. "Why didn't you tell me it was going to happen?"

"Honestly, because it doesn't happen all the time. It might not happen the next dozen times you try the same thing. However, I do know that a nightmare forms more often when you're not expecting it. But, you know what? You're now better-prepared to face off against things you'll encounter within the Dreamscape."

"Are you saying that I can beat the Sleepless Knight now?" Dave asked curiously.

"Nope," Bags said, shaking his head. "You'll get your ass kicked."

Dave cocked his head. "What can he do that I can't? Especially now."

"Well, she can put on deodorant, unlike some people I know," Bags said, sniffing and wincing as if he smelled something horrible.

Dave quickly sniffed his underarms then opened his mouth to say something, but as he did, Bags bit down on Dave's thumb. Dave released his grip on the weasel, and Bags quickly scampered away hiding underneath a bench.

"I can't believe you just did that!" Bags said, laughing as loudly as he could. "Did you actually expect to smell good after being wrapped in spit-covered notebook paper?"

Dave took a quick step toward the ferret, but Bags just backed further underneath the bench. "It was instinct, all right?"

"Yeah, sure. Whatever, boy," Bags said, barely containing his laughter.

"So, what now? Do I find another childhood memory to corrupt?" Dave asked, squatting to see where Bags was.

"Hey, listen to me, boy. You are going to see some strange stuff in the Dreamscape. Some of it is going to really freak you out. Think Beddy Tear is bad? You could run into your mom as a vampire or be abducted by an octopus brother or even worse. You have to prepare your mind to deal with things like Mr. Beddy Tear. If it had beaten you in your dream, it would have rooted in deeply within the very fabric of your mind and would be incredibly difficult to get rid of it."

"Wait a minute," Dave said, standing up. "It got Andy too. That means that it's in his dream as well, right?"

Bags smiled as he poked his head from underneath the bench. "Well, would you look at that? You actually thought something out rationally."

Dave looked down at Bags, his eyes half closed. "So, Beddy Tear is alive and in Andy's dream then. Just great."

"Yup and because you beat him here in your dream, he's stuck in only Andy's dream for now. That's a good thing! The fewer dreams your best desk-bound pal has to roam around, the easier it is to find it!"

"Bags, if it weren't for us, he wouldn't have this nightmare at all!"

Bags left the comfort of his bench and stood on his hind legs, adjusting the beret on his head. "Well guess what, Mr. Dream Walker? You have to go into Andy's dream and destroy Beddy Tear again. Otherwise, it will solidify its powerbase and make sure that it has complete control of Andy's dream. Then, Andy will be cursed with nightmares for the rest of his life."

"How could he beat Beddy Tear on his own? He—he's not a Dream Walker, so how is he supposed to do that?"

"You're always capable of overcoming your own nightmares, even if somebody else gave them to you. But, do you really want to wait and see if he can figure this out and risk truly giving your friend nightmares for longer than necessary?"

Dave paused and thought about Andy's personality for several seconds. "Well, Andy might want them. He's a pretty big horror freak."

"No, give the nightmare time and it will figure out exactly what makes you scream in terror. Andy may get a chuckle out of Beddy Tear, but what if Beddy Tear found out what he REALLY is afraid of. Beddy Tear will find out and use it against him," the brown haired ferret said nodding his head.

Dave took a deep breath and looked to the mall ceiling assessing the damage he had caused. "Okay, so tomorrow I come back and take care of Andy's nightmare. I'll be good and rest—."

"No!" Bags interrupted, tugging on his pant leg. "You will take care of this NOW!"

Dave looked down at Bags. "Aren't I going wake up soon?"

"Why the hell are you worrying about that? Aren't you worried about saving your friend?"

"Yeah, I am," Dave said. "But I want to make sure I have the time to do it."

"Time to do it?" Bags repeated, raising his voice. "It's your damn friend! Your friend is in danger! What do you do when your friend is in danger?"

"I...uh..."

"You what?" Bags said.

"I help them!" Dave said, nodding his head.

"That's right! You help them! So, let's do it! Let's go find Andy's Pathway," Bags said.

Going Down the Right Path

Dave looked around at the stores in the immediate area. "Sure, but how do we find it, though? It seemed so random before," Dave said.

Bags stared down the mall hallway. "Remember that the ones close to you are close by. Always remember that."

Dave nodded and looked around. "How do we find it? Even if it's close, that could still mean a zillion places."

Bags started walking and Dave followed. An older woman jumped out of the way screaming about a rodent infestation, which Bags ignored.

"The pathways like to make sense," Bags said. "However, they don't want to be obvious. They don't want to make it easy for a Dreamer to walk through one by accident."

"All right, so how do I get to Andy's dream?"

"Patience boy. Pathways are doorways, but again, they're not obvious. They're out of the way in a place where a dreamer probably wouldn't randomly stumble upon them. However, in the end, we're looking for doors," Bags said, accidentally knocking over someone's lemonade that had been left on the floor. "Now, where in the mall would you have no reason to go?"

Dave thought for a second while scanning the stores. Then, he saw a particular sign and smiled.

"The girl's bathroom!"

Bags nodded. "That actually makes sense, boy. Come on, let's go."

The two walked over to the girl's restroom and stood looking at it as if this was hidden treasure.

"Go on, boy," Bags said, his nose poking the swinging door.

Dave took a deep breath and walked in. The bathroom looked so strange to him. The women's restroom was much larger than the men's. While there were stalls, sinks, and mirrors like the men's restrooms, there were also nice comfy chairs and couches and what smelled like perfume. The walls were covered with actual live flowers. He could feel the rose and tulip petals on the wall. A bead of sweat rolled down his forehead, and he wasn't exactly sure what to look for. He opened the door a crack and found Bags looking up at him.

"Nice of you to let me in! Did you find it?" the ferret asked.

"I don't even know what I'm looking for!" Dave replied.

The ferret walked into the room with him and looked around.

"Boy, your women have some strange bathrooms," Bags said, sniffing the air.

"You're telling me! I mean, I've never been in one of the girl's rooms, but I can't believe they get couches. I never believed Eric when he told me about it!"

"Well, don't believe this room completely. If you've never been in one, this is what your mind is imagining that it looks like."

"I think the women's bathroom has flowers covering the walls?" Dave asked, peeling a petal from the wall only to see another petal underneath it.

"Yup. Freaky, ain't it, boy?"

Dave stayed silent, peeling another petal.

"Alrighty, kiddo. Take a look at those stalls. What do you see?"

Dave walked over to the bright pink stalls and stared.

"Uh, a nice paint job?" Dave said, shrugging.

"Do you see a name? Anything? Anything on any of the stalls?" Bags said, looking up at Dave.

"Nope, nope, nope..." Dave said, continuing on down the row of stalls.

Suddenly, the sound of a toilet flushing came from one of the stalls. The door opened and a large, middle-aged woman with short, black, curly hair stepped out. She turned to Dave with a confused look on her face. Dave recognized her. It was Mrs. Laffin, the school librarian.

The woman's face turned from confused to worried, "PERVERT!" she screamed.

"You've got it all wrong! I was just... I was just..." Dave couldn't come up with a good reason for being there. Not that he was given much time to explain. Mrs. Laffin swung at him with her pocketbook hitting him repeatedly on the shoulder. Dave quickly backed up and ran. Bags jumped and grabbed onto one of his legs as he rushed through the door, nearly knocking over a crowd of middle-school girls on their way in. They all gave high-pitched shrieks as he passed them. Dave didn't stop running until he rounded a corner several hundred feet away. Bags let go of his leg and dropped to the floor. Within a second, he was on his back laughing.

"I—hahaha—can't—hahaha—believe that just happened!" Bags said, laughing so hard he was crying.

"Shut up, Bags!" Dave said, peeking around the corner to make sure security wasn't coming for him.

"Well, I'll tell you something, that's something I'll NEVER forget!" Bags said continuing to laugh.

"Can we get serious? I'd like to help out my friend!" Dave said looking scanning the stores in this side hallway.

"Now he gets serious? Alrighty, boy! The bathroom is out," Bags said getting to his feet. "How about a store? What store don't you go into?"

"I don't know!"

"Come on, boy! Concentrate!"

Dave breathed out in a huff and shook his head. But, just as he did, a store caught his eye.

"There!" Dave pointed. "Johnny Narcisse. The preppy clothes store. There's no WAY I'm going in there."

"No taste for style, boy?" Bags asked, curiously.

"It's not that! It's way too expensive. It's where all of the rich kids or wannabes buy their clothes. I think I went in there once a few years ago with my mom. It was one of the few times I agreed with my mom. It's just not worth it."

"Poifect. Let's go in then," Bags said. "I believe you have a date with the girl's dressing room." Dave stopped and tried to think of a way out of it but decided not to fight it.

The two walked into the store and were instantly approached by an attractive name-tagged clerk named Mindy who tried to talk to him over the loud electronic music playing over the store stereo.

"Welcome to Narcisse, can I help you?" she asked, but Dave just shook his head and walked past her. He looked over his shoulder and saw the woman looking at him. He grabbed a random shirt off the rack and walked to the dressing room.

"This had better work," he said to the ferret. "I'm not going from store to store jumping into their women's rooms!"

Dave followed the sign for the dressing room and then turned right to head to the women's room. He breathed deeply and reached for the door. He quickly backed away as the door swung open. Dave took a few more steps back when Emma emerged from behind the door holding an armful of shirts. Her eyes lit up in surprise as she saw him.

"David! Were you just trying to go into the girl's room?" she asked reaching out and taking his hand.

131

"Uh. . .I. . ." he stammered. "Yeah, sorry, the guy's room is under construction. The girl out there told me to just go in the girl's room. I was hoping that nobody was in there."

Emma shook her head. "It was just me and—"

"Me!" Adrienne said peeking her head around the door before walking out.

"Adrienne? You shop at Narcisse?"

"No, Jimmy Chestnut shops at Narcisse," she said pulling out her stuffed alligator from a bag. The alligator was wearing a shirt from the children's section. "I just come along to keep him company."

"So, you're not all here together?" Dave asked.

Emma gave him a weird look. "What? No! She and I just happened to be at the same place at the same time. I was as surprised as you were seeing her here," Emma said as Adrienne began stroking Jimmy Chestnut's head.

"Oooookay. Listen, Em, can you make sure no one else comes in?" Dave asked.

"Sure, I can do that. There's a price though. One big smooch!"

Dave smiled, walked up to her, grabbed her lightly by the neck, and kissed her.

"It's too bad you're just a dream," Dave said motioning to Bags.

"Huh?" Emma said confused. "What is that supposed to mean?"

"It means—OW!" Dave jumped as Bags bit him on the ankle.

"Come on, kiddo. Remember what I said about talking with a dream. It'll get you nowhere!" Bags said, tugging on his pant leg.

"EEK! A rat!" Emma screamed clutching Dave.

"He's a ferret! Not a rodent!" Adrienne said.

"Yeah," Bags said. "I ain't no rodent!"

Emma shrieked. "It talks?!"

"Unfortunately, yes. It talks," Dave said in a monotone voice.

"I talk, he talks, she talks, we all talk. Can we go now?" Bags asked impatiently.

Dave smiled at Emma. "Guard the door, Em, okay?"

"'Kay," she smiled back at him.

Dave opened the door slowly and stepped in. He was quickly overcome with the same smell of perfume. Inside the room there was a long row of closed doors leading to small changing rooms. Like the bathroom, the walls were covered in flowers and the doors were painted in hot pink.

"The doors again, Bags?" Dave said closing the door behind him.

"Yes, genius."

Dave slowly approached the first door. Andy's name was written on it.

"It's Andy's! I think we found it!" Dave said excitedly.

Bags walked up and looked at the door. "Alrighty, boy. Go in and kick some Beddy Tear butt!"

Dave was about to open the door, but he stopped just before he turned the handle. "Hold on. I'm just curious."

He looked down the row of doors and saw Eric's name as well as Todd's, Cynthia's, Adrienne's, and Emma's. He opened Emma's door and saw her bedroom. He noticed a set of football shoulder pads lying on the floor.

"Oooh...I may have a co-starring role in Emma's dream tonight," he said smiling.

"Kid, you better get moving to Andy's dream," Bags said.

Dave let Emma's door close and opened Adrienne's door and his eyes widened when he saw his school, except that it was animated like a cartoon with all of the papers, pencils, books, teachers, and students singing a happy cartoon song as the birds and squirrels from outside sang along. He quickly closed the door, horrified but laughing at the same time.

"I have to keep going, Bags!" he said as the ferret sighed and lay down. "I have to see what they're dreaming about."

He opened Eric's door next but was blown back several steps by sheer crowd noise as he found himself looking at the middle of a stadium where two football teams were lining up.

"Cool!" Dave said as he closed the door.

He swung open Cynthia's door and was hit by a blast of freezing cold air. He looked in on a cave made completely of ice. He saw Cynthia standing in the middle of the cave dressed in a torn black hooded cloak, her face the only part exposed. She was wearing heavy mascara that had run down her face with tears. Feeling concerned, Dave began to walk in, but instantly felt a bite on his leg.

"Don't," Bags said. "Remember that it's a dream. Come on, let's go to Andy's dream."

Dave let the door close and shook Bags from his leg.

"Just one more door," Dave said going over to Todd's door. He put his hand on the handle, but just as he did, several large metal chains exploded from the sides of the door and crossed in front of it, a giant padlock placed where all the chains met.

"What the heck? Bags?" Dave asked, trying to turn the handle, but without success.

Bags walked up to the door and sniffed it. "Interesting!"

"What's going on with Todd's dream?" Dave asked.

"Kiddo, I think your friend Todd is an Exile," Bags said putting a paw on one of the chains.

"More terms for me to learn?" Dave said.

"Oh, har-dee-har-har...an Exile, genius, just means that he's barred from leaving his dream and people are barred from entering his."

"Why? Why Todd? I mean...he's just...Todd!" Dave said giving the chains a useless tug.

"I don't know," Bags said. "I don't know why you claim to be a friend of this guy even though he annoys the crap out of you, buuu-uuuut I do know that there's always a very good reason for keeping an Exile locked away from the rest of us."

"Why? I don't understand!" Dave said, suddenly concerned about Todd for the first time.

"Look kid, the Dreamscape is a weird place. Even I don't know everything about it," Bags said.

"But..."

"No!" Bags yelled. "Now, get your butt into Andy's dream and kick some Beddy Tear butt. No ifs, ands, or buts!"

Dave gave the chains one last tug and then kicked the door in frustration before moving over to Andy's door.

"Good luck, kid," Bags said as Dave took a deep breath, held it, and went through Andy's door.

Dave nodded, breathed in, and opened Andy's door.

Alter Egos

Dave stepped through the door and entered through the closet door of the inside of a wood cabin. He smelled damp earth coming through an open window that was also letting in a few drops of rain. He didn't recognize the place, but before he could look around, his body stiffened as he heard a door open to his left. He glanced toward the door from the corner of his eye and saw a familiar head of long curly hair and turned to face Adrienne. She looked both surprised and happy to see him. She quickly and quietly closed the door behind her.

"Dave?" she whispered. "You're not supposed to be here! This is my room!"

Dave smiled and looked around the room spotting Jimmy Chestnut on a pile of other stuffed animals on her bed.

"Oh, you know what? You're right! I'm so stupid! I should get going," Dave said shrugging and trying to get to the door behind her but finding her blocking the exit.

"You don't have to go yet, do you? Why are you up here?" Adrienne asked.

"Uh, I was just taking a short walk and kinda got lost," Dave said, hoping she would fall for it.

"So, you climbed in through the window? Why not just knock?"

Dave quickly tried to come up with a reason, but couldn't think quickly enough.

"Unless you were trying to sneak into my bedroom! Davey, I never knew you felt that way about me!" she squealed running to him and giving him a hug. "Here I was thinking that you were getting together with that Emma girl down at the beach, but you came to me instead!"

As soon as Adrienne mentioned the beach, he heard the distant sound of voices laughing and screaming as if a party were going on. He turned to look out the window as Adrienne shook her head.

"Daddy doesn't like the lake people. He says they're too loud," she said, raising her voice on the last word.

"Adrienne!" Dave heard a man's voice yell out from somewhere in the house. Dave could hear the wooden floorboards creak as the man walked toward the room.

"Oh no!" Adrienne said taking his hand and guiding him over to the window. "Daddy will get really mad at me if he sees a boy here."

Dave put a hand on the windowsill and remembered that Adrienne's father was not someone you wanted to mess with. The guy had a short temper and was overprotective of his little angel. "Yeah, I think seeing your dad right now would uh...result in me probably dying, so...it was nice seeing you."

Adrienne smiled and gave him a kiss on the cheek. Dave turned and smiled at her before he swung his weight up and over the windowsill. He tried to land gracefully but slipped in the damp earth coating him in chunks of dirt. He stood up, brushing the dirt off as he saw that he was in the middle of a forest, trees surrounding him in every direction. Just off in the distance Dave saw a cabin and an old, beat-up station wagon parked in front of it. Something about this seemed so familiar. He started walking away casually when he heard a deep male voice from behind him.

"Hey, you!"

Dave turned around to see an obese man with a giant grey beard leaning his head out the window. It was Adrienne's father.

"What the hell are you doing here, kid?" the man yelled with a voice that was scratchy from years of smoking.

"Uh, sorry, I went the wrong way. I'll get off of your property," Dave said, backing away as far as he could from Adrienne's father.

"You better or I'm coming out with my rifle and putting a couple holes in your little sock hop down at the beach," her father said, putting his hands in a position as if he was aiming a rifle at him.

"Uh, yeah, whatever, dude," Dave said, remembering Bags' advice to not argue with a dream.

"Tell your lake friends to shut the hell up or I'm coming down there. I won't show any mercy!"

Dave didn't bother responding as he walked away and Adrienne's father slammed the window shut. He turned and looked into the forest and then had a realization. Forest...beach party...light drizzling rain...this was the first time that Emma and Dave went public with their relationship back over the summer. They had dated for a few weeks but kept it relatively quiet except for their closest friends. This was the first time that they came to a party together. After that, everybody in school knew that they were boyfriend and girlfriend. But why would Andy dream about this?

Then, as he heard the sound of happy screams and loud music, Dave realized what this was about.

Seeing Dave and Emma officially together changed the whole structure of their friendship. Dave had started spending time usually spent hanging out with the guys alone with Emma. While this had bothered Eric a little bit, it had really gotten under the skin of Andy. He was even more miserable at the start of the beach party when he realized that Dave and Emma were spending most of the party away from him.

At some point, Andy started hanging out with Eric who had brought his sister Cynthia along. Eventually finding themselves alone together, Andy and Cynthia ended up talking and found that they had a lot in common and on top of that, their personalities meshed very well. Later, they ended up getting caught making out in the lake one night leading to Cynthia's classic nickname of Siiiiiiinthia. For the rest of the weekend, there wasn't a second when they weren't with each other. Dave remembered seeing Andy smiling for longer than a brief second for the first time in as long as Dave had known him. Andy was dreaming about the happiest time of his life.

He began making his way toward the noise, his feet crunching on old brown leaves and pine needles as he listened to the sounds of birds singing and trees moving in the wind.

"Private!" Bags yelled in his head. "What's the sitrep, over?"

"Bags?" Dave said, stopping his walk. "Why are you talking like a soldier?

"That's Sergeant Bags to you, soldier!" Bags said as Dave rolled his eyes.

"I ended up in Adrienne's cabin and had to get out of there first," Dave said pausing for the snide remark, but when it didn't come, he continued. "I'm in the middle of some forest, but I think I know where to go."

"All right soldier, get a move on."

"Okay, okay. I hear you," Dave said heading toward the music.

"Carry on, soldier. Be careful," Bags said purposefully slowing the last two words. "Over."

Dave found a path through the forest by following the tire marks leading to the station wagon in front of the cabin. As he walked, Dave twisted and turned, watching for signs of Beddy Tear, but he saw nothing except trees and falling leaves. As the path took a sharp curve, the forest canopy began to block out some of the sunlight, making the shadows grow longer and every step a little bit more worrisome.

Don't worry, Dave thought. *You beat it once, you can beat it again. Just use your sword and—* Dave then remembered that he left the sword behind in the other dream. As his thoughts drifted, something hit his shoulder. Dave jumped, swatting off whatever had just hit him. He raised his hands to defend himself from an attack, but just as he did, he saw that the thing that hit his shoulder was just a squirrel. The squirrel twitched its nose at him as it looked up from the pile of leaves that it had landed in.

"Get the heck away from me, squirrel," he said, his heart beating faster as he pointed down at the squirrel. "Get away from me or I swear I'm going to blow you away!"

As soon as Dave finished his sentence, a long black metallic cylinder appeared before him, hovering in the middle of the air.

"Soldier! Sitrep!" Bags yelled.

"Uh, a long black cylinder just appeared before me," Dave said, confused.

"Long black cylinder… is it part of the landscape?"

"I don't know. It's just floating in front of me!"

"Reaaaaalllly? Innnnnnteresting!" Bags said, his voice going a bit higher. "Tell me… what did you do or say right before it appeared?"

"I told a squirrel that I was going to blow it away," Dave said, not sure if he really wanted to tell Bags about it.

"A squirrel? A SQUIRREL?" Bags said, letting out a chuckle. "Come on, you've got bigger things to deal with."

"I know, I know, but he came out of nowhere."

"All right, all right," Bags said, holding back another laugh. "What is it?"

"Well, kiddo, it's one of two things. Either Andy's dream is just randomly making weird shapes appear or your mind just made a bazooka appear!"

"I what?" Dave said, his eyes opening wide.

"Kiddo, think about it. You wanted to blow the terrible squirrel away. Your mind was already panicked. It made something so that you could blow it away."

Dave quickly smiled for a second. "So, wait… I can make anything I want?"

"You're getting there, kid. It's harder to create things in another person's dreams, but luckily if you are close with the person whose dream you're in, it's a bit easier. Now you just need to do that on demand rather than having it happening randomly. Then you'll be able to kick some serious butt! Speaking of that, grab that bazooka! You'll need everything you've got to take down Beddy Tear!"

Dave reached out and grabbed the bazooka as the squirrel looked for acorns on the ground. The weapon was unnaturally light, like a balloon.

"Bags, I don't even know how to use one of these things," Dave said.

"Trust me, it's pretty simple, especially with your background," Bags said.

"Hey, I play a lot of video games that have these things in it, but that doesn't meant I know how to use it in real life!" Dave said, shaking his head.

"Your mind will never create something you can't use. It simplifies it so that it makes sense to you," Bags said.

Dave gave the bazooka a quick look over. Engraved on the side were the words:

AIM THIS WAY
TURN OFF SAFETY
PRESS TRIGGER
ONE SHOT

"I see it! I see the instructions! I—"

Dave stopped talking when a long rope of wet notebook paper descended from the tree canopy onto the squirrel. The paper stuck to the squirrel and it squealed in panic. The rope ascended back into the canopy and within moments, Dave heard a loud crunching of bones as the acorn that the squirrel was carrying dropped to the ground. Panicking, Dave aimed the bazooka into the canopy and fired. The rocket shot out with such force that it knocked Dave backward onto the ground. He looked up and saw an explosion of fire and wood

141

that sent dozens of birds flying. An unnatural, high-pitched screech came from the canopy,

"I got him!" Dave yelled.

"All right kid! Direct hit?" Bags asked.

"I think so!"

"You think so or you know so?" Bags asked.

"I...I don't know..."

Dave's eyes went wide as he saw Beddy Tear quickly scuttling down the tree, now with most of the bear portion furless, but otherwise completely intact.

"He's still alive!" Dave yelled.

Beddy Tear reached the ground and growled at Dave, a mere few feet away. Dave's mind and heart raced. He tried to imagine another bazooka, but the horrifying sight of Beddy Tear overcame him and he couldn't concentrate on it. Out of options, Dave ran through a crowd of trees, hoping that he could lose Beddy Tear. He looked over his shoulder and saw the nightmare scrambling behind him, the desk legs jumping onto the side of a tree to propel itself forward while the bear portion swatted away low branches.

"Bazooka, bazooka, bazooka!" Dave yelled, but as he did, he stumbled over a large rock. As he struggled to regain his balance, he felt Beddy Tear's massive body impact with his, the momentum sending Dave tumbling down a hill. He felt every bump, branch, and rock until he landed in sand at the bottom of the hill. Almost as soon as he stopped rolling, he felt a hand on his shoulder. He turned, ready to fight, but all he saw was Andy looking down at him.

"Andy?" Dave asked, not believing his eyes.

"Damn, you're pretty fast! I just saw you get thrown into the water!" Andy said, pointing behind himself.

Dave quickly stood up and saw dozens of people from his school standing around tents and campfires on a beach in front of a beautiful clear blue lake.

He saw that the party was basically set up like the cafeteria. Everyone was with the usual social groups—jocks with jocks, cheerleaders with cheerleaders. Even Rake's gang was there, hitting rocks with aluminum bats.

Dave looked over his shoulder and there was no sign of Beddy Tear. "Andy, you've gotta get out of here!" Dave yelled, turning back to face Andy.

Andy rolled his eyes. "Is this about my parents again? I told you before, I DON'T CARE! What, I can't spend the weekend with my friends?"

Dave opened his mouth to say something, but his heart jumped when he felt two arms grab him and lift him up.

Eric's voice calmed his heart down. "That's okay, Andy, I don't mind throwing him in again!"

Dave struggled against Eric's grip. "Seriously, we've got to get Andy out of here!"

No one seemed to hear Dave's voice. Suddenly, Jake's massive frame walked in front of him.

"Let's do this!" Jake said, a huge smile coming across his face as he grabbed Dave's legs.

"Guys! Seriously! Don't!" Dave yelled out in a futile effort to get them to stop.

Jake and Eric ran over to the lake, carrying a struggling Dave between them. When they reached the edge of the water, the duo looked at each other.

"One...two...three!" the boys counted together and launched Dave into the water in a huge splash. Dave panicked as he sank into the cold lake water, but he soon hit the bottom. He put his feet down and pushed off, rocketing himself toward the surface. As his head pulled above the water, he saw everybody on the shore laughing. Dave opened his mouth to draw a breath and say something, but before he could, the crowd went silent and pointed to his left. Dave turned ready to face Beddy Tear, but what he saw made his whole body shiver. He was looking at himself. Andy's dream of Dave.

The dream Dave's eyes were wide in shock. "What the heck is going on? Are...are you my twin?"

Dave swam back a few strokes from his dream twin. "Uh, nah, we look alike, but it's just a coincidence."

Dream Dave took a few strokes forward towards Dave. "No way! We look WAY too much alike! Heck, we've got the same clothes on!"

He pulled on his own soaking wet shirt and then pointed to Dave's shirt. Dave looked down and for the first time noticed that his clothing had changed since he stepped through the Pathway to Andy's dream. Dave moved his eyes back to his dream self and away again.

"Dude, chill out! Um, let's see... do you play football?" Dream Dave said.

"Uh, yeah," Dave said, getting closer to the shore.

"Where do you live?"

"Carter," Dave blurted without thinking about it.

"What?" Dream Dave said, his hand slapping down onto the water, sending a big splash towards Dave that he tried to avoid as much as possible. "That's impossible! I live there! I've lived there my whole life! I definitely would have seen you around! Man, wait till I tell Emma about this!"

They both stood as they reached a shallow enough area where it made more sense to walk than swim. Dream Dave reached out and slapped Dave on the back.

"Let's talk to my friend, Andy," Dream Dave said. Dave, however, turned toward his dream self with a look of horror and shock backing away quickly and falling into the water.

"What's wrong?" Dream Dave said as Dave got to his feet, staring nervously at him. "I..."

Dream Dave stopped and looked confused. He scrutinized Dave scanning him up and down. Suddenly, his face lost all emotion.

"You're not what you say you are, are you?" Dream Dave said, an angered look coming over his face. He lunged for Dave and grabbed one of his arms. "You must show me what you know! You must show me what you are!" Dream Dave said yanking one arm as

Dave tried pulling the other way. "David Calloway, I am you. I will be YOUR reality and YOU will be my dream. I will be FREE!" he said, his voice growing deeper and scratchy.

"Get off me!" Dave said, pulling away as much as he could.

Dave suddenly felt pain as he saw Dream Dave's fingers elongate into pointy tendrils that dug into Dave's arm. All he could hear was the sound of Bags screaming in his head.

"Kid! You've got to get out of there! He's becoming a wraith. In a few seconds, he's going to be waking up in your body!"

"I. . . want. . . out! I will not be held to this dream's rules!" Dream Dave said. Dave struggled to free himself, but Dream Dave's tendrils were holding him fast. He concentrated and tried to form a weapon like he did with the bazooka and the sword, but the pain was too much. He let out a scream of absolute agony as he felt the tendrils sliding through his arm and burning him from the inside.

Just when he couldn't take it anymore, he heard a loud splash right next to them. Dream Dave's tendrils withdrew into his hand as he turned around to see Beddy Tear rise from the water.

"Beddy Tear?" Dream Dave said, his eyes wide.

This Dream Dave doesn't know about nightmare Beddy Tear, Dave thought.

From the shore, he heard the sounds of dozens of people screaming.

"Oh crap! That thing again?" he heard Andy yell. "It's coming for me again!"

"Beddy Tear, what happened to you?" Dream Dave said, taking a few steps toward the nightmare, looking at the spot where Beddy Tear merged with the desk. Beddy Tear took a few sniffs in the air and cocked its head as it noticed the two Daves. Beddy Tear reached down with its paws and picked up Dream Dave, sniffing him.

This is bad, Dave thought. *Beddy Tear is bad enough, but Beddy Tear and a wraith? What if they teamed up? I can't let that happen!*

Dave reached into the water and found a small flat rock on the

145

bottom. He looked at Beddy Tear and back down at the rock. He took a deep breath and let the breath out, feeling his heartbeat calming.

"The stone is a ninja star, the stone is a ninja star, as sharp as the sharpest blade," Dave said, imagining the stone flattening out and becoming sharp as he reached back and then flicked his wrist forward to throw the stone as if throwing a Frisbee. As the stone left his hand, it gave off a shiny metallic appearance as it changed its shape to a four-pointed metallic blade. It spun over to Beddy Tear and sliced off one of its fuzzy ears. The ear came off and bounced down the bear's body landing right in Dream Dave's hands. Beddy Tear reached up to its ear, which was puffing out black dust, then looked down at Dream Dave and roared.

"Beddy Tear, NO! It wasn't me! It was him!" he said, turning to point to Dave. He turned back around just as the desk mouth opened.

"No, Beddy Tear! NO!!!" Dream Dave screamed.

Beddy Tear ignored Dream Dave's screams and shoved him into the desk mouth. The desk closed, chomping down on its victim as Dream Dave screamed from inside. The desk made an audible gulp and Dream Dave was no more. Dave could not relish the victory as he only had a second to ponder what happens to a digested dream or even HOW a desk digests things before Beddy Tear turned toward Dave and roared with both mouths. Dave backed up slowly, finally reaching land. However, just as he did, the nightmare charged. He tried to move, but he was just a bit too slow as Beddy Tear grabbed him by the leg and pulled him up dangling Dave in the air like a caught fish. The bear portion licked its lips in anticipation of a meal, opening its desk mouth wide, bringing the helpless Dave closer.

Suddenly, a glass bottle came twirling at the nightmare, hitting it right in the bear face, somehow just barely missing Dave. Beddy Tear roared in pain and dropped Dave into the muddy sand. Dave looked up, mud streaking his face, and saw Andy, but not the Andy he knew. Wearing black goggles, long spiked hair, and a black leather costume with buttons, hooks, and belts in random places, Dave only recognized him from the look and shape of his face and body.

"Andy, what the heck are you doing? That thing is going to eat you and then it's NEVER going to go away!" Dave yelled.

Andy stared straight ahead at Beddy Tear.

"That is why I must assume my true form. Andy never stood a chance, but Andruseth DOES!" he said, pulling a long oak pole from his back. He clicked a button on its side and a scythe-like blade appeared at both ends of the pole.

"Andy? What the heck?" Dave said, not believing his eyes. Andy had become his Lord Battler character.

"There is no Andy, only Andruseth, defender in the dark," Andruseth said, quickly glancing up at the bright sun with a cocked eyebrow before shaking his head and looking back at Beddy Tear. "This nightmare will harm you no more, David!"

"Andy, you've got to be careful," Dave said, standing and keeping an eye on both Beddy Tear and Andruseth. "That thing is really dangerous!"

Beddy Tear charged out of the water and lunged at Dave. However, Andruseth quickly stepped in the way and hit the nightmare with the flat side of the scythe. Beddy Tear stumbled back—mostly from surprise—and turned to face its attacker. It snarled at him raising its massive arms to attack Andruseth; but before it could, Andruseth jumped up and slashed downward with the blade of the scythe slicing through one of its furry arms. The nightmare howled as half its arm dropped to the ground, rolling to a stop on the water's edge as black mist sprayed from the wound.

Andruseth swung again, but this time, the bear managed to get inside the swing, getting lightly hit with the wood portion of the scythe. However, before the nightmare could do anything, Andruseth swung with the other side of the pole and slashed the bear from the stomach to the chest. As if an artery had been severed, black mist gushed from the wound. Beddy Tear took several steps back and looked down at the wound. Andy took the opportunity to charge and finish it off. Beddy Tear looked up and opened its desk mouth, spitting out a wet notebook paperball, the impact knocking Andruseth off his feet. The nightmare quickly jumped and landed on him with its legs splayed so that the weight of the desk pinned Andy's body to the ground. Andruseth weakly tried to swing the scythe, but the nightmare grabbed the pole and easily overpowered him, pulling the pole out of his hands and tossing it aside. Suddenly, Andruseth's body gave off a quick flash of light like his whole body was taking a picture. When the light died down, Andruseth was gone, replaced by just regular Andy.

Beddy Tear looked over at Andy hungrily, both bear and desk mouth drooling.

Dave had to help him. He looked around for the weapon that had hurt Beddy Tear. Finding it right at the water's edge, he sprinted to grab it. Just when he was about to pick it up, the pole gave off the same flash of light and changed from a pole to a large blue crab.

The crab looked up at Dave. "I've done what I can. You've got to save him!" said a high-pitched voice coming from the crab.

"What the...?" Dave said.

"Save him, Dream Walker!"

"Are... are you Andy's dream-guardian?"

"Yes and I've done what I can in this situation! Save my dreamer! Save my friend!" the crab said, quickly digging a hole in the sand and skittering into it.

Dave turned to face Beddy Tear who had picked up Andy with its one paw. Dave concentrated, trying to imagine the bazooka. The air shimmered before him and his eyes lit up as he could see the weapon start to take shape. However, a huge ball of wet newspaper launched itself through the shimmering image, dispersing it as the goopy paper hit Dave in the chest and knocked him off his feet. Beddy Tear, holding Andy in one hand, scrambled over to Dave. Dave tried to get up, but he slipped in the sand and fell. The nightmare moved on top of him, spewing the sticky notebook paper all over him, cocooning him up to his neck. He could not move.

The blue crab poked its eyes out of the hole. "Dream Walker! You can defeat this nightmare!"

Dave struggled against the notebook paper but found that he could not break free.

I need strength! I need strength to beat this thing!

Beddy Tear leaned closer, letting out what could have been a growl or a laugh, as the crab ducked into the hole.

That's what it wants, Dave thought. *Not just my dream, but it wants my fear as well. I'm not going to let it scare any of us anymore.*

I need strength.

I need energy.

I need power.

I need to destroy this nightmare once and for all!

Dave felt a warmth as he saw a bright blue light glowing from beneath the notebook paper cocoon. Starting at his feet and working its way up, the light burned away the cocoon as it moved. Beddy Tear took a few steps back dropping Andy to the ground.

As the cocoon burned off completely, Dave looked at his body and saw a bright blue shell over his body that quickly enveloped his head. He held his breath just in case.

"Boy!" Bags voice screamed in his head.

"Bags!" Dave screamed back.

"Calm down! This is you. This is your mind giving you the strength and energy you needed!" Bags said excitedly.

"Wh-what do I do now?" Dave asked, finally breathing normally.

"What do you think? You can kick that nightmare's ass! Your mind is finally getting off auto-pilot and letting you take control."

Dave smiled and stood up. Feeling empowered, he ran at the nightmare, throwing punch after punch at the surprised beast, targeting the area around its chest wound. With every hit a burst of black mist emerged and dispersed into the air. No sooner than Dave began to think that he could defeat Beddy Tear than the nightmare reached out with its good paw and grabbed one of Dave' arms. The bear lifted him with its enormous strength, dangling him like it had before. Dave flailed with his free arm and landed a solid hit in on the nightmare. However, Beddy Tear shook it off and roared, crushing Dave's arm in its immense grip. Dave screamed and the blue light around him flickered.

"Get... off me!" Dave cried.

Suddenly, several blue spikes pierced Beddy Tear's paw. Now black mist sprayed from these wounds as well. The nightmare roared in pain as its grip loosened. Dave climbed out it's grasp and landed on the ground as the spikes retracted from the blue shell around his arm, and the blue light flickered again.

Dave rose to his feet just in time to see Beddy Tear charge. It swung and connected with Dave's face in between flickers, the impact sending him end over end. He finally landed on his back. He reached up and felt hot blood streaming from a large gash on his cheekbone. His blue light flickered again as Beddy Tear snarled at him.

"Bags, what can I do? I can't keep this up much longer! This weird energy shield around me doesn't want to stay up. I don't know how to use it!"

"Kid, your mind is finally unshackling. It's your confidence, willpower, hopes, desires, and a whole mix of other things all rolled into one."

"Bags," Dave said, getting up and taking a few steps back as the blue shell around him disappeared for a second then reappeared. "I think I'm running out of confidence!"

"That means that you're feeding your confidence to Beddy Tear via your fear."

"What can I do?"

"There's one thing you can do," Bags said.

"What? What can I do?"

"Boy, I want you to focus all that energy in that shield. Calm your mind and focus it into your hand. Feel it move down from your head into your arm and into your hand. Feel it move up your leg into your stomach and then into your hand. You..."

Beddy Tear charged and tried to run him over, but Dave barely dodged it by rolling to his side. His shield flickered even more.

"How the heck am I suppose to focus?!"

The blue crab crawled out of its hole. "Dream Walker! You couldn't have come here without having the ability to affect a dream! I know you have the power!" The crab crawled back into the hole.

Beddy Tear stopped its charge and turned to face him, merely a dozen feet away or so. Dave closed his eyes and breathed out.

The sand under Beddy Tear is glue. The sand is glue! Dave thought. Beddy Tear cocked its head in confusion. It looked down and saw white goop mixed in with the sand around its desk feet. It tried to lift a leg up, but found that it couldn't. It reached down with a paw to pull a leg free, but whined in frustration when its paw stuck as well.

Dave closed his eyes and made a fist. He breathed out concentrating on his fist. He opened his eyes and saw that the blue shell around his body had moved to just his fist. It shone with a bright shimmering light as if his whole hand had turned into a giant blue sapphire. He looked back to the nightmare and knew exactly what to do.

"Beddy Tear, this has gone on long enough," Dave said, pointing his fist toward the bear. "This nightmare...is OVER!"

Dave's fist opened and unleashed a beam of blue energy that burst toward the nightmare. Beddy Tear looked up and let out one last whine as the massive energy carved through the air. It drilled and blasted through the bear's body. The nightmare exploded in a cloud of black mist that the remaining blue energy quickly dissolved.

Beddy Tear was no more.

"Bags, WE DID IT!" Dave yelled as the last bit of energy left him.

"Fantastic, kid!" Bags returned.

Dave's legs suddenly felt very heavy. His legs wiggled and then gave out as he collapsed on the beach.

Before Dave could speak, Bags started to talk. "Kiddo, don't worry. Your mind is exhausted. But, that's good because that means you're going to wake up very soon. And trust me, right now that's a REALLY good thing."

"Huh? Why?"

Bags hesitated. "She's here...in your dream. The Sleepless Knight is here right now and she's looking for you."

"What...I..."

"Kid, it's okay. I know you want to rush over here and save your ferret, but I'll be fine. Wake up and she won't be able to get to you. It's going to be okay. You did great today," Bags said complimenting Dave for the first time.

Dave smiled nervously as he tried to keep the sand out of his mouth. Looking up he saw Andy standing in front of him.

"Andy," Dave said as his friend knelt beside him.

"Yeah?" Andy said.

"When you wake up, apologize to Cynthia. I don't care whose fault it was. Just make up with her. Make things right. Can you do that for me?"

Andy smiled, one of the few times Dave had ever seen him do that. "I was already planning on it."

Dave nodded, smiled, and put his head down as his body faded away.

Fight! Fight! Fight!

Bzzzzz

Dave heard the buzzing of his alarm, but his eyelids were so heavy that he assumed that he was still asleep and dreaming.

Bzzzzz

Dave's head started pounding like someone was punching him on both sides of his head.

Bzzzzz

He heard the sound of his door opening.

"David, get up. You're going to be late for school!" his mother said loudly.

Dave forced his eyes open and immediately clutched his head. His mother, either oblivious to it or just plain ignoring the fact that his head was killing him, turned and left the room to start making breakfast. He flipped over and turned off the alarm clock with his elbow as if keeping his hand on his head would dull the pain. His eyes felt like they hadn't been closed in days and his body felt like Coach Weaver had made him run laps all practice. Even a hot shower and breakfast didn't seem to offer relief.

As he left for school, he ran into Andy who looked almost as bad as he did.

"I am so exhausted," Andy slowly mumbled.

"Me too."

"Krazy Koffee?" Andy asked as they fell in step together.

"Ah, yup," Dave replied.

As they walked in silence, Dave noticed that Andy was wearing blue jeans. On anybody else it wouldn't be a big deal. However, he hadn't seen Andy wear anything but black pants in the past five years.

"Rough night?" Dave asked.

"Nah, just woke up feeling this way. I must have been tossing and turning all night," Andy said.

Dave turned away from Andy and smirked. "I bet you must have had some weird dream, right?"

"Nope. I don't even think I had one last night," Andy shrugged.

Dave looked at his friend. "Nothing? Nothing at all?" he asked.

"No. Who cares?" Andy asked looking at Dave confused.

"Oh, uh...I figured that you would be dreaming about getting back together with Cynthia," Dave said, looking straight ahead down the road.

"Cynthia? Why? It's over between us," Andy said, no emotion in his voice.

"Oh come on, it's not like you guys really broke up!"

"True, but still...I guess I just don't see a future for us," Andy said. "Her constant prodding was a little too much for me."

The two walked by Emma's house. She saw them through her bedroom window and motioned for them to wait.

"Speaking of prodding," Andy said, narrowly avoiding a hard punch on the shoulder by Dave.

A smiling Emma came running out the door a minute later and caught up with them. She gave Dave a huge hug before walking to Krazy Koffee with them.

"So, Andy...Cynthia...Are you going to apologize?" Emma asked.

"Don't ask that, Em, I think Mr. Darkity Dark is playing stubborn," Dave said.

"Oh, screw you. I was unhappy, all right? It just took one extra push," Andy said.

"You were happier than I've ever seen you when you were with her," Dave replied.

"Yeah, well, I put on a good show."

"So, are you just going to avoid us at lunch then if Cynthia is at our table?" Emma asked.

"I've got other friends," Andy replied coldly. "I'll just hang out with Jake."

"Come on, man," Dave said. "Don't do this."

"Then stop trying to make me get back together with Cynthia, okay?" Andy said.

The trio reached Krazy Koffee and waded through the massive amount of students and teachers to get their caffeine. Afterward, Dave wanted to lighten the mood.

"So, Andy, get any further in ULB?" Dave asked, trying to get him to talk about his favorite video game.

"A little bit. But you guys don't want me going any further so I can't play much of the game that I bought," Andy replied.

"Well, it's going to be a lot of fun when we get together over the weekend," Dave said.

Emma poked Dave on the arm. "Just don't play the entire weekend. You better save some time for me!"

"You want to play Lord Battler too?" Dave joked as they reached the school.

They had a few minutes to spare, so they hung out in front of the entrance drinking their coffee as buses and cars were pulling up to drop off other students. Out of one of the buses stepped out Todd.

"Don't look, don't look, don't look," Andy said.

"Oh guys, don't!" Emma said, waving at Todd who made his way over. Dave and Andy stared at Emma.

"Hey guys!" Todd said as Dave and Andy grumbled hellos.

Andy turned to Dave to say something, but just as he opened his mouth, a lit cigarette butt flew by barely missing Dave's chest as it hit the ground. Dave flinched and spilled coffee on his shirt. The sound of Rake's gang hooting and hollering followed.

"Aw, missed it by an inch," Rake said, standing in front of his friends as he put another cigarette in his mouth.

Dave turned and walked up to him, his mind racing with what would happen if he swung at Rake right now. "Rake, what is your problem?" Dave asked.

Rake looked at him and answered with the cigarette dangling from his mouth. "Oh, sorry Dave. I was aiming for Emma."

That pushed Dave over the edge.

Dave shoved Rake who only remained upright with his friends' help. Rake came back and threw a punch nailing Dave right in the face and sending him to the ground. Suddenly, Todd let out a primal scream, and he tackled Rake to the ground. The two wrestled trading punches as a crowd of students formed a circle around them cheering on both sides. It only stopped when several teachers dragged the two apart and hauled them off to the principal's office. Dave and Andy came along as did Rake's crew. Emma wanted to come as well, but the teachers told her as well as the rest of the students to get to class.

The principal, Mrs. Rose Spriggs, sat down at her desk and looked at both of them with her pale blue eyes and thin white hair. All of the students called her Mrs. Sponge because she sucked all of the fun out of anything the students wanted to do that wasn't exactly by the book.

Both sides gave their versions of the story—Todd and Dave provided the accurate story while Rake tried to spin it so that Todd was the one who threw the cigarette at his friends. Finally, the principal had had enough and slammed her hand down on the desk knocking her pencil holder over and spilling its contents all over the desk.

"Enough! I've heard enough! Dave and Todd? Detention today. Raymond?"

"What?"

"I'm sick and tired of seeing you in here day after day. You're suspended for the week," she said, writing Rake's name on the suspension form with one of the pens that fell out of the pencil holder.

Rake looked over at Dave, Andy, and Todd. "Whatever... it just gives me more time for myself."

Mrs. Spriggs continued. "One more—just one more school incident and you will be expelled, Raymond."

Rake turned toward the principal. "Whatever you say. I don't need this place."

Mrs. Spriggs turned to Dave and his friends. "You three may go. Raymond and his friends will stay here for the next few minutes. I don't want another incident."

The three got up to leave, but Rake leaned back in his chair to get in Dave's way.

"It's not over between us. You know that, right?" Rake said.

"Get out of their way, Raymond," Mrs. Spriggs said.

Rake smiled and stared at Dave for a few seconds before leaning his chair forward and letting them go.

The trio walked in silence for the first few seconds as they roamed the virtually empty hallways heading toward their class.

"Hey Todd," Dave said as they walked down the hallway.

"Yes?" Todd said in a happy tone.

"Thanks... thanks for having my back," Dave said patting him on the back as Andy rolled his eyes.

"No problem. I mean, I would do it for any friend just like you would have done for me!" Todd said beaming.

Andy opened his mouth to say something, but received a punch on the shoulder from Dave.

Dave's head pounded throughout the day, and his body didn't feel any better even with the caffeine.

"Mr. Calloway?" It was his history teacher, Mr. Gavin, asking for his attention.

Dave shook his head to try to shake off the fog. "Yes?"

"What is the answer to my question? Who was part of the Axis in World War Two?" Mr. Gavin said pointing to a map of Europe.

"Uh... Germany..." Dave said immediately. He tried to think of other names, but as he did, his headache got worse.

"Good, you got the easy one. Who else?" Mr. Gavin said.

"Ummm..."

"Give me the two others," Mr. Gavin said, his face a combination of amusement and disappointment.

Dave knew the two countries. Every time he thought of them, it felt like a kick in the head. He looked up at the ceiling, but the halogen lights only made his head feel worse.

"Uh..."

"That's right Dave. Italy and Japan," Mr. Gavin said shaking his head.

Dave put his head down on the desk and tried to keep the lights out.

As Dave made his way to the cafeteria for lunch, he ran into Eric.

"Yo! I heard through the Emma-vine that you have detention today. Man, Weaver's going to murder you today when you show up late," Eric said.

"I know, I know—it's not like I planned it. Rake threw a lit cigarette at me again! I just... I dunno... I just snapped," Dave said.

"You snapped by pushing him? Dangerous man, you are!" Eric said, pushing Dave from the side. Dave stumbled and ran into somebody.

"Sorry!" Dave said before realizing it was Andy. Andy shoved him back almost slamming him back into Eric.

Eric stepped between them. "Don't worry, David. I know his ninja style!"

Eric threw a slow punch and let loose with a slow but loud kung fu howl. The punch connected with Andy's chest. Andy, however, didn't react. He simply turned and got in line for lunch.

Dave and Eric looked at each other. "I guess it proves that my awesome kung fu skills trump goth ninja skills!" Eric said, laughing.

"Whatever," Andy said, keeping his back to them.

"Andy, we're just joking around," Dave said, but Andy ignored them.

"What's his problem?" Eric asked, making sure to speak loud enough so Andy could hear.

"I don't know. He's been like this all morning," Dave said.

"Probably because he knows he'll never date a girl as hot as my sister!" Eric said loudly. Everybody in the lunch line stopped and turned toward Eric. It took a second or two for Eric to realize what he had said. "I probably shouldn't have said it that way. People go about your business! I don't think my sister's hot! Quite the opposite in fact!"

Some people laughed, some just shook their heads, but it did the trick. People returned to their conversations.

"Probably won't," Andy said quietly.

"What was that?" Eric asked.

"I probably won't get anybody like her again," Andy said moving down the line.

"Dude, don't worry about it," Dave said to Andy's back. "Listen, I think you guys were great together, but if it's over, then you'll find somebody else."

"Yeah, go find somebody who isn't my sister," Eric said as Dave shot him a look to shut up.

As they made it through the lunch line, Eric and Dave sat at their usual table. Without another word, Andy walked past them.

"So, we're no longer friends?" Eric said to Dave. "Andy's off to Jake-land for citizenship?"

"I have no idea," Dave said.

Andy walked past everybody and sat at an empty table. Jake looked over at Dave and made a drinking motion and shrugged. Dave chuckled and shrugged back. Even the shrugging was tough on his body.

Emma, Cynthia, and Todd showed up soon after. They were all laughing about something as they sat down with their trays.

"What's so funny?" Eric asked.

"It's about the push heard 'round the world!" Todd said, standing up for dramatics before sitting down again.

"The what?" Dave said, even though he had a good idea what this was about.

"Gang warfare! It's going to be awesome!" Todd said slashing the air with a plastic knife.

"Emma? Help me please!" Dave said. "What's going on?"

"Funny story, Dave," Emma said, smiling at Todd and then looking back at Dave. "Apparently, the rumor going around the school is that Dave and his cronies have formed a posse to take out Rake's gang."

"What? Like the old west? We're gunslingers?" Dave asked.

Todd's eyes lit up. "I've got a few paintball guns at home. I can—"

"NO!" Dave and Eric said at the same time.

"I don't want to have to deal with Rake," Dave said. "I mean, I'm not scared of him, but I don't want to get into trouble. Besides, it's not like we're some real gang or anything."

"True or not, it's going to build up around the school," Emma said. "I'm willing to bet that when Rake and his crew hear about it, they're going to be pissed! He's definitely gonna come after you."

Dave took a deep breath, but even breathing hurt. Everybody stayed silent for a few seconds and took a few bites of food.

Cynthia looked around the cafeteria. "So, can someone tell me why that goth-boy of mine is sitting by himself?"

Dave and Eric looked at each other. Dave simply shook his head and put his head on the table.

"Just let him be, Cyn. Just let him be," Eric said.

Detention Blues

When Dave showed up for detention, Todd was already there working on his creative writing homework. Dave saw several of the bullies and random jerks from school that always had to stay after class. Some were sleeping, some doing homework, and one guy was eating potato chips. As Dave sat down next to his friend, he leaned over and got Todd's attention.

"So, what do we do? Just homework, sleep, what?" Dave asked.

Todd put his fingers to his lips and pointed to the front of the room.

"No talking, Mr. Calloway."

Dave looked up to see Mr. Laws sitting at the front of the room

"Take out some homework and work on it for the next hour," Mr. Laws said.

Dave stared at Mr. Laws for a second and then grabbed his math homework and began doing it in silence. Mr. Laws mostly stayed at the front of the class. But he would occasionally walk the aisles, waking up sleepers, intercepting notes passed, and confiscating bags of chips.

The hour passed fairly quickly, but as people rushed from the room, Mr. Laws asked David to stay for a few minutes. Dave waved goodbye to Todd who packed up his stuff, smiled, and left.

"David, I have to say I was surprised to see you here today," Mr. Laws said.

"Yeah... well... it wasn't like it was planned," Dave said looking down at his own feet.

"I should hope not. Listen, I heard about what happened. Raymond is the kind of person that will try every angle to get under your skin. You have to somehow ignore him or utterly prove to him that you're not worth picking on. I recommend trying the former."

"Ignore him? When he's throwing lit cigarettes at me?" Dave said looking up at the counselor.

"Ignore him as much as possible. If he can't get a reaction out of you, it's not as fun for him and he may back off," Mr. Laws said. Seeing Dave's doubting eyes, he continued. "Now, I'm not saying that if he hits you that you should just sit there and take a beating. Self-defense is fine, but pick and choose your battles. However, if you do choose to fight, which I am absolutely not advocating, you must be ready to finish it. Prove to Rake that picking on you is not worth what you can give him in return."

"And how am I going to do that? He's got his whole gang around him all the time," Dave said.

"I don't know how you're going to do it, but today, tomorrow, next month, next year, or whenever, you will have to make a stand against him. I can guarantee you that he won't take this morning's fiasco lightly. He's actually quite good at what he does when he's serious about something. I'd like to think he could concentrate on his schoolwork and graduating rather than bullying and vandalizing, but we're working on it."

Dave and Mr. Laws stood silently for a few seconds then Dave eyed the door.

"What I'm saying is, be careful," Mr. Laws said. "While I can help keep it out of the school, I have a feeling that he's going to try and wait until teachers and parents are not around, in which case it may mean that you're on your own. Ignore him at school. But just be careful after you leave. Do you understand?"

"Yeah, I think so," Dave said as Mr. Laws nodded and patted him on the back.

"Very well then. Have fun at football. Good luck." Mr. Laws said, letting him go.

*
* *

Detention made him very late for practice. The coach was so angry with him that instead of having him participate with the group, he had to run laps and grueling drills. After about a half hour, his exhausted body and legs finally gave out and he collapsed. The coach, Tony, and Eric ran over to him as Michael, Cole, and the rest of the team burst out laughing.

After getting him some water and making sure he could see straight, the coach got him up and had Tony and Eric carry him over to the bench as practice wrapped up. He spent the rest of practice doubled over trying to catch his breath and not throw up.

Later, after a quick shower and an agonizing few minutes getting dressed, Eric and Dave met up by the bus driveway.

"Tough break today," Eric said. "Though I swear I told the coach that you were going to be late and he was okay with it!"

"Hey, we all know Coach doesn't like education getting in the way of football," Dave said, trying to stretch and rid his body of its pain.

"Now that's the truth. Still, you gotta wonder how Cole is still on the team," Eric said.

Before Dave could respond, a wet mound of dirt and grass hit the back of his head.

"Whooo! Touchdown!" Dave heard Michael Everway's voice behind him. "Hey Cole! I think ass-face and girly-man like you. I mean, like-like you!"

The two turned to see Michael and Cole standing behind them.

"Ummm... They're not like me, Mike," Cole said scratching his head.

Michael shook his head. "What do you think, Cole, diaper check?"

Cole smiled, revealing a grin with a tooth missing near the front of his mouth. He laughed and nodded as Mike slowly moved around behind Dave.

"Good answer, Cole," Mike said. "Get him!"

Cole reached out and tried to grab Dave, but he backed away a step, just out of his reach. However, Mike caught him, pulled the back of his of pants open and dropped in a huge mound of wet dirt and grass. Eric tried to move to help him, but Cole tackled him to the ground with ease and held him down with one hand while using his other to wipe Eric's face in the dirt.

Dave tried to fight back, but Mike shoved Dave to the ground as Cole got up.

"All dirty!" Cole said laughing and pointing at the two.

"Go take another shower, boys," Mike said, wiping the muck off of his hands and flicking it at both Dave and Eric before walking away.

Dave and Eric looked at each other. "One day," Dave said through gritted teeth. "One day, we're going to get those guys. We're going to get them so bad!"

"Sure we will," Eric said watching as his mother's car pulled up. "Sure we will."

Eric turned away as just one tear rolled down his cheek.

The ride home was spent in silence. Emma, seeing the dirt and miserable looks on their faces, stayed quiet for the entire ride home.

When Dave got home, he immediately ran upstairs and changed. While the pants could be salvaged, he didn't bother putting his boxers into the hamper. They went directly into the trash. He changed into some sweatpants and a t-shirt and went down to eat dinner.

Dinner was uneventful. His father showed up just as dinner was ready. They all went through the events of their day, but Dave glossed over the end of his. Immediately after dinner ended and he had helped clear the dishes, the phone rang. It was Emma.

"Dave, are you and Eric okay?" she asked as Dave went to his room and closed the door.

"Yeah, we're okay," Dave replied.

"Then... then, what happened?"

"Mike and Cole happened," Dave didn't want to go into any more detail.

"What did they do?" Emma asked.

Dave took a deep breath and exhaled loudly. "I don't really want to talk about it."

"Okay," she said softly, almost a whisper. "Maybe later then?"

Dave couldn't bear to shut her out. "Look, they beat us up, all right?"

"They did?" she said, still in that soft voice. "Did anybody see it?"

"I don't know," Dave said thinking about it for the first time. "But no one came to help, that's for sure."

"Okay... umm... is there anything I can do to make you feel better?"

Dave paused. "I don't know."

"Okay," she said, her voice returning to normal. "You just let me know."

"All right, Em," Dave said.

"Dave?"

"Yeah?"

"I'll make sure you're in my dreams tonight," she said.

Dave's heart skipped a beat. "What do you mean? Y-you can control your dreams?"

"Huh? What?" Emma asked.

"Can you control your dreams?" Dave said, almost regretting it as soon as the words left his mouth.

"Uh, I don't know. I was being cute and girlfriend-y, weirdo!" Emma said as Dave smiled and relaxed.

"Maybe I'll come visit you in your dreams tonight," Dave said.

"You better! How else am I going to make my other dream boyfriends jealous?"

"Other dream boyfriends? Like who?!"

"Oh, umm..."

"Todd?"

Emma laughed. "Yeah right, he's at the top of my list for guys I want to dream about. You know how it is."

"Very funny. Veeeery funny!" Dave said with a chuckle.

"Yeah, I know!" Emma replied.

"Hey, Em?" Dave said, closing his eyes.

"Yeah?"

Dave took a deep breath, held it, and let it out. "What if I told you that I could control my dreams?"

"I'd probably say whoopdeedoo and who cares," she said laughing.

"No, seriously. What if I could literally walk into your dreams tonight?"

"This isn't, like, a video game thing, is it? Because I'm really not into those that much."

"Nope, not a video game. I'm being serious," Dave said.

"Then, I'd probably think you're crazy and if you are serious, maybe a peeping Tom!" she said, laughing still.

"I'll make you a bet then. I'll bet you that not only will I be in your dreams tonight, but that tomorrow I can recite exactly what I said to you in the dream," Dave said.

"Uh huh, sure. And what's the prize if one of us wins?" Emma asked.

"How about a prize to be determined later as the winner sees fit?"

"Anything then?"

"Yeah, anything."

"Come find me in my dream and give me a kiss."

Dave's heart starting beating faster and he smiled from ear to ear, "I'll find you tonight, don't worry. I'll give you that kiss."

Emma giggled as they hung up.

Juggling Rabbits

Despite his exhaustion, it took Dave several hours of tossing and turning to fall asleep. When his eyes were open, it felt like lead weights were attached to them, but when they were closed, it was as if helium balloons were attached, making it nearly impossible to keep them closed.

Finally, after he fell asleep, he opened his eyes to see that he was in his house, surrounded by dozens of people in brightly colored pointy hats all talking and dancing with each other as loud holiday music blared over the stereo. Dave immediately got into a crouch to avoid any sword swings if the Sleepless Knight was waiting for him here. However, after waiting for a few seconds, he relaxed and looked around. He was dressed in festive bright clothes and everybody was dancing up a storm to some song from the 1980s that his parents always seemed to play when they were in a good mood.

Feeling something on his head, he reached up and took off a plastic hat that read "Happy New Year." He smiled, put the hat back on, and watched all his friends and family enjoying themselves. Then he noticed the hand that had just been holding his hat. The blue energy was there glowing brightly. He looked around to see if anybody noticed, but then shoved it into his pants pocket and walked over to the dinner table that was filled with soda, chips, and cold cuts. Piling some chips, turkey, and cheese on his plate with his non-glowing hand, he turned to watch the party.

"Hey kiddo."

Dave looked around for the source of the voice. It sounded like Bags, but he couldn't see the ferret. As he was looking around, somebody stroked his arm. He turned and raised his fist to strike. But, as he turned around, he saw Emma and relaxed.

"Come on, Davey, you're coming with me," Emma said, dragging him onto the dance floor, leaving Dave with a millisecond to put his plate down on a table.

They danced to a fast paced tune, some song that his parents always raved about during long drives. As they were spinning around, he saw Andy and Cynthia dancing, Todd dancing with Adrienne, and Eric dancing with some girl that he had a crush on, but Dave could not remember her name.

Emma put her hand on his hip and drew him in a bit closer. Dave and Emma smiled as they looked into each other's eyes. Their faces kept moving towards each other, their eyes closing, lips getting closer. It was then that Dave felt excruciating pain on top of his head. It almost felt like... claws. Little tiny ferret claws.

Dave drew back making Emma stumble forward a bit. She gave him a disappointed look as she opened her eyes. "Ruin the moment much?"

"Emma, excuse me for a minute," Dave said, quickly walking toward the bathroom. Frustrated, Emma went over to Eric and cut in, practically pushing the other girl away so that Eric would notice her.

As soon as Dave got into the bathroom, he closed and locked the door. He walked over to the sink and turned on the cold water. Grabbing the hat, he flipped it over and tossed it under the running water. A mere second after he did, a soaking wet ferret jumped out, landing on the sink counter.

"I'm going to kill you!" Bags screamed, trying to be as intimidating as he could, pathetic looking as he was with his matted wet ferret fur.

"Payback, Bags, payback," Dave said smiling. "I don't care if Beddy Tear was your way of training me. It was still pretty darn evil to do!"

"Yeah, well, evil or not, you learned how to fight in the Dreamscape!" Bags said shivering.

"Sure, whatever," Dave said as Bags quickly shook his body, spraying water all over the room, including all over Dave's shirt. "Hey! Watch it!"

"Don't blame me! I've got to get dry somehow!" Bags complained.

"Dave smirked. "All right, ferret. Want to explain to me exactly what happened last night?"

"Specifically?"

"The shell, the energy, whatever you want to call it. The bazooka. Heck, let's talk about the wraith. How about the black mist that came out of Beddy Tear?" Dave said crossing his arms.

"The black mist? Oh, that stuff! That's its energy. It's the life force of a nightmare. It's just as straightforward as that. And as for the wraith, well kiddo, I was actually worried for you there. However, good thinking about getting Beddy Tear to eat him! That was brilliant!"

"I didn't know what else to do," Dave said, rubbing his arm where the wraith's tendrils stuck into his body—not from pain, but just from the general creepiness of the wraith itself.

"Doesn't matter. It was brilliant. The nightmare ate the wraith. End of story," Bags said.

Dave breathed a sigh of relief.

"And about the shell, that's your mind, kiddo. Just like I said before. It's your willpower, your. . . look, the fact is that your mind is now getting used to the Dreamscape. Well, maybe that's not the right phrase. It's getting used to WORKING with you in the Dreamscape," Bags said, jumping from the sink, to the toilet, to the floor.

"So, I can form spiky bits and shoot energy?"

"Buddy, the sword, the bazooka, the spiky bits, the energy blast, the shell? It's all from your mind. Whatever you want to happen in your dream can actually happen," Bags said rolling around on the carpet to dry his fur.

"What are you saying exactly?"

"Are you dense? Wait a minute—what am I saying? Of course you are!" Bags said. "Kid, you're not limited to just those things."

"So, I can do exactly what? What can I do?"

"Kid, first, let's get rid of the shell."

"But...but...that's my mind, isn't it?"

Bags ignored him.

"Alright, let's start with something easy. Let's change your clothing. I want you to imagine what you wore today to school. I want you to imagine putting on every little piece of clothing."

"Why? I'm already wearing clothes," Bags said.

"Would you just trust me, boy?"

"Okay, okay. I'll try," Dave said concentrating. He imagined putting on his clothes—his underwear, his socks, his shirt, his pants, and his watch. He watched as the blue light moved from his hand as he concentrated and enveloped his body. The glow brightened as he saw his current festive clothes fade away. Just as they did, there was a knock on the door.

"Dave, are you okay?" Emma said from the other side.

"Yeah...yeah, I just felt a little dizzy. Just give me a minute, okay?" Dave said.

"Okay, but I want my arms around you on the dance floor when you get out, mister!" Emma said.

Dave didn't reply, but saw that the blue light had faded, leaving him standing in just his boxer shorts. "What the heck? Where did my clothes go?"

Bags broke out laughing. "Hahahaha! You've got to keep concentrating, kiddo! You let your mind drift off to other thoughts, naughty boy! Hahahaha!"

"Where did my clothes go, Bags!" Dave said, raising his voice, quickly looking around the room to look for his missing clothes.

"I see London. I see France. I see Davey's under—"

"Knock it off!"

"Don't think about your girlfriend while trying to form clothes, especially while you're still a rookie. . . in more than one way. Bwha-haha!"

Dave stared at the ferret, trying to ponder whether to strangle Bags or to just dunk him under the water again.

"Now, kiddo, concentrate again. As funny as it is to see you like this, we've got to get you ready for Ms. Sleepless."

"Mr. Sleepless isn't here, right?"

"She hasn't shown up yet. But, I think we'd know by now, eh? Anyway, concentrate!" Bags said.

Dave tried to concentrate, but Bags broke out laughing again.

"Bags! I said, knock it off!"

"Sorry, sorry, sorry. Go ahead," Bags said, covering his mouth with his paws, though from the way his chest was heaving, it was obvious he was still laughing.

Dave closed his eyes and let out a breath, trying to get rid of any tension. He imagined his clothes from school. He imagined putting the clothes on one piece at a time. Dave opened his eyes and saw his boxers glowing. He watched as the colors on his boxers changed to what he was wearing this morning to school and then the blue light spread out all over his body, stopping right at the bottom of his neck. Bags put his paws down and just nodded as Dave's shirt, pants, socks, shoes, and watch formed. The blue light faded and Dave was fully clothed.

"Fantastic!" Bags said. "No more looking at your ugly behind!"

Dave gave the ferret an annoyed look, but then looked at his clothes and smiled.

"Seriously, kiddo, you were one layer from blinding me!"

"You're about a second away from a ferret lobotomy!"

"Ooooh real tough! You can beat up a weasel! Well, I guess you needed to pick on someone your own size!"

Dave reached for the ferret, but Bags dashed behind the toilet.

"Come back here, Bags. I just wanted to see how far I could shot-put you, that's all!"

"Boy, if you throw me now, how are you going to learn how to make a sword, a bazooka, or something else that will give you a snowball's chance in beating Ms. Sleepy?"

Dave stopped trying to reach for the ferret. "No more jokes, okay? Truce?" He said, taking a step back to give Bags some space.

"No jokes," Bags said, emerging from behind the toilet. "Just insults, I promise!"

"All right, all right," Dave said. "Now, what's this about a sword? I mean, I made one at the mall when I was fighting Beddy Tear."

"Too easy. The bat and the sword were too similar. It's not too hard to alter its shape. I want you to make one from scratch," Bags said. "Remember how you did your clothes? It's kind of the same thing. Imagine making the sword. Imagine!"

"Bags, I don't know how to make a sword!"

"Nope, you probably don't even know how to tie your shoes either, right?"

"Bags, seriously!"

"Kid, remember the bazooka? Remember how your mind built it so that you could use it?" Bags said and then continued when Dave nodded. "As long as you believe it, your mind will figure it out. It might be created by a blacksmith in real life, but you actually think you make a sword through juggling rabbits. However, if that's how you believe that it's made, your mind will create it. It sounds weird, but you'll get it down."

"Wait, I can make a sword by juggling rabbits?"

"If you believe that's how it's made then, yes!"

"So, hold on. If I can create anything I can imagine, can I just create a weapon that automatically defeats the Sleepless Knight? Like a Sleepless Knight killer sword?"

"Hey, now you're thinking like I think you should!" Bags said.

"Okay," Dave said. "Now, do I do it the same way?"

"Yeah, yeah, but hold on. You can think of the Dreamscape kind of like playing cowboys and Indians as a kid."

"How so?"

"You can create a Sleepless Knight killer, but he can create armor that stops Sleepless Knight killer weapons. It's kind of like a cowboy shot an Indian, but the kid playing the Indian screams out that he has super-secret armor that prevents bullets from getting in."

"Wait, so that could mean that he's armored and protected against everything!"

"Depends on how strong her mind is, actually."

"How strong his mind is?"

Bags climbed on top of the toilet. "You can dream up whatever you want. However, the more complicated it is, the harder it is for your mind to comprehend it. Making a sword? It's pretty easy to justify a sword. Just juggle some rabbits. How hard is it for your mind to comprehend a blade and a hilt? I mean, yeah, yeah, those blacksmiths actually do put a lot of work into making it, but crap kid, at the very basic level, it's not too hard to imagine a sharp blade and a handle. However, making a sword that cuts through everything? You have to justify everything to your mind. It cuts through steel? Justify it. It cuts through diamond? Justify it. You'll probably have to do it every single night until your mind assumes that it's a basic part of your dream and automatically does it for you.

"I know that your knightly friend is heavily armored and power-ful, but in the end, her mind created the armor. She probably justified some neat things on the armor and sword, but she isn't some kind of Terror... well, I hope not, but if she were, she would have defi-nitely gutted you in your first dream. Besides, Terrors don't really fight with swords."

"Uh, Terrors? I'm assuming some big bad Dream Walkers?"

"You got it."

"Why don't they ever use swords?"

"Well, it's not like they never use swords, but swords are Dream Walker 101. Everybody starts off learning how to make one. That's why I think your sleepy stalker, while not some brand new Dream Walker, is relatively new to Dream Walking."

"So, he's beatable, then?"

"Technically, yeah. I mean, everyone is beatable, even the Terrors. You just have to find a way to beat her. I mean, in the end, she's human and I imagine someone that you know. Otherwise, she wouldn't have easy access to your dreams."

Dave sat down on the edge of the bathtub. It's not the first time the thought that the Sleepless Knight was someone he knew had crossed his mind, but hearing somebody else say it still shocked him.

"You mean that it could be a friend of mine?"

"Yup, or family or something that you see on a somewhat regular basis. Otherwise, it's tough as hell to find your specific pathway."

"But, it's possible, right?"

"Yeah, kid, but finding you once is one thing. Could be pure coincidence. Twice? Problem!"

"So, the Sleepless Knight is somebody I know. Great. Wonderful."

"Okay, going with that, who in the past few months have you started hanging out with?"

Dave's heart dropped. "Emma. I just started seeing her this summer."

"And so your pathways are now closer. Your hopes, desires, and dreams are now closer."

"Umm, I...wh...what about my plans with her tonight?"

"I would seriously advise against it. I wouldn't go out of your dream until we know for sure that she's not the knight."

Dave shook his head. "Oh come on. It can't be Emma. I mean, wouldn't she have tried every single night to get me?"

"I don't know what her plans are. But, dingbat, you could be walking into an ambush," Bags said, lightly tapping Dave's knee.

"It's just Emma!"

"It just could be Emma wrapped up in layers of Sleepless armor!"

He wanted to see Emma tonight. He wasn't about to let Bags stop him. "I'll be careful, okay. Show me the sword and I'll at least be able to defend myself."

"It's not going to be enough."

"Bags, come on."

Bags sighed. "You're digging both of our graves, but okay, fine. But, I'm doing this under protest."

"I understand. I'll take the risk. Now, how do you make the sword?"

"It's up to you to figure that out," Bags said, turning his head to not look at Dave.

"Cut it out! What do I need to do?"

Bags took a deep breath and rolled his eyes. "Remember, it doesn't matter how it's made in reality. In the Dreamscape, it matters how YOU think it's made. It matters that you believe in the method that it's made. Can you do that?"

"I can try, but why didn't I have to do this with the sponge rafter and the bazooka? Heck, what about the bat turning into a sword?"

"In your mind, you saw the bat turning into the sword. It's as simple as that. To your mind, you justified it."

"What about the rafter and bazooka?"

"Heh, a mind is a strange thing. Now that you're aware, you are in control of what your mind does in a dream. However, the mind still wants to be in control. It's used to having it! When you can't concentrate or when you are in a panic, the mind can slip through the cracks and reassert itself."

"And that means what?" Dave asked.

"Random things start to happen. Sometimes an entire dream will change. Sometimes random objects or people will appear. Usually it makes things appear to help you get out of your bad situation, whatever it may be. Now, when you're in somebody else's dream, you usually can't alter their dreams unless you're really close to them, but you can add to it."

"But, I altered Andy's dream by adding the glue to the sand to hold Beddy Tear in place!"

"You and goth-boy are good friends. It's only natural that you two can affect each other's dreams. It reflects the fact that you actually care about him and respect each other's hopes and dreams. Bah, I can't believe those cheesy words actually just came out of my mouth!" Bags said spitting on the ground.

"So, if I walked into Everway's dream, I couldn't do anything to his dream?"

"Do you give a crap about him?"

"Nope, can't say that I do!"

"Then, it's going to be extra hard to do it."

"Okay. I... I think I get it," Dave said. "So, the sword?"

"Do you juggle rabbits?" Bags said without hesitation. Dave let out a chuckle and shook his head.

"I... uh... sure," Dave said.

"No! You can't just do it half-heartedly. You have to make your mind believe it like you did with the stone that you turned into a ninja star! Use what you know. Use what you THINK you know ONLY if you believe it! Don't worry about whether it's over the top crazy. As long as you believe that this is the way you make your sword, then do it!"

Dave closed his eyes to concentrate and tried to think of juggling rabbits, but he started chuckling as he tried to imagine how he would form a sword. He then thought of Emma. He imagined Emma being attacked by the Sleepless Knight and he felt a wave of anger come over him. He needed to be able to defend her! He never felt so much anger toward somebody. He wanted to stop the Sleepless Knight at any cost. He breathed out to try to dispel his anger, but his rage overtook him.

He imagined himself at the top of an active volcano with lava bursting over the edges and cracks like ocean waves hitting a reef. The heat was unbearable, but he had to have something to defeat the knight and he knew there was a way hidden within the lava's depths. He looked at his hand and then at the lava. At any cost! He reached his hands into the lava and instantly howled in pain as his hands and arms began to burn. As his clothes burned away, he felt an object in the swirling liquid fire. He grasped it and pulled it up, screaming as the fire burned his arm down to the bone. He stumbled back, barely catching himself as he pulled out a gleaming orange and red sword that flickered like a fire depending on how the light hit it. He raised it into the air and let out a scream, releasing his anger and his pain.

"Wow, great going, kiddo!"

Dave blinked and realized he was back in the bathroom. His arms and clothes weren't burned or even singed. Resting in his hands was the fire sword. Dave nearly dropped it, but he soon realized that it was the same temperature as the room.

"Now boy," Bags said sniffing at the hilt while on his hind legs. "Don't go getting any crazy ideas that you're actually any good with that thing. But damn, I have to admit that it's pretty sweet!"

Dave looked at Bags and smiled as he slid the sword into a scabbard that appeared on his side. "Let's go find Emma."

Storming the Castle

It took Dave and Bags about a half hour to find Emma's pathway. They found her name scrawled in big white letters across the front door of Mrs. Patts' house, his neighbor from down the street. Mrs. Patts was an old and rather large woman who had lost most of her hearing. She always ran the TV or radio at the highest possible volume, which made the people next to her complain to her or the police almost nightly. She rarely came out of her house. She even paid some of the supermarket clerks in the area to go shopping for her and deliver her groceries. "Seriously? Mrs. Patts' house?" Dave yelled, trying to speak above the volume of the TV.

"What's the problem, boy?" Bags yelled back.

"So, when I open the door, I should see Emma's dream, right?" Dave said, peeking through a window and seeing Mrs. Patts sitting in a reclining chair and unwrapping a piece of candy as she watched TV.

"Yeah, just like a normal Pathway. Just like the girls changing room and just like the toilet. You nervous, boy?"

"I don't want to have to deal with the consequences of ticking off Mrs. Patts if it turns out that I'm just opening her front door!"

"Bah, what's the worst that could happen?"

"I don't know what she's capable of!" Dave said.

"You don't really believe your old childhood thing about her eating people, do you?" Bags said.

A creaking sound came from inside as Mrs. Patts stood and started walking toward the door.

"Who's there?" she called wheezing as she walked.

"Oh no!" Dave said, "We've got to get out of here!"

"Boy, it's just a dream! Go through this Pathway and you won't have to deal with the huge beast coming from the other side of the door. I may not want you to go, but crap, I can't stop you. Go now!"

The footsteps got louder as Dave looked between Bags and the door. Taking a deep breath, he reached for the handle and pushed it open. He closed his eyes and jumped in.

Dave opened his eyes to find himself just outside of a small run-down wooden house with dozens of men and women wearing medieval peasant clothing walked past him carrying bundles of wheat, buckets of water, along with sacks full of fruits and vegetables. They all looked exhausted and dirty. Dave soon realized that the people were all kids from his school.

I must be in some kind of medieval village, Dave thought. *How am I going to find Emma?*

A few drops of rain hit his face and he looked up into the sky and saw dark grey. As his eyes lowered, he could see a massive medieval castle straight out of one of his history books. Dave knew this was just a dream, but it didn't lessen the impact of seeing it.

Dave soon realized that many people walking by took a quick look at him and simply shook their head. He quickly realized they were looking at his clothes. He was still wearing clothes from his own dream. He quickly ducked into the house behind him and breathed a sigh of relief that it was empty, save for some rotting fruit in the corner which rats were picking apart. He imagined some of the clothing that some of the peasants were wearing. He saw his clothes give off a blue light as they slowly changed into a simple torn brown shirt and pants. Satisfied, he stepped back outside and collided with another person, both of them falling down the ground.

"Sorry, sorry, sorry!" Dave said as he looked to see if the person was all right. He then smiled as he realized that he had collided with Andy who was wearing similar, but darker peasant garb, but was covered in dirt and other unknown filth that wrinkled Dave's nose.

"Lord David, what you doing here?" he asked in a whisper as they both got to their feet. "You could get in trouble!"

"What do you mean? I'm just hanging around."

"What are you doing outside the palace? Princess Emma will throw a fit!"

"Princess Emma?" Dave said, restraining a smile. "Um, okay, I'll get back in, but why aren't you in there?"

Andy stared at him in silence for several seconds. "Don't play games with me. You know that I have been exiled from the palace for disrespecting Lady Cynthia."

Dave almost laughed aloud at that. "Ah yes. How could I forget?"

"Get back to the palace. If the guards see you, you're going to be in serious trouble! Use the secret entrance that we found."

Dave opened his mouth to ask, but Andy cut him off. "Remember the tune we used to sing as a kid about it?

On the west side
When you need a place to hide
Find the right rock and use two knocks
Tis the only way to open up the locks

"Ah yes. That tune," Dave said. "So, I guess I'll be going then."

"Yes m'lord, I understand," Andy said as he scurried away. "Please make sure to stay off the main road. Go through the fields. You will dirty yourself, but you'll avoid the guards and any other prying eyes who may be concerned that a lord is spending time with the peasants."

"Wait, I'm a lord?" Dave asked.

Andy cocked his head and his brow furrowed. "Y-yes, you are a lord. I believe you should seek out a doctor when you arrive at the castle. I believe you may have struck your head recently and it has caused memory loss. Please see the apothecary to get bled, my lord."

Dave smiled. "No, I'm fine. That won't be necessary. Thank you, Andy," Dave said as Andy nodded and walked past him.

Dave made his way through the small village and found the main road. Remembering Andy's caution, Dave found several small wheat fields that went alongside the road and made his way through them, trying to miss any guards. With each step his feet sank a few inches into the ground turned muddy from a recent rain. By the time he reached the castle, his shoes and the bottom portion of his pants were completely caked in mud.

Masses of people were going back and forth in front of the castle, mostly carrying sacks of grain or leading an cart-dragging oxen to markets or their homes. Two heavily armored guards stood in front of a massive wooden gate holding axes on long poles. One of the sack carrying men got too close to one of the guards and was pushed to the ground, spilling his sack of grain all over the ground. The man quickly got to his feet and ran away, leaving his spilled grain behind.

That, Dave thought, *is a good reason to not go through the front gate.*

Keeping his head down to not make eye contact with anybody, he headed down towards the west wall and soon found himself there staring up at the hundreds of feet of stone and sighed.

How the heck am I supposed to find the right rock? Dave thought.

He approached a random stone set into the wall and knocked on it twice. When nothing happened, he picked up a small stone and whipped it at the wall in frustration. He walked the perimeter considering his options. He could try the front gate, but given how irritable the guards were, he didn't think that would be the best course, especially in light of Andy's warning. Dave stopped in his tracks when he noticed writing on one of the stones.

EA + DC

"Emma Ashford and David Calloway. That must be it!"

Dave walked over and slowly knocked twice. His eyes lit up as he heard an audible click. The stones to the right opened like a hinged door, revealing a dusty, narrow, stone staircase ascending in front of him. Dave cautiously walked up the stairs ignoring a rat that scurried over his feet and darted into the open field. As he took his first few steps, the door behind him swung closed, leaving him in total darkness. His heart raced as he felt his way up the stairs, expecting something on the wall to come out and bite him. It felt like the walls were closing in on him. It felt like every step made the stairs wobble and shake, despite being solid stone.

Finally, he arrived at the top of the stairs. For a few seconds, he started to panic as he only felt solid stone and no door handle of any kind. However, with enough pushing and prodding, he found a small crack that ran up and down several feet. It was just barely large enough to fit his fingers into. He pulled and slid the stone wall just slightly, letting in a sliver of light. He pulled harder, giving himself room to squeeze through. After closing the door behind him, Dave saw that he had emerged through the wall of an enormous hallway. Several armored knights standing in front of him, including one in black armor, startled him, and he immediately drew his sword. However, Dave quickly realized that they were only empty suits of armor. Just to make sure, he flipped open the visor on the helmet and saw that no one was inside.

"Lord David, there you are!" a voice called. Eric strode down the hallway dressed in exquisite robes coming towards him.

"Eric, it's good to—"

"The princess has been looking for you, my lord," Eric interrupted.

Dave smiled. "Of course she is."

"Where have you been? You're covered in dirt and grime," Eric said, brushing dirt off Dave's shoulder. Dave looked himself over realizing that the walk through the field and the hidden staircase hadn't done his look much good.

"You must change clothes and do so quickly or the princess will be displeased," Eric said pointing to a doorway.

"Change in there?" Dave asked.

"Tis your room. Where else would you change?" Eric said, confused.

"Oh, of course that's where I change! It was just a loyalty test, you see," Dave said, turning away from Eric's stare.

"Very good, sir." Eric said.

Dave pushed open a heavy wooden door and entered the most extravagant rooms he had ever seen. While his bed, a few chairs, and a cabinet were made of dark oak, the bedposts were made of gold and encrusted with jewels. Everything in the room seemed to be adorned with sparkling gemstones or flowing with silk while beautiful marble statues lined the walls, making it seem like he was entertaining an audience.

He closed the door and took a few seconds to take it all in before going over to another wooden door in the corner. His footsteps echoed throughout the grand room. Throwing open the door, he saw rows and rows of fancy medieval clothing, all apparently made just for him. It was just like the clothes he saw at the renaissance fair he went to last year. He grabbed a random set of clothes and left the closet. As he took off his shirt, he saw one of the statues move slightly.

"Come out, whoever you are," Dave said reaching for his sword. He relaxed as Emma poked her head out.

"It is just me, my David," Emma said with a nervous smile.

"Emma, geez, you scared me for a second. I thought you were...I thought...well, it's just good to see you!"

Emma smiled as she came from behind the statue and blushed as she saw him without his shirt on. Dave smiled and left the shirt on the bed.

"Where did you come from, Em?" Dave asked.

"Like you don't know," Emma said with a smile.

"I know I should not be here, but I could not stay away once I heard you talking to Lord Eric," Emma said, trying to avert her eyes but failing.

"But, why would you stay away from me, Em?" Dave asked.

Emma looked into his eyes. "Because of Lord Everway, of course. He is to become my husband and ruler of the land."

"Lord Everway? You mean, Mike?" Dave said, raising his voice, irritated that Mike was even mentioned in this dream.

"Michael is his name, but he will be quite upset if you refer to him so informally," she said, looking aside momentarily before returning her gaze and taking a few steps toward him. "But, you know that you will always have my heart."

"Emma, heh, I know that this is just a dream, but remember our phone call tonight? This is me! This is Dave walking into your dream," Dave said standing inches from her.

"You have my heart and my dreams, my David," Emma said touching his face.

"I know, I know, but..." Dave didn't get a chance to continue as Emma kissed him on the lips. Her scent and her touch made him forget the bet as he grabbed her and pulled her closer.

"I love you, my David. Everway may have me as his wife, but he will never have my love. My true love," she said softly. Dave simply smiled and kissed her again.

Suddenly, yelling came from the hallway.

"You! Stop right there! That is for Lord Calloway!" Eric yelled from outside.

The large wooden door leading to the hallway exploded, sending wood chips flying everywhere. Instinctively, Dave covered Emma to make sure she wouldn't get hurt. He looked up in horror as the Sleepless Knight stood in the doorway, its massive sword drawn and pointed at Dave.

"Emma, you've got to get out of here!" David said, his eyes not leaving the Sleepless Knight.

Emma left his embrace and stared down the knight. "Who are you? This is my palace! You shall surrender to me or the greatest warrior in the land, Lord David Calloway, shall slay you!" Emma said in an authoritative voice.

The knight thrust with his sword. Dave pushed Emma out of the way and barely dodged the sword himself.

"I don't think he cares, Em!" Dave yelled. "Go now! Get help!"

Emma quickly crawled over to the passageway behind the statue. "Win with honor, my David," she said as she pulled the statue over to close the passageway behind her.

Dave drew his new sword and it sounded like somebody lighting a large match. The blade slid from the scabbard alight with flame for several seconds before dying down and leaving just the orange and red metal. The Sleepless Knight's blade dipped as if in disbelief. It only lasted a second, though, and the knight stabbed with its sword again. Dave swung the fire sword and connected with his opponent's sword. The impact blocked the sword, but Dave felt his grip loosening. The Sleepless Knight swung upward with the sword, and Dave fell backward to avoid the slash.

"Lord David, we are here to save your life once again!"

Dave recognized the voice. It was Mike Everway. *Michael*, Dave reminded himself. It was Michael Everway's voice. Dave and the Sleepless Knight turned to see Michael standing side-by-side with Cole and several other armor-clad people brandishing swords.

Michael pointed his sword at the Sleepless Knight, "I don't know who you are, but you're in MY place at the WRONG time!"

Cole also pointed his sword at the Sleepless Knight. "That's right, Lord Everway only accepts visitors from two to three pm."

Without hesitation, the Sleepless Knight swung its sword with one hand. Cole tried to block it, but upon impact, the Sleepless Knight's sword cut clean through his. The sword continued its path and lopped off Cole's head at the neck. His body shuddered and dropped. The soldiers behind Michael screamed and ran away dropping their swords.

"Cowards!" Michael screamed at them as he swung his sword to strike the Sleepless Knight, but the dark sword blocked the blow.

This is my chance, Dave thought. He charged with his sword, but before he could swing, the Sleepless Knight turned and used its massive reach to grab Dave by the neck. It lifted him into the air and choked him. Dave clutched at his neck and gasped for air.

"Lord David!" Michael yelled as he grabbed a smaller sword with his free hand and thrust it into the knight's armor stabbing right through the metal. The Sleepless Knight flung Dave across the room and then turned to face Michael. Dave's back felt like ten thousand needles were jabbing into him as he collapsed to the floor. The statue wobbled and fell over in Dave's direction. He rolled to avoid it as it smashed into hundreds of pieces on the ground.

"You're no mortal," Michael said withdrawing the blade. "What foul pit do you come from, demon?"

Michael swung down with both swords, but the Sleepless Knight swung up with its sword like a golf swing. The impact sent Michael's swords flying out of his hands. He watched helplessly as the Sleepless Knight slashed the sword down at him. Michael raised his hands to block it, but it was no use. The sword cut right through him from head to toe, his body dropping lifelessly to the ground. Its opponent defeated, the Sleepless Knight turned to Dave and pointed its sword at him with one hand as its other hand inspected the wound that Michael had caused.

Dave slid along the wall, holding his sword in front of him, hoping that it would stop one of the knight's hard swings.

"Who are you? What do you want from me?" Dave asked, trying to reason with whoever was in the armor.

The knight responded by charging and stabbing with its sword which Dave managed to duck and rolled behind the knight. He stood up only to have to duck another swing and then barely sidestepped another. Taking a deep breath, Dave concentrated and felt his will pooling into his hand. Before the knight could swing again, Dave raised his hand and let out a small burst of light into the knight's face. The knight's helmet erupted into blue flames as it dropped its sword to clutch at its face with one hand while swinging wildly with the other, trying to find where Dave was standing. Dave easily avoided those swings and moved behind his armored foe. Finally seeing an opening, he raised his sword and thrust.

Before Dave could connect, a small humanoid figure leapt out of the Sleepless Knight's armor itself, its body looking like little more than a shadow. A shadow with long claws and huge fangs. Dave tried to block the relentless slashing claws with his sword, but the attacks were too fast for him. It slashed Dave across the face and followed up with a slash to his chest. Dave cried out in pain as blood poured from the wound. Dave took a step back, but put his foot down on a piece of broken statue and slipped. As Dave fell, the shadow charged in to continue its assault, so intent on finishing Dave off, it didn't realize that Dave had raised his sword to stop the beast from reaching him. The creature screamed in agony as it impaled itself, the sword puncturing through its chest and bursting through its back. Dave quickly rose to his feet and tore upwards with his sword, ripping a massive wound in the shadow creature, spilling black mist into the air exactly how Beddy Tear's wounds reacted. The shadow faded away as the mist dispersed.

Dave only had a second to relish his victory before the Sleepless Knight swung down on him with its sword. He blocked it with his own sword, but the impact sent him up into the air backwards, tumbling him out the window. Instinctively, he grabbed the windowsill, dropping the sword which tumbled to the ground far below. As Dave struggled to pull himself up, the Sleepless Knight stabbed at him again. Dave did the one thing he could do: He let go.

Dave tried to concentrate as he fell imagining the ground turning to soft pillows to cushion his fall. However, he found that his mind couldn't focus. He kept thinking about the Sleepless Knight trying to skewer him. All thoughts, however, were jarred from his head when he finally smacked the ground. He slowly rolled onto his stomach, despite his body screaming in pain. As he got to one knee, he heard several armored footsteps rushing towards him.

"Lord David, are you okay?" a voice said as Dave stood up and found his sword embedded up to the hilt in the ground. Just as he freed his blade, the Sleepless Knight crashed onto the ground mere feet from where Dave landed.

"What the hell is that?" one of the guards said.

Dave blurted the first thing that came to mind. "He-he's the enemy! He killed Lord Everway and is trying to kill me!"

"That rotten cur!" the other guard said. "We'll stop him, m'lord. You get to safety!"

The guards pointed their weapons at the knight as it turned its head from guard to guard before staring at Dave.

"Go, m'lord! Go!" the guards shouted together.

Dave backed away then ran toward the wheat fields. As he ran, he heard the clash of steel on steel. Seconds later, the death screams of the two guards echoed across the fields.

"Kid!"

"Bags!" Dave said relieved to hear a familiar voice.

"You've got to find a pathway or else your flabby behind is going to get killed!"

"I'm trying, I'm trying! I don't know if I can reach my pathway!"

"Dummy, I said find a pathway. Any pathway, not just yours!"

"Bags, I gotta get out of here fast! I don't have time to look for other pathways!"

"And where do you think old SK will go?" Bags asked.

Dave thought about it for a second. *Of course the Sleepless Knight will try to follow me back to my own dream. That would be the first place he goes.*

"Then, where do I go?" Dave asked.

"Find another pathway? Is this thing on? Did you not just hear me?" Bags said.

"Where am I going to find one? The knight is going to catch up with me and kill me before then!"

Bags sighed. "You don't like listening to ferrets, do you?"

"What?"

189

"If your pathway is in the village, then chances are your friends are there as well. People that Emma hangs out with most often will be close by and if those people are close to each other as well in real life, they'll be close in her dream as well. You have to..."

Suddenly, the Sleepless Knight crashed down from the sky, landing mere yards away from Dave, the ground shaking from the impact. As soon as it landed, a jet pack detached from its back and fell to the ground. Dave raised his sword but took a step back as the knight did not draw its own. His opponent raised its arms to the sky and suddenly the wheat around Dave grew so tall it was above his head. The wheat darkened and thickened, turning into the same dark metal on the knight. Dave pulled on the wheat, but the shafts were as strong as iron bars. He was trapped.

He realized there was no top to the cage, but it was at least fifteen feet above his head. The knight advanced and slowly drew its sword relishing this moment. Dave looked to his left and right but saw nothing preventing the knight from finishing him. His foe swung the sword between the dark wheat, but Dave raised his hands up and thought of a shield that could stop the blade. Blue energy formed in front of him, creating a sapphire-like shield. The sword and shield smashed into each other, causing the shield to shatter and emit a blast of sapphire-like energy into the knight's chest knocking it off of its feet, its sword landing with the blade stuck in the ground.

Dave looked at the knight who was shaking off the hit and starting to get up

I need to get out of here! Dave thought as he looked at the top of the cage. *I need to get out of here fast! If only I could fly or something, I could get out here. Maybe like the jet pack that the knight was using.*

Dave felt an object form on his back, but before he could check to see what it was, a burst of fire exploded from it launching him out of his wheat jail cell, propelling him towards the village.

I'm flying! Oh my god, I'm flying! Dave thought. Just as Dave shook off the light-headedness, he realized he was descending from an extreme height. He wasn't flying anymore. He tried to will the jet pack to turn pack on, but he couldn't concentrate on much more than falling.

He screamed as he crashed through the roof of a rundown barn and into a large pile of hay. Small pieces of hay were launched into the air, and every piece of his body felt broken.

"Kid, your mind got you out of another jam, but I don't know how much it's got left of its own gas!" Bags yelled at him.

Dave tried to get up and failed, landing back in the hay. "I...can't."

"Get up now! You have to find a pathway! Your mind just bailed you out of a jam with that shield and with that burst to get you flying. I know you're a wuss and can't take a hit, but you're going to hurt a lot more if you can't get up!" Bags said.

Dave stumbled to his feet and instantly doubled over in pain.

"Suck it up!" Bags yelled. "Deal with the pain!"

Dave was about to yell something back at Bags when he was interrupted by a large crash outside the barn door. Screams from the villagers soon followed.

"Tis a monster! Run! Tis the Sleepless Knight! Sound the alarm!" Dave heard the villagers scream.

Dave backed away from the door, his hands trembling as he clutched the sword tighter. He was startled by something nuzzling his neck. Dave spun around, but only saw a brown horse, its head peeking over a wooden gate. Dave pushed the horse's head lightly. It gave him another nuzzle.

Dave turned around. "Horse, not now. I..." He saw a name on the gate. It read, ANDREW BAYS, but there was a long scratch through it as if someone was trying to cover it up.

"Strange, I found something with Andy's name, but..."

"It's a pathway, dummy! Go!"

Dave unlocked and opened the gate. The horse was not on the other side as he had expected. Instead, he saw a moonlit graveyard. He looked behind him at the front door and saw the knight's sword pierce it. Weighing his options, Dave decided to take his chances with the graveyard. He stepped through the gate and pulled it tight behind him.

Harvester

Dave stepped into the chilly night air. The moon illuminated a thick blanket of fog that clung to the ground, and a gentle breeze stirred the mist into a rolling sea of ghosts. Tombstones jutted through the shroud like rocky crags threatening ships in the night.

He surveyed this new landscape and realized he had exited from a large stone crypt. He backed away from the door, expecting a black sword to slice through the stone any second. He tried to slow his breathing, tried to do anything to prevent the Sleepless Knight from finding him, but he found that the more he slowed his breathing, the faster his heart beat. It was beating so fast he began to feel light-headed. He finally decided that breathing was the better option and inhaled. Despite the cold air, a bead of sweat rolled down his forehead and nose. Dave reached up to catch it before it dropped, nervous that even a drop of sweat could alert the Sleepless Knight to this new location. After several minutes, he finally relaxed.

"Bags, what do I do now?" he asked.

No one responded.

"Bags?"

Silence.

"Ferret, stop joking around! I need some help here!" Dave said, starting to shiver from the cold.

He started to panic. *What if something happened to Bags? What if the Sleepless Knight got him? What if during the time he spent waiting, the knight had gone into his dream and killed Bags? Can a guardian even die?*

Dave took another step back, but found that his left foot was stuck on something. He tried again, but something like fingers closed around his ankle like a vice. Dave stumbled as he tried to take another step, keeping himself upright only by catching onto a tombstone. He looked down through the mist, and his heart pounded again as he saw a half rotten hand emerging from the ground and gripping his ankle. He yanked as hard he could and soon heard a snap and a rip as the hand tore away from the arm. The hand still gripped Dave's ankle. Disgusted, Dave kicked his leg out again and again until the hand finally loosened and fell off. He took a few more steps when the dirt in front of him shifted and the upper body of a reanimated corpse dug its way out reaching for him with a clawed hand. He quickly drew his sword and swung at the zombie, connecting at the neck and slicing off its head with relative ease. He had seen one too many zombie movies and played way too many video games to not know how to destroy the living dead.

"Darn it, Andy!" Dave said, looking back at the crypt door just in case. "Why are you making my life difficult?"

Immediately upon saying that, a familiar noise sounded througout the graveyard. He concentrated and heard the noise again. It almost sounded like... a video game?

He didn't have any time to think about it further as another zombie launched itself from the ground and wrapped its arms around Dave's body from behind. He leaned forward and threw his head backward. His head sunk deep into the zombie's rotten skull. Unfortunately, that did not loosen the zombies' grip. The zombie cocked its head and opened its mouth to bite Dave. Its breath smelled of long dead meat and bone. Dave gagged against the smell as he struggled against the grip. He felt the zombie's mouth close on the back of his head, but he only felt gums rubbing up and down his head as the head-butt had knocked out what was left of its teeth. Dave used all his strength to reach for a tombstone, taking one slow step at a time as he dragged the snapping zombie behind him. His hands finally reaching the tombstone, he jumped up and pushed his legs off of it. The zombie held on to Dave, but the force of the push made it stumble backward. With a sickening crack, the zombie's rotten left leg bent in the wrong direction and finally broke pushing the bone through a hole in its skin. Dave collapsed onto the corpse, sinking into its rotten rib cage, coating him in putrid ooze. Realizing that the zombie had released its grip, Dave scrambled to his feet, quickly backing away as it reached out to try to snatch him again. But it could do nothing except crawl slowly towards him.

As Dave quickly put some distance between him and the zombie, the video game noise sounded across the graveyard again. Dave stopped and turned his head from side to side trying to find the source of the noise. He heard it again and pinpointed the direction from where it was coming. Before he could get moving again, a loud bang startled him. He jumped and spun around, expecting to see the crypt door slamming open, but he breathed a sigh of relief at the sight of another zombie pushing out of the ground. It had knocked one tombstone into another tombstone causing the noise he had heard. Another zombie burst from the ground, spraying dirt from its grave and launching the tombstone into the air. Dave backed away cautiously then broke into a full run as several tombstones shuddered and fell over. He kept running through the graveyard jumping over rotting hands that tried to grab him. The fog grew thicker as he ran, and it started rising higher and higher off the ground. Before long, the mist was over his head, making it nearly impossible to see more than a few feet away. He felt things clawing at his legs and feet, but he did not fall. He had to keep running toward that sound.

Finally, the mist thinned and faded completely. The sight he was left with made his jaw drop. He saw what looked like a massive TV screen, hundreds of feet tall, with giant speakers mounted to the sides. On the screen was an overhead shot of a graveyard with dozens of zombies standing around. It looked just like the graveyard he had run through. Occasionally, one of the zombies' bodies gave off a blinking light as it started to move around. Below the screen, he noticed that several hundred feet away from the screen was a person in a black trench coat standing and holding a game controller. Andy was controlling the zombies he had just fought. It was then that Dave came to a realization—he was playing Andy's video game.

"Andy!" Dave yelled while sheathing his sword, "Your zombies are way too easy! You can't dream of something better than that?"

Suddenly, he was hit from behind as a zombie emerged from the mist and collided with him. Dave turned as he fell, and the zombie fell next to him. Both started to get to their feet, but the zombie's rotten bones were no match for Dave's speed. He was up before the zombie was even getting to its knees. Before swinging the sword, he recognized the zombie. It was Eric. He hesitated, giving the zombie time to stand up fully. Reminding himself that it wasn't really Eric, he swung, taking off the head, and the body collapsing and becoming motionless.

"Andy, you and I have to talk!" Dave said as he shook the ooze from his sword. Andy remained motionless save for the occasionally finger and arm movements on the controller.

"Andy... a little help here? I think we have a problem," Dave said, hoping that his friend would be able to help against the Sleepless Knight like he did with Beddy Tear. Andy put down the controller and turned around. Dave's eyes widened when he saw that the person who turned around was not Andy.

It was Rake.

"You have no idea the trouble you're in!" Rake said tossing off Andy's jacket.

"Rake?! What are you doing here?" Dave said, taking a step back so that he was right against the wall of mist.

"Man, Lord Traum was right. A dumbass like you wouldn't know to ask the right questions, would you?" Rake said, smiling.

"What are you talking about? Where's Andy?" Dave demanded.

"Where's Andy? Bzzzz! Wrong!" Rake yelled. "The right questions would have been, 'Hey, Rake. You're so awesome and studly and stuff, but I have to ask: Are you a dream or a dreamer? Are you a dream walker?'"

Dave stared at Rake, his anger boiling over. "Where...is...Andy? What did you do with him?"

Rake smiled and pointed to his head. "He's all in here," Rake said, his grin growing as he raised his left hand to the sky. Suddenly, sharp spikes of bone burst from the ground, scraping the side of Dave's right leg.

"This is MY dream now just like yours will be soon!" Rake yelled as Dave grabbed his bleeding leg.

"Rake, you're the Sleepless Knight?! I'm going to kill you!" Dave yelled through the pain.

"Sleepless?" Rake said chuckling. "No, sorry, that position has already been taken. Lord Traum is going to make me the Tomorrow Knight in the Trauma Guild. Kinda suits me. Kinda like a dark fire. Speaking of that..."

A burst of flame that was a mixture of red, orange, and dark purple shot from the ground. It singed Dave's left pant leg as he barely rolled away.

"Rake, why are you doing this? You could be anything you want in here, but you chose to be a jerk...again!" Dave said, getting to his feet and making sure he wasn't on fire. "And who is Lord Traum?"

"No one a loser like you needs to know about," Rake said shaking his head. "Okay, time to take your dream! It's time I showed Traum that my plan was the right one."

Rake reached over his shoulder and pulled out a small wooden rod no more than a foot long. He clicked a small button on the side and suddenly the rod extended to the length of Rake's body, a scythe extending from each end. Dave recognized it immediately. It was Andruseth's staff.

Dave tested his wounded leg to see if he could put any weight on it. While the wound screamed in pain, the leg did not buckle. "How can you have his staff? That was a dream guardian!"

"Oh? That was a dream guardian? Interesting! Heh, I own his dreams. If it was in his dreams... if it was one of his ideas, I have it now!" Rake said.

Before Dave could respond, Rake charged and swung the scythe at Dave's chest. He took a step backward to avoid the swing and then had to duck another wild swing while also jumping over another aimed at his legs.

"I'm not going to get tired before I get you, Davey!" Rake said laughing. "I want that dream of yours!"

Dave jumped backward and drew his sword just in time to block another slash, much to Rake's surprise.

"Why? You think you can be a bully here too?" Dave said, saying the only words that were coming to mind while defending himself.

"I prefer to think of it as loser eradication!" Rake said as he swept Dave's feet, knocking him onto his back. Rake stood over him and raised his scythe into the air.

"Tomorrow Knight, here I come!" Rake screamed as he swung the scythe down at Dave's head. Dave moved his head at the last second as the blade of the scythe embedded itself into the ground. Dave swung his sword at the staff portion of the scythe, igniting the sword as it sliced through the wooden staff and cutting it into two pieces. He then kicked Rake in the stomach and slashed him with his sword cutting a deep gash from the bottom of his chest to his left shoulder.

Dave scrambled to his feet as Rake stumbled back clutching his wound. Rake looked down at his hand and saw his own blood. The scythe shimmered and disappeared as Rake looked back up at Dave, showing his bloody hand to him.

"You made me bleed, Davey," Rake said. "You're a dead man."

Dave's eyes narrowed in anger. "It really is you, isn't it Rake. You aren't some kind of freakish nightmare. Somehow you became a dream walker and took Andy's dream."

Rake stood up straight, the wound slowly closing. "Yeah, but his dreams suck," Rake said turning towards the video game screen. "What a crappy game. Is this all he's thought of with fat-ass Jake? Some cheesy-ass zombie game?"

Dave pointed his sword at Rake.

"What? Are you going to kill an unarmed man? Granted, an unarmed man who just insulted your boyfriend, but still!" Rake said, putting up his hands to show that he didn't have a weapon.

"If it gets Andy's dream back, then yeah unarmed or not, you're a dead man. And don't think that spikes or flames are going to stop me. You're losing Andy's dream to me!" Dave screamed as he charged.

A bone spike burst out of the ground behind him, which Dave dodged only to see the ground erupt with a blast of dark fire. He leapt into the air to avoid it and willed the jet pack to turn back on which this time it did. He saw the dark fire following him like a snake slithering out of a hole, nipping at his heels. He could feel the immense heat through his shoes. He had to think of something to stop it. Dave cleared his mind and imagined that the fire was actually a liquid and that it was cold enough to freeze. He imagined it becoming a long tube of ice instead of flame. Dave saw the flame begin to flicker as smoke coming from the flame turned to bright white steam. The flame quickly froze into a long tube of clear ice, a small candlelight flicker occasionally flashing from within the ice. The ice tube's momentum extended it just past Dave. He grabbed the ice with his spare hand and felt it freeze onto the tube stopping his momentum. He tried to pull his hand off the ice as he stopped, but he was stuck fast. The jet pack's quickly flickered out.

"The ice is fire! The ice is fire!" Rake screamed trying to start the fire up again. Dave heard the ice crack and begin to melt as the flickering fire grew stronger within it. However, the melting ice freed Dave's hand. He slid down the tube like a zip line into a lake and let go about halfway down. Startled, Rake couldn't move out of the way in time and Dave smashed into him as the tube of ice briefly turned to fire and then disappeared.

Dave lifted his sword to Rake's neck, but suddenly felt incredibly tired like he did at the end of the Beddy Tear battle. Using his powers against the Sleepless Knight and Rake must have drained his energy. Rake made a move to roll away, but Dave gathered enough strength to raise his sword and stop him from moving.

"It's over, Rake.'

Rake breathed deeply and yelled, "Get him, guys!"

Suddenly, three zombies burst through the ground behind Dave. As Dave got a good look at them, he realized that the zombies were all from Rake's gang from school, all with grey skin that was either rotting away or was missing all together, revealing bones and organs underneath.

Rake stood and moved behind his gang. "You almost had me there, Davey. But, like always, I'm going to beat you," Rake said, turning toward his gang. "Get 'em guys. Just leave him just barely alive for me. I want his dream."

The zombie gang lunged at him with their arms reaching for his neck. Dave swung his sword and slashed through a zombie's leg and cut it off at the knee. The zombie wobbled and collided with another gang member. Both of them toppled over. A zombie resembling Alexis, Rake's girlfriend in the gang, moved to attack, but a swing of the sword cut off her arm at the elbow. But she just kept coming, slamming into Dave with her whole weight, bringing both of them to the ground. Her good arm, if one could call a half rotten arm a good arm, grabbed Dave's sword arm, her icy grip chilling Dave right to the bone.

"Get off of me!" Dave yelled. "Bags! Where are you?"

Dave threw a punch, hitting her right in the mouth, knocking what was left of her teeth down her throat. He pulled away expecting her grip to lessen, but it stayed strong. He felt a pair of hands grab his feet as another pair grabbed him by his legs. Dave turned just as another managed to crawl over to him and grab his other arm. He was pinned down completely. Alexis dug her nails into his wrist. He screamed in pain and dropped his sword.

"See Davey?" Rake said as he stood over his fallen foe. "You're a loser! Andy was a loser. I'm sure Eric's a loser. Todd, hell, we know he's a loser. Cynthia? Loser! And Emma, she's not a loser. She's a skank!"

Dave's eyes widened as he tried to break free from the gang's grip but to no avail. Rake bent down and shook his head.

"You're helpless, Davey. Don't you realize that?" Rake reached out and plucked one strand of hair from Dave's head. He showed it to Dave and then let it slip through his fingers. He then lightly slapped Dave across the face. "See? You're pathetic!"

Dave spat at Rake and got him in the face, but Rake smiled and suddenly the spit transformed into a small rock that dropped into Rake's hand. He threw it back at Dave, hitting him in the forehead and opening up a small wound and making him momentarily see stars.

"Well Davey, I think we've had about enough. You've shown that you've got some ability in here. Fantastic! I can't wait to use your powers when I have your dreams! Why learn when I can just steal it from you!" Rake picked up Dave's sword and then pointed up at the large screen. It was showing an overhead shot of the fight. "Smile, Davey! Time to die!"

Before Rake could strike, a bright light lit up the night's sky. Dave and saw a golden ball of fire descending in their direction. As it approached, the ball seemed to unfold, revealing an angelic form with a golden body and wings giving off a nearly blinding light. Dave tried to see its face, but it was impossible to look directly at it for more than a second. He had to look away.

Rake backed up, still holding the sword as the angel landed. It stared at Rake and then turned its head slowly towards Dave. The angel's light grew brighter, making Dave squint even when he wasn't looking directly at it. When Dave opened his eyes, there was one less zombie holding onto him. He looked to the sky and saw the angel flying above him and holding the zombie in one hand by its neck. The zombie reached and tried to grab at its captor, but the angel held it just out of reach. Light started flowing out of the angel and into the zombie. It flowed through the angel's hand into the dead veins and arteries of the reanimated corpse. As the light reached its head, lights shot out from its eyes, mouth, nose, ears. There was a loud pop and the zombie exploded in a supernova of light. The light from the explosion flowed back toward the angel. It formed a ball of light between the angel's hands.

Rake took a few steps back and dropped Dave's sword as they watched the angel maneuver its hands as if holding a large ball. "Okay Davey," Rake said as his voice wavered, "I'll let you off this time."

The zombies released Dave from their grip and slowly marched toward their master. The angel raised the ball of light towards the sky. When Rake saw that, he turned and ran as fast as he could. The angel threw the ball of light toward Rake's gang, flying faster than they could run. Rake willed a body sized shield of dark fire between him and his minions, just as the ball of light hit the zombies, creating an enormous mushroom cloud of light, dissolving the zombies into black mist and shattering the shield. However, when the light dissipated, Rake had already disappeared back into the mist.

Dave grabbed his sword off the ground and pointed it at the angel, not sure whether he had any chance of lasting more than a second against this thing. The angel slowly descended to the ground while facing Dave who nervously backed away. Once it landed it pointed at Dave.

"David," it said with a voice that sounded like a little boy and little girl speaking at once.

Without thinking, Dave shot a blue beam from his hand. The angel closed its wings around its body as the beam struck it. Several shining feathers fell losing their light and turning into plain white feathers as they floated to the ground. Seeing that no further attacks were being attempted, the angel unfolded its wings. With a wave of its hands, several rings of light appeared around Dave. Dave moved to get out of them, but his arm touched the side of one of the rings and received an enormously painful shock. That was enough for Dave to realize that he would have to go up to get out of here. Dave used the jet pack to fly out of the hole, but the angel quickly caught him by his hair and pulled him close so they were face to face. Dave could only see the bright golden eyes of the angel, the rest of its face hidden behind a mask.

"David, I am here to help you," the angel said.

"Let me go!" Dave screamed struggling against the angel's grip on his hair.

"As you wish," the angel said, releasing his hold. Dave reached out to grab onto the angel as he fell, but his fingers only grazed the angel's robes before he slipped and plummeted to the ground. A wave of panic washed over him, but he quickly regained his sense as he looked at his sword. He took the hilt in both hands pointing the blade downward. He imagined that in the hilt there was a secret compartment housing a large parachute that came out whenever he fell great distances. In an instant, a large piece of nylon shot out of the bottom of the hilt almost smacking Dave in the face. The material formed a parachute with cords attached to the hilt. As it caught the air, the drag tugged hard on the sword, nearly pulling it from Dave's hands. As he struggled to hold on, the parachute drifted, bringing him by the giant screen. Dave watched the screen and saw Rake running through hordes of zombies who stood there unmoving, as there was no one using the controller to move them.

"What do you want?" Dave called to the angel.

"To help," the angel responded.

"Help me? Who are you?"

The angel paused as if it had to think of an answer. "That is not important. I am..." "Not important?" Dave said, cutting the angel off. "Why not?"

"It is rather hard to explain, but if you must call me something, call me Gabriel."

Dave chuckled. "Real creative angel name there!"

The angel simply folded its arms in response.

Dave stopped chuckling. "Are you a dream or are you a dreamer?"

The angel stayed silent.

"Are you a dream walker?"

The angel nodded.

"Then how do you know me?"

"David, Rake will not be gone long. He will find an opportunity to strike back," the angel said pointing off to the mist.

"Well, let's wait for him then. You can beat him with one hand behind your back I imagine," Dave said, looking down to see how far he had until he landed.

The angel paused, as if contemplating its response. "If you wish to survive in the Dreamscape, you must defeat Rake yourself. You must save your friend. You must help to find out why the Trauma Guild is so interested in your group of friends."

Dave took great interest in hearing about the Trauma Guild. "So, it isn't just some random attack by some dream walker jerk? This Trauma thingamabob is coming after me?"

"And your friends, yes."

"And...wait...have you been watching me?"

"And your friends, yes. I came here to look in on your friend Andrew and to see if his guardian was going to attempt to make him a dream walker. However, like you, I found that his dream had been taken over."

Dave looked down to see the ground fast approaching.

"Can I get Andy his old dreams back?" Dave asked, not remembering all the details Bags had told him a few days ago.

"Yes, but to do it, you must do to Rake what he did to your friend. Do you know what that will entail?"

"I...I have to beat Rake?"

The angel nodded in silence. "Defeat Rake, free your friend's dream, and take Rake's dream. With his dream, you may be able to find out the Trauma Guild's plan."

Dave safely landed on the ground as the parachute floated down on top of him.

"So how...?" Dave started to say something as he tossed the parachute off. However, as he saw the angel staring not at him, but something behind him. Dave turned and saw a large man standing several hundred feet away, covered in layers of black ripped clothes, a hood covering most of his face. Dave tried to see if he knew who it was, but saw that the face was covered in a dark shadow. Every time Dave moved, the shadow seemed to move as well to protect his identity.

"David," the angel said, "you need to go now."

"No, I'm ready! I'm ready to take on Rake, no matter what he looks like."

The man reached around his back and pulled out a machete covered in something that looked like dried blood and nightmare mist.

"This is not Rake, David."

"Then who is he? Another Trauma Guild member? Is it Traum?"

The man started slowly walking towards them.

"No, this dream walker goes by the name of Krieger and is one of the most dangerous people that I am aware of. He is an enemy to all other dream walkers.

"Then what do we do?" Dave asked, his heart beating faster.

"WE do nothing. YOU run!" the angel said raising its voice.

"What about you?"

"I...FIGHT!!" the angel said and launched a ball of energy at Krieger, hitting him right in the chest and setting off an explosion so powerful that the impact knocked David off his feet even over a hundred feet away.

Dave stood up, covered in dirt and grass thrown up by the explosion. As he got to his feet, he realized everything had become deathly silent. No birds, no crickets, not even one sound. He looked around for Krieger and saw that nothing was in the spot where it once stood, but a small crater. He turned to face the angel who looked at him and then pointed behind Dave. He turned around to see Krieger standing behind him, machete raised.

Dave's heart began pounding so hard that it felt like it was going to burst out of his chest. The sword slipped from his hands and his mind went blank as fear overtook him. Krieger swung the machete down at his neck.

The Big Break

Bzzzzz

Dave opened his eyes and immediately tossed off his covers, his eyes quickly darting around the room to see if Krieger was standing over his bed ready to swing down with his machete. He looked down at his shaking hands and only then noticed that he was covered in sweat from the fear that he felt from during the dream.

Bzzzzz

Dave slowly turned to his side and turned off his alarm.

"David! Get up!" his mom yelled after opening the door slightly.

"I know, I know," he responded weakly, his mother's voice bringing him back to reality. As his mother stomped away, Dave jumped into the shower and let his mind drift.

Who is Gabriel? Is it somebody I know, or is Gabriel just some random dream?

Will Krieger come after me again? Was he coming after me or was he going after Gabriel?

Who is the Sleepless Knight? Was Gabriel right about the Trauma Guild going after my friends?

The questions plagued David throughout breakfast. He ignored everybody around him, and his mother had to repeat her questions two or three times before David noticed she was talking to him. After assuring his mother that he wasn't on drugs and that he wasn't feeling sick, he grabbed his book bag and left for school.

As he left, he saw Andy leaving his house, but it wasn't the Andy that he knew. Dressed in a green collared shirt and grey pants, he was completely missing his usual gothic image.

"Andy, wait up," Dave said as Andy turned around.

"Yes, Dave?" Andy asked, his eyes bright and a smile on his face. It almost looked like he was cheerful.

"Dude, what's with the outfit?" Dave asked, looking him up and down, confused.

"What?" Andy asked, "Um, I like these clothes, why?"

"Well, this is the first time I've seen you in, you know, colors in years."

"So?" Andy asked, shrugging his shoulders and starting to walk toward school.

"So, how about your image, goth-boy?" Dave said matching his pace.

"Who cares?"

"Well, you for one. Why the change?" Dave asked.

"I didn't realize I had to run it by you," Andy replied.

"Well, you don't, but..."

"Look, who cares? Seriously!" Andy said.

"It's almost like you're a different person," Dave said.

Both stayed silent. Dave remembered what Bags said about a dreamer losing his dream to someone else. The dreamer's hopes, motivation, dreams, imagination, and inspiration all go away, given instead to the person occupying the dream. Rake took them all from Andy. Andy's whole identity had been changed just by taking away his dreams.

The two walked in silence until they passed Emma's house. She flashed Andy a weird look as she came out.

"Andy, what's the deal with the clothes?" Emma asked as Dave just shook his head.

"Oh come on," Andy said stopping suddenly. "Who CARES?"

"Are you feeling okay?" Emma asked.

"I'm...fine," Andy replied through clenched teeth.

They all walked in silence the rest of the way to school. Not one of them even looked at Krazy Koffee as they passed it.

"So Dave," Emma said trying to come up with a conversation, "I can't remember, why isn't your team playing tonight against Somerset? Isn't it supposed to be tonight?"

Dave almost forgot about the fact that he didn't have a game tonight. The football team almost always played their games on Friday afternoons or night. "Somerset was having some issue with the lighting. I can't remember what it was. Anyway, they couldn't do Friday afternoon, that's why we have to play on Saturday."

"Oh good, that means that I can go to my soccer game and not miss your game," Emma said.

"Are you going to root for me tomorrow?" Dave asked

"You or somebody cuter," she said smiling with a goofy grin.

Dave reached out and tickled her on her hip, her one major tickle spot. She giggled and stepped away.

"Oh, stop it!" Andy said. "Look, I'll see you later."

Andy walked away as fast as he could.

"What's wrong with him?" Emma asked as they slowed to allow Andy to get ahead of them.

"Probably just a head cold or something. Maybe we shouldn't do the boyfriend and girlfriend thing around him because of the whole Cynthia thing," Dave said.

Emma rolled her eyes. "Whatever. I'm not going to change my life for him," Emma said.

After a few steps in silence, Dave smiled. "By the way, nice castle last night."

"Huh?" Emma said, confused. "What are you talking about?"

209

"The castle. You know in your dreams, princess!"

Emma's eyes opened wide as Dave continued.

"Everway may have me as his wife, but he will never have my love," Dave said in his best Emma imitation.

"You've GOT to be kidding me! How did you know about that?" Emma said as her face turned red.

"I told you that I could do it. But, seriously, marrying Everway?" Dave said sticking his tongue out in disgust.

"Well, he'll probably be rich and famous someday. Can you blame me?" Emma said, shrugging and smiling.

Dave blankly stared at Emma. "Come on... Everway?"

"Whatever, it was a dream," Emma said. "But, seriously, you were in my dream last night? That's crazy! How the hell did you do it? Like, seriously, this is really amazing."

"Well, I..."

"Wait, that Sleepy Knight was there, wasn't he?"

"Sleepless Knight, and yes," Dave said, recalling the battle between them last night.

"How did you get away? I mean, did you beat him?"

"Ummm... yeah, I beat him. No more Knight. Umm... Knighty night?" Dave lied. He knew that he didn't need to lie, but scaring Emma at this point was not something he wanted to do.

Emma smiled, swung around, and gave him a huge hug. "Seriously? Does that mean you're going to keep the mean old Knight out of my dream every night?"

"Uh, sure. I mean, I beat him once, I can beat him again," Dave said, wondering what he was getting himself into.

"Will you come see me again? In... you know... my dream?" Emma said, breaking the hug.

"What? Real Dave isn't enough for you?" Dave said, smiling.

They both looked at each other and laughed.

In English class, Mr. Burke made everybody break into groups to discuss their latest creative writing homework. Dave was grouped with Andy and Todd. Their project was to give a paragraph description of a story that they would eventually flesh out over the rest of the semester.

Dave read his paragraph to the group. It was about a backup pro baseball player who is paid thousands of dollars by his Mafia-owned coach to injure a player on the other team. The player keeps injuring other players until the mob tells him to injure one of his own teammates. He refuses but ends up getting injured by one of his teammates who was paid to take him out.

Todd clapped after Dave finished. He loved it. Andy just sat there and shrugged.

It was Todd's turn next. He went beyond the required paragraph as usual, spinning a sword and sorcery tale about a group of veterans from some magical war who were being chased by multiple factions due to some super-secret mystery. Todd went into explicit details about the characters and some very specific plot points, but Dave couldn't remember anything beyond the first few lines. When it was over, there was silence for a few seconds before Dave realized that Todd was done.

"Good! Good! That was good!" Dave said, which made Todd smile. Thankfully Todd didn't ask for any constructive criticism on his text.

It was now Andy's turn. Dave turned and listened closely as Andy opened his notebook and read.

"Okay, there's this guy. He goes to a concert. He enjoys it and goes home."

Todd and Dave looked at each other. Dave stayed silent as Todd turned back to Andy.

"And then what?" Todd asked, trying to peek at Andy's paragraph.

"What do you mean?" Andy said closing the notebook. "That's it."

"Is there a bad guy or something like that?" Todd asked.

"Um, I don't think so. Maybe the ticket-taker? Those guys are usually jerks."

"So, the ticket guys act like jerks and what? They stop you from getting in?" Todd asked.

"Look, Todd, I'm sorry that I have a life and couldn't write a billion pages like you," Andy snapped back.

Dave leaned closer to Andy. "Calm down, man. He's just asking where the suspense is coming from. We're not trying to attack you, but you know what a pain Burke is for details."

"Uh, hello, the band might suck which they sometimes do," Andy said rolling his eyes.

Todd and Dave looked at each other again. Todd opened his mouth to say something, but Dave cut him off.

"Alrighty, good. Moving on."

Dave knew what was going on. This was fallout from Andy losing his dream. No creativity. He wasn't being himself at all.

Rake had to be stopped. Who knows how many people other than Andy had lost their dreams to him. What could be worse than a bully who steals all of your hopes and fears?

At lunch, Dave walked in to Emma and Cynthia already sitting at their usual table. He sat down with his tray of food, and just as he did, Andy walked in.

"Keep looking and talking to me, Cyn, okay?" Emma said. "Just ignore him."

"I take it that he hasn't talked to you, right?" Dave asked.

"Nope, not a word," Cynthia replied quietly.

Andy walked right past their table. As he got closer to Jake's table, Jake smiled and began to stand up to greet him, only Andy walked past him and sat down at an empty table. Jake looked over at Dave who just shook his head. Jake looked back over at Andy and then sat down.

"I don't really care about him anyway," Cynthia said.

"I'm sorry, what?" Dave asked, still looking over at Andy.

"About Andy, hello?" Cynthia said. "Has he...has he said anything about me?"

"I...it's complicated," Dave said turning and watching as Eric and Todd came out of the cafeteria line.

"Dave, come on, you know something, don't you?" Emma asked.

"What? No! Forget I said anything!" Dave said, trying to get out of the conversation.

"Come on, Dave! Spit it out!" Emma said as Cynthia turned to Dave.

"Oh come on, Cyn. You guys are perfect for each other. I honestly don't know what he's thinking. Just give him some time, okay?"

Cynthia drank deeply from her bottle of water instead of saying anything keeping a close eye on Andy. As Eric and Todd sat down, Eric leaned in close to Dave.

"Okay, Dave," Eric said. "Let's just say screw it and set fire to Everway's locker!"

Dave snapped out of his haze upon hearing that statement and chuckled. "Again with the locker?" Dave replied, putting his head down on the table next to his tray.

"Yeah, this way he might suspect us, but he will never know for sure."

"You really want to set fire to his locker?"

"Well..." Eric said, putting his fist to his chin, as if in deep thought.

"Are you really going to do it?" Dave said, looking up at Eric.

"Sure, meet me before practice!" Eric said. Todd and the girls started talking, occasionally looking over at them at every mention of fire.

"Dude, we're not setting fire to his locker!"

"But look what he did to us yesterday! The guy's gotta pay the price!"

"I know, but..."

"Come on! Fire's perfect! He won't know!" Eric said, smiling and pounding the table.

"How is that going to get him to stop harassing us?" Dave asked.

"Ummm...he might...ummm..." Eric couldn't come up with an answer.

"Your heart is in the right place man, but we need to come up with a plan that will get him off our backs. Maybe embarrass him and bring him down a notch."

"But how?"

"I don't know. I'll think of something," Dave said.

"No, you won't."

"Yes, I will!"

"You never do!" Eric said, raising his voice. "It's always, 'Maybe we'll do this...maybe we'll do that,' but you never go through with it!"

"Hey, neither do you!" Dave said.

Eric and Dave looked in opposite directions.

"Oh would you two just make out and get it over with?" Emma said, breaking the tension.

"Huh?" Eric and Dave said together.

"It's like you're married!" Cynthia said.

Dave smiled and held out his hand to Eric

"Oh darling, they've discovered our secret love! They've figured us out!" Dave said in a high-pitched voice.

Eric burst out laughing and the rest of the table soon joined in. Dave felt a lot of the stress from last night and this morning wash away. Just then, he felt a slap on his back. He turned around to Tony Krantz.

"Hey Tony, what's up?" Dave said.

"Sorry, Tony, table's all full, you know how it is!" Eric said, putting his feet up on the empty chair next to him.

"Well, boys, looks like you're going to get some serious practice time today," Tony said, ignoring Eric. "The principal is coming down hard on some of the guys who aren't doing so well in classes. He's having an after school meeting with them and that means both of you will get some playing time today."

Eric and Dave glanced at each other.

"That means Weaver's going to make sure you're in shape, Calloway. I'm sure the coach is going to test you too, Graham. So, guys... seriously... make sure you bring your 'A' game today to practice."

"I will, I don't know about Dave. He's kind of a slacker!" Eric said, stretching.

Tony ignored the comment and walked off.

"Holy crap, Dave, that rocks!" Eric said.

"Yeah guys, no pressure or anything!" Emma said, giving Dave a quick arm squeeze.

"And another thing about that TV show," Todd said, apparently continuing a conversation from earlier.

"Todd, Todd, we'll talk about that later," Cynthia said, waving her hand in Todd's face to quiet him down. "So, you could actually play in tomorrow's game?"

"Maybe," Dave said. "I mean, it depends if the principal stops the dummies on our team from playing. I'm sure Weaver's in there right now defending them."

"Dude, if I get to practice today... dude, I get... " Eric trailed off, his eyes wild.

"Huh? What?" Dave said.

"This is fate," Eric said.

The entire table turned to look at Eric who smiled and continued to eat his lunch.

The end of the school day could not come soon enough for Dave. When the bell sounded to let classes out, his whole body tensed in anticipation. When his math teacher, Mr. Erby, started erasing the whiteboard, Dave grabbed his bag and left.

He walked to his locker to put away the books that he wouldn't need for tonight's homework. As he opened the door, a rotten smell assaulted him from the locker. He looked down and saw raw ground beef splattered over the interior walls of his locker. Some of the bloody bits dripped down onto his books on the bottom.

"Gross," Dave said, reaching down to wipe off what he could.

On top of the pile of books was a note dripping with the messy bits. Dave opened it and read.

TONIGHT YOUR FRIENDS ARE GOING TO END UP LIKE THIS.

-YOU KNOW WHO

"Rake," Dave said under his breath, and he glanced left and right to see whether Rake or one of his cronies were watching, but he only saw random students walking toward the bus.

After cleaning up as best as he could, he looked at his watch and saw that he was going to be late for practice. He ran to the locker room after packing up his bags, but a familiar voice caused him to stop. Dave turned around to see Jake's huge frame rumbling towards him.

"Jake, hey, what's up?" Dave asked.

"Hey," Jake said between deep breaths. "What's up with our boy?"

"You mean Andy?"

"Yeah, I mean, I know we have shared custody of him and all, but he just told me that he doesn't want to work on our game anymore and that he's probably going to try to sell off his Zeus when he gets a chance."

Dave stared past Jake, trying to think of how to respond. Jake was a friend, but he never saw his pathway near Eric, Emma, and the rest of the gang. Was Jake a target as well?

Jake looked over his shoulder to see what Dave was staring at. Upon seeing just a few random people, he snapped his fingers in front of Dave's face to get his attention.

"It's... it's probably because of his breakup with Cynthia," Dave said, giving the easiest answer. "Give him some time."

"Wait, wait, wait. Andy's an emotional guy. I'll give you that, but come on. Completely avoiding his friends? Possibly selling his Zeus? He loves that thing more than life!" Jake said.

"Well, come on, I mean, it's not like the girls were all over him before, so this break-up hit him hard." Dave said.

"Yeah, but. . ."

"Listen, I'll have a talk with him," Dave said.

"Want to have a group intervention?" Jake said.

Dave looked at Jake with an amused look. "What? He's been ingesting too much goth, and we need to step in?"

They both laughed as Eric rounded the corner. Jake moved in closer to Dave.

"Talk with the dude. You know him best," Jake said.

Eric finally caught up with them.

"Who knows me best?" Eric asked, trying to put Dave in a head-lock. "Dave? He thinks he knows me. But, I'm much more mysterious then he thinks."

"What?" Dave said, fending off the headlock. "You? Mysterious?"

"Yeah, you think YOU have weird dreams with that knight guy? There I was, using my TV remote control as a death ray against some alien dudes in my backyard when all of a sudden some golden angel guy crashed through my back door while being attacked by some other guy with a machete," Eric said starting to walk down the hallway with Dave.

"Guys, I gotta catch the bus. I'll talk to you later. Dave, talk to Andy," Jake said, making a talking motion with his hand.

Dave ignored Jake and listened intently to what Eric was saying. "Angel dude and machete dude, right?"

"What?" Eric asked. "Oh yeah, angel dude and machete dude. Anyway, the angel dude grabbed machete guy and tossed him right back into the house. I did the first thing that came to mind. I shot the angel with my remote control, but it didn't do anything except for taking off a few feathers. The angel then looked at me and I swear I thought it was going to grab me and do the whole 'Hand of God' thing. Instead it turned to me and you know what it said?"

"No, what?" Dave asked.

"It said that I was in great danger, but the only one who could help me is David Calloway. He said that I need you and my Dream ummm...Dream Shield? Dream Blocker? Crap, what was it?"

"Dream Guardian," Dave said without thinking.

"Right, Dream Guardian. And I need to...hey!" Eric stopped and looked at Dave as Dave kept walking. "Hey, how did you know what I was talking about?"

"After practice, okay?" Dave said, breathing out a long breath. "You're going to call me crazy, but I promise you're going to think it's the coolest thing you've ever heard."

Tony was absolutely correct that there were multiple people who were stuck in that after-school meeting. There were enough people out that both Dave and Eric both were going to get a lot of playing time.

Michael and Tony led the team through some stretching before running a lap around the field. Eric and Dave stuck together, Dave slowing down to make sure Eric kept up.

"So, how did you know about the Dream Guardian thing?" Eric asked.

"Seriously, not now. It's going to really freak you out," Dave said.

"Oh come on. What, you had the same dream or something?"

Dave stayed silent, but he didn't have to say quiet for long. Someone stepped on the back of his shoe making him lose his balance and tumble to the ground. Eric immediately stopped to see if he was okay, but then they both looked up and saw Everway jogging by.

"Come on, ladies. Quit talking about your tampons and get moving," Mike said as a few of the other players chuckled.

Eric helped Dave up and helped him brush off the dirt.

"I swear I'm going to kick his ass before the day's over," Eric said.

"You won't hear me complaining," Dave said as they made their way to the center of the field where the rest of the team was lining up to listen to the coach's practice speech.

"Now, you may have heard by now that some of our players are not practicing with us today, and that they may not be playing with us tomorrow because some idiots on the team decided that they couldn't play football and learn how to dissect a frog on the same day," the coach said, his face turning redder and redder as he continued. "They decided they couldn't play football and learn who George Washington was. They decided they couldn't play football and learn how to even add two numbers together! Well, the principal has decided that due to them being dumbasses, we may be short a few people when we go up against Somerset tomorrow."

Most of the kids on the team groaned. Everway spoke up for the group. "Come on coach, you can't be serious. They kick our ass every time we play them and that's when the whole team is here. How are we supposed to even keep it close?"

Coach Weaver stared at Mike for a few seconds. "This is our starting quarterback, folks. This is the guy who is going to lead us to victory over the Scimitars," Weaver said, shaking his head. "Everway, you're going to lead this team to victory or so help me God, I will go back in time and break up your mom and dad, just so I can make sure you were never born!"

The entire team went wide-eyed at that comment.

"Now get on the field and PLAY YOUR DAMN HEARTS OUT!" the coach said as spittle launched from his mouth.

"Yes, Coach!" the entire team returned.

The team made its way onto the field. Eric and Dave participated in some practice drills, Eric and the rest of the defensive line endured some brutal strength drills while Dave and the third-string receivers lined up with Tony and repeatedly ran exhausing passing routes. After about an hour, the coach blew his whistle signaling that it was time for a scrimmage—the first-stringers and a few backups to fill in the spots left vacant by the principal against the remaining team members who were led by Tony Krantz.

Tony's offense went first. Dave received a hard slap on his shoulder pads from Eric before making his way on to the field to huddle up with Tony.

"All right boys. First play is a draw right up the middle to Nett," Tony said, nodding his head to Clayton Nett, the back-up running back. "Let's do it!"

The teams lined up. The defense called out adjustments as they saw what offensive scheme Tony had called. Dave jogged to the far end of the field to try to draw a few defenders his way. Tony hiked the ball and handed it off to Nett who tried to find a hole in the defense to run through, but the defense completely sealed everything that the offensive line tried to create. Nett turned to go in another direct, but he was hit from behind and tackled to the ground.

It was second down with about twelve yards to go to get a first down. Tony called another run. Tony took the ball and handed off to Nett. A linebacker let out a battle cry and charged through the line, tackling him for yet another loss of yards.

"You ain't going nowhere, Nett!" yelled Kurt Milardo, the linebacker who made the tackle. He wasn't as big as Cole, but it didn't make him any less intimidating to play against on the field—you always knew that the guy was coming after the war cry.

Third down and fourteen. With fourteen yards to go before getting a first down, it was an obvious passing play to the defense. That's what made it so tough. The defense knew what was coming.

Tony gathered the offense together. "All right boys, third down and long. Calloway, corner route, and it's coming to you."

Dave's heart beat faster as he lined up. He looked at his defender, a defensive back by the name of Brandon Keen, who had been playing football since he was in first grade. Brandon gave him some space, choosing to play a few yards deep, as he didn't care if

Dave caught a short pass. He just wanted to prevent him from getting fourteen yards and a first down.

Tony called the hike and Dave took off on his route, setting a decent pace. However, once he reached the part of the route where he changed direction, he revealed his true speed, getting behind Brandon. As soon as he did, Tony lofted the ball in his direction. It was a perfect throw and spiraled toward the exact spot where Dave was headed. Dave reached out his hands to catch it and heard an imaginary crowd chanting his name. Just before the ball hit his hands, Brandon rammed him with his shoulder from behind, sending Dave tumbling head over heels as the ball hit the ground.

Dave's first thought as he rolled onto his back was that he had dropped the ball. If he had been a little faster or a little taller, he would have caught it. As he got to his feet, he saw Coach Weaver slowly jogging over, his face red with anger.

"Damn it, Keen, you just got your team penalized and gave the offense a new set of downs! Great job, you just screwed the team!" Weaver yelled between labored breaths.

"But, Coach," Brandon replied, "It was that or give up the touchdown!"

"I don't give a crap! Get faster! Grow an inch or two! You play the ball, not the receiver!" the coach said, grabbing Brandon's facemask. "First down, ladies!"

The defense groaned and stared down Brandon as he made his way into the huddle. Dave smiled to himself and jogged back over to the offense.

"All right boys, hook pass to Parrish," Tony said, pointing to one of the other back-up receivers, Rob Parrish. Rob nodded as the huddle broke up.

The offense lined up as the defense stared them down. As Tony took the hike, Dave ran a short route to try to fool Brandon. After two seconds of running his route, he heard the whistle blow. Dave turned around to see Tony on the ground, Milardo on top of him, taunting him. Tony had been sacked for a loss of several yards.

221

Dave took a deep breath and jogged back. Tony stood and brushed the dirt off his jersey and huddled up.

"Come on guys, give me at least a few seconds," Tony told his offensive line. "Okay okay, out pattern to Parrish. Let's do it."

The offense lined up once again. Milardo paced back and forth, letting out a scream every other second. The noise distracted Dave and almost made him miss the fact that the ball was in Tony's hands. Tony tried to throw to Rob, but Milardo jumped up, blocking his view. Tony rolled out, moving over to the right side of the field to get a better view of Rob and threw it. Rob caught it and pulled the ball in just as he was hit by his defender, Jack Neuman. Dave noted that they were still about five yards short of the first down. It was third down and five.

Once more the offense huddled up. "Okay Okay, boys. Five yards to go. Screen to Calloway. You guys better block for him or I'm personally kicking all of your asses. Let's do it!"

Dave got onto the line of scrimmage. All he had to do was get five yards to get the first down. He looked at the first down marker, but then his eyes drifted towards the end zone. The ball was hiked and Tony reached over to hand it off. The defense thought it was going to be a running play and charged towards the running back. However, Tony pulled the ball back and tossed it to Dave who caught it in his chest. He ran forward and nimbly dodged and spun around numerous defenders. As Dave was in the middle of a spin, he saw Milardo's large shape coming his way. Milardo tried to grab him by the shoulders and drag him down. However, Dave came out of his spin and ducked down. Milardo couldn't adjust in time and missed. He stumbled and fell to the ground.

Dave then turned and saw a nearly empty field in front of him. Without a second thought he began to run and run fast. The defense tried to keep up with him, but Dave was too fast. He waltzed into the end zone and spiked the ball as the coach blew the whistle. He had scored a touchdown.

Dave's head was spinning, but he didn't know whether it was the fact that he was completely out of breath or the fact that he just scored. It was just a scrimmage, but this was the first time beyond simple drills that he had scored a touchdown on the team. Dave got a friendly slap to the back of the head by Tony. The defense was getting torn into by the coach for missing the tackles.

"Nice job, Calloway!" Tony said. "If you can turn on those afterburners all the time, man, Weaver's gonna put you in a few of these games!"

"You think?" Dave said, between deep breaths.

"He'd be stupid not to. Dude, you're fast. Like, really fast," Tony said.

Dave smiled and said nothing. Tony responded by shoving him a bit from behind.

"Just don't get too cocky on me, okay?" Tony said, jogging off.

"No guarantees," Dave said as he jogged over to the sideline to meet up with Eric who was donning his helmet.

"Dude, that was frigging sweet!" Eric said, adjusting his chinstrap. "Who knew that you had, you know... what's the word? Talent!"

Dave laughed. "Your turn. Give 'em hell!" he said as he slapped Eric's helmet.

Eric smirked and jogged onto the field. After a quick defensive huddle, the team lined up as the offense broke their huddle and did the same. As Mike surveyed the field, his eyes rested on Eric.

"Uh oh! Graham's on the field. Hey, o-line, you better watch out. We may have to pull two or three chicks from the soccer team to block him," Mike said, as the offensive line broke out in a laugh as they stared down Eric.

"Screw you, Mike. Let's see how you like it when I break your arm," Eric said glaring at the quarterback.

"I'm sorry. What did you say, Graham?" Mike said cupping his ear.

"I said, let's see... "

Eric didn't have a chance to finish as Mike called for the hike.

Matt Stromain, the person on the offensive line opposing Eric, lunging out with the full weight of his 275-pound frame and knocked him off of his feet, landing hard on the ground. Mike handed off to the running back, Nelson Biondo, charged through the Eric-less hole in the defensive line, running for fifteen yards before a defender caught up with him.

As Eric got to his feet, Coach Weaver turned red in anger. "Damn it, Graham, stay focused! Do you think Somerset is going to make it easier on you?"

Eric went into the defensive huddle and stayed silent. After the play was called, Eric slowly made his way to the defensive line.

"Uh oh!" Mike called as he lined up. "Graham's back! I think it's time for a bit more Stromania! I don't think you're any bigger than an appetizer for my boy here! More of a toothpick, really! Don't worry, we'll have you back on the sidelines with your loser boyfriend real soon."

Eric's face turned as red as the coach's was when he got angry. He stared at Stromain and breathed out, trying to focus. He saw Mike received the hike out of the corner of his eye. Stromain immediately lunged at him again, but this time Eric stepped slightly to the left. He swung his right arm up and connected just underneath Stromain's right arm, causing him to stumble, creating a hole for Eric to run through. The rest of the offensive line saw Eric go past them, but couldn't get off their blocks fast enough. Mike's back was completely exposed as he looked to pass downfield. Eric wrapped him up from behind, his full weight driving him into the ground.

As soon as Eric rolled off him, a smile spread across Eric's face. He got to his feet and pumped his fist into the air as he celebrated finally getting to Mike. He looked around and instead of people congratulating him, he saw that everybody was looking down at the fallen quarterback. Eric turned around and saw that Mike was clutching his arm in pain while still on the ground.

The coach and the team's trainer ran over to him as Mike got to one knee.

"It's my arm, coach. I think it's broken," Mike said. "That idiot broke it."

"Calm down, kid, calm down. Let the trainer take a look at it," the coach said.

"Graham, I always knew you were an idiot," Mike said through clenched teeth. "You just made this team a joke! There's no way we can beat Somerset now."

The comment raised murmurs throughout the team, especially the starters.

"Funny, Everway, last time I checked there's more than just you on the team," Eric said walking away. The rest of the team didn't know what to say.

"Graham, don't walk away from me! I'll get you..." Mike said.

"Focus! Focus!" the coach said to Mike, cutting him off. "Let's get you to the hospital. Tony, run the offense."

On the sidelines, Tony put his head down, but then nodded and put his helmet on.

They continued the scrimmage, but as Mike left the field, the energy of the entire team seemed deflated. The game against Somerset tomorrow went from a tough game to a game impossible to win.

After practice, Eric stayed silent through the shower. The entire team didn't really know what to say to him. Finally, in the locker room, Dave broke the silence.

"Eric, listen, it's going to be okay," Dave said as Eric put on his shirt.

"How do you know that? Dude, I just completely screwed the team!" Eric said slamming his door shut.

"I..." Dave couldn't think of anything to try to calm Eric down.

"I think I just made things worse! I mean, dealing with Mike and Cole is bad enough. But now I've got to deal with the entire team being pissed off at me? I'm a dead man!" Eric said punching his locker door. "Damn it, why did I let him get to me that much!"

"What do you mean? The guy's been on you since you joined

the team. Heck, it's not like he was the nicest of guys to you before-hand," Dave said.

Tony rounded the corner to where they were dressing. "There you guys are," Tony said, still in his gear.

"What's up, Tony?" Dave asked as Eric finished getting dressed.

"Just so you know, it looks like I'm starting tomorrow. Early word is that Mike's arm is broken."

Eric slowly bumped his head on the locker door and left it there.

"Eric, don't worry about it. Seriously," Tony said.

"Don't tell me what to think! I mean, I didn't like the guy, but I just screwed the team over!" Eric said turning his head away.

"Honestly, the guy wasn't all that great," Brandon Keen said, poking his head around the corner. "The guy throws a hell of a party and doesn't have a bad arm, but he ain't bringing us any championships anytime soon. I mean it sucks that the dude broke his arm, but he's not the entire team."

Parrish joined Keen. "Yeah and with him out, maybe somebody other than Bullington and Grasso will get the ball," Parrish said, tossing a football up in the air and catching it as it dropped.

Stromain's massive frame pushed Biando and Keen forward a few steps. "And maybe when we lose, Tony's not going to blame the o-line for not giving him ten seconds in the pocket."

"You mean you're not going to give me ten? You guys suck!" Tony said, narrowly dodging a punch by Stromain.

"Seriously, the dude couldn't see an open receiver even if the defense wasn't on the field," Stromain said.

Eric looked at Dave, then Tony, then the rest of the team. "So, you guys don't care that I broke Mike's arm? That seems a little weird!"

Tony smiled. "No, no, no, it's not that we don't care. It *really* sucks that Mike broke his arm. I mean, we're trash-talking him now, but he was the leader of the team. I have no idea what tomorrow's game is going to be like. We may get our asses kicked. But, you know what? Injuries happen. Hell, I broke my leg last season by slipping in some mud while doing punt returns. I wasn't doing anything but going forward. Stromain's gotten his nose busted a few times in scrimmages. Keen's just naturally stupid."

"What the hell?" Brandon said, pushing Tony into the locker as the rest of the team laughed.

Dave and Eric looked at each other and shrugged, though a smile did creep across Eric's face.

Weird Dream Magic
Hoo-Hoo

As Dave and Eric sat curbside waiting for Eric's mom, they waved goodbye to some of the other players.

"Wow, that was...strange," Dave said.

"Yeah, I didn't realize that breaking somebody's arm would earn you friends. Maybe there really is a future for me in the mafia," Eric said tossing a pebble into the driveway.

"Well, I don't know about getting invited to any parties anytime soon," Dave said, slapping him on the back, "but that was cool what Tony did."

"Yeah, he's definitely a leader type, that's for sure," Eric said.

Suddenly, something whacked Dave on the back. He reached his arms behind his back and brought back a soccer ball.

"Gee, there's a lucky guy out there somewhere who's dating a girl who can kick a soccer ball that accurately," Dave said, leaning backwards to see Emma standing over him.

"Did you win?" Dave asked.

"2–1! Guess who scored a goal?" Emma said, beaming.

"Uh, Valerie?" Dave said.

"Stephanie?" Eric said.

"Yeah, definitely Stephanie," Dave said.

"Funny!" Emma said as she sat down in between the two. "So, which one of you did the dirty deed?"

"What do you mean?" Dave asked.

"I mean, with Mike. I heard that somebody broke his arm. I figured that one of you snapped and went on a psychotic rampage," Emma said as she let her hair down from a ponytail.

"Talk to my friend here," Dave said pointing to Eric. "That's the man that broke Mike every way!"

Eric started to speak and then chuckled as he caught Dave's small joke about Mike's name.

"Thank you, thank you!" Dave said taking a miniature bow.

"Dude, be careful. I'm sure Cole's going to be pissed once he finds out about it," Emma said.

"Don't worry about Cole," Eric said. "The dude's on the warning list. Even dumbass Cole knows that he's on thin ice with his grades and all."

"I heard about that!" Emma said. "Hey, why doesn't this school do the old wink-wink nudge-nudge with their athletes like you always see in the movies?"

"I think you have to, you know, be in contention for championships in order for the principal to care *that* much," Dave said.

"Well, then just get better!" Emma said as Dave and Eric pulled on her hair from both sides. She let out a playful shriek and punched both of them in the ribs until they let her go.

As they calmed down, they sat in silence for a minute or two.

"Where the heck is your mom, Eric?" Dave asked.

"Getting her hair done? How am I supposed to know?" Eric responded.

"Hey, what are we going to do about Andy?" Emma asked.

"Get his hair done?" Eric said.

"The guy's changed," Emma said, "and I can't believe that it's *just* because of the Cynthia breakup."

"Nah, can't be," Dave said keeping his eyes to the ground.

"Well, what are we supposed to do?" Eric said. "I mean, if the guy wants to not be goth and not be our friends, then whatever."

"Yeah, but isn't it a little strange that it happened practically overnight?" Emma asked.

"Wow, just after the breakup with Cynthia? What a shock!" Eric said. "Maybe he's wanted to do this for a long time and wham! Here's his excuse."

"I don't know. Maybe. Dave, you've known him longest. What's going on?" Emma asked.

Dave thought about his answer for a few seconds. "He was kinda like this as a kid. I mean, the way he dressed and acted. Completely anti-social and didn't know where he belonged. It's like he suddenly remembered who he used to be."

"Well, I can see somebody doing that," Emma said.

"But, he hasn't been this way since he was about six years old!" Dave said.

"Oh, I didn't realize that when you said kid that you mean... you know... a kid, kid," Emma responded.

"All right, screw this Andy talk. He's not dating my sister and that makes me happy," Eric said. "What I really want to hear is how Dave knew what was in my dream with the Dream Blocker thing."

"Dream Guardian," Dave corrected him. "Umm... lucky guess?"

"Come on," Eric said.

"What are we talking about?" Emma asked confused.

Dave took a deep breath. "I keep thinking this is purely a weird dream I'm having, but even though it keeps getting stranger, it's starting to make more sense."

Eric and Emma looked at each other then back at Dave.

"You know how sometimes you can have a dream that feels so real even though you're on a pirate ship in the sixteenth-century, or you're designing nuclear missiles, or you're in a war on an alien world?"

"Yeah, except for the pirate ship, the missiles, and the war, but go on," Eric said.

"Eric, please shut up!" Emma said.

Dave faked a punch to Eric's shoulder. "Well, imagine if your dreams *are* actually real," Dave said.

"Uh, I've had the alien war dream and trust me, Dave, it's not real," Eric said. "Last time I checked, we haven't met any aliens in real life."

"I know I know... when I say real, I mean real in another dimension or something like that."

Emma turned towards Eric. "Dave was in my dream last night."

"Oh come on. That's so cheesy! Why don't you move in together?" Eric said.

"I'm serious!" Emma said. "Not only did he say what I was dreaming about, but what I said during the dream."

"What? I don't believe it," Eric said, looking away from them.

"All right, let's do this a little simpler," Dave said.

"Please do, my head hurts," Eric said closing his eyes.

"Okay, okay. Now you dream, I dream, we all dream," Dave said.

"We all dream for ice cream, yeah, yeah, yeah," Eric said as Emma punched his thigh. Eric tried to smile as he winced in pain.

"Now imagine if you could do anything you want in your dream," Dave said.

"Okay, done," Eric said.

"Now imagine that you can find a door or a pathway."

"Oooookay."

"And that you can open up that pathway and enter into Emma's dream."

Eric sat up. "Dave, you sly devil. Are you saying that you've been using weird dream magic hoo-hoo to get into Emma's dream?"

Dave looked over at Emma who looked back at Dave and smiled.

"I guess that's the best way to get his attention," Emma said.

"Uh, yeah, I did use the... um... weird dream magic hoo-hoo to get into Emma's dream."

"How? How did you do it?" Eric said. "I mean, assuming you guys aren't playing a joke on me."

"I think when another dreamer comes into your dream, it's like you're authorized to start learning how to do it to. It's kind of like a natural defense," Dave said, trying to remember the many discussions with Bags.

"Wait, if another dreamer comes into your dream, you can start learning how to do what? You learn how to walk into other people's dreams?" Eric said.

"Yeah, that's basically how I started," Dave said.

"So, why doesn't somebody just start walking into everybody's dreams? I mean, we can have this big rocking dream society!" Eric said. "You know... if you were telling me the truth and all."

"Well, cause not everybody plays nice in there," Dave said.

"Like the Sleepless Knight?" Emma said as Dave nodded.

"Guys, what I'm going to tell you has to stay between us," Dave said.

"Sure," Emma said as Eric shrugged.

"All right, if you believe me about the fact that I can walk around people's dreams," Dave said, eyeing Eric, "then please try to listen and believe this. There's a group of people, well, dreamers, out there that call themselves the Trauma Guild, led by some guy named Lord Traum."

"Trauma? Traum? Original. Really original," Eric said.

"Shut up, Eric!" Emma said.

"Anyway, the Trauma Guild is coming after us," Dave said.

"US?!" Eric and Emma said at the same time.

"What do you mean *us*?" Emma said.

"Yeah, why us?" Eric asked.

"I'm not sure why, honestly," Dave said.

"Wait, is this like some Freddy Krueger thing where if we die in our dreams we'll die for real?" Eric asked. "Because if it is, then this stuff just got real!"

"Not really, no, but..."

"Then who cares? It's just a dream!" Eric said.

"Yeah, seriously," Emma agreed.

Dave paused to collect his thoughts to make sure he explained this correctly. "If you die at the hands of another dreamer, you lose all of your dreams. All of your hopes and inspirations."

"Like I have any of those!" Eric said, laughing.

"Oh really? Like dreams of becoming a pro football player?"

"Well, duh, what guy doesn't have that?" Eric said.

"That dream is gone," Dave said.

"What? So, I don't know how to play football?" Eric asked.

"Oh, you'll know how to play, but you'll just go through the motions. No passion, no desire. Heck, you'd have no real drive to do what you did to Everway."

"What do you mean?" Eric asked.

"How many times have you fantasized about hurting that guy in some way? Burning lockers and all that," Dave asked.

"Duh, like a zillion times," Eric replied.

"Imagine having no desire or drive to actually do it."

"Like you and I have had since forever?"

"All of that motivation and desire to do it is gone. Doesn't matter whether or not you'd act on it, just the fact that you won't even have the idea," Dave said. "And the football thing that I was just talking about? Imagine you play football, but you have no drive or motivation to do any better. You don't try to do better or try to get a college scholarship because you don't have the dreams or desires to do so."

Eric stared at him, a concerned look on his face. "So, let me try to break it down into an edible portion for me. No dreams equals no fun?"

Dave smiled. "Yeah, all right, we'll go with that."

"Emma, what do you think about all this?" Eric asked.

"Before yesterday I'd say that Dave plays way too many video games, but he really freaked me out with the whole 'Hey, you were a princess in a castle last night' thing," Emma said as she put her hair back up in a ponytail. "He told me exactly what I was dreaming. I mean, exactly!"

"All right, so Dave, let's say you're telling the truth. What do we do?"

"I'm going to have to make sure you guys can defend yourselves," Dave said. "I've only had a few days of practice myself, but I can come to your dreams tonight and help you."

"Hey, wait, if you lose all your hopes and inspiration, then Andy..." Emma said, standing up. "That explains what happened to Andy!"

Dave nodded. "And now the people who did that to Andy are probably going to come after the rest of us."

"But, why us?" Eric asked as he sat up.

"I honestly don't know."

"Do you know who's in the Trauma Guild?" Emma asked.

"The Sleepless Knight is one."

"And he ganked Andy, right?"

"No, he didn't. Rake did," Dave said looking to see what Eric's reaction would be.

"Rake? You've got to be kidding me!" Eric said, standing up, and punching his left hand into his open right palm. "Oooo, count me in on anything that we can do to pulverize that twerp."

"Dave, is there anything we can do to save Andy? To change him back?" Emma asked as Dave got to his feet.

"Yes, we've got to defeat Rake in the Dreamscape. That's the only way," Dave said.

"All right! I get to dream about beating up the guy I've been dreaming about beating up for a...oh man, my head hurts!" Eric said.

"Dave, we'll do whatever you need us to do to help Andy," Emma said taking his hand.

"Guys, don't get me wrong," Dave said. "I'm telling you guys about this to hopefully protect you. If Rake gets his hands on you in your dreams and I'm not there, chances are...chances are you're going to lose your dreams. You will lose who you are."

"So, what do we do if we run into him and you're not there?" Emma asked.

"You run. You run as fast as you can. I'll find you. I'll save you. I'm going to make sure that whatever happens tonight Rake will never *dream* about trying to hurt us again."

Recruiting Allies

When Dave got home, he ran upstairs and did his homework, but found he could not even do basic algebra problems or even remember simple French words. Not only was he worried about what was going to happen tonight with Rake, but also the meaty smell of his books was starting to make him sick.

After finishing what he could, he slammed his books shut and went downstairs for dinner. Thursday was always 'do-it-yourself' night as his mother took the night off from cooking ever since both he and Nick were old enough to cook simple meals. As he went into the kitchen, he saw Nick blowing into a heated bowl of canned ravioli.

"Hey Dave," Nick said sticking his fork into a ravioli. He took a bite only to spit it out for being too hot.

"Hey, whatcha up to?" Dave asked.

"What does it look like? Dinner! Duh!" Nick said.

"Mom let you use the microwave?"

"I'm not a baby!" Nick frowned.

"I know, I know," Dave said. "I'm just surprised you didn't already burn down the house."

"I'm not a doofus either!" Nick said spearing another ravioli with his fork.

"I know, I know," Dave said. "But, it's an honest mistake. I mean you really do look like one!"

"That's 'cause I caught the doofus virus from you, doofus!"

"You're lucky I'm hungry for some ramen soup. Otherwise, you'd get a little of this!" Dave said raising a fist and smiling.

Of course, this was perfect timing for his mother to walk into the room.

"David! Stop whatever you are doing! Do not hit your brother!" his mother said.

"But, I didn't do anything!" Dave said putting his fist down as his brother giggled.

"I'm sure you were about to," his mother said walking to the fridge and grabbing a diet soda. "Did you do your homework?"

"Yes," Dave groaned.

"I'm serious, no football if you didn't do your homework!" his mother said.

"I seriously did my homework!" Dave said.

"No he didn't," Nick said in between bites and giggles.

"And how would you know?" Dave said, shooting him an angry brother look to shut him up.

"Well, I should check your homework. Bring it down," his mother said, motioning for him to go upstairs.

Dave thought about arguing, but just shot his brother an annoyed look and went upstairs to retrieve his homework. As soon as he brought it down, his mother started sniffing the air, smelling the meaty smell of his books. Before she could say anything, the front door swung open and his father came in.

"Family! 'Tis I!" his father said. "I—what's that smell?"

"I don't know, Steven. I just started smelling it myself," his mother said, kissing his cheek.

"Oh, ummm, that's me," Dave said, showing some of the meat splatter on his books. "I spilled my lunch on my books during school and it kinda went everywhere."

"Good one," his father said, patting him on the back, while going in closer to smell one of his books. "Raw meat, eh? Did you raid the cafeteria or something?"

Dave's mother immediately grabbed a wad of paper towels in her hand and snatched the books from him.

"These need to be disinfected immediately," his mother yelled. "Did you wash your hands? Did you put your fingers in your mouth after you touched these books? How do you feel?"

His mother reached under the sink and brought out a bleach spray, which she used all over the covers of the books.

"Mom, I'm fine. Isn't that bleach going to ruin the books?" Dave asked.

"Just let her work her magic," his dad said. "By the time she's done, it'll look brand new. Besides, that was the mystery meat at school, right? I don't think I really want to know exactly what it was when it was alive, if it ever was."

"Probably the same meat we had when we were your age," his father said. "So, why are the books down here?"

"I was about to check his homework," his mother said.

"Oh, let me take care of that," his father said, reaching for the books. His mother slapped his hand away.

"Are you going to check it or just fake checking it so you can talk sports with him?" his mother asked.

"Hmmm. . . " his father said, quickly trying to think of an answer. "Maybe your mother should check your homework this time then." His father shrugged towards Dave.

"It's okay, Dad. I think I'll be okay," Dave said.

"Your funeral!" his father said.

"Steven!" his mother yelled.

"Sorry, sorry!" his father said, waving her off.

The men laughed, but his mother shot them all an angry look as she pulled Dave away to check on his homework.

After an evening of dealing with his mother freaking out over all the wrong answers in his homework—that he had to correct—Dave decided to turn in. However, getting to sleep with everything he had on his mind was nearly impossible.

I have to get to sleep, find Eric and Emma, and train them before Rake gets to them. Could I actually train them? I mean I only have had a few days of experience in the Dreamscape. He could just imagine Bags laughing at him in a high-pitched ferret laugh when he told the weasel what he wanted to do.

When Dave turned over to his clock and opened his eyes, he saw that it was 11:30 pm. He had been trying to sleep for over an hour. Were Emma and Eric already asleep? More importantly, was Rake? He didn't recall even seeing Rake at school today, not that it would have stopped his buddies from dumping the meat.

Dave reached over to his clock radio and turned it on, spinning the dial to a talk radio station where some guy with a deep voice was talking about how some local politician was screwing up the economy. Within minutes, Dave's eyes felt heavy and with a blink, he saw something that nearly scared him to death—ferret, close-up to his face, sitting on his chest!

"Coochie-coochie coo! Awww... did him open his eyes. Did him? Did him?" Bags said.

"Get off me!" Dave said, rolling to the side as Bags jumped off. However, he rolled off whatever he was lying on, landing his shoulder on the hard ground.

"I guess I should have mentioned that you were on a bench," Bags said. "Well, you were on a bench."

Dave rubbed his sore shoulder and looked around. He saw that he was on a wooden porch. Everything here looked so familiar. Below the porch was a gentle grassy slope that led directly down to the docks and out to a lake. Dave sat up and chuckled as he felt summer air.

"This is Camp Cancrow. Wow, I haven't seen this place in years," Dave said, watching as a few young kids ran by with baseball gloves and bats in hand.

"I see," Bags said. "This is a camp for social misfits? The mentally deranged. . . the. . . whatever the hell you are, right?"

Dave looked around for the ferret, but found Bags well out of reach farther down the porch. "It's an overnight camp up in Maine. Wow, I haven't been here since I was about ten years old."

"'Cause everybody made fun of you?"

"You wish. My dad lost his job earlier in the year and couldn't afford to send me back. I wonder if the place is still around," Dave pondered.

"Okay, okay, okay, before you go down memory lane and get lost in traffic, let's talk about what happened last night."

Dave got back on the bench and looked over at the ferret. "You mean, when you bailed on me when I could have gotten killed?"

"Yeah, that's it. I bailed on you. It really serves my interests to have you die on me. Come on kid, get serious," Bags said.

"Okay, then what happened? I had to deal with Rake taking over Andy's dream and then deal with some weirdo angel and some machete freak," Dave said, raising his voice, and then lowering it as one of the older kids looked over at him before running past.

"I know what happened, but unfortunately not until you just came back."

"What? Wait, you didn't know what was going on?"

"Well," Bags said, turning his head away from Dave. "The thing is that if you go into your second dream other than this one, you lose contact with your guardian. We can't talk to each other."

"Wait, so if I go into Emma's dream then into Andy's, I can't hear you?

"Ding-a-ling-ding! You got it," Bags said.

"Something that would have been nice to know yesterday!" Dave said.

"Yeah, yeah, I know, I'm a bad weasel. But, we didn't really have time for explanations, did we?"

"All right, all right. Wait a sec...how do you know what happened then?" Dave asked.

"Once you pop back into your dream, all your memories and such flow into the Dreamscape for it to use in the dream. I, as your loveable and huggable dream guardian, have access to these memories. So, I checked out what happened. And by the way, nice catch—Emma, I mean."

"Yeah, I know. Hot, isn't she?" Dave bragged.

"Funny that your one big achievement in life is getting a hot girlfriend," Bags said.

"Bags," Dave said, feeling his annoyance with his ferret return. "Please remember that I know how to make swords now!"

"Okay sword-boy, serious talk time," Bags said, scrambling up onto the bench. "Let's talk about your best buddy, Rake."

Dave turned toward the ferret and stood up. "I've got to protect my friends."

"No, too much of a risk. I mean, yeah, it's noble and stuff to save your friends, but we still don't know who is in the Trauma Guild. We know Rake is, but what if one of your friends is?"

"There's no way that I can just sit back and let them take my friends," Dave said.

"Boy, listen to me and listen to me closely. We don't know who to trust here. At this point, it may be better to let Rake take them."

"What?!" Dave said, kicking the bench. Bags held onto the bench for dear life.

"The more friends he takes in the Dreamscape means less people that could betray you," Bags said.

"That's horrific! I'm not going to let my friends die!"

"I'm not saying to not go after Rake," Bags said. "By all means, go into Andy's dream and get his dream back. But about your other friends—remember, boy, they're only dying in the Dreamscape. You usually can get them back."

"So, they get tortured just to prove their friendship to me?"

"Boy, listen to me, it would be better at this point to avenge them rather than to protect them. You're risking too much."

"I don't care. I'm saving my friends."

Bags stared at Dave in silence for several seconds. "I can see that I'm not going to change your stubbornness. Fine. Be that way."

"You're letting me win?" Dave said shocked. "Okay, now I just need to find their pathways."

Bags sighed. "They're down at the senior camper bunks," Bags said, pointing his nose towards the left of the docks where a dozen large-floored tents stood, housing the fourteen- and fifteen-year-old campers.

"They are? How do you know? Don't tell me you always knew," Dave said, glaring at Bags.

"Nope, though it would have been a fun game to play. If you have plans to visit somebody else's dream before you arrive in the Dreamscape, I can find the pathways for you. Well, I can at least try. The more familiar you are with them, the easier it is for me to find," Bags said.

"But that doesn't make sense. I mean, what about yesterday? We still had to look for Emma's pathway. Why change your mind on this now?"

Bags sighed and lay down on the bench. "I didn't want you to go to Emma's dream. But, in the end, boy, I'm can't stop you from doing what you want. I'm hoping that I can talk some sense into you before you commit suicide. But, in the end, you now know how to find Pathways, with or without my help. I can preach and preach and preach, but if you don't want to listen, then what can I do? I can teach and teach and teach, but if you don't want to learn, then what can I do? I can..."

"All right all right all right," Dave said, walking down the steps of the porch. "So, down at the senior tents?"

"Yeah, that's right, dingbat," Bags said.

"Okay, hey, one more thing. The angel and the guy with the machete?" Dave said.

"Gabriel and Krieger you mean?" Bags said, looking up at Dave.

"Yeah, them and Lord Traum. What's up with them?"

"Dunno," Bags said, shrugging.

"Seriously?"

"Do I look serious?" Bags said, smiling.

"Come on, do you know them or not?" Dave asked impatiently.

"Most of the information I know about comes from your dreams and memories. We superior beautiful Guardians are born with the knowledge of how the Dreamscape works along with other vital details, but as for the majority of its inhabitants, we really don't know. I know of the Trauma Guild because the Dreamscape decided that I should know of them since the Sleepless Knight invaded our dream. As for the specifics about Traum or the Trauma Guild, I don't know. I do know that he's a Harvester. He goes after people to take their dreams and uses their dreams to grow in power. As for Krieger and Gabriel, well, if Gabriel were going to kill you, it would have done it like Krieger attempted to. But that's all I know."

Dave began walking down the creaky wooden stairs and then turned around and came back up. "Okay, so you don't know anything about those three, but what other 'vital details' are you not telling me? What else do I have to look out for?"

"I've told you what you need to know. Pathways, wraiths, nightmares, and controlling things in the Dreamscape are the most important. Things I haven't told you about like living dreams, Inochi Korai, the Terrors, well..."

"Well, what?"

"Well, if you run into any of those and they decide to come after you, it's not going to matter what I tell you. You're dead," Bags said, shaking his head.

Dave's face wrinkled as it took on a concerned look.

"Don't worry, boy. Living dreams are just a rare and I mean RE-ALLY rare kind of nightmare, quite literally a million-to-one odds. You'd have to basically break the Dreamscape to get to find an In-ochi Korai, and the Five Terrors, they're in a prison of sorts in the Dreamscape."

"Prison? Like Todd? Is that why Todd is an exile? Todd's a Ter-ror?" Dave asked.

"Todd? Ha! The last Terror was locked up about ten years ago. That would put Todd at about three or four years old, right? If you didn't know Todd to start with, I'd say maybe, but since you've known him your whole life, I'd say that Todd is definitely not a Ter-ror."

"Why would me knowing him for a long time have anything to do with this?"

"Because the Terrors are all immortal and have been around for a while. There's no way that Todd could have gained enough power to be a Terror when he was just out of diapers."

"The Terrors are immortal? They'll live forever? What are they, some kind of super-villain team?"

Bags paused for a few seconds, before letting out a chuckle. "Heh, comic books, no... in actuality, they're just five random peo-ple across history that have been, well, for lack of a better term, ter-rors for the Dreamscape. They have no relationship with each other other than the fact that they were terribly powerful and something had to be done about them. So, somewhere in the Dreamscape, they are waiting in their prison."

"In their prison? But, wait, if they are across history, how are they still alive? I thought that if you die in reality, your dream goes away."

"Your body dies and your dream goes away. That's the natural order of things. But, they found ways around it and used it to grow in power."

"Do... do you think Traum is trying to be another Terror?"

Bags laughed at that. "Maybe. Man, he's a pain in the ass, just like you! Before you start thinking about Terrors and such, find out more about Traum and the Trauma Guild."

"How?"

"Start with your dear friend Rake. You've basically beaten him before. Just watch out for his gang members and you'll be fine."

"But, what about Emma and Eric?"

"You know what I have to say about that," Bags said, a very serious look on his face.

"I'm still going after them."

"I know, I know, I know, I know," Bags quickly said. "Just don't die on me, at least not with me being a ferret. I swear I'll haunt you from my grave if that happens."

Dave and Bags met eye to eye and within seconds Dave cracked and laughed. "Okay, I think I've got it."

"Kid, you better. If you don't, I'm as good as dead," Bags said, not laughing along with Dave.

"What about me?" Dave asked.

"Yeah, I guess you'll be dead in here as well."

Dave just shook his head.

"Kiddo," Bags said. "Beat Rake and we'll talk more soon."

"Gotcha, wish me luck."

"I hope that you don't die horribly," Bags said cheerfully.

"Nice," Dave said giving Bags a smile.

Dave made his way down the hill, almost skipping along the way, remembering all the little nooks and crannies to avoid tripping over. He moved out of the way out of a group of younger kids, still wet from a dip in the freezing cold lake, running back to their bunks to dry off. When he reached the docks, he headed left and reached the long tents. While the younger campers received large spacious cabins, the older kids got nice, but cramped floored tents. The big benefit was that it was far away from the rest of the camp and didn't have the regular camp counselor supervision that every cabin had.

He smiled as he got to the tents. The only time he had been down here before was when the seniors were off on a day trip. He and some of the other campers raided their tents, taking candy, soda, and magazines from some of the tents. They took just enough so that the seniors noticed, but not enough to start an actual witch hunt.

As he started looking around for names on the flaps of the tents, a few seniors walked past him and gave him a strange look.

"Hey, are you lost?" one of the campers asked.

Dave looked at the guy and remembered him. He was some obsessive tennis jock that challenged and beat every single camper at the game, no matter how young.

"Uh, no, sorry. I'm just here to pick up some stuff from my tent," Dave said, his voice wavering.

"Really? I haven't seen you around here before. Which tent are you in?" the teenager asked, tossing his tennis rackets into one of the tents.

Dave looked at a patch that looked sewn into the teen's tent. It said *Eric Graham*. He walked a few steps further and looked around. He saw *Andrew Bays* on one of the tents, but the patch was tattered and nearly falling off. He saw right below it was a brand new patch with the name *Raymond Argus*. He wanted to jump into that tent right now to go after Rake, but he calmed down and looked around more. Across from Andy's tent was a tent named *Emma Ashford*. He noted that next to Emma's was a tent with what looked like metal bars across the entrance. He looked at the tent name and Todd Maggio's name was on it. He walked up to it and pulled on the bars, but they couldn't be pried loose. Knowing that he was being watched, Dave moved over to Emma's tent and opened up the flap.

"See you around," Dave said, waving to the tennis jock. He was motioning toward Dave while talking to one of the other seniors.

"Dude, that's not your tent!" one of the seniors said as Dave crawled in.

Dave entered the pathway and very nearly died on the first step. Immediately, he realized where he was. He planted his left leg firmly on the ground and tried to stop his momentum as he saw that he was on a very narrow ledge on the side of a mountain. Luckily for him, a blast of wind slammed into his chest and knocked him down onto the narrow strip of rock that he was on.

As soon as he got his breath under control, he surveyed his surroundings. If not for the fact that he had nearly died, this would be a beautiful scene. Blue skies with occasional big puffy white clouds that gave way to rows of snow-covered mountains almost made Dave lose track of what he was supposed to do.

Below him, his foothold gave way to hundreds, if not thousands, of feet of emptiness. It was a sheer drop to a rocky demise. There was no way to climb down on either side of him, and when he looked up, there was no end to the mountain. The narrow ledge where he stood seemed to be the only non-smooth part of this mountain. He looked to where he had emerged and saw a cave that went in a few feet before plunging into darkness.

As he tried to think of a way to get off the mountain, he heard the roar of what sounded like several small airplanes coming his way. He looked off in the distance and saw two small shapes flying around, but they didn't look like airplanes or helicopters. They looked like people! As the shapes flew closer, it became more apparent what was going on. They were people in jetpacks!

One of them has to be Emma! Dave thought as he waived both arms above his head, trying to get their attention. The two people flew past him in their bright red flight suits and helmets. They were going too fast for Dave to get a good look at them before they went behind the mountain and out of sight.

"They didn't see me," Dave said to himself. He looked around, trying to think of a way to get out of here. He could try that flying thing he did before with the explosion at his feet, but that was more of a catapult than flight. He looked down the side of the mountain and nearly brought up his lunch as he saw that he was at least a mile up. There was no way that he could do his catapult flight and actually survive the landing. He tried to concentrate and imagine building a jetpack for himself, but when he did, a blast of cold wind hit him in the face, breaking his concentration and making him realize how freezing cold it was out here. He would have to act fast if he wanted to survive out here.

"Okay, maybe starting with Eric would have been better," Dave said, turning around to go back into the pathway.

Before he could, the sound of the jetpacks came from the other side of the mountain as the two jetpack people curved around the mountain and slowed as they approached his small patch of rock. He saw them and raised his arms again, trying to get their attention. One of the people turned and waived as the duo slowed and landed. Dave backed up as much as possible to give them room.

As soon as they touched down, one of the people took off her helmet. Dave smiled as he saw Emma standing there in front of him. Emma smiled back and took a step toward him. The other person took off his helmet, revealing Mike Everway.

"We stopped for this dork?" Mike asked Emma. "Come on, we've got better things to do."

"Quiet, Michael," she said, rolling her eyes. "Dave, what are you doing here? Hell, how did you even get UP here without a jetpack?"

Dave shot Mike a cold look for a few seconds then looked back at Emma. "Remember, what we talked about at school?"

"We had school today?" Emma asked. "I've been doing this all day!"

"Yeah, dumbass," Mike said, putting his arm around Emma. "Emma and I have been doing this all day. Did you actually go to school? It's summer vacation."

Emma rolled her shoulder so that Mike's arm dropped off. "Dave, you didn't go to school, did you?"

Dave leaned closer to Emma. "No, remember that you and I have something to do?" Dave said, trying desperately to get her to remember.

Emma looked at Mike and then looked back at Dave confused. "What are you talking about?"

"Uh, remember, I'm here to help protect you and Eric against

Rake," Dave said, lowering his voice in the hopes that Mike couldn't hear.

Emma's eyes searched his for several seconds before her eyes went wide. "Holy crap! You're right!"

Mike leaned in between them. "What is he right about? Em, leave this loser behind. He probably can't even ride a jetpack."

Emma turned and smiled at Mike. She took a small step towards him and put her arms around him.

"Mikey-poo, I've gotta run. Okay?" Emma said.

"What? You're ditching me for this reject? What's with you? I know you've always had a crush on me. It's time for you tell everybody how you feel."

"Mikey?" Emma said in the sweetest voice she could work up.

"Yeah?"

"GET LOST!" Emma screamed as she hit the startup button on his jetpack. With a quick burst of fire, Mike launched up into the air screaming and cursing Emma's name.

"Whoa!" Dave said as he watched Mike shoot up hundreds of feet into the air.

"Come on, whatever you need to do, let's do it fast before he regains control," Emma said.

"All right, let's go. This way!" Dave said, grabbing Emma's hand. He led her through the cave and into the darkness.

"Where are we going? This is a cave!" Emma yelled as she slipped off the jetpack.

"Trust me! I know what I'm doing!"

Just as Dave's eyes adjusted to the lack of light, a blinding light appeared. He smiled and led Emma to it, stumbling out of the tent back at Camp Cancrow. Emma tripped over one of the ropes outside the tent and took a spill, taking Dave down with her. Emma landed on top of him. They looked at each other, embarrassed, but unhurt. Emma buried her head in his chest and laughed.

"Hey!" Dave heard the tennis jock say from behind the flap of one of the tents. "What the hell is going on? Where. . . where did that girl come from?"

When Emma heard the guy's voice, she immediately sat up and got to her feet, brushing the dirt from her flight suit. Dave rolled to his feet and looked over at the flap where the voice was coming from. He saw Eric Graham's name on the patch.

"Dave? Where are we?" Emma asked, looking around. "Is this where we had that party by the lake?"

Strangely enough, Dave's first thought was fighting Beddy Tear at the lake rather than the fantastic party. "No, this is where I lived my summers before you!"

"You lived before me?" Emma said playfully.

"Kid! Hey kid!" he heard Bags say as the ferret came racing down to the senior tents.

"Bags, over here. One down, one to go!" David said.

Emma looked around for the person David was talking to. David motioned down to the ground. As soon as she saw the ferret she leapt five feet back.

"A rat! Ew!" she screamed.

"I'm not a rat. I'm ferretus maximus!" Bags said, sitting down in the dirt.

Emma looked at Dave and then back down at Bags. "It-it-it talks?"

"Unfortunately," Dave said.

"Hey! Last time I help you out!" Bags said.

"All right, all right," Dave said, turning to Emma. "Em, meet my dream guardian, Bags."

"Your dream guardian is a ferret?" Emma asked, half-shocked, half-surprised.

Dave shrugged, "Well, he was your dog Max, then he was a snake, then he was a clown. I decided that a ferret might be better. Well, at least safer. So I chose to make him a ferret."

"Weird," Emma said, before her eyes lit up. "You know, with all the stuff you've been telling me about, why don't you make him one of those overly violent video game guys? I mean, at least you would have had someone to help fight that Sleepless Knight guy."

"Thank you!" Bags yelled, smiling at Emma. "Dave, I think I like this one! And by the way, why are YOU assuming that the Sleepless Knight is a guy? Seriously! Personally, I think the villain is a chick!"

Dave cleared his throat to get their attention. "Okay, back to the business at hand," Dave said, turning toward Eric's tent. "Bags, can you take care of Emma while I..."

Dave stopped and stared at Eric's patch.

"Sure kid, I'll take care of your hot girlfriend," Bags said, earning him a beaming smile from Emma. "However, my babysitting charges are very high. I AM a professional after all."

"I'M GOING TO KILL HIM!" Dave yelled.

"Dave, what's wrong?" Emma asked as Bags rose to his hind legs.

Dave pointed to the patch on Eric's tent. The patch had turned brittle and cracked since Dave went into Emma's dream. Just below it was a second patch: *Raymond Argus*.

"Isn't that Rake's name? What does that mean?" Emma asked.

"It means that while I was getting you out of your dream, Rake was in Eric's, taking over his dream," Dave said, moving towards the tent.

"Kid! Not yet!" Bags yelled.

Dave turned around, his eyes wide with anger. "Why not? He took Andy's dream and now he has Eric's! I have to go in there NOW!"

"I know! But, don't go in there without your sword. Remember how to get it!"

Dave reached down to his side, not able to concentrate through his anger. Suddenly, the sword appeared in its scabbard right where his hand was. He quickly took it out and a burst of fire came forth from the metal, the force of which knocked Bags and Emma off of their feet.

"I'll be back with Andy's and Eric's dreams or not at all," Dave said, diving through Eric's flap.

Showdown

Dave came through the pathway on his hands and knees and kept crawling until he felt linoleum on his hands.

"What do you think you're doing?" Dave heard a man's voice that sounded like he had the worst sore throat in history. Dave knew only one person who sounded like that. It was Mr. Grainy, the ancient school janitor. "What are you doing in a teacher's office?"

Dave stood up and looked around. From the yellow color of the walls and lockers, he was in the seventh grade building. Looking behind himself, he saw his old history teacher, Ms. Wallner's, name on the door.

Mr. Grainy looked down and squinted to see the sword at Dave's side, the metal glowing red-hot. "I...look, I don't want any trouble," he said, holding up his hands before quickly backing up, turning, and running.

Dave ignored the fleeing janitor and looked down each end of the hallway. Seeing nothing, he listened for noises, hoping for some indication of where Rake could be. There was nothing. Absolutely nothing.

He began walking down the hallway to exit the building. Just as he took his first step, he saw the locker to his right shake. Someone or something pounded from inside.

"Lemme out! Lemme out!" someone screamed from inside.

Dave looked in the slits of the locker door and saw Andy looking back at him.

"Andy? What the heck are you doing in here?"

"Lemme out!"

Dave pulled up on the locker door handle, but it wouldn't budge. There was a combination lock on the door that Dave had long forgotten about.

"Andy, hold on. Stay quiet and stay still," Dave said, aiming his sword at the door. He placed the tip of the blade below the lock. He focused his rage and energy into the sword, imagining the sword heating up. Soon, Dave smelled an awful odor as the sword began melting the door where his blade touched. He slowly brought the sword across, cutting through the metal. Once he cut all the way across, he backed off.

"Andy, be very careful, but kick the bottom portion of the door,"

A loud bang came from inside. The cut section flew off and narrowly missed Dave. Out from the locker stepped twelve-year-old Andy, dressed in a Null Spiders shirt.

"Thanks, I...Dave? Dave, is that you?" Andy said, looking up a good eight inches.

Dave smiled. Nowadays, Andy was several inches taller than him. "Uh, no, but he's my cousin."

"Oh, uh, well, thanks," Andy said, making his way quickly down the hallway.

"Hey, wait!" Dave said as Andy stopped and turned around. "Have you seen Rake?"

"Yeah," Andy said, looking down at the floor.

"Where is he? Do you know?"

"He...umm....stuffed me in the locker. I've been stuck there for hours," Andy said, his voice cracking a little.

"He stuffed you in a locker?" Dave asked, somewhat amused. His tension from the upcoming encounter with Rake was the only thing helping to hold back a laugh. "Did he say anything to you before he did it?"

"No, but he said that I wouldn't be alone," Andy said.

"What does that mean?" Dave asked. However, Andy looked up at him, meeting his eyes. He then turned and ran, taking a right up a flight of a stairs and straight out the building.

"Darn it, Andy. What did you mean?" Dave said, taking a few steps to follow him.

Suddenly, another locker started to shake.

"Lemme out! Lemme out!" shouted a girl's voice.

Dave looked into the slits and saw Emma.

Another locker started to shake.

And another.

And another.

And another.

Within seconds, all the lockers were shaking and rattling.

"Lemme out! Lemme out!" a multitude of voices yelled from their lockers.

That psycho put all the students in lockers, Dave thought.

Dave turned as one of the lockers near him pulled itself off the wall, bringing pieces of plaster with it. It screeched slowly across the floor. He could see a scared student's eyes in the slits. Suddenly, the locker launched itself into the air in Dave's direction. He tried to roll out of the way, but it clipped him on the shoulder, spinning him to the ground as he dropped the sword.

He heard another locker behind him start to pull itself off the wall, and it tumbled to the ground. Dave rolled and avoided it, but stopped just as another locker fell right in front of him. He got to his feet and saw two more lockers flying in his direction, one high and one low. With nowhere to go, he raised his hand and imagined a shield in front of him that could block the lockers. A cobalt blue shield formed in front of him and took the brunt of the impact, but it knocked Dave several feet back as it broke the shield apart.

"I'm going to get killed if I stay here much longer," Dave said as he fled up the stairs in the same direction as Andy had gone. As soon as he reached the top of the stairs, he turned around to see the lockers maneuvering to the bottom of the stairs, pushing each other out of the way to be the first up the stairs like they were students at the end of a school day.

"Lemme out!" More kids started to scream, their voices becoming louder and louder.

Dave's eyes widened as lockers launched themselves up the stairs. Dave ducked as two lockers passed overhead, smashing through the glass front door. Without a moment's hesitation, he ran through the now permanently open door and immediately turned to get out of the sight line of the lockers. Within seconds, several lockers burst through the front door, collapsed on the ground, and stopped moving.

Leaning against a wall overlooking the field used for recess, Dave rested, trying to catch his breath. It was only then that he realized it was raining. He looked into the grey sky and let several rain drops hit his face to help wipe away the sweat.

KSHUNK

Dave looked around for the source of the noise. It sounded like a ball being loaded and launched from a batting machine. Something then whistled across the sky sounding like the high-pitched firecrackers that people set off during Independence Day or whenever he and his friends got their hands on them.

A football hit the ground about twenty feet in front of him and began rolling his way. Dave stood still, not exactly sure what to do.

When it got within five feet, the ball exploded in a massive fireball. The impact hit Dave, launching him into the air and back up against the wall and knocking his breath entirely out of his lungs. He momentarily blacked out as he fell but was woken immediately by his body hitting the ground.

"Damn it!" Dave heard a voice yell from the distance. "Did you know that your idiot friend actually ran out to catch the ball?"

Dave shook his head to get rid of the cloudiness and got to his feet. He was covered in chunks of earth and black ash from the explosion. He quickly looked around. Finally, he saw what he was looking for. Standing on top of the gym building was Rake, dressed in Andy's black trench coat with Eric's football shoulder pads mounted on top of it, several metal spikes sticking out from the shoulders. Next to Rake was a football-launching machine that some teams used for receiving drills.

"It took me just about a minute to take over this loser's dream." Rake said, picking up another football. "He doesn't really have much going for him, does he? I mean, yeah, football's okay, but the guy obsesses just a wee bit too much. Tonight he was actually dreaming about playing football with you losers here."

Dave started taking a few slow steps forward. "Why does it matter, Rake? Why does Eric dreaming about playing football with his friends matter to you?"

Rake laughed. "You think I care? Nah, I think it's great that you losers could find each other. It'll give me great joy to know that all those precious moments are now locked up... inside my head. Maybe I'll even try out for the team. It was always Eric's dream to go pro, wasn't it?"

With that, Dave began to run toward Rake. Rake shook his head and dropped another ball into the football-launcher.

KSHUNK

The ball flew out toward Dave and hit the ground a few feet in front of him. Dave leapt over the ball as it rolled past him. A second later, an explosion from behind him caught Dave in the blast, making him stumble, but he stayed on his feet.

"Woohoo! That was a hell of a long bomb!" Rake exclaimed.

KSHUNK

Dave ducked as a football flew right by his head. Then he kept running. He heard the next explosion, but it was too far away to do anything except spray him lightly with bits of grass and dirt. Nothing was going to stop him from getting to Rake. His foe loaded another football.

KSHUNK

The ball sailed far over Dave's head. He was too close for the machine to get a good angle on him for a shot. As he got closer to the gym, he imagined being lifted to the gym roof. He concentrated and suddenly an explosion under his feet launched him into the air. However, unlike previous times, it was a softer launch and a bit more controlled. He wasn't going to travel for miles, just enough to land himself on the roof.

He landed feet first on the roof and immediately moved to draw his sword as he saw Rake rush him with an aluminum bat. Only then did he remember that he had left his sword back under the lockers in the seventh grade building. Rake swung and hit him in the stomach with a full swing, sending him into the air and off the building. Dave tried to catch the side of the building with his hands, but his fingers just clipped the edge and slipped off. He plummeted almost thirty feet to the ground, landing on his hurt shoulder and rolling several feet before lying still.

Dave opened his eyes and saw Rake jump down and land behind him, keeping Dave between him and the wall.

"Get up, freak," Rake said. Dave's mind tried to deal with the extraordinary pain in his stomach and arm.

His eyes focused on the weapon that Rake held. The handle looked like a normal aluminum baseball bat handle, but further up, the bat split apart into two separate bats and looked almost like a tuning fork.

Rake noticed Dave staring at the weapon. "Oh, you like it? Well, with ass-goth and you having weird weapons, I figured why couldn't I have one, too? I think it suits me," Rake said, caressing the bats as Dave slowly got to one knee. "Of course, I had to make sure that every hit... gave an extra oomph!"

Rake swung the baseball bat like a golf club, and it connected with Dave's chin, launching him over twenty feet into the air. He crashed through the gymnasium window, slamming into the hard-wood floor of the gym.

Dave clutched his chin in agony as a coppery tasting liquid filled his mouth. He spit out a mouthful of blood, but the movement made his chin feel like it was broken into hundreds of pieces.

"Kiddo!" Bags yelled in his head.

"Mbmgms?" Dave tried to say.

"Dummy, remember that I'm in your head. Imagine the words," Bags said.

Dave concentrated on his words.

"Rake's here. I'm getting my butt kicked! I think he broke my chin! He's going to be here any second!" Dave thought, getting to his feet, but he doubled over in agony and his stomach felt like it was turned inside out.

"Calm down, boy, calm down."

"I can't! It hurts too much!"

Dave looked up as the door to the gym burst open and Rake walked in, brandishing his bat in front of him.

"Awww... here's Davey-wavey!" Rake said, talking to his bat.

Dave winced as he straightened up. "Rake, I swear that if you take my dream now, I'll still find a way to beat you," Dave said through clenched teeth, struggling to talk through the pain of his stomach and jaw.

Rake chuckled and then clutched his stomach as he laughed. "You? Beat me? How? You're going to start over from scratch. You won't even remember that I took your dream!" Rake said, slowly walking towards Dave.

While backing away, Dave's eyes drifted to the floor and he saw some of the broken glass. He imagined a few small shards of glass standing up just in front of Rake's feet. Several small pieces stood up just as Rake's boot crunched down on them. Most of the pieces simply were crushed, but one sharp sliver cut right through the boot and into Rake's foot. His eyes opened wide as he yelled in pain and leaned over to look at his foot. Dave took the opportunity to launch all the glass pieces at Rake. Rake stumbled backward as the first few pieces slashed at him. Small cuts opened up all over his face. He screamed as he fell down, clutching his face.

Suddenly, the nets from one of the basketball rims ripped and fell on Dave. It expanded quickly into a human sized weighted net and pinned Dave to the floor.

Rake, wiping the remnants of glass and blood from his face, walked toward Dave. Several cuts were still bleeding. "That was a stupid trick and a waste of your energy. It's only delaying your death," Rake said.

Dave looked to the basketball net above Rake and made it fall, forming the same kind of weighted net. Rake looked up just as it fell on him.

Rake stared at Dave and then down at the ground. "Well, crap," Rake said, struggling to get out of the net while Dave did the same. "How the hell did you affect things in MY dream? Man, I swear once I take your dream, I'm going to get Lord Traum to show me how to do way more than just nets, fire, and zombies."

Dave legs were starting to feel heavy. "You may have this dream now, but you can never be its true owner. And that's my friend, Eric Graham!" Dave said, tossing off the net.

"That's so frigging lame!" Rake said, throwing the net off as well. "Now, let me get back to kicking your ass and taking your dream."

"Bring it, Rake. I'm right here," Dave said.

Rake and Dave stared at each other as a strong cold wind blew in. The nets rolled past them like tumbleweed. The lights began to flicker then dim, and the wind dropped the temperature in the room rapidly.

"A flare for the dramatics, Davey-wavey? Are you trying to intimidate me?" Rake said, rolling his eyes.

"That's not me, Rake," Dave said, suddenly even more concerned than he was before.

Suddenly, lightning burst from outside, lighting up the entire gym for a few seconds before causing all the lights to go out completely. With a flash, they came back on, but it was still very dim. Dave suddenly felt colder than he had ever felt before. Out of the corner of his eye, he noticed somebody was now standing on his left side. He turned and immediately jumped back several feet. Standing there was Krieger, machete in hand.

Rake AND Krieger? They're on the same side? Dave thought as he frantically looked for a way out.

"Oh lookee! It looks like Lord Traum sent me some help! Not that I asked for it," Rake said.

Krieger turned his shadow-covered face towards Rake slowly then back at Dave and raised his machete.

"Hey, freako! This isn't your fight! I need his dream!" Rake screamed.

Krieger slashed at Dave, who barely dodged it as the machete embedded itself into the wooden floor. Dave scrambled onto the bleachers. He wanted to create some distance between him and Krieger, but also not get too close to Rake.

"Stop it, you freak!" Rake screamed.

Krieger gave the machete a tug and freed it from the floor. He began to slowly ascend the bleachers towards Dave.

"Last warning!" Rake yelled.

Dave climbed to the top of the bleachers as Krieger followed. Dave could probably keep his distance, but soon he'd get too close to Rake.

"That's it! You're going down!" Rake said.

Rake concentrated and formed a baseball in his hand. He threw it up in the air and swung with his double-headed baseball bat, connecting with the ball and sending it sailing toward Krieger. It hit his side and exploded just like the football, sending him tumbling over the side of the bleachers.

Dave quickly hopped off the bleachers and sprinted to the other side of the gym. He was aiming for a door that led to the locker room and hoped to get out through the fire door nearby. However, just before he grabbed the handle, the door turned to ice, encasing the handle.

"You're not going anywhere, Davey," Rake said. "I'm not finished with you yet."

Both turned as Krieger rose to his feet and picked up the machete that had dropped during his fall.

"Dude, seriously. Traum's going to be pissed if he finds out that you're interfering," Rake said to Krieger.

Suddenly, Krieger flung the machete at Rake. Rake dropped to the ground with his head down as the machete embedded itself in the concrete wall behind him. Dave watched as Krieger slowly walked over to Rake, standing right above him. Unsure whether he wanted to help or hinder Rake, Dave said nothing as Krieger reached out, grabbed Rake by the back of his head, and launched him across the room. Rake slammed face first into the wall next to Dave. He slumped to the ground, his face a bloody smashed mess and his eyes glazed over.

Krieger walked over and reached for his machete. Dave concentrated and used Rake's trick from earlier to make the machete freeze over. A frustrated grunt came from Krieger as he glared at his frozen weapon. He grabbed it to pull it out of the wall, but Dave concentrated and made handcuffs of ice burst forth from the existing ice, encasing Krieger's hands completely.

Taking a step forward, Dave concentrated all of his energy into his right hand. He couldn't free his friends if he was dead. He had to get rid of Krieger before he could go after Rake. He saw blue energy pool into his hand. Krieger, seeing this as well, stood still for a second. Suddenly, the floor between them began to shake. The floorboards jumped up and down as black energy poured through the cracks in the wood. The floorboards exploded, as a black energy wave burst forth, slamming into Dave and crushing him with its immense force. The energy burned his skin. As it dissipated, Dave collapsed to the floor. As he did, Krieger turned the ice into steam and freed himself and his weapon. He removed the weapon from the wall and slowly walked over to Dave who rolled onto his back as the blue energy in his hand flowed back into the rest of his body.

Krieger was too strong. There was no way he could beat him, and there was no way could defend himself. Krieger raised the machete to strike Dave, but before he could swing, a bright golden shape flew into the broken window that Dave had made. It was Gabriel! He grabbed Krieger's arm.

"David," Gabriel said as Krieger struggled against Gabriel's grip. "I am sorry I could not arrive sooner."

Dave stood there in shock. "How? How did you know Krieger was here?"

"Why?" Dave asked the angel, his voice weak. "Why did he come after me?"

Gabriel stared at Krieger who was slowly rising to his feet and then back to Dave.

"Because he doesn't want it to end," Gabriel said.

Dave rolled over and raised himself on one elbow.

"What? He doesn't want *what* to end?" Dave said.

While holding Krieger back with one hand, Gabriel willed his golden glow to fade from his face.

It was Mr. Laws.

"What the heck?" Dave said. "You? You're Gabriel?"

"Not just Gabriel," Gabriel said as he pulled back Krieger's hood of shadows.

It was also Mr. Laws.

Before Dave could say something, Krieger managed to maneuver the machete a bit and cut Gabriel's arm slightly. Gabriel responded by flinging Krieger through the concrete wall. His body landed in a crater made by one of Rake's football bombs.

"Find me. Talk to me. I'll tell you what you need to know," Gabriel said. "For now, I must make sure that Krieger does no more damage."

Gabriel flew after Krieger, snatching him from the ground and taking him into the air.

Dave took a step to go after them. "Where... do you think you're going... loser?" Rake said as he rose to his feet, blood dripping down his face and his nose slightly bent to the left.

Dave turned in shock. "Rake, seriously. Give it up. Krieger left you in bad shape."

"Like you're any better." Rake said, pointing to the burned flesh. "I'm not going to be beaten by a loser like you!"

Rake bent and grunted as he lifted his weapon. He made his way slowly toward Dave. Dave backed up and began concentrating his energy into his hand. With a burst of speed, Rake screamed and swung down at Dave. Dave reached up and grabbed the bat with both hands. The impact drove Dave's feet through the floor, knocking him off balance. He fell to the floor, losing his grip on the bat.

"Aw, Davey-wavey has no weapon to block 'cause he was stupid enough to leave it in the seventh grade!" Rake said. "Maybe you can find your mommy and she can take you out shopping to buy another one."

As Rake raised his bat, something that he said caught Dave's attention: Shopping to buy another one? Another one! Why does it matter that he lost his sword? This is a dream! Not only that, but this is his friend's dream. He can do whatever he wants to if he can imagine it.

Dave went to his volcano. He reached his hand into the lake of lava and reached his hand into it and knew that this was exactly how his sword was made. He then reached his other hand into the lava and found something else.

"Goodbye, loser!" Rake said swinging the bat down.

Dave raised the sword and blocked the double-headed bat then turned the blade so that it was wedged between the two heads. He pulled down on the sword using Rake's own grip against him. Rake stumbled forward and Dave used that opening to plunge his newly formed dagger into Rake's chest.

Rake stumbled over Dave, dropping his bat. He pulled out the bloody dagger and looked at it.

"You son of a b—"

Rake dropped to the floor.

Dave got up on one knee and looked outside to see the flashes of light getting fainter and fainter, then turned back to Rake.

Is he dead? Did I beat him? Dave wondered to himself.

Dave looked back down at Rake just in time to see his body shimmer and fade away. As he faded into nothingness, he raised his middle finger to Dave in one final act of defiance. Immediately after Rake disappeared, he was replaced with three glassy orbs, each shimmering in a variety of colors as they rose into the air.

"Um, Bags?"

"You lived! Wow! I was beginning to wonder why I wasn't the guardian for some bully now."

"Bags, I beat him. I... beat him," Dave said, barely believing it himself as he stared at the orbs. He then looked up to the flashing lights in the sky as Gabriel and Krieger battled.

He doesn't want it to end? What does that mean?

Dave stared at the glowing orbs, not knowing whether to stay there or to find cover and wait for them to explode.

"Bags, what do I do?"

"Take one into your hand. Don't worry, unlike your ego, these things aren't fragile and unlike your acne, these won't explode."

Dave hobbled over to one of the orbs and grasped it gently. The first thing he noticed was that the orb kept alternating from almost too hot to touch to too cold to bear. Finally getting a good look at it, he noticed that the flashing lights he saw were not random flashes. They were actually images. He looked at the orb a little closer and then nearly dropped it.

It was the graveyard from last night, complete with giant video screen.

"Bags, I see the same dream I was in last night. Is... is this Andy's dream?"

"Ding ding ding ding ding! Unless Rake took down another guy with the same dream, you've got it!" Bags said.

Dave stared at the dream, rolling the smooth surface of the orb around in his hand. No matter how he held it, the dream was always right side up.

"Um, Bags? Now what?" Dave asked, smirking as a zombie stumbled across the dream and went out of sight.

"You have a choice now, an important one at that. Dunno if you can handle that kind of pressure."

"BAGS!"

"Release, Absorb, or Destroy. It's the best way to describe the process," Bags said. Before Dave could respond, Bags continued, "You have a choice to make with each dream. You can choose to release the dream. The dream will disappear and the dreamer will be released. Everything for that person will return to normal.

You can choose to absorb the dream like your friend Rake did which will take all of the persons dreams and inspirations away and will give you access to some of that person's memories.

Or you can choose to destroy the dream. That person's dreams and inspirations are destroyed utterly. No dreams are coming back from that one. I advise you to never do that unless you're absolutely sure."

Dave stared at Andy's dream. "So, how do I release a dream? I need to free Andy and Eric."

"As long as you're holding it, just will it to be free. Just imagine opening the orb and willing the dreams to fly away."

"That's it?"

"That's it."

"Andy," Dave said, concentrating solely on the orb. "Be free."

The orb floated out of his hand and began to spin rapidly. Different colors of light shot from the top half of the orb, through the roof, and out into the sky. Suddenly, it gave off a quick white burst of light, just like a camera flash. When his eyes could focus again, he saw that the orb was gone. In its place was Andy—not the younger Andy from earlier in his dream—this was the real Andy dressed in his black trench coat and Null Spiders shirt. Andy saw Dave and gave him a confused look.

"Dave? What the hell just happened?" Andy said as he gave the gymnasium a hard stare. "Why am I at school?"

"You're dreaming, Andy," Dave smiled.

"No crap, I'm dreaming! Why the hell would I want to come back here? I hate this place," Andy said as he walked over to the damage that happened from the fight. "I mean, look at this place! It's so run down! Um, speaking of run down, what happened to you?"

Dave ignored the question about his burnt skin as he bent down to grab another of the orbs, wincing a bit from the pain of his wounds. He looked into it and saw that he was staring at himself looking directly into the orb.

"Trippy," Dave said.

"What is that thing?" Andy asked. "It looks like something you'd buy at some novelty store or something like that."

Dave smiled. "Want to see Eric?"

"Not particularly," Andy said. "Why? Is he coming?"

"I'm going to snap my fingers and Eric is going to show up. When he does, I'm going to take both of you to a place where you can learn to defend yourself in your dreams."

"From who?"

"From anybody who's going to attack you here."

"This is one weird-ass dream, Dave."

"I know, I know. But, when you wake up, I want you to remember this dream," Dave said as he walked up closer to Andy. "Listen, tomorrow one of us is going to show up at your house and you're going to go to the game."

"But, I hate foo—"

"I know you don't like football, but I need everybody to be to-gether," Dave continued as he saw Andy open his mouth. "It's all going to make sense soon."

"Whatever you say," Andy said, shrugging before staring at the weighted nets on the ground. "Huh, I don't recognize these from school."

Dave didn't have a plan for what to do at the football game. He just wanted to make sure that all his friends were safe. If they remembered the dream, they'd remember that they have to go to the game. He smiled at Andy and snapped his fingers. In a flash of light, the orb disappeared and Eric stepped out in full football gear.

"Eric, welcome..."

Eric punched Dave in the face, knocking him to the ground.

"Eric!" Andy yelled.

"Screw you Rake. I've got you now!" Eric screamed as he jumped on top of Dave, and raised his fist to smash into his face.

Andy raced over and grabbed Eric from behind as both he and Dave dragged Eric to the floor.

"I'm going to kill you, Rake!" Eric yelled.

"Eric! It's us!" Dave yelled. "It's Andy and Dave!"

Eric looked at them both through his helmet, his eyes wild like he was just fighting for his life and then smiled as he exhaled. "I knew it was you all along," Eric said, pushing Andy off of him. "I was just playing around."

As they all got to their feet, Andy punched Eric hard on the shoulder, completely forgetting that Eric was wearing shoulder pads. The look of realization and pain on his face as his knuckles con-nected with the equipment almost made Dave burst out in laughter, but he held it in. Eyeing Andy for a second, he turned and slapped Eric's shoulder pads. "Listen guys. We're all dreaming right now."

"No crap, man!" Eric said. "You mean I'm not at school right now in real life? Come on."

Dave ignored Eric's wisecracks. "Here's the short story version of it. Your dreams aren't necessarily just for you anymore."

"Uh, what?" Andy said, looking over to Eric who looked just as confused.

"Think of it this way," Dave said, trying to come up with an analogy on the fly. "Imagine your dream as a room in a giant mansion, but none of the rooms have obvious exits."

"I was at one of these places a few years ago for one of my cousin's weddings. I spent hours trying to find secret passages." Andy said.

"All right, good! Now imagine that each room has a zillion secret passages, each one leading to another person's dream," Dave said. "That's how I got to your dreams tonight."

"Dave, I'm really confused about all this," Andy said. "Assuming this is all real and all..."

"It's not real. It's a dream," Dave said, picking up the last orb. Looking closely at it, he saw what looked like a disco ball spinning within the orb. While a little surprised by seeing a disco ball, this had to be Rake's dream.

"So, it's a real dream?" Eric asked, getting himself even more confused.

"NO!" Dave yelled, looking down from the orb. "Look, it's a dream, that's all it is. But, it's possible not only for someone else to walk from their dream to your dream, but for that person to literally take over your dream."

Dave looked at his friends. Eric seemed confused. Andy seemed more interested in the weighted nets. He had to get them to understand it and take it seriously.

"Anybody can take over your dreams. Somebody like Rake."

The look in Eric's eyes showed that he finally got it. "Hey, this is the stuff you were talking about after practice today!" Eric said, his voice echoing in the gym.

"Yup, that's it," Dave said, happy that Eric remembered. "That's exactly it."

"Holy crap," Eric said as Dave saw his face sink. "Rake got me, didn't he?"

Dave nodded. "Yeah, but I got you back."

Andy laughed. "You lost to Rake? You suck!"

"Dude," Dave said, stepping between Andy and Eric just in case. "You lost too."

Eric smirked and Andy looked at Dave. "I did?" Andy asked as Dave nodded. "When? I mean, I think I would have remembered him taking me out."

This got Dave curious. He didn't actually know if Andy would remember getting taken over or not. "So, you don't remember seeing him at all in your dreams? Like, in the past few days?"

"Uh, no," Andy said.

Dave thought about the situation for a few seconds. He then remembered at the lake that Rake was there. "Do you remember fighting a giant teddy bear at the lake a few nights ago?"

Andy thought about it for a few seconds. "Kind of. I remember. Wait... I remember getting attacked from behind and knocked to the ground. By the time I looked up, all I remember seeing was a giant two-headed baseball bat coming down on my head."

Dave nodded. "That's when he got you. That's when he got your dream. Darn it, I was there. I could have stopped it!"

"You were there in my dream? Damn it, why didn't you stop him? You let Rake take my dreams?" Andy asked.

"I didn't realize he was there. Seriously. Besides, I used up everything I had beating that Beddy Tear monster."

Eric cocked his head. "Beddy Tear? As in, your childhood teddy bear?"

Dave and Andy looked at Eric. "Wow, you actually remember that?" Dave asked.

Eric shrugged. "I guess my mind remembers little details."

"Okay, well, yeah, it was my teddy bear that became a monster and went into your dream, Andy. I went in there to destroy it."

"Wait, does that mean that *you* let it in?" Andy asked.

Dave looked down at his feet. "Uh, yeah, kinda. Not on purpose though, but yeah. But, I promise that it won't ever happen again."

"You better. I can't believe you did that!" Andy screamed.

Dave quickly changed the subject. "Okay, we've got to go back to my dream."

"Why?" Andy asked.

"I need to talk to my dream guardian."

"Your what?" Andy asked as he and Eric joined Dave as they headed out the door.

"Dream guardian," Dave said, noticing that the flashes of light from outside were gone. Was the battle between Gabriel and Krieger finished? Was there only one remaining? Were they both Mr. Laws? Why didn't Mr. Laws tell him that he was a Dream Walker? "Uh, think of it like a teacher, but the subject is dreams."

"Oh crap!" Andy said. "I knew that sounded familiar. I think I have one of those things as well. It started talking about some kind of danger in my dreams. I guess that was Beddy Tear."

"Or Rake," Eric reminded him.

"I know your guardian. I met it when I was in your dream with Beddy Tear," Dave said.

"Oh yeah? What was it then?" Andy said.

"A really ugly poodle," Dave said. "It said that it represents the real Andy."

Eric stopped and turned toward Andy who opened his mouth to say something. Before he could, Dave cut him off.

"Sorry, that was somebody else," Dave said as Eric faked fainting. "What I meant to say is that it's a blue crab. Kind of scared of its own shadow."

Dave looked at Andy and could see that he wanted to deny it. "Yeah, that's him. That's Frank."

"Frank?" Eric asked.

"Frank," Andy said.

"Frank," Dave repeated.

"Well, Andy," Eric started to say with a big grin on his face.

"Careful, buddy," Dave said.

"Quite *frankly*, your dream guardian sucks!" Eric said as Andy picked up a scrap of a burnt football and flung it at him.

"Dude, I don't see your dream guardian anywhere," Andy said. "Probably cause it's tiny, just like your..."

"Guys, guys, guys, chill out," Dave cut in, trying to stop them.

"I'm sure mine is around here somewhere," Eric said, looking around.

"Guys, seriously, it's actually going to be good to find your dream guardian, but right now, it's more important to get you trained. Emma is over there waiting for us."

"For what?" Eric asked

"My dream guardian is waiting there to train you guys to defend yourselves," Dave said as they made their way into the seventh grade building.

"Defend us against Rake?" Eric asked. "Awesome, 'cause I'll kick his ass when I see him."

"No, not against Rake. I took care of him," Dave said as he showed off the orb. "This is what's left of his dreams."

"Really? Let's smash that sucker," Eric said as he reached for it, but Dave pulled it away at the last second.

"No, I've got to keep it. I've got to ask Bags a few questions before I do anything."

"Bags?" both friends asked.

"Yeah, Bags—my dream guardian."

"So, Frank is a ridiculous name, but Bags isn't?" Andy said as the friends laughed and entered the seventh grade building

They all walked in silence for a few seconds as they encountered dozens of fallen lockers. Unsure whether the lockers would still move, he kicked one of them and waited for several seconds. Seeing nothing moving, he and his friends continued past the lockers.

"What happened here?" Eric asked.

"Locker fight," Dave said, shrugging as they slowly made their way into the hallway.

"Okay, so we're being trained to defend ourselves from what?" Andy asked.

Dave took a deep breath and closed his eyes. "The...Sleepless Knight."

"The WHAT?!" his friends said.

"Sleepless Knight," Dave responded.

"You mean, like the guy that kicked your ass in ULB?" Andy asked.

"Yeah," Dave said, almost embarrassed by it. "Look, somebody is going around to people's dreams looking like the Sleepless Knight and trying to take their dreams. Apparently, Rake was working either with or for it."

"So, somebody is dreaming that they're the Sleepless Knight?" Eric asked.

"Basically, yeah, and whoever it is, guy or girl, is *really* dangerous," Dave said.

"I'm sure whatever it is, we'll kick its ass!" Eric said, pumping his fist dramatically.

The trio arrived at the entrance to the pathway. Dave turned and opened up the door. Behind the door was nothing but darkness surrounding a four-foot bright triangle that showed the campgrounds beyond.

"What the hell?" Eric said, looking through.

Dave started to step through the hole. "This way to my dream," he said as he turned and smiled at his friends and went through.

Through His Eyes

Immediately as his friends stepped through the pathway, Dave mentally called out for Bags. Leading his friends passed a few wide-eyed seniors, the trio met up with Bags and Emma in the field between the senior tents and the rec room.

"Dave, where are we? Some kind of cult hideout?" Andy asked.

"Cult hideout? Seriously? Dude, it's my overnight camp from a few years ago," Dave said.

"Like I'd know that," Andy said as Bags made it down from the porch.

Eric looked down at Bags. "Sweet! You had ferrets at your camp? My uncle has a few of these guys," Eric said, reaching down to pick up Bags.

"If you value your life, boy, you won't come any closer," Bags said, showing his fangs.

Eric jumped back a few steps. Andy flinched but then laughed at Eric's reaction.

"Guys, this is Bags," Dave said, leaning down near the ferret. "He's my dream guardian."

"Your dream guardian is a ferret?" Andy asked.

"Long story, but yeah," Dave said.

274

"Ferret, clown, snake, dog, rabid machine gun spewing anteater, whatever. Who cares?" Bags said. "What Dumbass here has decided to do is to bring all of you into his dream so that I can train you to defend yourselves against threats like the Sleepless Knight, which I hope that my big dummy over here has explained, right? By the way, Dummy, you look like hell," Bags said, looking up at Dave who rolled his eyes and nodded.

"Good, great, wonderful. Any questions before I torture you?" Bags asked.

Eric and Andy looked at each other, but Dave simply presented Rake's orb.

Bags looked up and smiled a weasel smile "Ah, a dream. Why did you bring it here?" Bags asked.

"This is Rake's dream," Dave said.

"Annnnnnd you didn't destroy it or absorb it, why?"

"Well, that's the thing. What happens if I absorb it?"

"You get his dreams and inspirations and such, like I've told you a billion times before," Bags said.

"If I get all of his dreams, I get to see what he has seen before in the Dreamscape, right?"

"So, if I absorb his dream, I might be able to find out what exactly Rake was after. Maybe find out what the Trauma Guild's plans are."

Bags' eyes opened wide. "You know what, boy? You finally came up with a good idea."

Dave stared at the orb. "Bags, you take care of my friends, okay?"

Emma walked over to Dave and put her arm around his waist. "Dave, is this dangerous?"

"I don't know. Bags?" Dave asked.

"Listen, it's only a matter of time before any dream walker associated with Rake will know who took his dream. I imagine it's mostly going to be Trauma Guild members. But, at this point, what's the risk? They're coming after you anyway! And simply experiencing Rake's dreams are no serious risk to you."

"Okay, okay. All right, Bags, I'm going in. Treat my friends right. I kinda like them, you know?"

Bags faked a vomit.

"Dave, be careful all right?" Emma said.

Dave turned and took her by the waist and kissed her the longest kiss they had shared. It was fitting that this kiss was only a dream, even if they both remembered it in the morning.

As they separated, Dave concentrated on the orb and imagined the orb flowing into his body. He watched as the orb slowly melted into his hand, creating a thick cool liquid that quickly evaporated in his hand. Dave closed his hand to try to catch it, but as he did, his vision was suddenly filled with hundreds of images.

Rake in a dojo beating up three karate masters.

Rake in an ice cream store flinging ice cream at customers.

Rake in a misty throne room staring at a man in really fancy black armor and flanked by several other armored people.

Rake in racecar zooming along the track.

Rake walking down the street with his arm around two hot girls from school.

Rake turning into...

"Bags! How do I turn it off?" Dave yelled, blinded by the visions.

"...ou—ust—centrate—cific—eam!" Bags yelled, but Dave could only understand some of it.

Rake diving into a pool filled with ping-pong balls.

Rake skateboarding with his gang.

"Conce—drea—" Bags yelled.

"What?" Dave yelled.

"CONCENTRATE!" Bags yelled.

He tried to concentrate on one of the dreams. There were so many dreams. So many memories.

Dave blinked and suddenly he realized he was no longer at the camp. He was hugging a tree for dear life.

"Dude, you gotta keep up," he heard a woman's voice say.

Suddenly, his body was moving, but he had no control over it. He was slowly climbing up the tree. His head turned and stared off into the distance. It was nighttime and the sky was absolutely clear. Dave could see dozens, if not hundreds, of stars.

"Rake, come on, man!" a woman's voice called to him again.

"Shut up! I'm coming!" Dave said, but it wasn't his own voice.

Rake? What did she mean by that? Am I Rake? Dave thought to himself. He tried to open his mouth to say something, but he couldn't.

Dave climbed, but as he did, Dave noticed the arms of the person who was climbing. They were skinnier then his own arms. Almost bony. Almost like...Rake.

I'm in Rake's body. Oh my god, I'm in Rake's body! Dave thought. Now what?

Finally, he stopped climbing. He looked up to see Alexis, Rake's girlfriend, sitting on a huge branch that extended out from the tree.

"Come on over here, Rake," Alexis said.

Rake made his way over to her and sat down.

"You know," Rake said, "when you said you wanted to climb a tree, I thought you meant that you wanted to..."

"Look at all those stars," Alexis said, pointing to the sky. "Do you think there's life out there?"

"Like friggin' aliens?"

"Yeah, friggin' aliens."

"I don't know. I guess so."

"What do you want to do when you're older?" Alexis asked. Dave had never seen her curious. He had always seen her as a bully that kept vandalizing the school and harassing people.

"Same old stuff. You planning on doing something?" Rake said.

"Yeah, *I* plan to. I don't know about you, but *I'd* like to do something with my life beyond this petty crap that our gang does," Alexis said.

Dave felt Rake's anger rise in him.

"What, like I don't?" Rake said.

"I didn't mean it like that, but dude, you've gotta have a plan. It's what my mom always told me."

"Screw your mom."

"I'd bet you'd like to."

Dave felt a tickle, almost like his body was trying to laugh.

"That's a scary thought," Rake said. "But a guy's got duties to perform, so I guess I'll get right on her... I mean, get right to it."

"Dude, my mom?"

"You're the one who told me I had to do it!"

Rake and Al laughed as he put his arm around her.

Seriously? This is what they talk about? Dave thought to himself. *I always assumed they were performing blood sacrifices or something.*

It was then that Dave felt warmth, like he felt when he and Emma were together. It was then that he realized it wasn't him. It was Rake's emotions.

He quickly thought about the other dreams. What about how Rake got involved with the Trauma Guild?

He blinked and suddenly he was running down a school hallway. Coming around the corner was Dave himself. Rake kept running, heading straight toward him.

Rake, stop! You're going to run straight into me! Dave thought as he thought about what he just said.

Happiness mixed with anger.

Rake dipped his shoulder and rammed it into Dave's stomach, doubling him over. Rake stood up and brought a knee up into Dave's face, knocking him onto his back.

"Please. Please no more," Dave said.

Rake ignored his pleas and grabbed Dave by his hair, pulling him to his feet. With a smile, Rake threw Dave headfirst through the window, sending him into the courtyard, glass flying everywhere.

"Later, dude," Rake said as students scrambled to get away from him.

Satisfaction.

Suddenly, students at one end of the hallway started screaming.

"Don't worry," Rake said. "It's Calloway I was after. That guy deserved it!"

The students pointed beyond him, down at the other end of the hallway as the lights flickered and went dim.

Rake turned around to see a masked person walking down the hallway clad in black armor and a white metallic mask. The armor, while definitely metal, seemed to ripple as the person moved, as it seemed to flow backwards in rivers of black.

Rake took a step back, "What the hell are you?" he said, looking up at the mask. The white mask had a smiling face on his right side and a frowning face on the left, almost like the comedy and tragedy faces in theater. Behind the mask, Rake could see no eyes.

"Mr. Argus, I have been looking for you," a deep voice came from the armor.

"Me?" Rake said, "Who the hell are you?"

Fear quickly overcame his anger.

"My name is Traum. Lord Traum," the person said, stopping mere feet away from Rake.

"Is that so?" Rake said, backing away. "Well, Traum, you'll have to make an appointment."

Traum watched as Rake backed away a few more steps. Suddenly, there was a loud crack and crunch as the floor, walls, and ceiling behind Rake came together as if some giant hand had pinched them together.

"What the hell did you do?" Rake asked, his voice cracking and nervous.

Terror.

Traum stayed silent for a second. "My will."

Rake backed up, but he tripped on his own feet and fell down as Trauma took a step forward.

"What do you want with me?!" Rake yelled.

"I'm here to make you an offer," Trauma said.

"An offer? To me? What could I do for you?" Rake said, his voice still cracking.

Scared, but curious.

"I understand that you have issues with Mr. Calloway."

"Yeah, so?"

"I am in the process of dealing with a dilemma that involves Mr. Calloway," Traum said with an eerily slow voice. "I am offering you a chance to deal with your issues with them."

"How? I mean, there are only so many times I can beat them up before I get kicked out of school."

"What if I told you that you could be their literal worst nightmare and you could never get into trouble?" Traum said, continuing his slow pace.

Rake looked at Traum and slowly smiled.

Happiness.

"I'll take that smile as your acceptance of my offer," Trauma said. "Very well, let us find your dream guardian. It will explain all that you need to know about the Dreamscape..."

Dave's vision suddenly blurred. When it cleared up a few seconds later, Dave was back at the campsite. As he took a step, his body felt stiff, as if he hadn't moved in ages.

He looked over and saw that Andy had formed his double scythe blade and was chasing Eric who was forming a green light in his hands that quickly faded away, formed again, and faded away.

"I can't do it, Bags! I can't do it!" Eric yelled.

Suddenly, a red leather whip wrapped around Andy's feet and

yanked him to the ground. Emma leaped up and shrieked in victory as she ran over to her fallen foe.

"Got you!" she yelled.

Dave smiled as he felt a paw on his foot. He looked down to see Bags.

"Kid, what did you find out?" Bags asked.

"Where the heck did I just go?"

"You were right here the whole time, boy. When you're viewing somebody else's dream, that's all you can do," Bags explained. "Now, what did you find out?"

"I...I know what Traum looks like. I saw him recruit Rake," Dave said as his limbs began to loosen.

"Good, but that's it? Seriously, you have access to all of his dreams."

"I was watching the dream where Traum recruited him, but then suddenly I was back here! What do you want me to do?"

"Are you able to concentrate better then you were doing before?"

"Yeah," Dave said, as he realized he could see normally again. He smiled as he noted a few roses and a few slithering snakes. "Now what do I do?"

"Good, now you've gone through the hard part of absorbing a dream. Now here's the thing. Think of his dreams as having been catalogued. You can now find anything and everything he's ever dreamed about. You just have to concentrate and you'll find it."

"Anything?"

"Anything that he's ever dreamed about."

Dave concentrated.

I want to see when Traum tells Rake his plans.

Dave blinked and suddenly he was walking down an old stone hallway. Cobwebs lined every inch of the room which was dimly lit with a torchlight every ten feet or so. Finally, after what felt like hours, he reached a large wooden door. Rake reached out and pushed it open. As he did, a thick white mist poured from the room into the hallway.

Fear.

"What the hell?" Rake said.

"Do not worry about the mist," Traum said from somewhere in the room. "It is merely there for effect."

Rake was amazed by what he was seeing. The room was very long and fairly wide, with dozens and dozens of suits of armor lining the walls on either side of him. He went up to one of them, an armor made of what looked like glassy black stone. He looked at the label below the armor:

TOMORROW KNIGHT

"Do you like that armor, Raymond?" Trauma said.

Rake shrugged, "It's all right."

Rake looked at the armors and noticed that some were made of rocks and gems, some out of metal, others out of substances that Rake couldn't even begin to ponder. He walked up to armor that seemed to have swirling shades of green liquid moving through it. It didn't even look solid, but the liquids did not drip off it. He reached out to touch it.

Amazement.

"I would not do that, Raymond," Traum said, "unless you wish to die horribly."

"What? Is this like some kind of museum?" Rake asked. "Like, if I touch something, some guard is going to come out and try to kick my ass?"

"No," Traum said. "That armor was made to end the life of who-ever touches it."

"Seriously?" Rake said, staring more closely at the armor. "That's friggin' sweet! Why isn't it being used?"

Curiosity.

"The armor ends the life of whoever touches it, but also slowly kills the user. Its drawback was something that its owner did not realize until it was too late."

Curiosity deflated. Fear.

Rake backed a few steps away from the armor and walked further into the room. At the end of the room sat Traum dressed in the same armor as before, sitting on a throne that seemed to be made of the same material as his armor. It gave the appearance that his throne and his armor were all one piece. On each side of him stood three people clad in armor.

On his left stood one whose armor was made of a solid ruby, another person whose armor made of pure silver, and another was wearing armor that resembled the 'snow' that you would see on a TV channel that didn't work.

On his right stood one whose armor looked like it was made of a solid emerald, another person whose armor looked like it was made of pure gold, and another person who had black armor whose metal glittered like stars.

"My knights and I are pleased that you could meet us. I trust that your guardian showed you the way?" Traum said.

"Who? The talking car?" Rake said. "Yeah, he showed me the way."

"Excellent. You must learn to rely on your dream guardian. It will serve you well. Never underestimate what it can do or what it can teach you to do."

"Whatever. It's a talking car that told me about the Dreamscape and how to go into other people's dreams."

"And the fact that you can walk into other people's dreams does not impress you?"

"Oh yeah, neato. I can now see that my friends are dreaming about picking flowers and dancing around with forest creatures. Whoopee," Rake said, rolling his eyes.

Boredom.

Seriously? This guy is bored? Dave thought. *No wonder he can't stay interested in class if he can't even keep excited about the Dreamscape.*

Suddenly, the knights started whispering all at once, each one saying something different. Traum looked to his left and then to his right. The whispering stopped.

"You seem to be able to keep calm in unusual situations, Mr. Argus," Traum said.

Confidence.

Rake stared ahead at Traum. "Okay, what do you want?"

Overconfidence.

The whispering started up again. Traum looked to his left and then to his right. The whispering stopped.

"We are looking to find a particular person," Traum said. "Do you know this boy?" Traum asked.

"What boy?" Rake responded.

Rake noticed that something was in his hand. He looked down to see a photograph.

"What the hell?" Rake said. "How did I get this?"

Amazement.

"Do you know this boy?" Traum repeated.

Rake looked at the photograph and nodded as Dave's eyes widened.

It was a picture of Todd.

"This loser? Yeah, Todd Mackio or something like that," Rake said, tossing the picture onto the ground.

"Correct, that is Todd Maggio," Traum said.

Rake shrugged. "So, you want me to kick his ass or something? Crap, you don't even need to ask me that. I was planning on doing that sometime this year."

"I'm afraid you misunderstand. I don't need you to find him in reality. I need you to find him here in the Dreamscape," Traum said.

Rake paused. "What, so I have to just find his hallway, right?"

"His pathway," Traum corrected.

"Yeah, whatever. Is that it? Why me then? You guys have eyes, right?"

The whispering started and stopped again.

"I am afraid it is not that easy. Mr. Maggio is an exile."

"An X-File? Like an alien?" Rake said, his eyes going wide.

Confusion.

"An exile," Traum repeated, enunciating each letter.

"Okay, what does that mean?"

"It means that Mr. Maggio is not allowed out of his dream and nobody is allowed in. He is cut off from the rest of the Dreamscape," Traum said.

Curiosity.

"Okay, so? Why do you need loser boy then? Is he your buddy or something?"

More whispers.

Fear. Slight, but there.

Traum slowly stood up. "No. I want his dream opened. I want it opened because I want his dreams as my own."

Traum wants Todd's dream? Dave thought. *Why? Why Todd? Just because he is an exile?*

Rake paused. "Oh crap, I remember the car telling me about this. You can take over somebody's dreams. But, Todd? Why would you want that loser's dream? So you can learn how to play Dungeons & Dragons better?"

Traum walked up to Rake, mere inches from his face. Rake tried to look straight into Traum's mask, but he ended up looking off to the side. Dave could feel Rake shivering slightly. He didn't need to even think about Rake's emotions. He knew that he was scared by the mere stare of Traum.

"Over the course of history, people have walked the Dreamscape. Nobody knows exactly how many dream walkers there are roaming around. It could be hundreds, it could be thousands, and it could be millions."

Traum continued, continually staring at Rake. "While there are many powerful dream walkers, every once in a while a dream walker arises that lives to only terrorize the entire Dreamscape. Whether they have a formal plan such as to rule the entire Dreamscape or simply doing it out of pure madness, they are nearly impossible to stop. They are called the Terrors."

"Terrors?" Rake asked.

Traum stopped speaking and stared at Rake in silence for a several seconds before continuing. "While all Terrors are eventually stopped or killed, usually when other powerful dream walkers band together to battle them, there are a few of these powerful Terrors that have learned to cheat death, albeit a half-life, by living eternally within the Dreamscape after their physical body had wasted away. They became, for all intents and purposes, immortal."

Curiosity again.

"Immortal?" Rake asked. "They'll never die?"

"Correct," Traum said.

"And Todd is one of these immortals?"

"No, he is something different."

"What is he?" Rake asked.

"Throughout history, there have been five known immortal terrors. I am sure there are more immortals than that, but only five terrors have become immortal. These five, for lack of a better term, are known as the Five Eternal Terrors, or just the Five Terrors. Luckily for the Dreamscape, each time a new Eternal Terror appeared, the Dreamscape survived. It could not kill the Terror, but it could seal it away. It did so by not only gathering many dream walkers to face it, but by also choosing a champion. It chose one whose mind was open and free and gave to its champion a piece of itself. While in the Dreamscape, this person is in fact, an avatar of the Dreamscape. He is the living embodiment of the Dreamscape itself."

Shock.

"Wait. Are you saying that Todd is this avatar thing?"

"That is what I believe," Traum said.

"Wait, but Todd is only fourteen years old. I'm no braniac, but it's not like he's been around for hundreds of years."

"Every time the avatar dies in real life, the Dreamscape chooses a new avatar who is sealed up within his or her own dream to make sure that they are safe until a new Terror arises or an old Terror emerges."

"So, what? Are you going to free a Terror to open up the dream?"

More whispers followed by more silence.

Dave stared at the six armored figures and then his eyes narrowed. "Or... are you planning on becoming a new Terror to get that pathway open?"

Traum spread his arms. "No one, at least no sane person, sets out to become a Terror. My goal is simple. I want to see what the Dreamscape sees. I want to feel what the Dreamscape feels. I want to know what it is to be in control of the hopes and desires of every living being."

Rake looked a Traum, not exactly sure what to say. The whispers began again and then went silent.

Fear.

"I-i-if you're not going to become the Terror thing, then how am I supposed to get into Maggio's dream?"

"It has been said that while the Dreamscape wants to prevent the avatar from getting out, in the end, it mainly wants to protect anybody else from getting in. However, if the avatar truly desires to emerge, it can."

Rake gave Traum a confused look. "But, how do we make Maggio... I mean, the avatar want to emerge?"

"By going after the things and people he cares about," Traum said without hesitation.

Rake smirked and nodded. "Calloway and his crew. That's where they come in."

"By threatening his dear friends, we can force Mr. Maggio to emerge from his rabbit hole. It is then that I will strike and claim his power for my own."

More whispers.

"But, how do you know that I won't just take Toddio for my-self?"

Traum leaned in closer. "I do not doubt that you will become a powerful dream walker. But, if he is truly the avatar, then you will be no more than a speck of dust on the floor to him."

"Oh come on. I can beat Todd."

Traum ignored him and sat back down his throne. "In reality, that might be. But in the Dreamscape, do not assume everybody is as they are in real life. Your dream will die a quick death if you underestimate a dream walker just because of who and what they are in reality."

"Wait a sec," Rake said. "How do you know that Todd's an avatar? Just because he's an exile?"

"I have my reasons," Traum said.

The knights began to whisper again and then went silent.

"What the hell is with the whispering?" Rake asked.

"In order to join with me, you must follow orders without ques-tion. However, I would be foolish to not listen to the opinions of those that serve."

"So, I get to tell you what to do if I ever become one of those guys?"

"Tell me? You will never tell me what to do, Rake, but if you earn a place as one of my Knights, I may listen to what you have to say."

"Whatever. Okay wait a minute. This avatar thing...you don't know for sure if Todd is this avatar thing, do you?" Rake said. "How long have you been searching for the avatar?"

"For many years now," Traum said.

"And you want me to help you? Why not just use these big guys here?" Rake said, pointing to the knights.

"Each knight performs a specific duty for me. We must prepare for the battle with the avatar, but also must continue our search for further exiles. But, you shall have aid in not only your mission, but also to train you to make sure that you are as powerful in the Dreamscape as you are in reality. You, Rake, will be a squire for the one that is called the Sleepless Knight."

The Sleepless Knight stepped forward and pulled out its sword, mere inches from Rake's face. Dave actually tried to flinch for him.

"Whoa, whoa, whoa!" Rake said, nearly tripping over his own feet.

Dave wanted to reach out and punch the Sleepless Knight, but he couldn't in Rake's body.

"You and the Sleepless Knight will venture forth. I want you to terrorize the friends of Todd Maggio. I want you to torture them. I want you to hurt them. I want you to take over their dreams to taunt his remaining friends with and to grow in power. I want you to force him to emerge from his cave so that I can absorb his essence and become one with the Dreamscape!" Traum said as the knights began whispering again.

The Sleepless Knight sheathed its sword and offered its hand to Rake.

Rake looked down at its hand and back to Traum.

Fear. Curiosity. Confidence. Terror. Overconfidence. Happiness.

"Terrorizing those losers in here, and it's never going to get me in trouble with teachers or the cops?" Rake smiled. "Sign me up."

Rake and the Sleepless Knight shook hands.

Dave's vision blurred as he found himself back at the campsite. As his limbs loosened, he watched as Eric kept trying to form something made out of green energy in his hands, but couldn't. Andy smirked, retracted his scythe blades and swung it at Eric's feet, knocking him to the ground.

"Damn it!" Eric yelled. "Screw this! This sucks!"

Bags bounded over to Eric and bit him on the flesh part of the arm.

"OW! What the hell, ferret?" Eric yelled.

289

"If you don't get this right, you're dead!" Bags yelled, walking up to Eric's face.

"I thought you said that we'd just lose our dreams!" Eric said.

Bags put his nose right on Eric's nose. "If you're some unimaginative idiot who has no dreams or hopes, then you know what? It probably won't matter much. But, just imagine if playing football brought you no joy because you have no dream about going pro sometime. Yeah, you've got no talent now, I know, but that's not what drives you. What drives you is the desire to be a great player. With no motivation, hopes, or dreams, how much longer do you really think you're going to play? It wasn't Mommy or Daddy who forced you to do this. You are doing this because you *want* to do this. You are doing this because you *hope* to win a game for your team. You are doing this because you *dream* about going professional. All of this is *gone* if the Sleepless Knight or any member of the Trauma Guild gets you."

Bags turned away and walked back over to Dave. Eric stayed on the ground as Bags' speech and its importance registered in his head. Andy, meanwhile, turned away and got Emma's whip snapped at his face. He raised his staff to block it, but the whip wrapped around the middle of the weapon. With a quick tug, Emma try to snatch it away, but Andy resisted as his scythes extended again.

"No use, Andy! I'm winning this one!" Emma said, smiling.

Andy smirked. "I don't think so!"

Suddenly, black goggles appeared where Andy's eyes were. His long hair became sharp and spiky. His black cloth trench coat turned to a tight black leather costume with buttons, hooks, and belts in random places.

"Holy crap! That's friggin' Andruseth!" Eric screamed, rolling to his side.

"Who?" Emma turned to ask.

Andy used that opportunity to twist the staff with his hands. The staff suddenly broke into two separate scythes, the whip falling harmlessly to the ground. He charged at Emma who quickly started backing away.

"I've got you now!" Andy yelled.

"Eek!" Emma squealed, laughing as she fell down. "You got me! You..."

Emma disappeared.

"What the hell?" Andy said as his costume reverted back to his original clothes. "I swear I didn't do anything."

Bags stepped forward. "Don't worry. She just woke up. It's just as well though. You kids are catching on... slowly, but catching on nonetheless, much quicker than dingus Dave over there. You just need to get some practice."

Dave stepped forward, ignoring Bags. "Andy... that was Andruseth! Cool!"

Eric got to his feet. "Dave, you saw that? That was awesome! How did you know to do that?"

Andy looked in the other direction, "Frank told me how to do that."

"The crab?" Dave asked.

"Yeah, the crab, do I know anybody else named Frank?"

"All right, shut the hell up, dumbasses," Bags said. "What did you find out, boy?"

Dave took a deep breath. "It's Todd. The Trauma Guild is after Todd."

"Todd? Seriously? They can have him!" Andy said, rolling his eyes.

"Todd... Todd Maggio?" Eric asked. "Why the hell would anybody want him?"

"Good question," Bags said. "Boy, would you care to answer?"

Dave stared at Bags. "Traum thinks Todd is the avatar of the Dreamscape. He wants to steal Todd's dream to gain his power."

"Oh, crap," Bags said.

Dave looked at Eric and Andy. "He's sent Rake and the Sleepless Knight after us to lure him out. He wants Todd to try and save us so that Traum will be able to go after him."

"Oh, crap," Bags said.

"What happens if Traum gets Todd's dream?" Andy asked.

Bags looked deep in thought.

"Bags!" Dave yelled.

The ferret looked up at the trio. "If Traum absorbs Todd's dream, we will have a Terror unlike we have never seen. We will have a Terror with the power of the Dreamscape. That kind of power in the wrong hands...he'll be unstoppable."

Bzzzzz

Dave opened his eyes.

Bzzzzz

Dave shut off his alarm and sat up.

It's Saturday. He wouldn't be able to talk with Mr. Laws about Gabriel and Krieger.

Bzzzzz

Dave remembered what Bags said to him before he absorbed Rake's dream. Any dream walker associated with Rake will know who took his dream.

Traum will know who took Rake's dream. He will know that I know his plans. He'll be coming for me, Dave realized. *He'll be coming for me as soon as possible. He'll be coming for me tonight.*

A Chance to Shine

Dave jumped out of the shower and started toweling off. As he was combing his hair, there was a knock on the door.

"Yeah?" he asked, covering up just in case his family did the knock and enter without waiting for an answer thing.

"I think someone was trying to call you or something," Nick said as he opened the door just enough to slip Dave's cell phone in.

Normally Dave would yell at Nick that he'd take it when he was finished in the bathroom, but today was different. Dave grabbed the phone and closed the door. There were several text messages:

EMMA
Did that really happen last night? Were u actually in my dream last night?

ANDY
If that really happened last night... Todd? Seriously?

ERIC
Be ready at 11 AM for the game.

Dave looked at the time on his cell phone. It was 10:45 AM. He rushed out of the bathroom and grabbed his gear along with a bottle of water and wolfed down a quick bowl of cereal.

"Don't eat so fast, David. I'm sure Eric's mother will wait," his mother said as his father noisily flipped to another page in the newspaper.

"Okay, Mom," Dave said as he tossed his dishes into the sink and slung his gear over his shoulder.

"We'll see you at the game. Good luck today," his father said from behind the paper as Dave left. "Remember our rule. If you fumble, you're out of the family."

Dave snagged the pile of newspaper sections to the left of his father and tossed them on the kitchen counter, just far enough away that his father would have to get up to get them. His father put down his paper, looked at the pile on the counter, and then continued to read.

"That's okay. I already took those into the bathroom with me," his father said. Dave looked down at his hands as if they had toxic waste on them.

"Dad, gross," Dave said, starting to laugh as his father did the same. His mother simply shook her head as Dave made his way outside.

It was fairly cold outside, probably close to freezing. He almost went back inside to grab something warmer to wear before the game, but opted to try to suck it up and deal with it.

He took out his phone and called Emma.

"Hi, sexy!" Emma said almost on the first ring.

"Hey!" Dave said, not having a proper comeback to that. "Are you coming to the game today?

"Against Somerset? Wouldn't miss it for the world!"

"Awesome. Can you do me a favor?"

"Can I make sure to not check out the other player's in your game today?" Emma said. "I'll try, but I'll make no guarantees."

Dave smiled and paused, trying to quickly think of a comeback. "I think I can make the guarantee that I won't be checking out their butts," Dave said, quickly continuing when Emma didn't laugh, "but anyway, can you take Todd and Andy to the game today?"

"Todd *and* Andy? Seriously? Todd would go nuts for the invite, but Andy, if we can get Andy to *come* to a football game, would probably kill Todd on the way over. Why?"

"Remember last night?"

There was silence over the phone for several seconds before Emma spoke. "Oh sweet! It was definitely real?! That's so awesome! Okay, I'll see about Andy, but why Todd?"

"Remember?"

"No, why Todd?"

"Oh yeah, you woke up before I talked about it. Todd's in the same situation that we're in. Maybe even worse."

"Todd? Oh, okay," she said, not really sounding like she was taking it seriously. "Listen, Davey, you and I can do sooooo many things if we can spend time together in the dream world."

"I know that, but..."

"Sooooo many things," she slowly said.

"I...I mean..."

Emma giggled. "I'll see what I can do with Andy and Todd, okay? Worst case scenario, look for me in your cheering section!"

"Uh, yeah. Thanks, Em!"

Dave hung up just as Eric's mother pulled her car up and Dave hopped in after putting his gear in the trunk.

Dave and Eric were silent for the first minute or two.

"So, do you think we'll actually get to play today?" Eric asked.

"Depends on whether those guys from yesterday are still out," Dave said. "And whether Weaver strangles you or not, of course."

"Yeah, how could I forget?"

The boys went silent again.

"Hey, Eric?" Dave asked.

"Yeah?"

"Last night. . . do you remember your dreams?"

Eric thought deeply for several seconds and then his eyes showed that he realized what Dave was trying to hint at.

"Oh crap, that was real?" Eric asked.

"Yeah, you let Emma attack you with the whip and Andy with the scythe."

"What are you boys talking about?" Eric's mother asked.

"Nothing, just Lord Battler stuff," Eric quickly responded.

"Oh," his mother responded and went back to listening to the radio.

"I called up Emma before you picked me up. She's going to try to get Andy and Todd to come to the game."

"She's going to actually get Andy to come to a football game?"

"Yeah."

"Andy Bays? The same guy who walked a half-mile to go home from my house and play on his Zeus rather than hang out with us to play some football in my backyard?"

"Yeah, that Andy. I'm figuring after the events of last night, Andy may want to stick a bit closer to us."

"Why? Is that Balm guy going to shank us or something in real life?" Eric said, as his mother's head almost turned completely around, giving Eric a very concerned look.

"Just a joke, Mom," he said as she continued to stare, "Seriously!"

His mother stared for a second, before turning around and swerving to avoid a car in the lane that she had drifted into.

"Traum?" Dave asked.

"Yeah, him."

"I don't know. I don't think so. If he wanted to, it's not like we know what he looks like. I guess that explains all of the masks that I've been seeing."

"Huh?"

"There are four people that I've met in the Dreamscape so far other than my guardian: Sleepless Knight, Gabriel the Angel, Krieger who's some creepy harvester..."

"Harvester?"

"Someone who just likes to take people's dreams."

"Oh."

"Annnnd Traum, head of the Trauma Guild. All masked. I can't figure out who they are. I don't know if they're people we know or not."

"All bad guys?"

"As far as I can tell, Gabriel isn't. The rest of them, definitely."

"Wait, could those masks be like a super hero identity thing?" Eric said, meeting his mother's eyes in the rear view mirror and shrugging to her.

"Exactly what I was thinking. They keep masked so that it's hard for anybody to get any retribution on them."

"But, what your ferret was telling us last night..."

"Dave, you have a ferret?" Eric's mother asked.

"Mom, we're talking about a game on the Zeus, okay?" Eric quickly said.

"Oh, sorry, I don't know what you boys are talking about anymore," his mother said.

"Anyway, your ferret," Eric continued.

"Bags."

"Right, Bags. He said that if a person takes over another person's dream, that the victor's name goes on the pathway thing. So, how can anybody hide?"

Dave looked out of the window. "I guess the masks are there just in case they try and fail. If they get away, there's no way that you can identify who they were."

"There's no way?"

"For all I know, the Sleepless Knight is you," Dave said, turning to face Eric.

"Dude...that sucks," Eric said. Dave turned back to the window as they arrived at school. "Is there anybody you can trust now?"

Dave thought about it for a minute, but could not think of anybody.

The team bus was already waiting for them when they climbed out of Eric's car. Most of the bus was already filled with players and gear, so Dave and Eric had to find seats on different ends of the bus.

Dave had to sit down next to the linebacker, Kurt Milardo, who shot him an irritated look before leaning over to talk to some of the defensive linemen behind him.

He noticed that there were still a few players missing, most notably all the same players who were missing yesterday. Dave stayed silent, but smiled to himself. He actually might get to play today.

His smile lasted for several minutes until the bus door opened and let in Cole Dutton. As he got on the bus, he stared down Eric. Eric met his glare for several seconds, before looking away.

Milardo turned around to see him. "Dutton? No crap, man, they let you back in?"

"Yeah, coach said something to the principal," Cole said as he made his way to the back of the bus. "Put me on prohibition if I turned in some paper before the game."

"You mean, probation?" Milardo asked.

"Huh?" Cole said, looking confused. "No, it was on the Prohibition."

Milardo started to say something, shut his mouth, and started to talk again. "Oh, who gives a crap? At least now we have a chance against Somerset," Milardo said. "Here, I saved you a seat."

Kurt was pointing to Dave's seat. Cole walked up to the seat right in front of Dave and stared him down.

"Calloway. Get out of my seat," Cole said.

Dave looked up at Cole and fought the urge to start a fight.

"Why don't you get your own seat, Cole?" Eric said from the front of the bus.

Milardo stood up. "That has to be Graham defending his boyfriend."

Cole turned around and started making his way down the bus to go after Eric. Just at that second, the bus door opened and let in Coach Weaver.

"Dutton, take a seat," Weaver said, trying to defuse the situation.

Cole looked down at a seat and back at the coach.

"Coach, isn't the bus driver going to get mad if I take one of his seats?" Cole asked.

The coach looked at Cole, trying to figure out if he was joking, but just shook his head. "Cole, sit down."

Dave had already used the opportunity to switch seats, sitting with one of the tight ends. Cole turned around and saw the open seat with Milardo and sat down.

"Okay team, we've got a little news. I managed to broker a little deal with the principal and we will be getting at least some of our players back for today's game as long as they turned in some extra credit project or something. Any rate, they're on probation and have to get their grades up ASAP to play after this week, but the principal knows how important this Somerset game is."

Dave's heart sank. With most of the team being there was little to no hope of him playing.

"Here's the other piece of news. As you know, our quarterback, Michael Everway, got hurt in practice yesterday. Unfortunately, it looks like the arm is broken, so Everway is done for the season. However, before you get all pissy and moany, our backup QB, Tony Krantz, will be starting today. Tony's a hell of a QB so don't go and think that the season is lost. This is a new beginning for our team and it begins by crushing Somerset! YOU GOT ME?"

The team screamed in agreement.

*
*   *

"...and Milardo with the tackle. It's now third down with four yards to go. Coach Weaver calls a timeout. That's their final timeout. Somerset is on Carter Middle School's forty-five yard line with not much time left on the clock. If Somerset gets a first down here, the game is over. Carter needs a stop here."

As the announcer stopped talking over the PA system, Dave looked up at the scoreboard. 24–20, Somerset was leading. Tony had played brilliantly for somebody who was starting his very first game, spreading his passes around to every receiver on the field, not just Michael's favorites, Bullington and Grasso. Not sure who to defend, the Somerset defense decided that rather than trying to figure out who Tony was passing to, that they'd just go after Tony time and time again. After the third sack in the first half and being down 17–3, coach Weaver decided to run plays around short passes which took advantage of Somerset's aggressive tactics. Carter ended up tying the score at 17 by the end of the third quarter, but now with so little time left and being down by four points, it didn't look good.

"Well, at least we're not going to lose by much this time," Eric said as Dave rolled his eyes.

Dave saw Pat Kimmel, one of the starting defensive tackles come over after the last play and lay down on the grass, clutching his calf. The trainer quickly went over and started working on his leg. Weaver took a look down at Kimmel and then down at his clipboard.

"Graham, get your ass up here!"

Dave looked at Eric who didn't even notice that he was called.

"Graham, are you deaf?" the coach called again.

Eric looked over at the coach and as soon as they made eye contact, he realized what was happening. He put on his helmet and jogged over to the coach who grabbed him by his facemask.

"You're going in for Kimmel. They're going to try to run this ball right down your throat. If they do, I want you to take that ball and spit it into their backfield. No one gets by you and no one pushes you around, you got me!"

"Yes coach!" Eric yelled.

300

"That's my boy!" Coach Weaver said, slapping him on top of the helmet. "Now get in there!"

Eric made his way onto the field and into the huddle. Milardo rolled his eyes.

"Is Weaver serious?" Kurt said. "Crap. All right guys, what do you think?"

Cole smirked. "Four-three kill the guy with the ball?"

Kurt nodded. "I like the plan. Let's hope Graham doesn't screw it up for us."

The team broke the huddle and lined up.

Eric lined up against one of the most massive guys he had ever seen. It's not like the guy was muscular. It was all just mass, mostly fat.

Somerset's quarterback took the ball. As he did, the fat lineman slammed into Eric, pushing him over to the left, opening up a huge gap. The quarterback handed off to his running back who headed toward the gap.

All Somerset needed was three yards... nine feet... one hundred-eight inches... and the game would be over.

The running back reached the gap. Just as he did, Eric freed himself from the lineman and dove at the ball carrier, managing to get a hand around his ankle. Eric dove and managed to get a hand around the running back's ankle. While it wasn't enough to bring the guy down, it caused him to stumble. Waiting for him was Milardo and Dutton. Milardo grabbed him high while Dutton did the same, but lower, putting his helmet right on the ball. The ball popped out and hit the ground. One of the Somerset players tried to pick it up, but it squirted out of his hands and rolled along the ground, right next to Eric. As soon as he saw it near him, he reached out and grabbed it, pulling it close to his body. The big lineman lumbered over to try to get it for himself, but Milardo, recovering from the tackle attempt smashed into the lineman, knocking him off his feet.

The referee saw that Eric had possession of the ball and gave the signal that it was the Cougar's ball.

The entire bench erupted in cheers as did the Cougar fans that made the trip to Somerset. The whole team surrounded Cole, Kurt, and Eric as they made their way to the bench. Dave got up to congratulate Eric, but was grabbed by the arm by Tony who dragged him over to the coach.

"Coach, we've got maybe two plays left, but we need a touchdown."

"No crap, Krantz, so get in there and kick some ass!"

"Coach, I know that we've got players with more experience, but we don't have anybody who is as fast as this guy here," Tony said, motioning toward Dave.

"Calloway? He's fast, but I'm not going to put in someone who hasn't played in a game yet when the damn game's on the line."

"All I want him to do is run straight. Nothing trickier than that. We'll still have Bullington and Grasso in if he can't get open."

The coach breathed deeply and stared into Tony's eyes. "It's your ass if he screws up."

Tony smiled. "Hey, when have I ever let you down?" Tony said as he slapped Dave's back, and they both jogged onto the field.

"Today wouldn't be a good place to start!" The coached yelled to them.

As Tony and Dave jogged over to the huddle, Dave looked over at the quarterback. "Why me?" he asked.

"What? You think I was joking about your speed? These bozos on Somerset are going to be tired. You'll pass them in an instant," Tony said.

"Well, no, but still! I mean, all I've done is catch a couple of passes in practice."

"Hey, the way that I'm thinking is that Somerset knows that Bullington and Grasso are the go-to guys. They don't know you at all. You go in, you run straight. Worst-case scenario, you pull a ton of guys to follow you and that'll give Bullington and Grasso a shot. Best case? They pretty much ignore you and if that happens, trust me...we win."

Tony and Dave huddled up and called the play. Bullington would get the ball about twenty yards down the field unless Dave was wide open.

"What? Calloway? Seriously? He ain't as fast as I am," Grasso said.

"Are you talking about on the field or alone with a picture of Dutton's mom?" Tony said

The players laughed, even Grasso.

"Listen, I'm not going to talk about how even if we lose we win or some cheesy crap about teamwork, sooooo let's just win, all right?" Tony said as the other players nodded.

"Cougars on three!" Tony yelled as the team put their hands together.

"One... two... three!"

"COUGARS!!"

The team broke the huddle and lined up.

Both sides' fans, cheering like crazy while they were in the huddle, began to quiet down.

Dave saw that the defender covering him was a good ten yards away. The defender didn't care about giving up ten yards. He wanted to make sure that he didn't give up a bigger play.

Tony called the hike and Dave took off. The defender initially just jogged back a few steps to keep pace with him, but his eyes widened as Dave's speed easily outpaced his own. Tony looked to Bullington but saw that he was well covered. He turned and saw that Dave had the defender beat by several steps and launched the ball into the air. The safeties on Somerset saw the ball get thrown and realized it was going nowhere near Bullington or Grasso. They ran as fast as they could to catch up with Dave.

Dave saw the ball descending, slowing down slightly or he was going to overrun the ball completely. He reached out, opened his hands, and caught the ball. He sped back up, heading for the end zone.

He reached the fifteen-yard line.

He reached the ten-yard line.

He reached the five-yard line.

It was at the one-yard line that one of the safeties caught up with him and dragged him down just short of the end zone. Dave looked up as the referee was already setting up a ball for the next play. He heard Tony screaming from behind.

"Get up Calloway!"

The safety got off Dave as Tony gave the signal that he was going to spike the ball, giving up the next play to stop the clock so that they could have time to plan for one more play. As the team lined up, Dave—completely out of breath—got to his feet, lined up, and looked to Tony for him to spike the ball. From the corner of his eye, he noticed one of the defensive linemen was wobbly, like he was out of breath just from running down the field. Dave was tired from his sprint down field, but he was used to running. A gigantic lineman though? He must be exhausted.

Unfortunately for the defensive lineman, Tony, as well as the Carter Cougars' center, Jessie Cicero, saw it as well.

Tony called the hike and faked the spike. As he did, Jessie lunged out and knocked the tired lineman off his feet. Tony then followed Jessie and the opening he had created and ran untouched into the end zone as the clock expired.

"TOUCHDOWN COUGARS! THE COUGARS WIN THE GAME, 26–24!!!" the announcer yelled.

The entire team as well as the entire Cougar fan base erupted in cheers as they ran onto the field.

Eric ran over to Dave and slapped his helmet.

"We won!! We beat Somerset!!" Eric screamed.

"We beat Somerset!" Dave screamed back as he tore off his helmet.

Suddenly, someone grabbed him from behind and put him in a headlock.

"I told you!" Tony said, grinding him in the headlock. "I told you that putting you in was a good idea!"

He let go as the offensive line picked up Tony and paraded him around the field in celebration.

"All right, I have to admit, that was kind of neat," Andy said as he, Emma, and Todd reached Dave and Eric in the middle of all this chaos. Emma put her arms around him, a bright smile on her face.

"Congratula—" Emma was cut off by Dave's kiss.

The friends stood there awkwardly for several seconds as the kiss continued.

"Well...okay," Eric said, turning away.

"Aw, let them be," Todd said.

"Why are you here again?" Andy asked.

"Emma invited me, why?" Todd said.

"Whatever...doesn't matter," Andy said. "Anyway, Eric, I have to admit, fighting off that two tons of terror guy—that was pretty sweet."

"Yeah, I thought the dude was going to knock me down and eat me!" Eric said.

Dave and Emma broke their kiss. Emma's face was completely red. Smiling and bright eyed, but completely red-faced.

"WHOOO!" Dave yelled, feeling the adrenaline.

"Yeah, I second that!" Eric yelled. "WHOOO!"

"WHOOO!" Todd yelled.

"Aw hell," Emma said. "WHOOO!"

Andy looked around as his friends smiled and looked at him, "Whooo?"

They all laughed.

"Ah, Andy...so energetic...so passionate," Dave said.

"Whatever," Andy said, waving it off. "So, what's the plan?"

Dave put his arms around the shoulders of Eric and Andy and had Emma and Todd lean in, listening to the other players cheering.

"Tonight," Dave said, "meet at Eric's place. We're taking down the Sleepless Knight... and if he's there, we're taking down Traum as well."

"Cool!" Todd said. "Lord Battler it is then!"

As the friends looked at Todd, Dave thought, *Does he even know? Does he even know that he's being targeted by the Trauma Guild? Does he even know that he's an exile? Does he even know that he may be the avatar of the Dreamscape? What does he know?*

Dave tried to put those thoughts behind him. He wanted to take this moment in. His team won, and he had played a huge part in that victory.

*
* *

Dave threw open the door to his house and dropped his gear in the entryway. As soon as he turned to close the door, Nick ran down the stairs.

"Dave, Mom and Dad are taking us to see Grueber tonight!" Nick said, his whole face lighting up.

Dave smiled. "The vampire movie? Sweet, but I've got plans tonight."

Nick frowned. "Aw, come on!"

"It's going to be just as good without me," Dave said, slapping his brother on the back.

The sound of a newspaper rustling came from the kitchen. "How did you do today?" his father asked.

Dave walked into the kitchen to see his father reading the paper while his mother did the crossword puzzle.

"We won! We beat Somerset!" Dave said as the adrenaline rush returned.

"Wow, that's the team that always kicks your butt, right? Did you play?" his father asked.

"Not only did I play, but I'm the guy who set us up for the winning touchdown," Dave said, rolling his head as if he was working out some kinks in his neck.

"You didn't score?" his father said, disappointed.

"No... not this time," Dave said.

"Slacker," his father said, hiding a laugh by drinking from his coffee mug.

His mother looked up from the crossword puzzle. "And why aren't you coming tonight?"

"Um, because we won. My friends and I are going to celebrate."

"Like, a party?" his mother said, squinting her eyes at him.

"Lisa, I'm sure he'll have booze and sugar cubes laced with LSD," his father said, rolling his eyes. "Let him go out with his friends."

"Steven, this is a family outing," his mother said.

"It's Saturday and we're just going to a movie. If he wants to hang out with his friends, let him hang out with his friends," his father said as he turned to Dave. "But, Dave, you owe your mother one."

Dave nodded. "Sure, whatever."

"Fine," his mother said, smiling. "Tomorrow, you and I are going clothes shopping for winter clothes."

Dave looked on the floor, trying to think of a way out of it.

"Ouch!" his father said. "Oh well, Dave. I bet movie night with the family is looking pretty darn good right now!"

Dave grimaced at his father. "I... sure... but..."

"Sorry, pal, you made your choice. You chose to get tortured by your mother tomorrow rather than spend time watching a scary movie with her tonight," his father said, barely holding back a laugh while drinking his coffee.

Dave tried to think of something witty, but before he could, his mother stood up and went to the sink to wash out her coffee mug.

"Ten o'clock tomorrow morning. Sweaters and slacks," his mother smirked.

As soon as it started to get dark, Dave made his way over to Andy's house. Andy opened the door decked out in his black trench coat, black pants, and black shirt. Andy's true self was definitely back.

"Hold up a sec, I've gotta grab my memory card. I've been playing ULB since we got home and I want to show you guys what I've opened up in the game."

"And how has dear Andruseth been?"

"Crappy, actually. They changed some of the combo moves from before. So, the stuff that Andruseth was good at in Lord Battler isn't that good in Ultimate Lord Battler."

"You didn't change anything?"

"No, why would I?"

"You didn't, you know, experiment with some of the new stuff?"

"Meh, I'll get to that once I beat the game with Andruseth,"

"Oookay, whatever."

Andy went over to his Zeus and grabbed the memory card.

"All right, let's go," Andy said.

As they walked down the street, they talked about some of the things Andy had discovered in Ultimate Lord Battler. But, in the end, it was just random small talk for Dave. He kept thinking about what could possibly happen tonight.

"And so after you beat the second boss, all of these shops, training halls, and side quests come up and..."

"Hey, Andy, what do you remember about when your dream was taken over?" Dave interrupted.

"Like, how it happened?"

"Yeah."

"Welllll, I'll do my best. Uh, I remember fighting some weird teddy bear creature in school. I—"

"That was the night before."

"No, that was the night that..."

"Trust me, Andy, I was there. You were eaten by a big teddy bear."

"Oh...oh yeah."

"S'okay. If it makes you feel any better, I was eaten as well," Dave said.

"Really? Aren't you supposed to be trained to dream fight or whatever it's called?"

"It was like my second day or something like that. Besides, Bags was showing me a lot more stuff than just fighting. I wouldn't have found you guys if he was just showing me fighting."

"Whatever," Andy said. "Anyway, so it was the lake thing, right?"

"Yeah, the lake thing."

"So, if I'm remembering right, I just took down the bear freak."

"Well, it was me who took it down, but no big deal," Dave said.

"That's not what I remember, but whatever. So, you and I took down the bear, but then you disappeared and I was left alone with Frank."

"Yeah, your blue crab dream guardian."

"Yeah, him. So, pretty much as soon as Frank introduced himself, WHAM, something struck me right in the back and knocked me on my ass. Felt like somebody just clubbed me in the back. I looked up and there's a two-headed baseball bat coming for my head," Andy said, rubbing the back of his head.

"Dude...that's brutal,"

"Yeah, next thing I know in my dreams, I'm walking out into the middle school gym with you."

Dave stopped walking as Andy kept moving. "You do know that if I could have, I would have stopped him."

Andy walked several steps in silence. "Yeah, I know. It doesn't change the fact that Rake had my dreams, even if just for a little while."

Dave looked down at the moonlit street, breathed deeply, and walked faster to catch up with his friend.

The two friends went around to the back of Eric's house and opened the sliding glass door. Eric was in there watching a college football game.

"'Sup?" Eric asked without turning around from his couch.

Andy and Dave walked into the room, Andy sitting in his usual chair, and Dave plopping down on the couch with Eric.

"Can we toss in Lord Battler?" Andy asked.

"Noooot yet. Lemme finish watching this," Eric said, pointing to the television.

Andy sat back in his chair, not taking his coat off.

"Where's Emma?" Dave asked. "I talked to her earlier and she said that she was on her way.

"Upstairs with my sister."

"Cynthia?" Andy asked, sitting forward.

"Yeah, do I have another one?"

"Hey, why didn't Siiiiin-thia show up to the game?" Dave asked.

"Mom was pissed. Apparently she flunked some test," Eric said, dunking a chip in some salsa and stuffing it into his mouth.

"Hey," Andy said, turning toward Dave. "Why didn't we bring Cyn into this whole dream thing? Isn't she in danger?"

Eric put in the effort to turn his head towards Andy. "Do you think anybody wants to mess with my sister if they get her angry?"

"The Trauma Guild has gone after only the people in this room so far, but that doesn't mean that they won't go after her," Dave said as he heard the basement door open and people coming down the stairs. "But for now, Traum is going to know that I took Rake's dream. Unless Traum is an idiot, he'll realize that I can figure out what his plans are. That means that Traum is going to have to come after me as soon as possible."

"Who's coming after you?" Cynthia said, coming down the stairs with Emma.

"Nothing, Cyn," Eric said.

"Let me guess. Something that Andy got on the Zeus?" Cynthia said.

Andy looked at Cynthia and reached over to the game case for Ultimate Lord Battler and starting reading the instructions.

"So, anybody know when Todd is showing up?" Dave said.

"I told him to be here about sevenish," Emma said, looking at her watch. "It's seven now, so aaaannny minute."

Andy tossed the instruction manual back onto the table, looking agitated. "Come on, Eric, let's put in the game."

"Dude, wait a few minutes!"

Andy's leg was bouncing as if he was nervous about something. He looked down at the game case again and then back at Cynthia. Andy quickly stood up, took Cynthia by the hand, and led her outside, closing the sliding glass door behind them.

Eric turned his head away from the game to look at the two talking just on the other side of the door.

"Holy crap, what's he doing?" Eric asked.

"I dunno," Dave said.

"Oh come on, guys," Emma said. "He's got to be apologizing to her."

"Seriously? I don't want him with her!" Eric said.

"Aw, playing the big brother part tonight is Eric Graham!" Emma said as Dave let out a loud laugh.

Andy hadn't let go of Cynthia's hand as they kept talking in low voices.

"I think I can make out what they're saying," Dave said.

"Ahem, so can I," Eric cleared his throat, trying to do his best Andy impression. "Oh dearest Cynthia, I completely forgot that I'm a total loser whose best hope for getting some this century before I met you was the fat and smelly dude from the message board on the Zeus page that claims he's a hot sixteen-year-old chick. Please, I beg of you. . . take me back! Without you, I suck!"

Dave started to clap, but Emma jumped in. "Oh Andy, you are so hot and manly with your black on black outfit and complete lack of emotion as well as your desire to do nothing but sit at home and play video games. Please come upstairs and make a woman out of me!"

"Hey, that's my sister!" Eric yelled.

"It's...oh wow!" Emma said, pointing to the window. "That's your sister making out with our goth-boy!"

Eric stood up and turned around.

Andy and Cynthia were lip locked, Andy still holding onto Cynthia's hand. After a few seconds of kissing, Todd rounded the corner from outside.

"Hey guys!" Todd said, loudly enough to be heard through the door.

Andy gave Todd an angry look and nodded his head towards the door.

"When did you guys get back together?" Todd asked.

"Todd, go the hell away!" Andy said, opening the door.

As the door opened, Dave and Emma began clapping.

"Andy, dude, we're playing Ultimate Lord Battler now," Eric said, turning on the Zeus.

Andy, Cynthia, and Todd walked into the room. From the look of Cynthia's makeup, she had been crying.

"Cyn, you okay?" Emma asked.

Cynthia rubbed her eyes a bit. "What? This? Oh, yeah, everything's fine. Listen, my mom's going to kill me if I don't get back to my room. So, um..."

Andy kissed her again. After a few seconds, she pulled away, smiled at Andy, waved goodbye to everybody, and went upstairs.

Dave slapped him on the back. "Good job."

"Yeah...I know," Andy said, grabbing a controller and putting his memory card into the Zeus.

"Okay, okay, okay, let's play," Eric said. "I want to burn the image of my sister kissing somebody out of my head."

"Can I create a character with you guys?" Todd asked.

"Do you even know how?" Andy snapped back.

"Dude, chill," Dave said. "Todd knows. Come on over."

Todd pulled up a chair and grabbed a controller. "Cool, I've been planning out a sweet character for ULB."

As Todd starting creating his character, Dave watched him.

"Hey Todd, random question for you," he said.

"Yeah, what is it?" Todd said, stopping his character creation.

"Dude, you don't have to stop, keep going. I want to actually play tonight." Andy said, impatiently as Todd kept creating his character.

Dave glared at Andy who just shrugged it off.

"Todd, do you remember your dreams?" Dave asked.

"Yeah! I had a sweet one yesterday that I was in school and the principal was telling me to take these pills or else I'll never get rid of the measles. So I took them and it turned out that I was the only one to do it and everybody else died."

"That's sweet?" Eric asked.

"I woke up and put it in my journal. It's a cool idea! I mean, nobody trusted the pills, but I took them and survived."

"Even the principal died?" Eric asked.

"Well, sorta. The principal turned into a two-headed demon with violin strings for arms, but whatever. I beat him by convincing measles that the demon was the real enemy. Then it ate him."

"What ate him?" Eric asked.

"The measles."

"The measles ate the principal?"

"Yep. Like I said, pretty sweet!" Todd said.

Todd finished his character and chose his archenemy—some undead woman floating in mid-air with a noose around her neck.

"Sick! Do you see her?" Todd said, pointing to the screen.

"Yeah, yeah, we see her," Andy said.

"Todd, one other question. Does the word *exile* mean anything to you?" Dave asked.

Todd looked at Dave. "Do I know what it means?"

"In your dreams, I mean."

"Uh, no. Should I?" Todd asked.

"How about Traum?"

"Nope."

"Avatar?"

"Nope," Todd said as Eric chowed down on more chips, and Andy glared at Todd impatiently.

"Dreamscape?"

"Uh, nope."

"Sleepless Knight?" Dave said, trying anything to get Todd to tell him something about the Dreamscape.

"Like from Lord Battler?"

"Yeah."

"In my dream?"

"Yeah, have you ever seen or heard of it in your dream?"

"Uh...nope."

Dave looked at Andy and Eric.

Eric leaned over towards Todd. "What captain butthead is trying to ask is...can you go into somebody else's dream?"

Todd looked over at Eric. "What? Go into somebody else's dream? I wish! We all could go on some adventures!"

"Yeah, wouldn't that be a joy," Andy said.

"Yeah!" Todd said, raising his voice.

"He doesn't know anything, guys," Emma said. "Leave him alone."

"What a surprise. Todd's not the answer," Andy said.

Todd put down the controller. "What's going on? Why all the questions?"

Dave looked over at Todd. "Todd, this is going to sound weird, but tonight someone might be coming into your dream."

"What? Really? Cool! Why?" Todd said.

He didn't even question it, Dave thought.

"Someone believes that you're something you're not," Dave said. "And he will do anything to get to you."

Todd's eyes widened. "So... so, what do I do?"

"I don't care if you see something cool or weird. If you see something that's out of the ordinary, you run. Just get away, okay?"

"Uh, okay. But, how do you know it's going to happen?" Todd asked

Dave looked over at Emma who shrugged. "Don't worry about how I know. Just remember, run first. Okay?" Dave said.

Todd looked around the room. "Sure, I'll run, but only because you warned me to."

Around ten-thirty that evening, Eric's mother came downstairs and told everybody that it was time to go home. The friends watched as Todd's parents picked him up, and they waited for Emma's parents to show up.

"Guys, listen up," Dave said. "We've got to be ready for them tonight, okay?"

"Yeah, but how?" Emma asked.

"Yeah, what do you want us to do?" Andy asked.

"Safety in numbers is my plan. With four of us, even if we're not experts, maybe we stand a chance."

"All right, I can do that. After all, I'm the expert in the group," Eric said, smiling.

"Hey, if you can do to the Sleepless Knight or Traum what you did to Everway, there's NO contest."

"Damn right!" Eric said.

"So, what do we do? Where do we meet?" Andy asked.

"Meet in my dream," Dave responded.

"How?" Andy asked.

"Look for a door somewhere in your dream that has my name on it. It should be a door that you usually would never go into or is a bit out of the way. It could be the girls' bathroom if you're a guy or maybe it's the men's bathroom if you're a girl. Maybe it's a port-a-potty."

"Is it always a bathroom?" Eric asked.

Dave laughed. "Not always. Remember that we came through a tent last night."

Eric nodded, remembering the events of last night.

"If you don't see my name, but you see somebody else's name from this group on a door, chances are my name is nearby. Do this as soon as you fall asleep."

"Got it. But then what?" Andy said.

"What do you mean?" Dave asked.

"Do we go find Traum and the Sleepless Knight?"

Dave thought about it. "I don't know where they are."

"Then what do we do?"

"We wait. We wait for them to come to us," Dave said. "Yeah, that's what we're going to do. If they could have gotten Todd before, they would have. That means that they need us for some reason. So, we wait. They're going to have to come to us."

Dave looked out into the night as it lit up with the headlights of Emma's mother's car.

"And when they come, we're going to pay the Trauma Guild back for every last bit of pain they've given us."

When Dave got home he stood in the hallway on the second floor. He stopped before he entered his bedroom and listened. His parents were watching TV in their room, usually some sketch show that they loved watching on Saturday night. He smiled as he listened at his little brother's door and could only hear the occasional sounds from his Poseidon, a handheld game system. He wasn't supposed to play it after he was in bed, but what his parent's didn't know didn't hurt them.

Dave went into his bedroom, lay down on his bed, and thought about what he said before he left Eric's. *It was time to pay the Trauma Guild back for every last bit of pain. But, do we have a chance against them?*

True Intentions

David opened his eyes and saw that he was standing at the front door to his middle school. It was unbearably hot, hotter than any summer day he could remember. Within a few seconds, Dave began to sweat.

"School again?" Dave said aloud, wiping his brow.

Something looked a bit different though. He looked to his left and then to his right. The standing door was all that was left of the school besides piles of rubble where the walls should have been. Behind him was a parking lot full of buses and cars, most of them wrecks or at very least, missing their windows.

"What happened here?" Dave said, slowly making his way over to the parking lot.

Looking into the first car, he jumped back. There was a skeleton in there staring back at Dave, one hand on the steering wheel.

Suddenly, a shape jumped out of the car and landed on his shirt, digging with its claws into Dave's chest. He screamed as he fell and slapped whatever it was off of him. As he knocked it away, he felt the familiar feeling of fur.

"Bags! I swear, I'm going to kill you!" Dave said as the ferret snickered and ran underneath another car.

"Yeah right. What, do you need to warm up for your execution?" Bags said from behind a tire.

"My execution? Positive reinforcement, Bags, I can always count on you for that."

"Hey, what are little furballs good for anyway?"

Dave pointed to the cars and to the school. "What happened?"

Bags bowed his head. "This is what happens if you don't save it."

Dave looked down at the ferret. "It? Huh?"

"The diamond."

"Who?"

"You know... the blue diamond," Bags said.

"What blue diamond? You're not making any sense!"

"Saving the blue diamond is what you'd normally be doing in this dream if you weren't going to charge off after ol' SK," Bags said, poking his head out from behind the tire. "But, you and your friends have illusions of grandeur and are off to take on the Trauma Guild. So, I guess it doesn't matter."

"Bags, get serious!" Dave said, squatting down and look at the ferret.

"You expect, dingbat Eric, darkity-dark-dark Andy, and itty-bitty girly-girl Emma to take on *at least* the Sleepless Knight and possibly even the rest of the Trauma Guild, *including* Lord Traum?"

"We're going to try. That's all we can do, right? I mean, there's always a chance we could do it," Dave said.

Bags looked up at Dave and walked out from under the car. "Good. That's what I wanted to hear. Never be too afraid to try and never be too confident that you think you can't be beaten. No one is unbeatable. Even the Terrors know that much."

Suddenly, a car alarm in the middle of the parking lot sounded. Dave looked down at Bags and then took off running toward the alarm. Dave summoned his fire sword into his hand. As they made it over to the alarm, Dave smiled as he saw Andy looking at the noisy

319

car. Andy looked at Dave and then back at the car. He shook his head and kicked the tires.

"Stupid car. I didn't realize that when I went through the door to the room that had all the putters for Ted's Mini-Golf that I'd be crawling out the trunk of a car."

"Dude, I know. I've seen some weird stuff too," Dave said, slapping his friend on the back.

Bags bounded over, climbing up on the hood of a nearby car.

"You boys wanna do something about the noise? It's giving me a piercing headache," Bags said.

"What? You mean destroy the car?" Dave asked.

"Or cut the alarm, whatever," Bags said.

"Destroying it would be more fun, I have to admit," Andy said.

"But, wouldn't that wreck your Pathway?" Dave asked.

"Like I was planning on going back there tonight," Andy said as he pulled his staff from behind his back.

"Riiiiight," Dave said as he raised his sword.

Bags just shook his head. "You dumb pieces of... listen, weapons are all good, but do you really think that *just* weapons are going to help tonight? You can attack with weapons anytime. This time, I just want you to be more creative in your... well, in your destruction. No sword, no freaky looking staffs of death. I want you boys to destroy this with... well, pure imagination."

"Like what?" Dave asked.

Bags stayed silent and walked away.

"Seriously, what do you mean?" Andy asked.

Bags looked back at them but just shook his head.

"Okay okay. That car alarm is pretty annoying," Dave said.

"Yeah, loud and obnoxious," Andy said. "Kinda like Eric."

"Heh, so let's treat this car like we would Eric," Dave said, smiling.

Andy chuckled. "That might be a bit too painful,"

"Nothing's too good for *our* friend!" Dave said. "He isn't watching, is he?"

Andy laughed and shook his head.

"All right, how do we beat up Eric?" Dave asked.

"Well, first we have to make him shut the hell up!" Andy said.

Dave imagined the car alarm to be a small speaker in his car. It made sense to him that a security feature in the car would be hooked up to this small speaker hidden somewhere in the car. He imagined this small speaker melting and turning into a big puddle of ooze.

The constant whining from the alarm became distorted and then stopped.

Andy shot Dave a confused look. "Did you do that?" he asked.

"I think I did actually. That alarm is just a big pile of sludge now."

"Cool, wanna crush the car now?"

Before Dave could say anything, the door to the car next to them threw open and Eric slid his way out, covered in some kind of green slime. Dave and Andy ran over to Eric and pulled him to his feet.

"Ugh, this is friggin' disgusting!" Eric said, wiping the slime from his face.

"What the heck is it?" Dave said, wiping his hands on the car next to him.

"Hell if I know. I was on some television set and some kooky chick was asking me questions that I didn't know about and suddenly WHAM! I'm covered in green slime."

"Seriously, you're... you're disgusting!" Andy said as Eric wiped the slime out of his hair.

"You're telling me?" Eric said, flicking slime at Andy and getting some of it on his shoulder.

"Gross!" Andy said, quickly wiping it off.

"Guys! Chill!" Dave said. "The car alarm is off and we have Eric. All we need now is Emma. Let's look around for Emma's pathway."

"Okay, how do we do that?" Andy said. "Any tricks you want to show us?"

Dave looked down at Bags who just smiled back at him, not saying anything. "Bags? Wanna tell us?"

Bags smiled and shook his head.

"Looooks like no. No tricks. We're going car to car. Let's split up," Dave said, moving to the next car over after faking a kick motion to the ferret.

"Hey, what if the Sleepless Knight attacks us while we're split up?" Eric asked.

"Eric, we're not going to be far away. Just scream like a girl like you usually do," Andy said, walking over to another car.

"Guys, enough. Just look for a car with Emma's name on the door of it, okay," Dave said.

Dave then thought the worst.

"Hey guys," Dave said. "If you see Emma's name, but it's crossed off and there's some other person's name underneath, don't touch the door, okay?"

"Why?" Eric asked.

"Because that means we've already lost her," Dave said, looking down as he moved onto the next car.

As the three spread out, Bags climbed up on the roof of the car that Dave was inspecting.

"You know, boy," Bags said, leaping onto the next car, "one of those two could still be the Sleepless Knight."

Dave looked up at Bags and then back down at the car. "I know, I know, but what do you want me to do? I can't assume that they're evil. Well, the bad kind of evil, I mean. Andy's goth-evil. Kind of different."

"Andy can't be evil-evil?"

"Well, I guess he could, but come on, he let himself be captured? Why would he do that?"

"To lure you into a false sense of security?"

"Come on, Bags, now you're talking like an idiot."

"Am I? Crap, you must be rubbing off on me."

"Seriously, the knight could have taken me out a long time ago. Why the con?"

"You're looking at me like I know what the Trauma Guild is up to! Why the hell do people travel in between dreams... why the hell do people harvest... why did the Terrors do what they did? You know why? It's because people walk in all shapes, sizes, and personalities. Whoever the knight is, they must have a reason why they didn't constantly come after you day after day. I mean, if they didn't get you on day one then why not get you on day two?"

"I don't know. I really don't know," Dave said.

"It's either because it was a completely random harvester walking into your dream or you've got somebody who is playing games with you. Based on the fact that the knight has gone after you multiple times, I'll bet all the fur on my back that it's someone playing games."

"Either way, I'm not going to assume that my friends are the enemy."

"Fine, don't assume, but don't drop your guard around them, you got it?"

"Yeah, I got it," Dave said.

"FOUND IT!" Eric screamed from the other side of the parking lot.

Dave, Andy, and Bags made their way quickly to a large red minivan. Dave quickly looked at the name. Written in nice cursive writing was:

EMMA ASHFORD

Dave breathed in and turned to his friends. "Guys, it's game time," he said. "Get ready. It could just be that Emma can't find the pathway. But we have to go in for her just in case she's in danger."

Andy nodded and concentrated. In a burst of black lightning, Andy transformed himself into Andruseth, pulling the double scythe staff from his back.

Eric smiled, closed his eyes, concentrated, and...nothing happened.

Andy rolled his eyes. "Dude, stay here. You're going to be useless in there."

"What?!" Eric said, looking from Andy to Dave.

Dave slapped Eric on the shoulder. "Andy might be right. Listen, come with us to Emma's dream, but stay back by the Pathway so that if things get rough, you can bail."

Eric smirked. "If you think I'm the type of guy who is just going to hang back and do nothing...well, I'm not going to be that type of guy. Maybe I can't do things like you can. I can't form a scythe or a sword. But I've got something better."

"The power of stubbornness! I'm too darn stubborn to listen to any of you!" Eric said, sliding open the door and entering the van, disappearing into the pathway.

As Andy and Dave stared at each other dumbfounded, Bags chuckled before nipping at Dave's ankle.

"Go on, boy. You wouldn't want stubborn boy to get lost."

Dave slapped Andy on the back as they both entered the van.

Dave rolled out of a very narrow pathway onto a huge pile of flowers. As soon as he made contact, the flowers exploded into a mushroom cloud of petals, spraying a variety of colors in every direction. He stood up and as he brushed petals from his hair, he noticed that the entire ground was covered with millions of flowers. The sky was literally raining petals blown in from a field of colorful flowers. He turned around to see that his pathway was a small door set into a large tree. Around him were dozens of similarly sized trees, including one with large metal chains around it.

That must be Todd, Dave thought as he saw Andy and Eric standing by the tree.

Dave jogged over to them, watching Andy tug at the chains.

"Is this...is this Todd?" Andy asked.

Dave nodded.

"He's locked up? For what?" Eric asked.

"If the Trauma Guild is right, for being the avatar of the Dreamscape," Dave said.

"The what?" Eric asked.

Dave turned to say something snarky to Eric, but as he did he saw something flying at them from the corner of his eye.

"Get down!" Dave said and the three ducked. A large spiked metal ball flew at them, barely missing Eric. It stuck in a nearby tree and as it did, the tree began to wither and die.

"Holy crap! Did you just see that?" Eric yelled as they got to their feet.

The three watched as another tree suddenly began to transform from a large oak tree into something humanoid. The tree bark darkened into black glittering armor and one of the large branches became a large black sword.

The Sleepless Knight had arrived.

As soon as it appeared, screaming came from another tree nearby. Tied to the tree with chains of the same black glittering metal as the Sleepless Knight's armor was Emma.

"Dave! Andy! Eric! Anybody! Help!" screamed a familiar female voice.

"Emma!" Dave yelled.

As soon as he yelled, the Sleepless Knight pointed its sword in his direction. Dave pointed his sword right back at him. Andy raised his scythe and Eric took a few steps back.

"I know why you're here," Dave yelled. "You're here for Todd."

The Sleepless Knight cocked its head to the side.

"Yeah, that's right," Dave continued. "I know that Traum... heck, the entire Trauma Guild is after Todd. You guys think he's the avatar of the Dreamscape. Traum wants to harvest him so he can gain a direct connection with the Dreamscape. He's trying to become the most powerful dreamer, even possibly stronger than the Terrors. Am I right?"

The Sleepless Knight stared at Dave. Then it did something Dave did not expect.

It spoke.

"If he is the avatar," a deep male voice said from within the armor, "then he will be brought out of his prison and given to Lord Traum. However, while I will complete the quest that my master has set before me, what I truly desire is more dreams. Traum wants to harvest the avatar to become one with the Dreamscape. I want to harvest because I desire the dreams of those with powerful dreams.

"I have allowed you three to grow in power for one reason and that is so I can add your dreams and your power to my own. Taking the dreams of regular dreamers only does so much. I have harvested many, but Traum has shown me that harvesting dream walkers can increase my power to levels beyond imagination. Why try to learn new techniques and powers when I can let you learn them and then I can take them when they have developed? I allowed you to develop into dream walkers so that I can feast upon them."

"What the hell?!" Eric said, taking a few steps forward to line up with his friends.

"You son of a bitch. You think we're just going to let you take our dreams?" Andy said, getting into a stance ready to fight.

"This is all a game to you, isn't it? How long have you been doing this?" Dave said.

"Long enough," the knight replied. "And there are plenty more dreamers to develop and dreams to harvest at school after your dreams are mine," the Sleepless Knight said.

Dave re-gripped his sword, feeling his hands shake in anger. "Don't think we're going down without a fight. You'll find that allowing us to gain power is going to be your downfall." Dave said.

The Sleepless Knight laughed, a metallic echo coming through his helmet.

"I have planted the seed of your power," the Sleepless Knight said, raising his sword to the sky, "and now it is time to harvest!"

With that, the Sleepless Knight slammed his sword into the ground, which erupted with a wave of black energy, tearing up mounds of earth and flowers as it made its way towards them. The three dove out of the way and the wave struck a tree behind them. The wave of energy cut the tree in half. The top half slowly toppled over onto them. Dave imagined that the tree was lighter than air as it fell over. As it fell, he saw a name carved into the bark.

DAVID CALLOWAY

The tree stopped just short of Dave's face and then began to float away. Dave breathed a sigh of relief as the three got to their feet.

"A simple trick," the Sleepless Knight said. "Try to defend against this!"

Suddenly, the tree burst into thousands of small dagger-like pieces of wood and plummeted to the ground like falling icicles. A piece of wood hit Eric deep in his shoulder darkening his shirt with blood. Dave pushed Eric to the ground and stood over him. Dave's sword ignited in flame as he began to spin it wildly above his head. The fire burnt the wood instantly to a crisp, landing harmlessly on Dave and Eric's body. Andy, seeing what he was doing, began to spin his staff above his head in a circular motion. Wind poured forth from his staff, forming a wind tunnel above Andy's head. The wood blew up into the sky and scattered amongst the trees and flowers.

"Eric, get up!" Dave said.

"I can't do it! I can't do anything to that guy!" Eric said, wincing as he pulled the piece of wood from his shoulder.

"Eric, listen to me. Andy and I are going to attack the knight. When he's distracted, save Emma!"

"What if he comes after me?" Eric said.

"Damn it, Eric," Andy said. "Don't worry about the what-ifs all the time! Just save our friend!"

Eric looked over at the knight and then at Emma. He nodded to Dave and Andy.

After the last bit of wood finally dispersed, Dave concentrated and a solid wall of stone burst from behind the knight. Sleepless turned to see what had happened behind him and Dave charged with his fire sword. The knight raised his own sword to block Dave's charge, but before Dave could reach him, Andy lowered his spinning weapon and the wind tunnel to face the knight. The wind tunnel flew at the knight, cutting a path through the flowers and earth. Sleepless raised his sword and blocked Dave's fire sword and then faced the wind tunnel. A mound of earth burst from the ground to block the wind tunnel. However, it was too late to stop the initial burst. It slammed into the Sleepless Knight, sending him crashing into the wall of stone. The wall broke on impact and the stone collapsed on top of him.

"Eric, now!" Dave yelled.

Eric ran toward Emma, his eyes not leaving where the Sleepless Knight had fallen.

Andy charged at the fallen knight. The knight kicked one of the stones at Andy who ducked it. Just as it passed him, the stone exploded, sending Andy tumbling forward. As the Sleepless Knight got to his feet, Dave charged, but a swing from Sleepless's massive sword forced him to stop his charge and block. While his sword did block the attack, the strength of the swing knocked Dave to the ground. The Knight bent down and picked up Andy by his neck, raising him to the sky. The clear blue sky became clouded and dark, rumbling with thunder.

Sleepless Knight heard a commotion coming from his right as Eric freed Emma from her imprisonment.

"No, no, no, you don't get her that easily," the knight said.

He stared at the two for a second and suddenly a figure leapt out of the knight's back, resembling the shadow of something not quite human with long claws on its hands and horns on its head. It was the same shadow creature that had attacked Dave back at the castle a few nights ago. The creature screeched and charged Eric and Emma. Eric saw the creature and put himself in front of it. The shadow creature tackled Eric, slashing him with its claws. Eric raised his arms to block the attacks, blood pouring from new wounds on his arms.

"That's better. Now, where were we?" the Sleepless Knight said. "Ah yes, hand of god attack. Goodbye!"

Hand of God? Like the Lord Battler attack? Dave thought.

Dave put his sword on the ground and suddenly a path of fire tore its way through the flowers and lit the Sleepless Knight's foot on fire. The knight screamed in pain and threw Andy to the ground as the fire quickly turned to water and soaked into the ground.

"You don't get to do that again, Calloway," the knight said, stomping over to him.

As Dave got to his feet, he saw Andy get to one knee clutching his throat. "Andy, save Eric. That shadow thing is going to finish him off without our help. I'll hold off Sleepless."

"What?!" Andy said.

"Just do it!" Dave yelled.

Andy looked up at the Sleepless Knight and then over at Eric.

"Damn it!" Andy said as he turned and ran to help Eric.

"All you could do before, Calloway, is run away. Do you really think you could do anything else to me?"

"I may run away, but you'll never be able to catch me," Dave said, raising his sword.

The Sleepless Knight laughed, raising his sword to touch the tip of Dave's. "You don't realize it, do you?"

"What don't I get?" Dave said, taking a step back.

"Do you really think that I just let you go? You walked into my squire's dream."

"Rake..."

"Yes, Rake, my squire. You either beat him and take his dreams then get harvested by me, or he beats you and just when he thinks he's getting powerful, I harvest *his* dreams."

"You'd take out your own guy?"

"In order to reach my goal, I would harvest a thousand squires. You may run away from me, but eventually you'll tire. You may try to fight me, but eventually you'll lose. It doesn't matter how it happens. I will have your dream!"

Eric howled in pain as he felt his arms being torn to shreds. Emma picked up a rock and threw it at the shadow creature. It bounced harmlessly off the creature who simply glanced at Emma and growled.

"Emma!" Eric wheezed. "Run!"

The shadow dove at Emma, claws outstretched. Emma shrieked and took a few steps back, nearly tripping over something round at her feet.

There was a soccer ball. It was ticking.

Emma smiled and kicked the ball at the shadow. The shadow caught it in a clawed hand and then screamed in agony as the ball burst in flames, blowing off its hand in the explosion.

As the thing rolled around on the ground, trying to put out the fire that engulfed its body, Eric got to one knee and looked around for a weapon as blood oozed from his arms.

"Finish him off, Em!" Eric yelled.

Emma looked around for more soccer balls and then looked at Eric, confused.

"Em, remember what that ferret told us yesterday? Use..."

Suddenly, the shadow, free of the flames, dove at Eric. It knocked Eric down and pinned his arms down to the ground, lunging at him with its fangs. Eric struggled to get out of the hold, but the creature was too strong. Expecting the end to come, Eric suddenly felt the creature's grip loosen. He looked at the creature and saw that it had the blade end of a scythe sticking through its chest. In a burst of black dust, the creature dispersed into the air, revealing Andy's smirking face.

"You owe me one," he said, turning toward Dave's battle. "Come on, let's help Dave."

Andy ran over to help Dave as Eric got to his feet.

"Em, I may need to get about a billion pints of blood after this, but what do you say?" Eric said. "Wanna go kick some Sleepless Knight ass?"

Emma smiled as they both ran over to help.

Dave rolled out of the way of the Sleepless Knight's sword swing, but stopped short of rolling into daggers that popped out of the ground, pointing in his direction, waiting for him to roll right onto them.

He looked over at the Sleepless Knight and made the ground beneath the knight turn into thick mud. As the knight sank into the mud, Dave sprang to his feet and swung his sword. The knight reached up to block the swing, but with Dave's momentum, the impact knocked the sword from the knight's hand. Dave swung again and the Sleepless Knight blocked with its arm, and a large chunk of metal flew off. As Dave recovered to swing again, the knight burst out of the mud and grabbed him by the throat, lifted him into the air, and squeezed just enough to make Dave struggle to breathe.

Suddenly, the Sleepless Knight stumbled a few steps, clutching its back with its free hand, as Andy struck the Knight with his scythe, carving out a chunk of armor.

"Drop him!" Andy yelled as he prepared the scythe for another attack.

However, the Sleepless Knight simply turned and used Dave as a shield.

"Hurt your friend. Come on Andy, Andruseth, or whatever you're calling yourself these days. You don't like anybody. You never do. Everybody is merely an annoyance to you. Their opinion, their gossip, whatever they like, it's all just meaningless to you, isn't it?"

"What?" Andy said, reaching back to strike.

"Why don't you join the Trauma Guild, Andruseth? You have the right mentality for it and you have the skills. I need another squire, after all, since Dave killed Rake."

The Sleepless Knight offered its hand while Dave struggled to breathe.

"You've got to be kidding me!" Andy said. "You're offering me a deal while you're in the middle of killing my friend?"

"Well, I tried," the Sleepless Knight shrugged.

Andy swung the scythe but had to pull up short as the knight

331

continued to use Dave as a shield. As Andy hesitated, the knight used the opportunity to grab Andy by the neck and lift him into the air.

"Look what I have here," the knight said. "Two losers for the price of one. Which dream should I take first? Who is going to be the first to die?"

"You are," a voice said.

"Huh?" the Sleepless Knight looked down just as Eric swung with an uppercut directly to the knight's helmet, hitting with a thunderous clap, knocking the helmet from the Sleepless Knight's head.

The Sleepless Knight dropped Dave and Andy to the ground as Eric clutched his hand in agony, screaming that it was broken.

As Dave and Andy struggled to regain their breath, Emma finally rejoined the group.

"Guys," Emma said, pointing toward the knight.

The four looked at the Sleepless Knight as it stood with its face finally revealed.

It was Cole Dutton.

"Cole?" Dave asked, not believing his eyes.

"Ha! It's a guy!" Bags said in Dave's head. "Well, at least it's not one of your friends!"

Cole bent down and picked up his helmet. Seeing that most of it had been crushed, he tossed it aside.

"That's fate for you," Cole said. "You plan out protection against swords, guns, and such, but forget a simple thing like someone punching you in the face and BOOM, someone punches you in the face."

Cole slowly bent down and picked up his sword. Dave and Andy, still shocked from the revelation did nothing but raise their own weapons just in case there was an attack.

"You know what the really crappy thing about this is?" Cole said, stretching his arms. "Now I have to get rid of all of you. You all knowing who I am isn't going to do me any good."

Suddenly, the earth opened up beneath them, forming a deep pit.

Andy and Dave fell, but managed to catch the side. However, Andy had to let go of the scythe and watched it fall into the darkness of the pit. Emma fell, but grabbed Dave's leg, nearly yanking him down into the depths. However, after slowing her descent by hanging onto Dave's shoe, she reached out and grabbed a large root sticking out of the pit's walls. Meanwhile, Eric narrowly avoided the fall and managed to jump to safety. Unfortunately, he landed near the Sleepless Knight.

Eric looked up just as the Sleepless Knight lashed out with his hand, grabbed him by the throat, and lifted him into the sky. Dave and Andy lifted their heads above the pit just as the skies opened up and a beam of light blasted down on Eric. Their friend screamed as his body quickly dissolved in the light.

Bouncing down onto the ground and rolling into a small patch of grass was a glowing orb—Eric's dreams.

Dave and Andy pulled themselves out of the pit and helped Emma up. As they saw the orb come to a stop, Dave put his head down. A friend was lost.

The Sleepless Knight raised his sword to the sky. "I've always wanted to use that. Ever since the Sleepless Knight came up as my archenemy in Lord Battler. Oh, wait. That was Randall's dream. Or was it Keith's? I've taken so many dreams, it's hard to keep it straight.

"Now, who else wants the Hand of God? Step right up!" Cole said, offering his hand, but holding his massive sword above his head, ready to swing.

"Cole," Dave said, "I don't know how, but we're going to take you down."

Cole laughed. "Do you think that just because you beat Rake you can beat me? Rake was nothing!"

Dave thought about what he had to do to beat Rake. Net versus net. Broken glass. Sword versus baseball bat. Something clicked in Dave's head. Something about Rake's weapon that had never occurred to him before.

Suddenly, Rake's two-headed baseball bat formed in Dave's free hand.

"Andy, take this," he said, handing the bat off.

Andy took the bat and looked at Dave. "Rake's bat? Why?"

Dave smiled. "I've got a plan," he said.

"Care to fill me in?"

Dave pointed to the bat, looked at Cole, and then back at Andy. "I want you to catch the sword."

Andy opened his mouth to say something, but the Sleepless Knight charged, swinging his blade. Andy was caught off-guard, but Dave swung his sword up to block the swing. As Dave struggled to fend off the strike, Andy swung and caught the Sleepless Knight in the stomach with a baseball bat swing, knocking Cole back a few steps and freeing up Dave.

Dave charged with his sword, but the Sleepless Knight raised his free hand and a beam of dark purple light shot from his palm, striking Dave in the right arm, spinning him around and knocking him off his feet. He could smell his flesh burning from the beam before he even looked at the burnt skin of his arm. Cole raised his hand again and shot more of the same purple light at Andy and Emma. Andy tackled Emma to the ground as some of the shots hit his back, burning right through the trench coat to the skin causing Andy to yell in pain.

"Aw, he protected a friend. Ain't that sweet?" Cole said as he slowly marched over to Andy, his sword raised to the sky.

Cole swung his sword down, but at the last second, Andy raised the bat straight up. Cole's sword wedged between the bat heads. Andy twisted the bat as he slowly got to his feet, staying close enough to Cole that he couldn't pull the sword away and didn't have the angle to firmly grab his neck. Cole resisted the twist, by trying to twist back the other way. The bat, however, proved to be stronger as Cole's blade snapped in half.

A startled Cole stumbled back as Andy swung the bat up as hard as he could, hitting Cole's sword hand and knocking the remaining half of the sword out of his hand. Dave used the opportunity to throw his fire sword at Cole. Just as it was about to stab through Cole's stomach, the knight caught it.

"You're not finishing me off that easily, Calloway," Cole said, smiling.

"Yes I am, Dutton," Dave said.

Suddenly, the fire sword exploded, shattering Cole's armor, sending shards of glittering black armor everywhere. The impact sent Cole end over end, slamming into a tree several feet behind him. Dave and Andy ran to Cole, Dave forming another fire sword as they ran.

"Awesome, kid! Finish him off!" Bags exclaimed.

Cole sat against the tree, the only remains of his armor forming a trail of metal starting from where he was hit. He looked up at the two as Dave pointed the sword inches from his face. Dave saw it in Cole's eyes. He knew he was beaten.

"Tell me why." It was all that Dave could say or do.

Cole let out a huge breath and put his head down. "Everybody in school knows me as the big dumb jock," Cole said, looking back up at the two. "That's all I am, right? You heard the coach. If I can't play football, what am I good for? Think anybody cared? Nope, it was 'Got to get ready for the game Cole! You'd better get that football scholarship Cole!'"

"Why are you telling me this, Cole?" Dave asked.

"Shut up, dork." Cole said. "Man, I love football. I mean really love football. I wanna be a pro football player. But, I don't want to be just known as that idiot Cole."

"Then I became a Dream Walker somehow. I found out that I could take other people's dreams. . . smarter people's dreams. . . and take their ideas. . By taking other people's dreams, I could get the same ideas that people way smarter than me have. That was my way to change things. I'll get some ideas that will make people think I'm more than a dumbass. Jack in shop class had an idea on how to build this neat tree house. Now that idea is mine and I can build it. Hell,

335

the Sleepless Knight idea I took from some guy from my English class. It was his archenemy from some dumbass video game. Now his idea is mine and stupid me can actually try and do something more than just play football."

Andy laughed. "But, you're ruining other people's lives by doing it! Those are other people's dreams and ideas! Jack no longer has the idea of building that thing in shop class!"

Cole shrugged. "Did you ever want something so badly that you didn't care what happened? Your friend Eric wanted revenge on Everway and he broke his arm. He may have even ruined his quarterback career depending on how it heals. Was that worth it? Andy, you dated and broke up with Cynthia, your friend's skanky sis, worth maybe ruining your friendship with Eric?

The three stood there in silence for several seconds before Dave spoke.

"But wait. After all this, you still were the same guy in reality. You were still the same Cole that I knew. Failing tests, bullying, and all that."

Cole nodded. "It's what Traum wanted. Don't change overnight to the people that know you or they'll get suspicious, especially if one of them is actually a dream walker. Luckily, Traum showed me who else in the school was a dream walker before I—"

Suddenly, a thin ray of black energy pierced Cole's head. His eyes widened as blood came out of his nose and ears. He fell to the side, his eyes slowly closing. Dave instinctively reached out to grab him, but the Sleepless Knight's body disappeared, and dozens of orbs floated into the air. It was Cole's dream as well as the dozens of dreams he had harvested. Standing there was a familiar swirling black armor. Dave found himself staring at Lord Traum himself.

Traum and stared at one orb in particular. "Hmph, Mr. Dutton's dream," a deep male voice said from within the armor. "My assumption was that a man of his lower intelligence would have simply followed my orders and not have taken his own initiative."

Dave raised his sword as Andy dropped the bat and formed the staff scythe.

"Traum," Dave said, keeping his distance, as the leader of the Trauma Guild looked over at the two.

"That is Lord Traum to you, Mr. Calloway," Traum said. "And before you awaken from this dream, you shall see the birth of a new avatar."

Lord Traum made a crushing motion with his hand and the shards of Cole's dream along with all of those that he had harvested turned to dust and drifted slowly to the ground.

Avatar

As the last of Cole's disappeared into the ground, Dave felt his body go numb. He had no love for Cole, but in one instant, Traum had crushed all that Cole had wanted to be. No one, not even Cole Dutton, deserved that. Slowly, he could feel his cold numbness being replaced with a white-hot fury.

"Oh, Mr. Dutton, you poor fool," Traum said as he slowly walked toward Dave. "You were only supposed to threaten them, but you allowed your prey to gain in strength to a point where the prey could defeat the predator."

"Just threaten us?" Dave said, backing up a few steps with Andy and Emma, his arms spread to the side trying to give his friends some protection. "I think he went a little overboard with threatening. He's stolen people's dreams!"

"To better himself, Mr. Calloway," Traum said. "If you cannot achieve your dream, we do not let them go to waste. The Trauma Guild will achieve them for you rather than letting them wither and die."

"That's crazy!" Dave said. "My dreams are what make me my own person. Even if I don't achieve them all, they're mine to hope and wish for."

Traum went silent for the longest second that Dave had ever felt. Then Traum laughed.

"What's so funny, Traum?" Dave asked.

"Your dreamer-self is quite motivated. When I take your dream, your motivation should do quite well when merged with mine," Traum said, raising his hand and pointing at Dave with one finger. "Goodbye, Mr. Calloway."

A beam of black energy shot out of Traum's finger and raced towards Dave. Instinctively, Dave pulled his arms in front of his face for protection. He imagined a shield protecting him from the beam and a shield of blue energy appeared before him. Dave only had a second to relax, confident in his shield's power to protect him before the beam split apart, going around Dave.

Andy gasped.

Emma screamed.

Dave turned to see two orbs in place of his friends as he let his shield drop. He quickly turned back around to see Traum standing a mere foot away. Dave thought about his volcano and imagined drawing out his fire sword. However, before Dave could draw his weapon, dozens of inky black tendrils emerged from Traum's armor, as if the armor itself was alive. The tendrils lashed out and grabbed Dave by his arms and legs. Dave inhaled to scream, but another tendril wrapped around his neck, lifted him up at least ten feet into the air, and tightened. Dave's chest pounded as he felt his dream slipping from him.

"You fought well, Mr. Calloway. Defeating the Sleepless Knight as well as his squire, Rake, was no easy feat. After this ordeal is over, I will extend an offer to you to join my Trauma Guild."

Dave felt the tendril around his neck loosen, just enough for short breaths and loud whispers.

"You want..." Dave coughed, trying to catch his breath, "you want me to join the Trauma Guild?"

"Yes, that is my offer."

"And dream only of stealing other people's dreams?" Dave said. "Not in my lifetime!"

Traum began walking toward Todd's pathway, the tendrils carrying Dave in mid-air. Traum reached out as if to touch the chains, but stopped short and turned to Dave.

"Harvesting is not a requirement to be a part of the Trauma Guild."

"But, you don't care if your people do?" Dave said, raising his voice as much as the tendrils would allow him.

"Those people that lose their dreams will dream again."

"By letting their real dreams die?"

"If it serves our purpose, yes," Traum said.

"And what's in it for me?" Dave asked.

Traum walked toward Dave, his armor rippling with every movement. "Power. With your ability, you will never have to worry about your normal life anymore. When you sleep, you will be one of the most elite dream walkers in existence and part of the most powerful organization that the Dreamscape has ever seen," Trauma said.

"Power in service to you, I assume?" Dave said.

"You will use your power to suit my goals, yes."

"And what is *your* goal?" Dave asked.

Traum peered up at Dave. Dave found that the tendrils were loose enough to look down at Traum's face. It was still covered in the strange smiling and frowning white mask.

"My goal is simply to become the avatar of the Dreamscape," Traum said. "I simply desire to join with the Dreamscape and become a part of it."

"Why? Why do that?" Dave asked.

Traum stood up. "To become anything, anywhere, anytime within the Dreamscape. To be omnipresent."

Dave smirked. "So, you want to be a god in the Dreamscape? Why not start doing some mustache-twirling, you psycho."

Traum turned his back on Dave. "Call it becoming a god if you will. I consider it a side effect."

"A...side effect?" Bags said. "What the hell is he talking about?'

"Wait...if becoming basically a god in the Dreamscape isn't your goal, then what is your goal?"

Traum turned towards Todd's pathway. "I'm doing this because I don't want it to end."

Dave looked away from Traum. *That's almost exactly what Gabriel had said.*

"You don't want what to end? The Dreamscape?" Dave asked.

"No, not the Dreamscape. The Dreamscape is eternal."

"Then what?"

"Mr. Calloway, I am a patient man, but unfortunately we are wasting time," Lord Traum said. "I need you to summon the avatar here."

"Me? How the heck should I know how to summon the avatar?" Dave said as he tried unsuccessfully to wiggle an arm free of the tendrils.

"It's simple," Traum said in a voice almost as quiet as a whisper. Suddenly the tendrils around his arms and legs tightened. Pressure and pain coursed throughout Dave's body as he let out an uncontrollable scream.

Traum turned toward Todd's pathway. "You see, the Dreamscape is very protective of its avatar. It keeps the avatar in its own dream, almost like a mother holding its child. It won't let the avatar out unless the Dreamscape itself is threatened or," Traum paused as he tightened the tendrils even more, "the avatar's will to save one of his friends grows too strong for the Dreamscape to control."

As he finished his last word, the tendrils whipped Dave through the leaves and branches of a nearby tree, opening up what seemed like endless cuts over Dave's body. He tried to scream, but as he opened his mouth, the tendril around his neck closed, cutting off his breath completely. Just as Dave's vision began to fade, the tendril loosened, allowing Dave to breathe once again.

"Beg for your friend to help, Mr. Calloway. Bring the avatar to me," Traum said as he continued to stare at Todd's Pathway.

The fact that Dave's own body felt like it was on fire was bad enough. Add the fact that the pain Dave was suffering was merely a means to an end for Traum made Dave even angrier. He struggled against the tendrils, but it was useless. He was helpless.

Kiddo! Bags yelled in his head. *You're right, you are helpless up here! But you're not limited to just up here!*

What do you mean? He's too strong. I can't do anything to him! Dave thought back.

Maybe not you, but maybe someone... or something else? Use your memories, dummy!

Dave's thoughts raced as he tried to think of something that could deal with Traum. Then the idea finally came.

"Ask the Dreamscape to free your friend, Mr. Calloway," Traum said. "It's the only way that you can save yourself."

"You're right, Traum, I'll call out to my friend. Just not to Todd,"

Traum was silent as he turned to look up at Dave and the tendrils began to tighten again.

"Beddy Tear, go get him!" Dave yelled.

"What?!" Traum said. Suddenly the ground erupted directly next to Traum as the giant teddy bear desk creature reached out and grabbed Traum's legs. Traum tried to resist the creature's strength, but was soon pulled off his feet. Traum turned and shot a beam of black energy at Beddy Tear and put a hole directly in the bear's forehead. Dave smiled as fluff burst out of the other end. This was not a nightmare. This was Dave's own creation.

The creature growled as some the fluff landed on the back of the desk. Traum raised his finger to shoot another beam, but Beddy Tear opened his mouth and spit out a wad of notebook paper onto Traum's hand. Before Traum could figure out what to do next, Beddy Tear dropped down into the hole bringing Traum tumbling down into the hole with him. At the last second, Traum grabbed onto the edge of the hole with his one good hand as Beddy Tear growled and howled from below.

At the same time, the tendrils released Dave dropping him onto the ground, landing on his back. As Dave tried to shake the stars from his eyes, he saw the tips of the tendrils turn into spikes and embed themselves into the ground. Traum was using the spikes to try to pull himself up. With a quick thought, the fire sword was back in Dave's hand. He took a deep breath and pooled as much energy as he could into his sword.

"Not today Traum," Dave said as he plunged the sword into the ground. Suddenly, the earth surrounding Traum exploded like a volcano with lava shooting everywhere. His tendrils dug into the lava and then let out an animalistic screech as if they were alive, and then retreated into Traum's armor. With his leverage gone, Traum hung on with his five fingers. One finger slipped off the edge of the hole. Then another. Finally, one after the other, his fingers released their grip and Traum disappeared, screaming into the depths of the hole.The lava quickly cooled and transformed back into normal earth as if it were never there.

Silence.

"Holy moley, kiddo, you did it!" Bags said as Dave collapsed to his knees, smiled, and then collapsed as his body gave out on him. He was completely spent.

"Don't move a muscle, boy, just wait until you wake up," Bags said. Dave didn't have the energy to respond. He simply blinked a few extra times, imagining that it was some kind of Morse code communication back to Bags.

Suddenly, a black tendril emerged from the hole and snapped Dave off the ground. Dave's eyes widened as Traum floated out of the hole, covered in Beddy Tear fluff.

"No, I beat you," Dave managed to get out before another tendril whipped around his throat.

"I won't be beaten by a toy," Traum said. "Don't you realize, Mr.

Calloway, that my strength is equal to that of an avatar? I won't be beaten by some newborn dream walker."

"Funny," a voice said from behind Traum. "How do you know you're equal to the strength of an avatar if you've never faced one?"

Traum turned to see Todd standing in front of the door to his open pathway, wearing a plain red t-shirt and blue jeans. Traum released Dave, and hundreds of tendrils emerged from his armor.

"Your look insults the Dreamscape's gift to you, avatar," Traum said in disgust.

"My look?" Todd said, looking at himself. "This is the Dreamscape, Traum. I can look like whatever I want. It doesn't judge nor care what I look like."

Traum almost growled at that. "Avatar, you know what I am here for," Traum said. "And you know that I have the power to take it."

Todd smiled and shook his head. "You do? You let a newborn dream walker almost beat you. You do realize that I am a part of the Dreamscape itself. Whatever it can do, I can do."

Suddenly, black beams of energy blasted from not only Traum's hands, but also from each of the hundreds of tendrils. Todd waved his hand and the beams of energy turned into harmless cool water that splashed all over him.

"Very refreshing!" Todd said. "But now I'm wet. That just won't do."

Todd looked up to the sky and suddenly the clouds that had stuck around since the Sleepless Knight had arrived moved away from the sun. Todd looked at Traum and then back at the sun.

"The sun. It looks so small from here," Todd said, smiling. "But it looks so close. It's almost as if I tried, I could just pluck from it from the sky."

Todd reached out towards the sun and with his two fingers plucked it from the sky, showing the sun, no bigger than a quarter, to Traum. The heat from the sun quickly dried Todd's skin and clothes.

"That's better," Todd said.

Traum concentrated, put his hands together and then released a gigantic ball of dark energy towards Todd. The ball tore up the ground as it soared towards the avatar.

Dave saw the look on Todd's face. Todd was still smiling.

"I knew you weren't powerful enough," Todd said.

Todd blew on the sun and a gigantic eruption exploded forth from the star, instantly dissolving the energy ball and erupting into Traum. Traum screamed in agony as the impact launched him into the air several hundred feet. Todd swung his hands and suddenly an open doorway formed in mid-air facing down. Traum helplessly flew into the doorway and the door closed behind him, chains forming around it.

"Good luck getting out of that one, Traum," Todd said with a smile as the door stayed aloft in the sky. He continued to smile until he looked down at his fallen friend "Oh crap, Dave, are you okay?"

Dave moaned a response. It was the best he could do. Todd got his arm around Dave and lifted him to his feet.

"Traum... is he... gone?" Dave asked.

"Don't worry about Traum. He's been exiled."

Dave tried to raise his fist in victory, but he just didn't have the energy.

"You were amazing, Dave. Seriously! The Dreamscape is totally impressed," Todd said, slapping Dave on the back, the strength of which knocked Dave the ground. "Sorry, sorry, sorry!" Todd said, picking him back up.

"Is... he gone... forever?"

"Traum? Not sure. I tossed him into an exiled pathway. If it was anybody else, I would say yes, but his whole Trauma Guild has been opening up exiled pathways for a long time. It's only a matter of time before Traum or his goons figure out a way to escape. And when he does, we'd better be prepared."

"Why? You... you beat him so... so easily,"

"He was overconfident and underprepared. He didn't know what he was in for. But, whoever Traum's dreamer is, he's not a fool. The next time he shows up, I can guarantee it won't be as easy. Next time, he's going to bring the entire Trauma Guild. And now that he knows he can use you to lure me out, I have no doubt that he is going to try it again with you or somebody else in our group," Todd said.

"But, you're the avatar. He can't beat you!"

"Anything in the Dreamscape can be destroyed, including me. The Dreamscape wouldn't be foolish enough to give someone complete and utter power. I can be killed just like you can.

"Do you think we can take him? Traum I mean." Dave said.

Todd shook his head. "Maybe, but I think you took him by surprise this time. He'll be more prepared. Besides, it doesn't have to be you next time. He'll need a dream walker, but that means that he doesn't need you. He could get Eric, or Andy, or even..."

Dave felt his heart sink. "Emma."

"Exactly," Todd said. "But there is something you can do."

"What's that?" Dave asked.

"Grow strong," Todd said. "You and the others. Learn and master all that you can about the Dreamscape and the abilities that you have. You already started down that path with that camp training. You've already shown skill that would have taken other dreamers years to develop. You've got some natural talent to go along with a great guardian who has helped bring that talent out."

Dave didn't say anything. He knew Bags was smiling.

"I wish I could help you with all of your training," Todd said, "but the Dreamscape strongly frowns upon me coming out unless it's the direst of circumstances. But, you're strong. Your bond with your friends is strong. Train with them until you can rival even the strongest members of the Trauma Guild."

Dave paused to think of a reply, but could only nod.

"And Dave, one more thing. Never think that you've seen all that the Dreamscape has to offer. Never quit imagining the possibilities while you're within here. You wouldn't believe what amazing things you'll find in here. Just remember: everybody dreams."

Dave smiled. "So, what you're saying is that I should keep living the dream?"

Todd stared at Dave for a second and then started to laugh.

"Sorry, I just had to say it," Dave said. "I couldn't resist."

Both let out a few more chuckles.

"See you at school tomorrow?" Todd asked extending his hand.

"You bet," Dave said, grasping Todd's hand and shaking it. "And maybe after school we can throw down with Lord Battler."

Todd's eyes widened. "That would be awesome. As long as I don't get the Sleepless Knight as an enemy again."

Dave's eyes widened. "You too? What the heck?" Dave started to rant and saw that Todd had a huge grin on his face.

"Kidding, kidding, kidding!" Todd said.

Dave gave his friend a playful punch on the arm as Todd disappeared. He must have woken up.

"There's something else you can do, David," a voice said from behind Dave. Dave turned to see Mr. Laws.

"You!" Dave yelled out. "You knew about Dream Walkers this whole time? You didn't warn me or anything?"

"What was I supposed to say? Tell a student that there's a magical world where you can walk into other people's dreams? If you were like most people in school, you just had a vivid dream. I had to be sure first."

"Sure about what?"

"That you can help me, David. I know you've seen Gabriel and Krieger's true identities."

"Yeah, they're you!" Dave said. "I really don't understand what's going on."

"Many years ago, I fought against Chimera, one of the most powerful Terrors that the Dreamscape had ever seen. After a long battle that saw the destruction of a great many dreams, I managed to defeat it, but in doing so, I fractured my dream self into several pieces."

"You can fracture your dream?" Dave said in amazement.

"Yes, and I need your help. I need you to help put my dream back together. This fracture is causing me to have nightmares every single time I sleep. I need you to end this."

"So, Gabriel and Krieger. They... they are part of your dreams?"

"Yes, they are part of my fractured dream. When I sleep, they become Dream Walkers themselves. But there's one other fracture."

"Who?" Dave said. But Mr. Laws didn't answer. He was just looking up. He was looking at Traum's Pathway.

"No. No way," Dave said.

"David, I know I'm asking a lot of you. But I fear there is little time."

"Why?"

"Chimera has returned."

It was the last thing he heard before his alarm woke him to a new day.